Outrageous
FORTUNE

Outrageous
FORTUNE

Meredith Land Machin

ST. MARTIN'S/MAREK
NEW YORK

OUTRAGEOUS FORTUNE. Copyright © 1985 by Meredith Land Machin. All rights reserved. Printed in the United States of America. No part of this book may be used or reproduced in any manner whatsoever without written permission except in the case of brief quotations embodied in critical articles or reviews. For information, address St. Martin's/Marek, 175 Fifth Avenue, New York, N.Y. 10010.

Design by Laura Hough

Library of Congress Cataloging in Publication Data
Machin, Meredith.
    Outrageous fortune.
    I. Title.
PS3563.A3115509   1985   813'.54   85-2672
ISBN 0-312-59189-6

First Edition

10 9 8 7 6 5 4 3 2 1

For my parents, Emmette and Kathleen Land,
and for my husband, Rick

To be or not to be: that is the
    question:
Whether 'tis nobler in the mind
    to suffer
The slings and arrows of
    outrageous fortune,
Or to take arms against a sea
    of troubles,
And by opposing end them?

—*Hamlet,*
    Act III,
    scene i

PROLOGUE

1968: The Crash

Kate refused to leave the house. Her husband was coming home. It was bad enough that she had to be out all week; worse yet that she spent her days in that dreary building on Delaney Street where the concept of office camaraderie had yet to be introduced. She hid in her cubbyhole and, as often as she thought she could get away with it, called home. She did not want their reunion to begin on the telephone, but not knowing if he was home yet was worse. There was never an answer.

At five o'clock she would rush out, and the drive home was unbearable, the suspense exhausting. Calling out "Hello?" as she came in, she was greeted with only silence.

But now she had the weekend, a golden Saturday and Sunday in late May, two precious days away from Delaney Street, and she vowed that nothing would take her away from this house. He could come today, or tomorrow, and she would be here. She wouldn't consider the real possibility that he might not come until next week. She would deal with that, if she had to, on Monday.

She didn't want to think, period. To think was to worry, and there had been months of that. Today she needed action, so she ignored the lure of sunshine and warm air, the first real summer day after a bitter Chicago winter. Instead, she scrubbed floors that were already spotless, wiped invisible dust from the furniture, and again changed the sheets. She defrosted the freezer and watered the plants. At two-thirty, when she found herself needlessly scouring the sink, she gave up, changed into a bathing suit, and carried a plastic lounge chair out to the backyard. She stretched out her winter-pale, thin legs. She'd never had a weight problem, but now she was thinner than she'd ever been. She'd had no appetite at all lately.

With her forearm shielding her eyes, she breathed slowly and deeply, forcing her muscles to relax. It was a technique she had mastered these past months. As long as she was busy, at the office

3

or at home, she could keep her balance. It was the nights that gave her trouble, when she lay in their bed alone, or the odd moments of the day when she could find nothing to do, when even the juiciest novel was not enough to distract her thoughts. Then the demons would begin to circle, and sleep was the only escape. In, out, in, out, deeper and slower breaths, in, out, there, it was working. She was slipping away from them.

"Asleep?"

Kate started in her chair.

"Oh-oh, I guess you were. Want me to leave?"

"No, no, that's all right." Kate smiled quickly. "I wasn't asleep, just pretending."

"I know, it's too hot to do anything, isn't it?" Jane dropped down on the grass. "No word yet?"

"No. I was hoping it'd be today, but . . . Where's Ted?"

"Playing golf, the idiot, in this heat. Do you believe it's still May? This summer is going to be awful."

"Where's Scotty?"

"Mercifully delivered from me for the afternoon," Jane said. "The pool opened today, and Sharon called, volunteering to take all the kids. Bless that woman."

"Your turn will come," Kate said lazily.

"I know, I know. Meanwhile, let me enjoy this afternoon, will you? Now, tell me. Is the castle ready for the returning king? Everything in perfect order? Is the royal carpet rolled out?"

"Stop teasing," Kate said mildly. "Yes, everything's ready, except . . . well, I was thinking this morning . . . I was thinking it might be nice to have a party, a sort of welcome-home thing—"

"It's about time. I've been waiting for weeks for you to say that. Of course you should have a party! We'll make a poster—no, a big banner, 'Welcome Home, Jim.'" Jane spread her arms wide. "In red letters, I have a spray can in the basement. And piles of food; oh, I know, steaks on the grill—"

"Wait a minute." Kate squinted at her neighbor against the glare of the sun. "I was thinking of something a little simpler . . . cheaper."

"Mmmm, right, sandwiches, beer, but a cake at least, Kate. You have to have a cake."

4

"I'll make a cake." Kate closed her eyes. "Of course, it'll have to be short notice since I'm not sure when he'll get here."

"Let's have everything ready, poster up, food in the freezer—"

"It's more than that, Jane. I—I'm afraid he might extend again, for another six months, or who knows how long. I'm afraid instead of him coming in the door any day now, or being here when I come home from work, I'll just get a letter, and he'll say he's staying."

"Nonsense. He won't do that."

Kate marveled at her friend's confidence.

"Katy, he's been over there almost nineteen months, he must be sick of the place by now. Besides, you told me the only reason he extended his tour before was that they promised to send him to language school, and they never did, so why would he fall for that again? Listen, he's probably on his way home right now.

"Tell you what. When he gets home, just let us know, that's all I ask. And you enjoy that first night alone, uninterrupted, but I'll alert everybody. We'll have the party at our house the next night, a real celebration! I can't wait!"

"Neither can I." Kate brushed a strand of her long brown hair away from her face.

If Jane caught the doubt in her friend's reply, she didn't acknowledge it. She said easily, "It's going to be perfect. He'll be so proud of you for the way you've managed without him. You've told him, haven't you? About your job?"

"Yes." Kate sighed. "I can't afford to quit until he finds something."

"Well? What'd he say?"

"Oh, you know Jim." Kate kept her tone light. "His letters are so vague. Half the time I'm not even sure he gets mine. He's never really mentioned the job."

"How much did you tell him?"

"As little as possible," Kate said humorously, but it wasn't a joke. "Nothing about Mr. Ingram and his passes. I just said I needed something to keep me busy. I didn't want him to think I couldn't manage with the money he was sending me."

"It barely covers the house payments. He knows that. I'd think he'd be proud of you. And when he—what's that? There's somebody at your front door."

5

Kate was out of her chair in an instant. "Ted should be home by now," Jane said. She got to her feet. "I'll go comfort the weary golfer. Call me—if it's not Jim, you're coming for dinner tonight, remember? Six-thirty."

Kate hardly heard her. "Right, see you," she said, and she pulled on her shirt. Jane slipped through a gap in the hedge separating her backyard from Kate's, and Kate ran through the back door into her living room. Three feet from the front door, she stopped.

Through the screen she saw a figure in uniform, medals splayed across the chest, posture erect, and for a brief second, she let down her guard. She was safe, they were safe, he was home; here, at last, was her husband, Corporal James Downing, United States Marine Corps, and Vietnam was behind them forever.

"Mrs. Downing? Mrs. James Downing?"

What was this? That was not Jim's voice, he wouldn't—then who—?

She took another step toward the door, then another, and peered through the screen. This man was too short, too dark. He wasn't Jim.

And then she didn't want to know who he was. It didn't matter. She didn't even want to look at him or hear his voice, but she couldn't avoid it. He was saying her name again, she was nodding, opening the door, and, terrified, she was unable to jerk her eyes away from his clean-shaven face.

The brown-and-white tile on the floor in the front hall was suddenly icy beneath her bare feet.

He removed his hat and introduced himself, though she forgot his name instantly, and said he was from a Marine Corps Reserve Infantry unit in Waukegan. She said yes and nodded again.

She invited him into her immaculate living room. It was tiny and uncluttered, with a picture window looking out into the small backyard. There was a fireplace, swept clean, and narrow bookshelves on either side of it, crammed with mostly hard-covered volumes. There was a multicolored braided rug on the floor.

"Nice place, ma'am. Very nice." The Marine officer settled into a flowered easy chair.

Kate perched on the edge of the couch, the only decent piece of furniture in the room. It had been a gift from her parents, and the cushions were still firm, the beige wool upholstery unworn. She clenched her hands together and wished she hadn't been caught in her swimsuit because, even with the shirt on, she felt naked, as if her terror were as exposed as her body. She was defenseless against this buttoned-up, uniformed, blank-faced military man. Defenseless and beaten.

She clamped her feet together and stared at his lips. She would not look at the black band he wore around the sleeve of his dress-blue uniform.

He was telling her quietly, oh, so kindly—how many times had he done this? Kate wondered; did he spend every day like this, going from house to house, wife to wife?

—What? A plane crash.

Not a gunshot wound? No enemy fire? He was what?

She had not spoken a word since they'd entered the living room, but it was as if he were hearing her questions.

He was in a plane crash—mechanical failure, they thought, but they couldn't be sure. It was at sea and—

Well, but how did they know he was dead? Jim could swim—

There were no survivors; yes, they were certain, and he would like to offer his condolences.

Kate stared, dry-eyed, at his fingers. She found a crack in his superhuman armor. His nails were bitten to the quick.

He rose and she felt herself coming to her feet. She actually thanked him for coming as she walked to the front door with him.

What?

No, there was no need for him to call anyone. She was fine, thank you. Fine.

He had thrust a card into her hands. It identified him as Captain Samuel F. Berger, United States Marine Corps, Inspector Instructor Staff, Company H, 2nd Battalion, 24th Marines, 4th Marine Division. Kate crumpled it in her hand until it was soaked with perspiration.

He could come back, he assured her, to answer any questions she might have, and to help in any way he could. She was to call him if she needed anything, anything at all.

What would I need? she thought. Another stone-faced robot like you?

On the coffee table back in the living room was a package of information describing all the death benefits to which she was now entitled. There would be a five-thousand-dollar check coming soon from the Serviceman's Group Life Insurance, plus a few months' basic pay and she couldn't remember what else. She had that. What else could she need? There would be a letter too, from her husband's company commander in Vietnam. Also, any personal effects would be sent to her as soon as possible.

Personal effects? What could this robot possibly know about personal effects?

She stood in her bare feet on the cold tile, hugging her elbows, watching him walk down the sidewalk in the late afternoon sunshine. He put his hat back on and tugged at his jacket to smooth it in the back. His posture was so stiff he looked like a toy soldier.

I certainly made that easy for him, Kate thought, staring after him. No screaming, no hysteria, not even any tears. My behavior was absolutely proper, she said to herself. Probably the easiest one he's had all day.

She watched him get into his official car at the curb. He started his engine and drove slowly away, down to the end of the block. He turned at the corner and was gone.

Kate thought, I must call Jane, I certainly can't go out for dinner tonight. She scraped her nose a little against the screen as she turned toward the kitchen.

"Jane? I'm sorry, I can't come tonight." She was thinking how polite she was. She was always polite, just as her mother had taught her to be. She was totally unaware that her voice, normally low and a little scratchy, had risen two octaves.

"Well, it's Jim—" Her voice cracked. "It's Jim. He . . . he's—" and she couldn't say it. She couldn't finish. There was something in her throat stopping the words, and now there was a roar in her ears blocking the sound of Jane's questions. She couldn't speak and she couldn't hear, so she hung up the phone and leaned against the cool, metal-edged counter, trying to breathe.

In, out, in, out, she told herself, but it wasn't working. She hadn't perfected the technique after all. Everything was plugged up. She couldn't seem to get any air, and then came the scream, because the demons were no longer imaginary. They were real and the scream went on and on and on. . . .

Later, her memory of the weeks that followed would be sketchy, compartmentalized. She would recall quite clearly that both Jane

8

and Ted were there, holding her, comforting her, and she'd been grateful that she wasn't alone, though of course she really was alone. She would remember the drive to O'Hare but not packing her suitcase, and the flight itself was gone from her mind completely.

The two days she'd spent in Seattle with Jim's parents had the same quality. There were flashes of clarity interspersed among total blanks. Their apartment was a dismal place; she had slept on a lumpy couch in the front room and killed cockroaches in the bathroom, that much was vivid, but how had she arrived at the place? She had no idea and she doubted she would be able to find it again.

There had been a memorial service. They called it that because there was no body. She remembered nothing of the service, but she could still hear the inane remarks of the guests who had come to the apartment afterward, friends of his parents mostly, and one or two young men who had played high-school basketball with Jim.

She had found the whole scene preposterous, a party, for God's sake, people laughing and drinking and filling their plates with ham as if the world were still all right, as if Jim's death made no difference at all. She had sat, tight-lipped, in a dark dress she would never wear again, knees pressed together, hands gripped in her lap. If they came apart, surely, so would she, her composure would dissolve, but as long as they stayed together, she would be all right, she would not scream out loud at this monstrous charade. She found herself nodding like a puppet whenever anyone addressed her. Because she was the widow, she was permitted to act strangely, she hoped.

Jim's parents, too, seemed bewildered by it all. They were strangers to her, almost. They had come for the wedding and she hadn't seen them since, but they were kind to her. She knew that she would never see them again. The only thing they had in common was Jim, and now he was gone. They had received the same sketchy information that she had. There had been a plane crash; there were no survivors. Once they exhausted that topic, there was nothing left to say.

Then she was back in the house on Rolfe Road, the house she and Jim had shared, and she found it comforting. She felt lost without him and she kept asking him, sometimes out loud, what should I do about such-and-such? What should I do with your clothes, Jim?

What should I do with this car that keeps breaking down? What should I do about this leaky faucet? Although she had lived alone for two years, it had been only temporary, she'd thought. Soon Jim would be back: He would take care of things. He was good at making decisions, at dealing with people and problems that baffled her. Now, all the things she had postponed, shoved out of the way, came rushing at her, demanding answers, decisions, solutions. She felt weighed under by it all. Shoulders slumped, eyes red from crying, she dragged herself out of bed in the mornings, threw on whatever was handy, and drove to work.

At least her job, boring as it was, filled the days. But how had she passed those eternal nights, those endless weekends? That part was a blur, except that Jane had been there every day, without fail, and often Ted was with her. Somehow they had tolerated her constant weeping, her lethargy, her self-pity. And then there was Benjamin Cramer.

They were in Kate's kitchen, drinking coffee, as they had done nearly every evening since Kate's return from Seattle a few weeks before. It was Wednesday and it was raining again. The air, hot and sticky, demanded iced tea, but Kate felt frozen inside, and she was drinking coffee as if it could warm her into feeling normal again.

"Well, Kate, what's new on Delaney Street?"

Kate shrugged. "Same as always. Nothing exciting."

"How's Ingram?"

Kate rolled her eyes. "The same."

"Still itching to compromise your virtue?"

"That's a nice way of putting it. Mr. Ingram is Mr. Ingram, Jane. He never changes. Apparently, a widow is fair game, too."

Jane shook her head in disgust. "Still paying you the same pittance?"

"Yes," Kate said slowly. She wondered where this probing was leading.

"Still have you doing the same boring work? Typing figures? Filing and cross-filing meaningless reports? Is he still timing your lunch hour?"

"Jane, so what? It's a job, and you know I can't afford to quit."

"I know," Jane said, and Kate could almost feel her friend getting

10

ready to pounce. "In fact, you're barely making ends meet, aren't you."

It wasn't a question, so Kate didn't answer, but she admitted it to herself. Her salary was just enough to cover the mortgage payments, utility bills, and taxes, and to buy the coffee. She had put the money from Jim's insurance policy into a special account. She knew exactly how she was going to spend it, and it wouldn't be going for groceries or car repairs. She owed a debt to a kind old man named Hiram Wilcox, and the moment she felt she could manage without that emergency backup, she would send him the money.

But when would that time ever come? Right now there wasn't a penny extra, not for clothes or a good haircut or even—but what difference did it make? She had no one she wished to impress, no one to look pretty for. Jim was gone, he wasn't coming back, and she no longer cared much—about anything.

Jane rose from the table and went to refill their coffee cups. When she sat down again, she leaned forward on her elbows.

"Kate, it's time."

"Time for what?" Kate said it automatically and immediately wished she hadn't.

"Time to start living again." Jane's voice was gentle, but Kate had heard that note of determination before. This time she met it head-on.

"I'm not ready to start living again." She said it flatly, almost defiantly. "Sounds awful, doesn't it? Well, I don't care. There's no reason to live." Kate realized she was crying again. Why could she not conduct a single conversation without breaking into tears? She did it everywhere, at the office, at the filling station; every time she turned around, she was crying. She sniffed loudly, not politely at all, and said, "Jim is dead. He was my reason, the best I ever had, but he's gone and that's it."

"Will you please listen to me for one minute?" Jane gripped her arm. "I don't want to talk to you like this, but I have to. There's nobody else to do it. You have to start again, and I think we can help you. There's a job. . . . How would you like a new job?"

That reached Kate. She said carefully, "What kind of job?"

"Just what I said. Interesting. Challenging. I think you should go after it, and Ted thinks so, too."

11

"Ted?"

"He's the one who told me about it, silly. Listen, I don't know all the details, but there's a man in Ted's building—"

"It's in Chicago? Forget it. I hate the city. You know that."

"Oh, Kate." Kate could hear the exasperation in her friend's voice. "Will you just listen? His name is Crater, or Carter, something like that."

"You don't even know his name?" Kate knew she was making it hard, and that was unfair to Jane, but she couldn't seem to help it. She did not want any changes in her life. What was the point?

"The man's name doesn't matter. He's an investment counselor, or a financial consultant, something like that, I forget his title. You know, he's a whiz at making money and he tells other people how to do it. Finance, Kate, do you hear me? Finance. Think about it."

"Finance," Kate repeated. "My experience at the bank . . ."

"You bet, sweetie," Jane said triumphantly.

"The bank," Kate said again, her voice sinking. "Some recommendation that would be."

"Stop that foolishness. None of that was your fault, and I doubt he'd check on it anyhow. He'll give you a typing test and hire you, period. Honey, you just tell him you once worked in a bank, tell him all the departments you were in, just enough to let him know you can add and keep accurate records. That's all he needs to know.

"And listen, there's something else. This guy, Carter or whatever, well, Ted did an appraisal on some property for him and when Ted saw him today, Carter mentioned he needs an assistant. Not a secretary, Kate, an 'administrative assistant,' he said. He was moaning about the employment agencies because they've sent him three losers in a row, and—"

"Sounds like a lovely man to work for." Kate was still thinking of the Elwood National Bank, the pride she had felt walking through its doors on hot summer mornings, the crisp clickety-clack of her heels as she crossed the polished marble floor, her father by her side, tall and distinguished, smelling of shaving lotion. . . .

"Kate?" Jane snapped her fingers. "Listen to me. You can imagine the dizzy broads they've probably sent him. You can outtype and outthink every one of them. He's probably looking for somebody he can depend on, someone he doesn't have to stand over every min-

ute. He wants someone who's more interested in the rate of infla-
tion than the color of her nail polish."

"I don't wear nail polish."

"That's my point," Jane answered with infinite patience. "He'll
hire you in a minute."

For the first time, Kate was tempted. Just a tiny bit.

"Just think, working for a man who respects your intelligence
enough to give you something besides forms to type. Ted says he
has a beautiful office, right on La Salle Street—"

"Oh, yes, right in the city. No, thanks anyway, Jane, but I
really—"

"You are impossible! What do you have against Chicago?"

Kate didn't hesitate. "It's dirty, there are too many people, the
wind comes in off the lake and hits you in the face every time you
turn a corner, and I hate commuting."

"How would you know? You've never tried it. Take the train,
dummy. Twenty minutes, twenty-five tops, and the station is a couple of blocks from the office. Remember? He's in the same building
as Ted. You and Ted could take the same train the first few times.
Ted could take you by the hand and lead you to the office. And I
could come in and meet you for lunch."

"Would you?" For the first time in weeks, Kate's large gray eyes
showed a spark of interest.

"Here's the number." Jane whipped out a slip of paper from the
pocket of her shorts. "Call him tomorrow, when Ingram's making
his move on one of the other secretaries. Ask for a Friday appointment, then Friday morning call Ingram and tell him you're sick.
Ted will go in with you and show you where the office is. Do it.
What can you lose?"

Kate couldn't think of a good answer to that question, so the next
morning she waited until Mr. Ingram left the office for a minute and
called the number. Somewhat to her surprise, a very efficient
woman answered and gave her an appointment for an interview the
next day.

So much for dizzy broads, Kate thought. There was a catch in
here somewhere. Probably the guy was an ogre, or maybe he was
another Ingram, every secretary another conquest. Well, she had an

13

appointment. She might as well check it out. It was hard to imagine working for anybody worse than Mr. Ingram.

She refused to acknowledge it, not even to herself and certainly not to Jane, but she felt a tiny surge of anticipation. Surely it was too soon to feel remotely excited about anything? She was still in mourning, after all. It wasn't suitable.

So, in the rush of Jane's enthusiasm, she remained outwardly calm as they planned what she would wear, what purse she would carry. Not that she had much choice. Her closet was full of wool skirts and sweaters and corduroy jumpers, perfect for an eighteen-year-old girl going off to college, which was exactly what she had been when she'd acquired those clothes five years before. Since then her circumstances had drastically changed, and there was very little that looked appropriate for a twenty-three-year-old professional woman to wear to a city executive's office. Finally they selected the least objectionable dress, a sleeveless beige shift with a jacket two inches too short for the current style, but Jane lent her a striking red-and-blue scarf that helped a little. Friday morning, Jane saw them both off, her husband and her friend, kissing them as if they were embarking on a month's journey. Ted sat with Kate on the train, telling her how nice she looked and giving her a few pointers.

"The one thing he demands is punctuality, Kate. Whatever you do, be on time."

He left her in the lobby of the old and imposing office building, where she sat rigidly on a green-cushioned bench and watched all the well-dressed men in their three-piece suits and the well-dressed women with their coiffured hair arriving for work. She felt more inadequate by the minute. It was a long way from the little insurance office on Delaney Street, and the distance was more than a train ride.

She looked all wrong. Everything about her said "college girl," not "career woman." Her hair was as she'd always worn it, in long waves falling past her shoulders, and she touched it nervously. No more long waves, she decided. Too girlish. And her dress, her shoes were hopelessly out of fashion, bought on sale last summer when she had gone to work for Mr. Ingram.

Well, she had known all along that she didn't belong in the city,

14

certainly not in this rarefied atmosphere on La Salle Street. What was she doing applying for this job, anyway?

When it was time for the stores to open, she escaped from the lobby and ventured down the street to a book shop, but she was afraid of getting lost, so she didn't wander far. When she realized she was checking her watch every two or three minutes, she returned to the office building, took one of the elevators to the tenth floor, and arrived for her interview ten minutes early. To her surprise, she was immediately ushered into the inner office.

The moment she met him, she had to abandon all her preconceived notions. Instead of a stubby, wizened senior citizen, the man who rose from behind the massive mahogany desk was under thirty. He did have a slightly receding hairline, but he was of medium build, slim and athletic-looking, dressed conservatively in a dark blue suit. She could detect no oil in his reddish-brown hair, no sickly smelling cologne, and not a flicker of a leer in his steady gaze. His eyes were a brilliant blue, unclouded and correctly remote. She knew immediately that these eyes missed nothing, and although there was nothing challenging in his look, it nevertheless unnerved her and sent her remaining shreds of confidence running for cover.

This man could not keep a secretary for long, she thought, and, as the interview progressed, she knew why. He was stern and demanding; he had no time for small talk, for superfluous pleasantries, for anything inconsequential. He abhorred sloppy work, he told her, and did not tolerate careless errors. He described the position as primarily secretarial but it could—here his voice became cautious—it could evolve into administrative assistance. Kate sensed that he hoped it would, but had been stung before, so he wasn't making any promises. It would depend on her, she realized. . . . If she were capable, if she were bright, efficient, a workaholic . . . oh, there were too many ifs.

She nodded occasionally. I must be the world's champion nodder, she thought, but he did not welcome interruptions, so she said nothing.

Then he asked her about her background. She had anticipated this and had decided to keep it brief. She described her present job with the insurance company on Delaney Street, out in the suburbs, but omitted all the grim details except the low pay and the dull routine. She mentioned her two years at Northwestern University. He didn't ask why she had left, and she was relieved not to have to explain.

Then she described the jobs she had held in her father's bank. She did not tell him her father had owned the bank, only that she had worked there for three summers and had been given the opportunity to learn as much as possible. She was barely conscious that, as she discussed the various bank departments, a quiet enthusiasm colored her voice.

When she was finished she sat, hands in her lap, and tried to meet his gaze. His face expressionless, Cramer—Cramer, she said to herself, I have to remember his name is Cramer—paused only a moment before he mentioned a salary figure that was exactly twice what Ingram was paying her at the insurance office. Would that be acceptable?

Kate could not hide her astonishment.

"Mrs. Downing, if you're the person I'm looking for, you're worth that much and more. But if you're not, you're not worth a quarter of that. What do you say to a two-week trial? If it doesn't work out, I'll help you secure another position. Can you start a week from Monday?"

Kate was not prepared for this. She'd assumed that she'd hear from him in a week or two, at least a notification that he'd hired someone else. Instead, he was offering her the job on the spot. She had the feeling that if she hesitated, if she asked for time to consider it, he would find someone else. She thought of Mr. Ingram and his ugly innuendos, the demeaning way he treated his secretaries. She thought of her house and the mortgage payments that were such a struggle. With the salary Mr. Cramer was offering, she could easily make the payments, pay all the bills, and still have something left over for clothes, for movies, for taking Ted and Jane out for dinner. She thought, too, of Jim, wondering what he would think of this man across the desk from her. Jim had been so confident, such a good judge of people; she wished he were here to help her decide. But of course he wasn't. If he were, she would not need this job at all.

"A week from Monday would be fine, Mr. Cramer. What time?"

"Nine o'clock, sharp. See you then," and as he stood up she real-

16

ized that the interview, such as it was, was over. It had lasted all of fifteen minutes, and he had not asked her to take a typing test.

The first thing she did was to find a pay telephone and call Jane, who, after the cheering was over, instructed her to go up to Ted's office and demand to be taken out for lunch.

It was not until the next week, enduring the last of Mr. Ingram's leering glances, that fear took over. What had she done? She was giving up a boring but perfectly secure job for who knew what? Mr. Cramer, she was positive, would be impossible to please, and though he had promised to find her another job if she didn't—how had he put it?—"work out," she was afraid now that she had been incredibly naive. She had nothing in writing, not even a guarantee of that fantastic salary. In two weeks she could be out on the street looking for another position, with the mortgage payment due and no reference. Terrific. She went home on Friday convinced she had made a terrible mistake.

At the end of her first week with Benjamin Cramer, she still felt that way. He demanded nothing less than perfection. He worked at a breakneck pace and her own work load was more than she could handle. Yet the work itself was little more than what she had done for Mr. Ingram, typing and filing. Twice there had been no time for lunch, and Friday night she stayed until nearly eight o'clock, calling Ted first to be sure there was a late train home.

"Take it easy, Katy." Jane, as always, sounded supremely confident. "It's only the first week. The man deals with money, remember? Other people's money. Naturally he's cautious. Know what I think?"

"What?" Kate said, rubbing her eyes.

"He's testing you. He said he'd give you two weeks. This week he threw everything at you, to see if you'd complain. Did you?"

"I didn't have time," Kate said wearily.

"Okay, so far, so good. This week he's gonna toss in a few extra goodies, he's gonna ask a little more. You just stay in there. You do it if it kills you. By Friday, he'll tell you you're in, he wants you to stay. What do you want to bet?"

Kate laughed in spite of her doubts. "If he says that, I'm taking you and Ted out for dinner. If he doesn't, I won't be able to afford my own dinner, so it'll be your treat."

17

"That's a deal."

A week later, Kate paid the bill for three steak dinners, but she felt she had won the bet. She had survived the trial and Cramer, just as Jane had predicted, had waited until Friday afternoon, then called her into his office.

"Mrs. Downing, I'm very pleased with your work." He didn't smile, but he wasn't exactly grimacing either. "As far as I'm concerned, the position is yours. Is that satisfactory with you?"

"Yes, sir." She was too tired to think of telling him that she was exhausted, that he was asking too much, that she doubted she could keep working at this pace. She simply nodded and went back to the stack of work on her desk.

After that the burden seemed to lift a little, but she knew the work load wasn't getting any lighter. She was simply catching up to him. She dragged out her old portable typewriter at night and practiced until her back ached and her fingers were numb. Jane and Ted took turns dictating fictitious letters so she could improve her shorthand. The previous secretary, gone "to a position more to her liking," Cramer had explained briefly, had at least left the files in perfect order.

And there was something else. There was Benjamin Cramer, a polite if rigid man with a zeal for his work that was contagious. Kate wanted to meet his expectations of her, so she stuck with it. Occasionally she shuddered at the memory of Mr. Ingram, and was grateful that Benjamin Cramer was always businesslike, even distant, in his demeanor. He never volunteered any personal information about himself, and he never asked her anything about herself or her life away from the office. She found it a relief to keep matters so simple.

At Christmas time, nearly seven months after Jim's death, she closed another chapter in her life. On a Friday night, home alone as usual, she was going through her bank statements and she realized that her savings account was now up to a thousand dollars. It was enough, she decided. The next morning, in the bitter cold, she went to the bank and closed the special account she had opened with Jim's insurance payment. It had accrued a little interest, and she withdrew that too, taking the entire amount in the form of a check made out to Hiram Wilcox. She put it in a stamped envelope, along with a brief note she had written the night before, and dropped it in the mailbox outside the bank.

The debt was paid, though it was her father who had incurred it, and when the envelope slid down the chute she straightened her shoulders and marveled at how much easier it was now to stand up straight. She saw nothing charitable in the act. That money was death money. She'd done nothing to earn it and she refused to profit from it. Hiram Wilcox had been a friend and he had been cheated. Though she knew the money could never obliterate her shame, she hoped it would, in small measure, correct the injustice he had suffered.

She spent New Year's Eve that year, as she had the past two years, with Ted and Jane. It was the end of 1968, the year of the Tet offensive, the year of her husband's death, the year, in a sense, of her own death and rebirth. She was twenty-three years old and she was alone, but she had survived the year. For the first time in months she realized she did not need a cup of coffee to warm her.

"Happy New Year, Kate!"

"Happy New Year," she replied, and she began to believe it.

1973: The Meeting

The sun had disappeared behind the pines when Cramer heard the automobile outside. It was moving slowly, the driver feeling his way along the ruts that passed for a road. Inside the cabin, Cramer put down the detective novel he had been trying to read and went to freshen his drink at the cabinet near the door. He poured three fingers of bourbon into the glass and added a single ice cube. Then he stood at the end of the counter, facing the only door, and waited.

He did not hear the car door slam—he never did—and it was several minutes before the door of the cabin swung open.

"Mr. Cramer." The visitor nodded, closing the door behind him, and Cramer let out his breath slowly. He nodded in return, saying nothing, and went back to the sofa. He did not offer the visitor a drink, but he left the bottle and a clean glass on the counter, in plain view. Once, thought Cramer, just once, I wish he'd break the pattern and have one. It would show a tiny weakness. But no, the man settled into a chair across from him, ignoring the bottle, ignoring the book on the table at the end of the sofa, ignoring everything except Cramer.

Cramer always forgot how big the man was. He was well over six feet and he had black hair and a thick black mustache. Cramer could hold his own in most encounters, but this man matched him stare for stare, demand for demand. He never cracked, never gave ground. His black, horn-rimmed glasses, the lenses tinted an amber color, were a shield Cramer had found impossible to penetrate.

Well, this was the last time, Cramer thought. After tonight it'll be over and then I don't care what the hell the man does. I'll never see him again. I wonder if I should speak his name. I'm really sure this time. I'd like to see his face when he realizes I know.

"Talk, Mr. Cramer. I want to know everything." The man leaned back in his chair and crossed his legs, making himself comfortable; but Cramer knew that, at least, would change. Before they were through, the man would have crossed and uncrossed his legs twenty times, he would have perched on the edge of the chair, and he would have paced the floor.

Cramer began as he always did. "First the papers."

"First your report," the man replied automatically. It was almost a game, a ritual played out only because Cramer never stopped trying to gain even a tiny advantage.

"You have the papers with you?"

"You'll get them before I leave."

"I have your word on that?" Cramer's voice was sarcastic.

"That's right," the man said shortly, tiring of the game. "Now the report. And don't leave anything out."

Cramer was tight-lipped. "I never do." He took a healthy swallow of his drink and began talking. His voice was even, emotionless, as flat as he could make it. He was reciting facts, he told himself, and he distracted himself by counting the number of cigarettes the man across from him smoked. The man seemed more restless than ever this year. He interrupted constantly, asking for clarification, more details. What he wanted, Cramer knew, was for Cramer to convey his own feelings about the facts, and that he refused to do. He would give nothing he didn't have to give.

In fact, this year he was going to hold something back. It was a risk, but not too great. Cramer had tested him on other, smaller matters in the past, to see if the man had any way of verifying the facts Cramer gave him or withheld. Last year, for instance, she had bought a new car, and Cramer had deliberately refrained from mentioning it. The man had never given any indication that he knew about it, so Cramer felt reasonably certain that he was the only source of information.

This year she had gone back to college. She hadn't told Cramer about it, but he knew. If she wanted to keep it a secret, that was fine with him. And he had no intention of sharing it with anyone, particularly the man here in the cabin with him tonight.

So he kept his tone as bored as possible, and for nearly four hours he related the exceedingly dull facts he knew the man wanted to hear.

"No dates?"

"Only a few, and never the same man twice."

"You're sure?" Cramer nodded. "Hard to believe. Still, keep an eye on it. Anything else?"

"That's it." Cramer was exhausted and trying not to show it. He kept his eyes on the man. "Now, the papers, please. All of them."

The man was silent, his back turned to Cramer as he stood near the fireplace. Cramer could do nothing but wait.

"Mr. Cramer, you've done a good job. Real good; so I'm not quite ready to terminate our arrangement." He still had his back turned, smoke curling around his black hair as he puffed incessantly.

"What in the hell are you trying to pull?" Cramer got up from the couch.

"I need you a little while longer. You'll get the rest of the papers when I'm ready. Here, just a sign of good faith." He turned around, holding out a white business envelope. Cramer had no idea where it had come from, but the man must have had it stuffed in his jacket. He took the envelope and tore it open, pulling out three sheets of ruled ledger paper filled with dates, names, and dollar amounts. He looked through them rapidly and swore.

"Where're the rest?"

"Not yet."

"But you gave me your word." Cramer kept his voice low, but his rage was building. "Five years, that's all I agreed to, and the five years are up. I want the rest of those papers."

"I know you do." His voice was unperturbed. He sat down in his chair again and ground out the stub of his cigarette in the overflowing ashtray.

"Mr. Cramer, I think you have a pretty good hunch who I am." He watched Cramer closely for any response, but Benjamin Cramer had not become a millionaire by revealing his surprise at anything he heard. He stood, fists clenched, glaring at the man. "And I wouldn't doubt it at all if you'd even thought of going to the police. All you have to do is turn me in; they lock me up and you're home free. So why haven't you done it?"

He smiled and pointed to the papers. "That's why. I have the rest of them, in a safe place. When I'm ready, you'll get them. But for now . . ." He leaned back in the chair and lit another cigarette. "You've got quite a reputation, Mr. Cramer. I've been reading about you. What would all those hotshot clients of yours do if they knew about those papers? Maybe they'd run into that fancy office and tell you it doesn't matter. They'd still trust you with their life

22

savings, right? Sure they would, and God's in His heaven, too. You believe that, Mr. Cramer?"

Cramer was ready to explode, and it took every trick he'd ever learned to hide his raging desire to kill this man.

"How much longer?" He was not conceding, he told himself, only stalling, exploring options.

"Five more years. What's it to you? You're Mr. Big on La Salle Street, and it costs you one night a year when you're on vacation anyway. Still, I suppose you might be bored with it. Tired of those three-martini lunches and ten-course dinners, sick of the penthouse apartment and the Caddy. Maybe you're thinking what fun it'd be to start all over, change your name, move to another city, and hope nobody recognizes you. So what's it going to be?" He flicked his ashes in the direction of the ashtray.

"I don't own a Cadillac." Why Cramer chose that particular point to argue was beyond his own reasoning. His fury was consuming his logic. "I don't drink martinis, either," he added absurdly.

The man waited. There was a protracted silence.

Cramer broke first, as they both had known he would.

"Five years."

"That's the deal."

"And then you could change your mind again. How stupid do you think I am? I won't do this forever."

The answer surprised him. "No, you're too smart for that, but you're too smart to panic now, too. In five years you'll be so rich you can tell those phonies who pay you to do what they're too dumb to do themselves to kiss off. You won't need them anymore, I won't need you, and everybody'll be happy."

There had to be a way out, but for the life of him, Cramer couldn't find it.

"Get out of here," he whispered, no longer containing his loathing, "get out before I—"

"Kill me?" The man rose from his chair, easily, and he smiled again. "You're not a killer. You're a thief and a cheat and a fraud and a liar. But you're not a killer."

He strolled across the room, his back to Cramer as proof that he believed his own assessment. At the door, he paused.

"You know who to call if you need me. But I don't think you will. You're taking care of things just fine."

Cramer stood there, helpless. The man stepped out onto the sagging wood porch and breathed deeply of the night air.

"See you next year, Mr. Cramer." He closed the door softly behind him.

Then Cramer did something that Kate Downing would never have believed, even if she had seen it. He picked up his empty glass and threw it against the door.

1

March 1978:
An Orderly Life

■

Kate had taken Ted at his word. "Be on time," he had said that first day, and so she had, every single morning for nearly ten years—until today. She had been up until nearly three, studying for a test on the history of U.S. banking, and had dozed off on the couch with the textbook still in her hands.

She awoke at eight, frantic at having overslept, but she took the time to dress carefully, as always, choosing the pink wool suit and winding her hair into a neat knot at the back of her head. All the way into the city on the last express train, she fretted over what Mr. Cramer would say. In the relentlessly scheduled world of finance, he understood the value of time and the necessity of using it wisely. She knew he lived in the city, in an elegant condominium at the edge of Lake Michigan, because he could walk to the office from there. No haphazard public transportation for Benjamin Cramer.

Kate knew he would already be in the office. Even when she arrived early, which was most of the time, he was always there, already engrossed in his work, but she prided herself on her own punctuality. It was one of the many things he had taught her.

His clients and associates, she thought wryly, had been forced to learn the same lesson. A late arrival for an appointment with Benjamin Cramer only shortened the length of their time with him. She knew this practice had cost him a few clients, but not many. He got away with it for a simple reason: None of his clients had ever lost a dime by following his advice. He was cautious and prudent and as clever as any investor on La Salle Street. And she was his right arm, as efficient as he was, and what was he going to say about her being twenty minutes late?

He said nothing. He only looked up calmly when she poked her head into the inner office. In an uncharacteristic rush of words, Kate said, "Oh, I'm sorry I'm late, I overslept, so stupid, I don't know how it happened, I'll get right to work," and she ducked back to the corner in the outer office to hang up her coat before he could say a word. It was a cold, sunless morning, and she poured a cup of coffee before she sat down at her desk to see how much work had accumulated in the hours since she had left it yesterday evening. Plenty, she decided; a bad morning to be late, but she would catch up somehow. Within an hour, she was into her routine, feeling calm again, and not minding at all that she would be working straight through her lunch hour.

Around ten-thirty, he buzzed her on the interoffice phone.

"Mrs. Downing, it's the tenth of March. Time to make the cottage reservations with Weaver. Will you take care of it?"

"Of course. The usual time?"

"Yes."

It was an annual request, the only duty of a personal sort that he did not perform himself, and Kate dispatched it with her usual competence. She looked up the number in her office directory and called the Weaver Real Estate Company in Eagle Hill, Wisconsin, asking for Rodney Weaver.

"Good morning, Mr. Weaver. This is Kate Downing calling for Benjamin Cramer in Chicago."

"Aha! Mrs. Downing! Good morning!" Weaver was his ever-ebullient self. He and Kate had never met, but they were comfortably acquainted by telephone. He was always friendly and joking, and Kate often wondered about him, what he looked like, if he was married. He probably was.

"Mr. Cramer would like to make the usual arrangements for his cottage for the first three weeks in May. Is it available?"

"Yes, yes, you know I always save it for him, and I hope you won't think I'm presumptuous, but I took the liberty of checking it personally just last week. It's in fine shape. It'll be all ready for him."

"No, Mr. Weaver." Kate was smiling a little. "That's not being presumptuous." It seemed that Mr. Cramer's love of routine was known everywhere. Another woman might have laughed about it with Weaver, but not Kate. She was intensely loyal to Mr. Cramer. She said only, "I'm sure he'll appreciate your efficiency."

"Yes, well, there's another thing I should mention. Heh, heh, probably won't matter, but the rate has gone up a bit. I hope that's not a problem?"

"Tell me the amount, please," Kate said. "If it's agreeable with him, I'll mail you the check this afternoon."

She jotted down the figure and said a quick good-bye. She had no time for idle telephone chat today, but she was still smiling. She doubted that the increased rate, or anything else, would keep Benjamin Cramer from his appointed rounds. She buzzed the inner office.

"Mr. Weaver reports that the cottage will be ready, but the rate has gone up ten dollars a week."

"Thirty dollars?" he said, after a pause.

"Yes," Kate answered, and waited again.

Finally, "Oh—all right. Send the check, if you will."

"Certainly, Mr. Cramer."

Kate was glad he was in his own office and couldn't see her puzzled face. This was none of her business, and Mr. Cramer abhorred intrusions into his personal life. Still, it seemed odd that he would pause for concern over a thirty-dollar increase on a cabin rental.

Ah, well. She began to see the humor of it. A man whose daily business involved tens of thousands, even hundreds of thousands of dollars, concerned about a measly thirty! Suppressing a grin, she wrote out the check from the account she was authorized to use, addressed the envelope to Rodney Weaver personally, as she did every year, and tossed it into the outgoing mail basket. She looked up to greet the next appointment of the day. He was right on time.

"Good morning, Mr. Rissman." Kate smiled with genuine delight. She always had time for idle chat with Milton Rissman, Benjamin Cramer's attorney. Of all the interesting people who came through the doors into Benjamin Cramer's office, Rissman was one of Kate's favorites. "Still cold out there?" she asked dryly.

"Hmmph!" Rissman said from behind a red wool scarf. He was a short man, a little overweight, with unruly, curly dark hair. He did

27

his best to look ferocious, as befitted a Chicago lawyer, but his eyes betrayed that facade. He found nearly everything in life amusing. He dumped his briefcase on the floor and began to struggle with the scarf.

Kate laughed. "You need help! This thing must be ten feet long." She helped him unravel it, then took his coat to hang on the rack in the corner.

"Cold, Mrs. Downing, is hardly the word for it. Thank you for your assistance, but please—spare me the jokes about that damn scarf. It keeps me warm, and besides—"

"A Christmas present?" Kate guessed.

"From my wife," Rissman said ruefully.

"I like it," Kate told him. "Very practical. Coffee?"

"Two sugars, no cream." Rissman didn't bother to sit down. He knew Cramer was waiting for him.

"Mr. Cramer's ready," Kate said, handing the lawyer his coffee.

"Surprise, surprise," Rissman whispered as he walked past her, and Kate smiled again, but she said nothing. Her day was back on track, running smoothly, just the way she liked it.

The first three weeks in May were a slow-moving blend of boredom and freedom for Kate. With Benjamin Cramer away on vacation, there was much less activity in the office. In the beginning she had scheduled her own vacation time to coincide with Cramer's, but in recent years they had mutually decided that one of them should always be in the office. It was not an equal partnership: Cramer was still the boss, Kate the assistant. But she knew the steady clients and their portfolios nearly as well as he did, and he wanted her there to deal with them in his absence.

That was fine with Kate. She had no relatives to visit and she rarely traveled away from the city on her vacation. Besides, she enjoyed running the office by herself.

This year there were a few reports that Cramer wanted completed by the time he returned, and she typed them herself because she had done most of the work of preparing them and because she had the time. She cleaned out the files, throwing little away but organizing their contents until they were in perfect order. She cleaned her typewriter, answered the phone calls and the urgent mail, and scheduled appointments for the weeks after Cramer's return.

She also, with a free conscience, studied for her upcoming exam. In a few days, God and her professor willing, she would have her bachelor of arts degree in business. It had been a long time in coming, but it was worth all the nighttime and Saturday classes, the deluge of busywork that had often seemed to take more of her time than the accumulation of practical knowledge. She had worked hard. When this last exam was over and she had that diploma in hand, she was going to march into Mr. Cramer's office and ask for a substantial raise.

She could hardly wait to see the look on his face when she showed him that diploma. She hoped it would be a look of pride, for it was he who, however unwittingly, had given her the courage to aim for it. He had believed in her from the start, once she'd proved herself during those first two weeks, and then he had taught her, encouraged her, praised her work. It had not been easy, earning his respect, so as it came, it was all the sweeter.

He had begun by explaining bits and pieces of the reports she was typing, then, very slowly, giving her tiny assignments, which she accepted on top of her regular work load. The volume of business increased and, along with it, Kate's fascination with what Jane called "the heady world of finance." They reached the point where they were understaffed, but Cramer was reluctant to hire a third person. It would mean moving to a larger office, which he could certainly afford, but he liked this one. He liked the calm, unruffled atmosphere, he said.

At last, when Kate was working late every night and coming in most Saturdays, he announced that he and two other men in the building were forming a typing pool. They were renting an office down the hall and hiring three or four typists to handle the overflow work. Kate was delighted. She, too, loved the routine they had established, but she needed more time off, she thought.

And then, in all that free time, all those long evenings and two-day weekends, she found herself sinking into depression. It was almost as if Jim had just died and left her alone with time hanging, waiting to be filled. Only there was nothing to fill it with. Jane and Ted and their little boy, Scott, were gone, Ted having jumped at the promotion his company offered, even though it meant relocating to New York. New neighbors had moved in, of course, but the easy camaraderie she had shared with Jane was absent. So she sat there in the house Jim had loved and remembered the way things used to be. It was the worst year since Jim's death.

Then, with an offhand remark, Benjamin Cramer once again rescued her from self-pity. One day he said casually, "Mrs. Downing, it's a shame you never finished school. With a degree in business, you could write your own ticket."

It was only his way of praising her. Perhaps, she thought later, he had been only joking. But the remark kept coming back to her, and a month later she took his advice. She had the money; she had the time; she certainly had the incentive. She applied for readmission to Northwestern, was accepted, and attacked her studies with the same fervor she'd applied in the early months of working for Cramer.

Now, nearly fifteen years after she had entered college as a freshman, she was in her last semester. She had taken her time, been careful not to overburden herself, and had done well. Next month she would graduate with honors.

She hoped desperately that she hadn't outsmarted herself. What if her degree priced her right out of his office? It would be foolish to stay if she could earn a higher salary and carry greater responsibilities elsewhere, and yet she dreaded the idea of leaving. She truly loved working for Benjamin Cramer.

She was, in fact, quietly proud of the life she had made for herself. She had learned to enjoy living alone, arranging her furniture and her time exactly as she pleased. There were few men in her life—that was a void, she admitted, but one she preferred to live with. She had been burned once. She was never surprised when the men she dated seldom asked for a second meeting. She kept them at a distance, and there was never, ever, any sex. She was, she knew, ridiculously out of step with the times, but she couldn't shake her old-fashioned suit of moral armor. Once or twice, on those rare occasions when she saw a man more than once and was beginning to get to know him, she had toyed with the idea of inviting him home. Caution always prevented her. She did not think she could expose her body without baring a bit of her soul, too, and that she refused to do.

30

She supposed Mr. Cramer knew her as well as anybody did, which was ironic, because he knew nothing about her life away from the office. But he knew her laugh, and he knew how her mind worked when they discussed a business proposition. He knew, if he'd ever bothered to notice—which she was certain he hadn't—her taste in clothes and perfume. Somehow she didn't mind him knowing these things. She felt safe with him. She was happy being in the office with him, and most of the time she was happy away from him, too.

Only in her secret dreams, when she unexpectedly faced an empty evening stretching ahead of her, only when she could not avoid it, did she find herself recalling her past and questioning all the upheavals. Only then did that monster, self-pity, make her wonder what she could possibly have done to deserve the things that had happened to her.

And, reliving those nightmares, she would recall all too vividly the weight they had placed on her, crushing her spirit. She realized now that on the day she had met Benjamin Cramer she had been close to suffocation. She wondered how long she might have fought the demons in her head, the ones encouraging her to give up. What might have happened if Jane had never mentioned the man who worked in Ted's building?

Even now she shuddered whenever she remembered the night she'd returned from Seattle, Ted and Jane finally sent home with her assurances that she was fine. Standing in front of the medicine cabinet, she had gazed at the bottles of pills, aspirin and Empirin and cold tablets, and wondered how many she would have to take. Her fingers were closing around the first bottle when there was a pounding at the door downstairs. It was Jane, calmly announcing that she was spending the night, and where was an extra blanket?

Kate had known then that she couldn't do it, not in her own house, because Jane would be the one to find her, and Kate couldn't bear that. She would have to go away, maybe check into a motel somewhere, so she began planning, even as she went back to work for Ingram. As soon as Jane and Ted stopped hovering, gave her one free day, she would leave.

And then—oh, then, thank God, there had been Benjamin Cramer. After facing leering Mr. Ingram in that shabby suburban insurance office every day, what a genuine pleasure it had been to

31

come here and work with Mr. Cramer. He cared about his work. He had a sincere if businesslike concern for his clients, and he treated her with the same proper courtesy. She shared with him what she considered a perfect and rare working relationship.

She had never had dinner with him, unless you counted sandwiches in the office, and she didn't. They ate lunch together only occasionally, when he sensed that a business meal was the best way to woo a client and wanted her there to take notes. She had visited his apartment only once, to deliver some papers when he was ill. He had answered her ring and thanked her for making the special trip, but hadn't invited her in. Kate supposed he lived alone because he never mentioned family. Once in a great while she saw his picture in the newspaper society pages, attending a charity benefit with a woman on his arm. But it was never the same woman twice.

She knew he was generous with his raises. He possessed a wry, almost cynical sense of humor, especially about himself. He had a brilliant mind, was a good dresser, and she knew he played tennis every Sunday morning. Beyond that, he was just Mr. Cramer, the man she worked for.

So during those three weeks in May when Cramer was fishing in Wisconsin there was a certain emptiness in Kate's life, but she certainly didn't think of it as a personal one. She adapted to the change of pace rather well, she thought. On Friday of the third week she readied the appointment schedule, arranged the mail in order of importance for Cramer to attend to, and surveyed the office with a critical eye. No doubt he would come in before she did on Monday morning and she wanted it to look perfect for him. It did.

Walking to the train in the warmth of the spring evening, Kate reflected, not for the first time, that Mr. Cramer, Mr. Organized, was slipping. He had forgotten to send his usual postcard from Wisconsin. She received one every year, during the second week of his vacation. It was always a scenic view of the north woods and a lake. Kate had kept each card after the first. The message on each was the same, and that was why she saved them.

"Dear Mrs. Downing—" followed always by a dash, not a comma; punctuation was still her job, not his; "I trust all is well in the office. Weather here is pleasant. Weaver sends you his regards. BTC."

Once, in a perverse streak of curiosity, Kate had searched the newspaper for weather conditions in northern Wisconsin. It had

32

rained for six straight days. She had laughed and decided that Benjamin Cramer, true to his own efficiency, kept a mimeographed form from which he copied his annual card.

But this year it had not come. She wondered if it had been lost in the mail, or if the fishing had been so extraordinarily good that her boss had simply forgotten to send it. Well, it was hardly necessary, she chided herself, as she boarded the train and allowed herself to be jostled by the other commuters until she could grasp a strap. The card never said anything of importance anyway.

Still, as the train churned through identical suburbs in the spring twilight, she became aware of a tiny knot of uneasiness in her stomach. Kate's life was built on its own pattern of schedules. More than anything, she valued its security, it unchanging and predictable order. The absence of the annual postcard had nudged that order a bit out of line. She would feel better when Cramer was back at his desk.

Monday morning would be the same as always, she told herself. Mr. Cramer would glance up from his desk when she came in from the hallway. "Did you have a nice vacation, Mr. Cramer?" she would ask. "Yes, very pleasant," he would say. "Any problems while I was gone?" "No," she'd answer, "but this Burlington file has some gaps in it, I believe," and they would immediately be immersed in their work. That was the way it always was. Everything would be fine on Monday.

As she stepped off the train and walked to her car, she decided that after her final exam was over and she had more free time, maybe she would start walking to the station in the mornings and home in the evenings. It was only a mile's distance, and she needed the exercise. She was no longer as thin as she'd been ten years ago, but her figure was still trim—she took after her father in that respect—but she knew she was terribly out of shape. Jogging did not appeal to her; her mother's old admonishment that "ladies do not sweat" overruled the current craze. But walking—now that was a perfectly proper activity for any lady.

Kate slid behind the wheel and pulled out into the traffic. On Rolfe Road she relaxed a little, as she did every evening when she neared home. This neighborhood, where she had lived for fourteen years now, was her own oasis, a refuge from the noise and crowds in the city. She liked Chicago no better than she had when she'd first

33

gone to work for Mr. Cramer; she was no longer afraid of it, but she only tolerated it, and was glad she had kept this house. When she entered the driveway, she felt a surge of pride. Her house. Her yard. She had labored to hang on to them because she felt certain that Jim would have wanted her to. He would be proud of me, she told herself. He would.

She ate a bowl of soup and a piece of chicken at the kitchen table, bent over her books and notes. Her final course, the one on U.S. banking procedures that had caused her to oversleep that one morning back in March, was still challenging her. She spent the evening studying graduated returns on various types of investments.

She was up early the next morning, reading and memorizing again, and she took a break in the afternoon to work in the garden. Sunday was the same. When Monday came, she had not spoken to another person since Friday, but that was not unusual. She had built this life, and she was satisfied with it.

2

Monday, May 22, 1978: The Postcard

•

Kate rose early on Monday morning, not on purpose, but because she had been restless all night and was unable to stay in bed any longer.

"Pre-exam jitters," she told herself as she showered and dressed, and, indeed, she was mentally going over the material she had studied all weekend. She refused to admit that it was anything else.

The weather was gray and unusually chilly. Kate, who through sheer self-discipline did not experience great swings in mood, found herself irritated by the rain. Today, of all days—well, it was the exam. She didn't relish sitting sopping wet in a classroom for two or three hours tonight while she tried to astound the professor with her knowledge.

By the time she left the train station and began the short walk to the office building, it was raining determinedly, and she frowned as she battled the rush-hour crowds on the sidewalks. She entered the building shivering, and felt a trickle of water run down her back. In the elevator she removed her scarf and tried to check her appearance in a mirror, but the elevator was crowded, too, and when it finally reached the tenth floor and she had squeezed her way out, she felt she'd achieved a major accomplishment in managing to arrive at work on time and in one piece.

She walked down the hall as she always did, at a rather brisk pace, but certainly not a hurried one, and her face was composed.

The aloof manner she projected had begun years before as a pose, a defense against her feelings of inadequacy and inferiority, but now it was simply a part of her. The men who had offices on this floor admired her, but from a distance. Her manner distinctly said "Hands off."

She put her hand on the doorknob and, as if on signal, the knot in her stomach was there again; the same sense of uneasiness she had felt on Friday washed over her. The door was still locked.

She stood there dumbly for a few seconds and glanced at her watch. It was seven minutes before nine and Mr. Cramer was not here yet. Impossible. He was always in the office by eight, sometimes earlier. She tried the knob again. It wouldn't turn.

She dug in her purse for the office keys she'd been using the past few weeks—she never needed them when Mr. Cramer was here—and unlocked the door. It swung open to reveal a dark office. She flicked on the lights and walked across the gray carpet to her desk. It was as she had left it on Friday, clear of clutter, neatly organized. She looked around her, bewildered, half expecting her boss to pop up from behind the couch opposite her desk. He didn't, of course. His humor was not of the slapstick variety. The coffee maker, on a small table in the corner near the door to Cramer's inner office, was unplugged, cold.

Finally she put her hand to the door of the inner office. Feeling absurd, but not knowing what else to do, she knocked gently. There was no answer.

"Mr. Cramer?"

Silence.

"Mr. Cramer?" She knocked again, louder this time. "Mr. Cramer, good morning, are you in there?"

She paused, then muttered, "Oh, this is ridiculous." She was still grasping the keys in her hand, and she inserted one in the lock and pushed open the door. The blinds at the window were partially open; thin slats of gray light cast striped shadows over the desk, bookshelves, chairs, and carpet. The room was empty. Kate put her hand to her forehead and pressed her fingers hard against her skin.

Dear God, something is wrong. He should be here and he's not, and something is very wrong. She leaned against the doorframe, and the knot in her stomach curled up like a fist and made her draw her arms to her sides and hunch in her shoulders. She stood, alone,

36

and thought, this can't be happening again. Life does not repeat itself like this. Still she stayed there, frozen, and it was a long time before she moved.

The month was the same; it was May again. But she was in the office on La Salle Street, not at her house on Rolfe Road. She was older, more mature, but for all the distance she thought she had traveled, she found herself as she had been ten years before: alone, deserted, lost.

And this time not even Ted and Jane were here to hold her up, to tell her what to do. They were in New York and their correspondence had dwindled to a card at Christmas. She could hardly call up and say, "Jane, this is Kate; Mr. Cramer is gone." Yet there was no one else to call. . . .

Kate raised her head, blinking rapidly to hold back the tears. She wanted to scream, but she swallowed it, pushed it back in her throat and willed it to stay there. She looked again at Mr. Cramer's office. The rain was a dull, steady beat against the window. She switched on the lights and saw, on his desk, the letters she had stacked there Friday afternoon, everything arranged as she had left it.

Kate rubbed her forehead and realized she was dripping on Mr. Cramer's rug. Drops of rain were running off her coat and umbrella. She felt a smile tugging at the corners of her mouth. Mr. Cramer definitely would not approve of a puddle in the middle of his new gray carpet. She shrugged out of the coat and hung it with her umbrella in the corner of the outer office. She closed the door to the hallway and went to her desk.

It was stupid to compare this to ten years ago. Ridiculous.

She punched the button on the recorder attached to the telephone. Perhaps Mr. Cramer had called earlier, before she arrived, and left a message. . . . But no, the tape was silent; there had been no calls at all over the weekend.

She turned off the recorder and sank into her chair, frowning in concentration. Was she worrying over nothing? Her boss was a few minutes late for work. So what?

Well, he was never late for work, that's what. Never. His cardinal rule, punctuality, was as strong now as it had always been. So there had to be a reason, some logical explanation. Could he have overslept? No, not possible, but still . . . She flipped through her telephone file and called his apartment. The phone rang twelve times before she slammed down the receiver in frustration. Of course not. Benjamin Cramer never overslept.

He could be ill. Yes, that was a possibility, but still, he would have called. . . . Maybe he'd become ill in Wisconsin, out in that cabin. There was no telephone there; that was one reason he liked the place. No interruptions. So if he was ill and couldn't get to a telephone, then . . .

She knew only one person to call. Near the end of her directory she found Rodney Weaver's number and she punched the buttons on her telephone with a fairly steady finger.

"Mr. Weaver, please." If she had been aware of her own voice, she would not have believed it could sound so calm and controlled, perfectly businesslike. Inside she was screaming.

"I'm sorry, Mr. Weaver is out. May I help you?"

Kate swallowed. "Yes, please, this is Benjamin Cramer's office calling, from Chicago. I was expecting Mr. Cramer to return this morning. Do you happen to know if he's ill?"

"Um, Kramer. Benjamin, did you say? I'm sorry, that name doesn't sound familiar. . . . You must have the wrong number."

"No, no, please, wait a minute—" Kate sensed the woman on the other end of the line was about to hang up. "Benjamin Cramer; surely you know the name. He's rented a cottage through your agency for years, somewhere on a lake, I believe. Rodney Weaver always makes the arrangements himself. Are you sure he's not in?"

The voice on the other end was patient. "Mr. Weaver's on vacation. But—if he's handled this account, there must be something in our files. I'll check. May I call you back?"

"No, I'll wait, thank you." Kate's grip tightened on the receiver. Her tone was more authoritative than pleading.

"Yes, ma'am, all right. That was Kramer with a *K*?"

"No, *C*. C-r-a-m-e-r."

"Yes, please hold." Kate sat at her desk, pressing the receiver to her ear. She glanced at the clock: 9:05. Five minutes passed—oh, he wasn't going to be happy when he saw this phone bill, Kate thought.

"Excuse me, are you still there?"

"Yes, I'm here. Did you find the records?"

"No, I'm afraid not. We do manage several lakeside properties, but none have ever been rented to anyone named Cramer. In fact,

38

his name isn't anywhere in our files at all. Are you quite sure you have the right agency?"

"Of course I'm sure." Kate heard her own voice rising and she paused a moment to bring it under control. "I call your office every year, in March. I've done it for years. I always speak to Rodney Weaver and I reserve a cottage for Mr. Cramer for three weeks in May, and then I always send you a check. I can't understand why you don't have any record of all this."

The woman's voice took on a defensive note. "I'm very sorry, Miss—what did you say your name was?"

"Kate Downing; it's Mrs., and I'm sorry, too, but I'm worried about Mr. Cramer. He always follows a schedule, and it's not at all like him to be late and not let me know."

"Mmm, I know. Mr. Weaver is somewhat like that himself. I wonder—have you tried calling his home?"

"Yes, there's no answer, and—well, this is so unusual. I'm afraid he might be ill or—"

"You should try the hospitals. If he had an accident—"

Kate sucked in her breath. Oh, no, not an accident. . . . "I never thought of that," she managed to say. "I should—can you give me the number of the hospital nearest you?"

Kate jotted it down, thanked the woman—she had been very kind, really—and rapidly punched the numbers. A car accident, she thought. He could be alone in some hospital, swathed in bandages, he might even be—

"Eagle Hill Public Hospital."

"Hello, I'm trying to find out if a certain patient has been admitted. His name—"

"One moment, please."

There was a series of clicks. "Admissions."

"Yes, can you tell me if you have a patient named Benjamin Cramer?"

"Kramer, with a *K?*"

"No, *C,* Benjamin Cramer with a *C.*"

There was only a brief pause. "No, we have no Cramer listed."

"Excuse me, but I'm looking for—for a missing person." That sounded overly dramatic, even to her own ears, but she didn't know how else to put it. "He may have been in an accident. Could you check the admissions for the last several weeks? Any emergency victims, or someone with no identification . . ."

"Certainly, I'm looking now. There were two accidents this weekend, let's see . . ."

Kate held her breath, almost hoping his name was on the list. Then at least there would be an explanation, but if he'd been hurt—

"No, they've been identified, no Cramer here. I'm sorry."

"Thank you." It was automatic courtesy, bred in Kate from childhood, that produced this calm remark instead of a shriek. She replaced the receiver slowly, struggling to keep her mind clear. This was no time to succumb to panic.

She tried to think logically, to keep her imagination from veering off into terrible visions of what might have happened to him. He hadn't sent the postcard, so it was possible he'd been injured before the second week of his vacation. Maybe even before he left Chicago. But he would have sent word to her, she would know, unless . . . She read in the papers all the time about unidentified accident victims, people who were unconscious for long periods of time. . . . Oh, it was too fantastic. Still, what other possible explanation . . . ? No, she would not think about that.

She swung around in her chair and pulled out the Yellow Pages from the shelf behind her desk. Good lord, she'd never known Chicago had so many hospitals. Spreading the book on her desk, she called them one by one, asking the same questions, receiving the same negative answers. When the last call yielded the same result—"We have no patient by that name, no, no unidentified patients—" Kate told herself she should feel relief, but she didn't. She thought he had driven up there, and suppose he'd had an accident along the way? He could be anywhere between Chicago and Eagle Hill.

The outer door swung open. Kate looked up, hopeful that it was Benjamin Cramer, but it was only Ernie, the mailman.

"'Morning, Mrs. Downing. Sorry, the mail's a little soggy today." He handed her several slightly damp envelopes, glanced at the empty OUT basket on her desk, and turned to go.

"Know you're busy today, boss back in harness, see you tomorrow," and he was gone, the door closing behind him.

Kate flipped through the envelopes automatically. There were bills, a few envelopes with letterheads familiar to her, from regular clients, and—a postcard. A picture postcard with a photograph of tall pines and a painted blue lake. Her eyes widened; she turned it over to read the message. It was a little blurred because of the rain, but she could decipher it.

Dear Kate,

I've decided to stay an extra week. The weather is bad, but the fishing is fine. Please reschedule appointment with J. A. McGavin for Tuesday, 30 May.

As ever,
Benjamin Cramer

Kate's mouth opened in astonishment. What on earth . . .?

She peered at the postmark and was able to read the date: The card had been mailed on Friday, May 19, three days ago. But the city and ZIP code were smeared by the rain, unreadable. Was the state Wisconsin? Were those letters WI? She couldn't be sure.

Underneath her desk, Kate's knees were pressed together and her toes curled up inside her shoes. She gripped the card with both hands and stared at it blankly. She was beginning to feel cold inside, icy cold. Benjamin Cramer had never postponed a meeting in his life.

3

Tuesday, May 23, 1978:
The Man and
the Mountain

■

The surface of Baker's Lake was a glassy blue on Tuesday morning, smooth and undisturbed in the cool dawn of another cool day. The breeze from the west had died in the night and the pine trees rimming the lake stood tall and still, unbending and majestic. It was a small lake by Wisconsin standards, only a mile wide, perhaps four miles end to end, and it was not known for good fishing. The townspeople disdained it, but occasionally a northern pike swam to the surface and dove again, reveling in its possession of a home untroubled by humans.

There were three or four cabins scattered in the woods bordering the water. They had all seen better times, though none had been showplaces when new. Gradually the various owners had sold out to a real estate firm, relieved to be unburdened of poor investments, and the cabins had steadily disintegrated into decay. . . . All but one, which in outward appearance resembled the others: Built of wood, unpainted, weathered by Wisconsin's hard winters, it was fronted by a sagging porch and surrounded by weeds and unattended clumps of bushes, pines, and white birches. It was situated awkwardly in its little clearing, with the porch facing neither the lake nor the narrow access road but leaning east, toward the dense growth of trees that swallowed up the road. The only outward sign that this cabin was different from the others, and it would have taken a sharp eye to spot it, was an old LP gas tank at the far side of the porch, securely attached to the side of the cabin.

Even a casual observer, however, given a quick glimpse inside the structure, could have told immediately that this cabin was in use. It was clean and simply furnished, with sturdy pine tables and chairs, an overstuffed couch, and good reading lamps. The stove and refrigerator were old but serviceable. In a tiny, separate room were a double bed, made up with plain white sheets and two heavy blankets, a built-in dresser, and a homemade closet that some amateur handyman had nailed to an inside wall. On the floor of the closet, resting on an old newspaper, was an outboard motor, and, on top of that, two orange life jackets. There was a small bathroom with an old footed tub; the place had running water piped in from its own well. All the windows were covered with faded blue curtains.

To reach the cabin from the county highway was a chore hardly worth the effort, so it was seldom attempted. An unmarked dirt road left the highway eight miles north of town, meandered through the trees in a haphazard path around the lake, and finally dissolved into a double row of tire tracks, which ended thirty or forty yards from the lake on a high point of ground. The only reward for reaching the end was this seemingly worthless pile of lumber leaning slightly toward the east, held together with rusting nails and the faint hope that some fool would patch it up enough to keep it standing through another winter. Someone had, but he hardly thought of his investment as foolhardy. His name was Rodney Weaver, and for the past ten years his business interests had extended beyond small-town real estate.

Around the corner from the porch, on the side of the cabin facing the lake, was a small wooden boat equipped with oars. It was beneath a scraggly row of bushes and covered with an old tarp. The cabin, lost in the pines and humbly serene in its isolation, was barely visible from ten feet out in the lake. It was, intentionally, a private place, maintained in a manner to attract no attention whatsoever.

At the edge of the lake, down the slope from the cabin, there was a strip of sand and a crumbling wooden dock. A few yards away, half in and half out of the water, lay a man. He had a bullet in his left thigh and a wound from another that had torn through his left shoulder. He had lost a great deal of blood and by all rights he should have been dead. Anger—a raging, savage, animal anger—had kept him alive.

The man's name was Benjamin Todd Cramer. When the first rays of sunlight topped the pines and found his face, he opened his eyes and knew he had lived through another night. He almost wished he hadn't because the pain seemed more than he could bear, but then his anger saved him again and he gritted his teeth in determination. His feet and legs were freezing; they had lain in the water all night, and he knew he had to move. He brought his right arm up and underneath his chest and hunched himself forward a few inches. The pain shot through his left side and he collapsed on his right arm, gasping for breath. In a few minutes the pain subsided a little, he could breathe again, and he spit the sand out of his mouth. He dug his elbow into the sand beneath him and moved a few more inches out of the water.

Ten minutes later, his feet were on the sand, but still numb, and he allowed himself to rest again. He raised his head and squirmed ahead a little more, and then he could make out the cabin, but between him and the cabin was a mountain strewn with trees and bushes and boulders that prevented him from moving in a straight line to the door.

No, he told himself, not the door, they'd have locked it, and they've closed the window, I can see that. Not that I could stand up to crawl through it anyhow. Got to get to the key. Oh, God, if that key's gone, I'm dead. It's got to be there.

He wiped the sand from his mouth with the back of his hand and shifted his body a few inches to the right, so he could view the cabin from a slightly different angle. He couldn't be sure, but he thought he saw a patch of canvas, the tarp, and he could only hope that they hadn't hauled away the boat. It had to be underneath that tarp. He raised himself on his right arm again and began to claw his way up the mountain.

It was not a mountain, of course, only a slope, but it might as well have been a cliff. It took him six hours to reach the tarp and another twenty minutes to pull it back—thank God, the boat was there; he actually grinned at their stupidity—and then, lying at an impossible angle, feet twisted behind him, head rammed against the side of the boat, he lifted his right arm and groped blindly for the seat. Underneath, secured with masking tape, was the key to the cabin door, exactly where he had put it three and a half weeks ago. The sound from his lips was intended to be a laugh, but it was more of a bark, the utterance of a wounded animal incapable of any other expression.

Then he had to rest again, and his fingers curled around the key, grasping it as if it were a lifeline, which in a real sense it was. They must have been in a hurry, once they thought he was dead, and so anxious to get away that they'd overlooked the one item that could save him. His own sense of efficiency made him grunt at their ineptitude: They'd spent hours in that boat, but they hadn't found the key. He blessed his own foresight, though he'd hardly dreamed he'd ever be this desperate. He always locked the cabin whenever he left it, even for a few hours of fishing; he was an urban man, and locking doors was a way of life. Once, a few years earlier, he'd locked himself out of the cabin and wasted hours tracking down Weaver to get another key. The next day he'd had an extra key made and, every year, his first task when he arrived was to tape it to the bottom of the seat in the boat. Now he had it in his hands; it was all he needed and he was only a few yards from the door. . . .

But the strength to move was just not there. He would have to rest a little longer. His medical knowledge was limited, but he'd learned a few basics in the military, years before. If he didn't at least clean these wounds soon, the damage would be beyond correcting.

He lowered his head to the ground and tried to find a comfortable position. Impossible. He moved his head. The pine needles scratched his cheek and he swore silently.

Cramer was using his anger again, consciously now, to keep himself awake. It was better than indulging in self-pity or second-guessing. Never once did he think "What if I had left on Friday?" or "If only I had listened to Weaver." His worst mistake, once again, had been overconfidence. He believed in the power of money—and why shouldn't he, when he wielded that power so successfully every day? He had been so sure that he could buy off the man in Hong Kong that he hadn't even bothered to send his usual postcard to Kate Downing. He had believed, foolishly, that he'd be back in Chicago early, even, possibly, within the first week.

Because this time he had come to the cottage prepared for the encounter with the man from Hong Kong, the man who hid behind amber glasses and what Cramer now knew was a black wig. This was the tenth year, the arrangement was to end, and Cramer was supposed to receive, finally, all the pages from the ledgers. Ha! Cramer knew, at last, that the man would never keep his promise. But he had naively thought that the man would appear as usual one night and listen to Cramer's report, which Cramer had made duller, safer, every year. Then he would produce a few more pages from the ledgers, tell Cramer he needed more time, turn his back, and walk out.

Well, this year Cramer had planned a surprise for him.

"One hundred thousand dollars," he was prepared to say just as the man was putting his hand on the doorknob.

Cramer had calculated the amount very carefully. He had determined how many shares of which stocks he would have to sell and on which property he could secure second mortgages, arousing the least suspicion on La Salle Street. The last thing he needed was a flying rumor that he, a financial consultant, had money troubles of his own. Then, when he made his offer, if the man laughed in his face, Cramer was prepared to go higher. Step by step, dollar by dollar, he had planned how he could do it, which properties he would have to sell outright. He'd even made a list of potential buyers for each property, men he knew were likely to have loans easily approved, men who coveted certain prizes in his collection of real estate holdings. It would take some haggling, but he was confident he could come to an agreement with the man from Hong Kong.

Five years ago he had said he needed more time. To Cramer, that meant he needed more money. Well, Cramer was running out of time, but now he had plenty of money. He would pay for the remaining pages from the ledgers.

Then the race would be on, the best man would win, and Cramer never once doubted the outcome of that contest.

But this year, with Cramer for the first time actually eager for the annual encounter, the man from Hong Kong had once again snatched away the advantage. He simply never appeared.

Always, by the end of the first week, he had come and Cramer had given his report. The encounter left him feeling dirty, and he would spend the next two weeks at the lake trying to shake that sensation of filth. On the Saturday at the end of the first week,

Cramer had not left the cottage at all. Saturday night, he had barely slept. Sunday, he paced the floor, ate and drank too much, and sat up all night in the chair by the fireplace.

Monday, he drove to the nearest town and called Rodney Weaver. He was not certain how much Weaver knew—was he a simple go-between or an accomplice?—so he was brief.

"Where is he, Weaver?"

"Now, Ben, calm down, calm down. You're on vacation, remember?"

"Cut the bull. Where is he?"

"Well, as a matter of fact, he told me you'd be calling." Weaver paused, sensing his momentary advantage.

Cramer, who hadn't smoked in years, suddenly felt an intense craving for a cigarette. He was standing in a phone booth near a gas station, and he could see a cigarette machine inside the office.

"Ben, you still there?"

Cramer grunted.

"Well, don't you want to know what he said?" Weaver sounded positively gleeful.

Cramer thought a moment. What leverage could he use?

"Rodney, when was the last time you were audited by the IRS?" His voice was casual, as if he were making idle conversation.

"Uh?" Weaver said. "What do you mean? Out in the sun too long yesterday?" He chuckled, but there was an edge to it, and Cramer had found the leverage.

"I have a friend named Darrell Shandstrom," Cramer said. "Roomed with him in college, matter of fact. Right now he's an up-and-coming agent in the IRS. Fraud division." This was the truth. "I happen to have his telephone number in my pocket right now." This was a lie.

"Ben, wait a minute, what—"

"Tell me what you're supposed to tell me, Rodney. I don't like games."

"He isn't coming," Weaver snapped. "He said to wait until you called and then tell you he isn't coming."

"Anything else?" Cramer was slumped against the glass enclosure of the phone booth, staring blankly at the cigarette machine across the way.

47

"What d'you think I am, your answering service?" Weaver's voice was a whine.

"Exactly. Anything else?"

"He just said he wasn't coming this year. The rest of it's your problem." Weaver slammed down the phone.

Cramer hung up and walked over to the filling-station office. He nodded to the mechanic, dropped some coins in the slot, and walked out with a package of Camels. He got behind the wheel of his Mercedes and drove away, puffing.

The next morning, he went to a different phone booth and called Weaver.

"Call him, Rodney," Cramer said, without identifying himself. "Tell him four words. Tell him 'One hundred thousand dollars.' I'll call you tomorrow." Cramer hung up, went back to the cottage, and spent the day fishing.

Wednesday morning, he called Weaver. Weaver said the man had laughed.

Cramer paused. He wanted Weaver to believe he had to think about his next offer, though, of course he didn't.

"Tell him one-fifty, Rodney."

The man in Hong Kong laughed.

"Two hundred."

"No deal," said Weaver.

"Tell him five hundred, Rodney. And tell him something else. Tell him if he doesn't accept, his chicken in the suburbs is flying the coop."

"His what?" Weaver seemed totally confused.

Cramer repeated the message. "Tell him to think about that, Rodney. I'll be at the cottage."

A week later, on Friday of the third week, Cramer was still waiting, for a counteroffer, perhaps; a response of some kind. It was still early when he heard a car pull up outside and he went out to meet it eagerly. It was Weaver, who saw the question on Cramer's face and shook his head. Cramer turned abruptly and Weaver followed him into the cabin. There was a fresh pot of coffee on the stove, its rich aroma masking the stale odor of cigarette smoke. Weaver, without asking, poured two cups and joined Cramer at the wooden table.

48

"He hasn't called, Ben," Weaver said. There was no glee now, no gloating.

"Did he laugh?" Cramer was gazing out of the window that faced the lake. His voice was emotionless.

Weaver said nothing.

Cramer looked at him and saw that the smug, unctuous Weaver had disappeared, and in his place was a local, small-town real estate agent who suddenly knew how insignificant he was.

"You can tell me, Rodney."

Weaver nodded and took too big a gulp of coffee.

"He laughed. Then I told him the part about the chicken and he stopped laughing. He said he'd call me back, but he hasn't."

"Yet," said Cramer.

"Ben, I don't know what the hell's going on, but I don't like it. Why don't you drop it?"

Cramer believed him. Weaver knew only as much as the man in Hong Kong deemed necessary, and that wasn't much. He was paid to keep this cabin livable but inconspicuous, and to rent it only to Cramer—he had bragged about that several times. "You're the only tenant, Ben," he had said. "Come up whenever you want!" The man in Hong Kong wanted no one else to know of this place. Weaver had his telephone number, occasionally his instructions, and that was all.

"It's not a joke anymore," Weaver was saying. "Look, what do you say I call him back? I can tell him you changed your mind. I can convince him."

Cramer looked steadily out at the lake, blue and calm in the morning sunlight. He knew his position was impracticable, possibly even dangerous. But he had waited too long already, years too long, and now he was committed to this course of action. Nothing Weaver said, not even his veiled references about the volatile nature of the man in Hong Kong, made Cramer think anything else.

"You can call him," he said finally, "but it won't change anything."

After Weaver left, Cramer sat at the table, idly fingering a splinter on the corner of it, letting his coffee grow cold. His well-honed business instincts told him this deal was going sour. The smart move was to go after Weaver and say he'd changed his mind. That might let him off the hook, at least temporarily. . . .

No, it wouldn't. He knew as well as, if not better than, Weaver did the kind of man he had been dealing with all these years. He had been forced to accept the blackmail, but he had fought back in his own ways, protecting her when he could, which hadn't been often, by withholding information from the man. And he had determined, from the very beginning, that he would at least learn the identity of his enemy.

That had been the hardest task. It had taken him many months to find a man he could trust with such a dangerous secret. Finally he had hired a young and discreet private investigator named Randy Daniels. Daniels did not work fast, and he did not promise miracles. His fees were enormous. "By the time I'm forty," he told Cramer during their first interview, "I'm going to find some quiet corner, sink into it, get married, and raise kids. Until then, I'm working my tail off. You'll get your money's worth."

Cramer, who often harbored a similar secret vision of his own future, was convinced. And Daniels had been relentless, following the slimmest of leads and vague clues that never panned out, filing detailed reports with every monthly bill he sent to Cramer's home address. Finally it was Cramer himself who turned up the crucial bit of information that led Daniels to the truth—that, and a dangerous two days Daniels had spent following the man as he left the cabin late one night in May six years before, sticking with him on the interstate down to Chicago, abandoning a car he never did recover at the airport, somehow managing to get the last seat on the plane the man boarded for Hong Kong, only to lose him as he sped away from Kai Tak airport.

Cramer knew more about the man now than he'd ever wanted to know, and he wanted to be rid of him. Five years ago the man had suggested an alternative. He could start over, move to another city, change his name. . . . And Cramer had hurled a glass across the room in his helpless rage.

Now he let his mind play with the idea. He could do it. He knew he could. It would be a challenge, and there was nobody better able to meet a challenge than Benjamin Todd Cramer. He had capital now, a small amount compared to what he was aiming for, but still, it was substantial. He could do it.

But it was not part of his nature to retreat. He had issued this new challenge; that much was done, and somehow he could not regret it. Once, ten years ago, he had buckled under, and he was paying for it still. That was the action he regretted. He vowed he would never retreat again.

So pride was part of it. So was honor. He supposed it was outright hypocrisy to think of that term, but, he told himself, he did have a sense of honor. To sneak off, pretend he was someone he wasn't, deny whatever good things he had done, all in an effort to escape the bad—the entire notion repulsed him.

What's more, she would never go with him, not under those circumstances.

The splinter broke off in his fingers. He tossed it into an ashtray and got up.

It was time to sell off a few shares. He wasn't panicking. He didn't believe the market was crashing. But he was going to diversify one of his holdings.

He strode into the bedroom and pulled out a postcard from the top drawer in the dresser. It was several years old. He had found a bargain on his first trip up here and laid in a supply. He was quite aware that his postcards to Kate Downing always said the same thing. He had done it on purpose, establishing a routine that she would have to notice. He had done it so that if any trouble ever arose, he would have a means of sending her a message. He had always been vague about what sort of trouble might arise, and he'd known he might not have time to get word to her. But now it happened that he did.

He would have to word his message very carefully. The name, of course, was the key; he had to give her the name that bound them all together, her and the man from Hong Kong and himself. But he did not want to alarm her. In all likelihood, he'd be back in the office Monday. But if—well, if he weren't, he had to give her a lead to follow.

The name was John Anthony McGavin. He lived not ten miles from this cabin, but Cramer had never met him. He was the missing link, and when Cramer had stumbled on that possibility, Randy Daniels had gone to work, taking pains to confirm that he really was the link they were searching for.

Cramer went back to the table and pondered for several minutes before he wrote out the message on the postcard. He addressed it, found a stamp, and drove into town to mail it.

After that he felt so relieved that he stopped in at the local hotel for a late breakfast and managed to carry on a perfectly normal, if impersonal, conversation with the hotel owner. He was a gossipy old man who had once, in a previous conversation, totally unwittingly given Cramer the information that had proved so valuable. He had mentioned John Anthony McGavin. Cramer had picked up on it almost idly, sure it would lead to nothing, but he'd got as many details as he felt he safely could without arousing the owner's suspicions. Then Randy had earned his fees.

The hotel owner had made possible the message Cramer had sent this morning, and his rambling, leisurely conversation with him, when he was suddenly anxious to be back out fishing at the lake, was Cramer's private way of expressing his gratitude. He gave no sign that he even remembered Cramer, or the time they had met before. Once again, Cramer managed to steer the conversation toward mention of McGavin, and the hotel owner's enthusiastic remarks assured Cramer that using McGavin as the link was an acceptable risk.

Then he returned to Baker's Lake and spent his last weekend there, fishing and reading by turns. He was a little on edge, but by Sunday afternoon he decided nothing was going to happen, nothing at all. The man in Hong Kong had finally decided he no longer needed him.

Cramer relished his last few hours out on the lake until the sun was low and he knew he had to go in. In spite of the terrible circumstance that had first brought him to this place, he had come to appreciate its beauty, the isolation it gave him from his frantic business routine in Chicago. He dreaded the long drive back to the city, but it was time to leave. He motored slowly back toward the dock, trolling one of his lines, and in the near darkness he didn't see them until he was only a few yards from shore. Then he had no choice; he had to go on in and meet them.

Weaver was there, a sickly, uneasy smile flickering on his lips. With him stood another, bigger man—and Cramer sucked in his breath. It was him! He looked the same, with his black hair and mustache, the amber glasses completely hiding his eyes in this dim light. He was not smiling.

Weaver was babbling, greeting Cramer heartily, tossing the loop at the end of the towline around a sagging wooden post, reaching to help Cramer out of the boat. Cramer collected his fishing gear and endured Weaver's prattle as the three of them climbed the sloping path to the cabin.

"Got your key, Ben? Here, use mine. Say, where're all the fish? They outsmart you today?" Nonstop, the words poured out; Cramer heard panic in every one of them.

He had his own keys in his hand, and he used one to open the door. It led into the kitchen area, and Cramer moved aside a bottle of bourbon and dumped his fishing gear and the keys on the counter that separated the kitchen from the rest of the room. He went to the sink to wash his hands. Behind his back, the man from Hong Kong quietly closed the door and leaned against it.

Cramer supposed he should have been terrified, but he was actually elated. The man was here to deal. Let's see, what was the last offer he had made? Five hundred thousand dollars, right, and he knew exactly how he was going to raise that amount. But it would take a little time. He had to make that clear. He dried his hands on a paper towel and turned to face them.

"All right, let's get down to business. Five hundred, right?" He was rubbing his hands together as he went around the end of the counter.

"You don't understand, Mr. Cramer." The man from Hong Kong spoke calmly. "You never have understood. It's time to terminate our arrangement."

Cramer turned around and saw Weaver shrinking against the stove. The man was still leaning against the door.

"Fine," said Cramer shortly. "It's over. Give me the rest of the ledgers." He leaned his hands on the counter, facing the man.

The man from Hong Kong began to smile, and Cramer felt a twisting sensation in his stomach.

"I don't like threats," the man said. "Just where do you think the chicken in the suburbs is going?"

Cramer swallowed. So that was it.

"She's free to go wherever she wishes. My God, it's been ten years—"

"I decide where she goes, and when. Not you." He sighed, as if he was already tired of explaining the obvious. "You made a mistake when you fell in love with her."

Cramer couldn't hide his surprise, and the man said sharply, "You think I didn't know? I probably knew it before you did, but I thought you were smart. I thought you'd know that it's impossible. She's not going with you or anyone else."

"You have no right—"

"*You* have no rights, Cramer. You made a big mistake. I was going to let you off this year. It's safe now. Like you said, it's been ten years. So I figured, what the hell, I don't need you anymore, she's not going to make any changes in her life. And then you foul up the works. Dumb mistake."

"But the ledgers—"

"I'm entitled to a little insurance. I said to myself, as long as I've got the ledgers, Cramer's not going to do anything stupid. He's not going to mess up that nice little life he's made for himself. And then you blow it."

"So you were going to leave me hanging," Cramer said. "No ledgers, nothing. Limbo."

"I was, but you ruined it. It's your own fault. All you had to do was leave her alone."

"Ben," Weaver said urgently, and Cramer glanced over at him, surprised. He had almost forgotten Weaver was there. "Ben, look, we can work this out. Just do what he wants and—"

Weaver stopped abruptly and Cramer looked back at the man leaning against the door. He was pointing a revolver straight at Cramer's head.

"It's too late for that," he said. "I don't trust you anymore."

Cramer did not plan what he did next. There wasn't time to think; there was time only to make one desperate move. He grabbed one of the fishing rods off the counter in front of him. It was the one he had trolled with on his way into shore. He swung it as hard as he could, ducking behind the counter as the rod whipped through the air. The end of it caught the gun as it went off and the shot went wild. Cramer didn't see the line come loose from the rod. The hook at the end flew into the man's eye as another shot went off.

"Weaver! Take the gun! Damn you, Cramer! Ahh!" It sounded as if he was in pain, but Cramer didn't stop to find out. Still in a crouch, he moved over to the window facing the lake, his body still hidden by the counter.

"The barb!" The man was yelling with rage. "Get the barb out of my eye!" There was a scuffling noise, and Cramer took his chance. He shoved the window open and leaped through it, landing on the pine needles with a thud. The man was shouting, "Get him, Weaver! Never mind my eye, get Cramer! Don't let him get away!"

Cramer heard the door at the side of the cabin opening, and he knew he couldn't get around to his car. He didn't have the keys anyway; they were back in the cabin on the counter. The woods, then—

A shot rang out and he staggered hard against a tree. A bullet had torn past his shoulder, slicing through his light jacket, his flannel shirt, and his flesh. The pain seared through his arm, but he didn't dare stop. He was a target, leaning against this tree. If not the woods—

He turned, crouching low, and plunged through the bushes toward the lake. As he splashed into the water, another explosion filled the air. Cramer cried out. This time the bullet had not just brushed him; it had lodged in his leg. He dove, moving deeper and deeper into the icy water, away from shore, away from the men who had come to kill him.

The darkness had descended completely now, and the moon had not yet risen; it was his only defense. It had probably saved him, throwing off Weaver's aim. He counted to forty, then rose to the surface, his head emerging from the water. He let out the air slowly, not making a sound, and listened. Above the pounding in his ears and the sound of water lapping into shore, he could hear the man from Hong Kong ordering Weaver to help him into the boat. His eyes followed the sound, and he could make out two dim figures near the crumbling dock, arguing as they tried to start the motor. Their voices carried clearly across the dark water.

"Weaver, you idiot, I can't see, you'll have to steer this thing. Pull the rope harder; he just turned it off, it has to work. Pull harder!"

Finally the small motor roared into life, and Cramer knew it was over. He was in bad shape; they had the boat, and even if one of them couldn't see well, there were still two of them. Weaver probably knew this lake as well as he did. There was nowhere he could go, nowhere he could hide.

Was this what it came to, then, he wondered? Ten miserable years of hating himself, of being a coward, so he could sink to the bottom of this lake and die? Or, worse yet, be finished off by the man who had made him so miserable?

He shook his head. He would not make it so easy for them. He had not come this far to give up so readily. He had rights, plenty of them, and one of them was the right to keep going, foolhardy or not. Let them come after him. Let them find him, if they could.

He sank again and propelled himself through the water with his right arm. His legs were dead weights behind him; he couldn't seem to move the right one without moving the left, and that sent waves of pain through his body. He came up for air again and saw the boat ten feet away from him. Without pausing to take another mouthful of air, he sank and stayed right where he was, not moving, not risking even a tiny disturbance on the surface of the water. He started counting to forty again—why he had selected that number as the proper one to aim for, he had no idea—but this time he couldn't make it. He was at only twenty-seven when he knew his lungs were going to burst; they were burning a hole in him, he had to go up for air. Slowly, slowly, his head broke the surface. He had already expended all his air, so he drew in slowly, filling his lungs, his head, even his limbs, it seemed, with a fresh supply. The boat was perhaps fifteen or twenty yards away from him. It seemed to be moving away, so he submerged again, slowly, silently, and headed for the reeds a hundred yards downshore, in the opposite direction. Several times he had to come up for air, but he reached the spot he'd aimed for. When he felt the sandy bottom of the lake beneath him, he rested, head just above the water, weeds in his face. He was gasping now, and had the boat turned back, he would have been discovered; he couldn't have moved another foot.

But his enemies had overestimated him and while they circled the middle of the lake in the boat, Cramer lay near the shore and listened. It was only a few minutes before the whir of the motor came closer. He peered through the weeds and saw the outline of two figures. One was steering the boat and the other was holding a hand over his eye.

"Look, it's useless." Cramer could hear Weaver pleading. "You've got to take care of that eye; it's still bleeding—"

"Are you sure you got him?"

"Yes, yes, I know I did, but—"

"Then find him! We're not leaving until . . ." His voice faded away as the boat moved off.

Cramer pulled himself out of the water and sat on the soggy ground, hidden by the reeds surrounding him. He shrugged out of his polyester jacket and tied it around his leg, now numb with pain and cold, hoping the material would be enough to stop the bleeding. The left sleeve of his flannel shirt was already torn and it pulled away easily. With his right hand, he wound it around the injured shoulder and used his teeth to secure the knot.

He heard the motor across the lake and he slid back into the water. He edged his way along the shore, away from the cabin, as far away as he could get, deeper into the backwater of reeds until he thought he was in the thickest growth. Then he waited.

He waited all of Sunday night while they searched the lake. Twice they came so close to him that he was sure they would spot him; how could they miss him? He held his breath, willing his muscles to stay still for fear a single reed moving even slightly would give him away. Their voices sounded only a few feet away.

"Why did we have to kill him?" It was Weaver, still not understanding the rules of the game he had chosen to play so many years ago.

"You better hope he's dead," came the angry response. "Poke the oar in those weeds."

Weaver struggled clumsily with the oar. Cramer shrank back and watched it move right in front of his face.

"Nothing?"

"Of course not," Weaver snapped. "I shot him, remember? He's somewhere on the bottom of the lake. This is useless."

"Keep going. Down there. Try the oar again."

Cramer, doubled up in the weeds, was enduring a pain he hadn't thought possible. He let out his breath only when they slowly moved away.

The night went on. They came back again and again, and the pain, especially in his leg, grew even greater. He was angry, furious at Weaver for his spineless obedience to the man from Hong Kong, but he was even angrier at the man himself. He swore that if he lived, if, by some miracle, he actually survived this double cross, he would repay him in the way it would hurt most. Cramer knew exactly what he would do, and, to keep himself alert, to divert his mind from the pain, he planned it in meticulous detail.

They came again, much later. Weaver was still whining.

"This wasn't part of the deal. I'm a respectable businessman, I have my broker's license."

"The only reason you're here at all is to help me clean up the cabin, in case the police come. If it hadn't been for that damned fishhook, we'd be out of here by now. Do you think I like this stinking place?"

Cramer stayed doubled up in the reeds, not moving, as the dawn came slowly. Still they would not give up. They kept circling the lake, crisscrossing it, back and forth, around and around, but the motor couldn't operate in the tangle of weeds, so each time they bypassed him. They stopped only to add gas to the engine. Around noon, Cramer heard the echo of their voices downshore, toward the cabin. They were swearing at each other as they struggled out of the boat. He listened to their grunts, carried across the water to him by the gentle wind, and he guessed they were hauling the boat out of the water and dragging it up the hill. Were they leaving? Were they giving up the search at last?

He couldn't believe it, so he stayed where he was, trying not to move. He heard the cabin door slam and two automobile engines starting.

They're taking my car! Oh God, how in hell will I get out of here?

But both cars were leaving, he was sure, and that meant they were both leaving, too, satisfied that he was dead, either killed by the bullets or drowned in the lake. He didn't know if he'd won or lost.

They think I'm dead, but I can't walk. How am I going to get out of here?

He stayed in the reeds until dusk, anticipating their return. Surely they would think of something they'd forgotten, some detail overlooked, and come back to take care of it. He drifted in and out of consciousness, aware of a hollow space in his stomach. He hadn't eaten since the afternoon before.

Hunger finally pushed him out of the reeds. He had left a few tins of soup in the kitchen cupboard and he thought there was the end of a loaf of bread somewhere. If they hadn't taken them, if they had overlooked just that one detail . . . Slowly, half floating and half pushing with his right arm, he bobbed along near the shore toward the cabin. When he felt the gravel and then the firm sand solid beneath him, and he could see the dock a few yards away, he knew he was there. He stopped to rest, just for a moment. . . .

It was late in the day when he awoke, not in the sand at the edge of the lake but on hard ground at the rear of the cabin. The burning in his shoulder and leg was more intense than ever, and his entire right side was numb, asleep from the weight of his body, but in his fist was the key. When he was fully awake he cursed himself for his weakness. He'd made it up the hill but he had wasted the entire afternoon, let it slip by as he lay there unconscious. Hours, life-giving hours, wasted! He had to get inside the cabin. The food was there, he hoped, and bandages and antiseptic in a first-aid kit supplied, ironically, years ago by Rodney Weaver. He had to at least clean his wounds, do what he could to stop the spread of infection. Beyond that, he had no plans. He was almost beyond caring. One thing at a time. He would reach the inside of that cabin before he rested again.

Clutching the precious key in his fist, he inched his way around the boat and along the back of the cabin. He rounded the corner, panting hard, dirt in his mouth and eyes, and kept going until his arm bumped into the bottom step of the porch. Instead of slowing him down, it seemed to spur him on—he was so close, he couldn't stop now—and, using his right arm and right leg, he hauled his body up the steps, one, two, three, four—there, that was the porch; he could feel blessed splinters in his arm. It was dark, but he was nearly blind with pain anyway, and he could feel his way. The fingers on his right hand were bleeding, raw from clawing the ground, and the key felt slippery in his hand. He had to use his left hand to uncurl his fingers from around the key and then, grunting at the spasm of pain that fired through his body, he raised his right arm, stuck out the key, and poked it at the door, feeling for the keyhole. At last it slipped in and he turned it, twisting at the knob with his thumb and index finger. The weight of his body falling against the door pushed it open and he went with it, landing hard on the floor of the cabin. His face smashed into the wooden planks, but he hardly felt it. He had made it! He was inside the cabin. He was safe.

He lay on his stomach, feet sticking out onto the porch behind him, and tried to catch his breath. He told himself he wasn't resting; no, he couldn't afford that. He was only gathering his wits. It was very important now that he plan every motion; there could be no wasted time, no fruitless expenditure of what little strength he had left. The key was still in the door; it seemed miles above him. He squinted at it through bleary eyes and asked himself, do I really need to remove the key? No, let it be. They're not coming back, and if they do, they'd find me anyway. The key in the door would give away nothing. Besides, they aren't coming back, no one is. They think I'm dead. For all I know, I am, and this is the hell I never believed in.

It was cold on the floor. He had spent two nights out-of-doors and he knew he had to get warm. The only light was the glow of the moon filtering through the open door. They must have closed the curtains. Well, he would have to close the door, but not before he found food. The cupboard under the counter was at his elbow and he found the knob and pulled on it. Inside—ah, they'd missed it! That was their second mistake, first the key and now the soup. In the drawer above his head was the can opener and he reached up, pulled out the drawer, and felt through the few utensils it contained until his fingers closed around the can opener and a spoon. It took him a minute to figure out how to brace the can and use the opener with only one hand; his left hand seemed to be useless. He had no idea what kind of soup he'd opened until the first spoonful slid into his mouth, and then he didn't care; it tasted awful and delicious all at once and it didn't matter that the bread was gone. He found two more cans, opened them, and devoured their contents, hardly tasting them. He had to hurry, before he passed out again.

Now, what if they'd taken the first-aid kit? He kept it in the bathroom, but he could hardly walk in there to check. The liquor bottle! He'd left a bottle of bourbon on the counter. If only it was still there, if only he could reach it. Check the cupboard first. If they had seen it and decided to leave it, they would have put it there, and he groped inside the cupboard again, feeling in the back corners. Yes! That was it; his fingers grasped the bottle and pulled it out.

Now, what else? Well, he had to get to the bedroom sooner or later; that was where the only blankets were and he was freezing cold. He could stop in the bathroom on the way; the sink was lower in there—no, the bathtub; he could use that faucet. He stuck out his right leg and kicked the door shut, then started dragging himself across the floor, rounding the cupboard with the liquor bottle clutched in his right hand. His head bumped into something, hard. He reeled back and, in an involuntary motion, his right arm came back to brace his body. The liquor bottle smashed against the cupboard and broke. He could feel liquid running over his hand, burning the cuts.

It was too much. Tears spurted from his eyes, leaving tracks in the dirt on his face. The neck of the bottle was cutting into his palm and he flung it away from him. Damn! He couldn't do it! If the first-aid kit was gone, he had no antiseptic, and if there was no antiseptic, then there was no use in going any further. It was over. He'd given it all he had, more than he'd ever dreamed he could, but it was no use.

But even as he thought it, he was crawling again, scraping his way across the floor of the cabin, bumping into furniture, knocking over an end table, crying and grunting his way into the bathroom. He didn't pause to think what kept him going until much later, when he was sprawled on the bed with the blankets pulled to his chin, shivering uncontrollably. Then he could see her face swimming before him. She looked exactly as she always did, smooth and unperturbed. Her eyes, more gray than blue, pained him even in remembrance, because they were the one thing about her that hadn't changed.

He still remembered that first day when she had ventured into his office. He'd been appalled by her appearance. He knew he was a snob, so he tried to make allowances, but even so she did not present the polished image he wanted in his front office. The only reason he'd proceeded with the interview at all was that he'd had no choice. And then an amazing transformation had taken place. He had watched a nearly emaciated, dull woman come to life when she discussed finance. Her demeanor lost its hesitancy, a hint of color tinged her cheeks, and he spotted her potential. He had to hire her, that was a given. But it was due as much to her own efforts as to his that she had stayed on. He recognized quality when he saw it. She was that rare creature, rare in his experience, anyway: an assistant who was as punctual as he, and blessed with the sense to know when to speak and when to keep her silence. She most frequently chose the latter. He admired and respected the business sense she

61

had slowly acquired, and he trusted her to keep her mouth shut outside the office about the confidential financial portfolios with which they dealt every day.

True, he had pushed, demanded, and, just often enough, encouraged her. As subtly as he could, he'd brought in women clients who knew how to dress, how to carry themselves, how to project an image of businesslike yet nonthreatening assurance. And she had missed nothing. He had watched all the transformations, the improvements, over the years, silently rejoicing in each step she took.

But the dull gray disappointment had never left her eyes, even when she laughed. It was as if something had permanently turned those eyes away from hope, and her mouth, generous when she smiled, her skin, glowing with newfound pride in her accomplishments, nothing could hide the disillusionment in her eyes.

He no longer remembered when he began to love her. It might have been the day, soon after she began work, when an old man named Gavin Harris had come into the office and she had been kind to him in a manner that conveyed respect. Or perhaps it was the first time she giggled—actually giggled!—at one of his rare jokes.

Well, it no longer mattered how it had begun. But it was then that he hired Randy Daniels and began to see a glimmer of hope in the whole miserable mess. His own greed and stupidity had led him into the mess, but now, with her, he saw what his future might be. Someday he would come back from this cabin free and clear of the blackmail that had brought them together and then cruelly kept them apart.

But he'd made a terrible mistake. He should have known that his opponent had too many years invested in this scheme to allow Cramer to dictate his own future. And he had found a perfect robot in Rodney Weaver. Weaver had, out of—what? Friendship? Some remaining shred of decency?—tried to warn Cramer, and Cramer had ignored him. Had Weaver known on Friday what the man was planning? Now, shivering in the lumpy bed, sick with fever and regrets, Cramer guessed that he had, but the knowledge did him no good. It was too late. Cramer had chosen to deal with the matter in his own way, and the fact that he wasn't dead right now was due not to his own cunning or intelligence, but to luck.

He thought of the postcard he'd sent. At the time it had seemed a clever ploy, but now he couldn't even remember what he'd written.

It had been an oblique message, he was sure of that, but she was smart; surely she would decipher it. He hoped he'd been right in leading her to McGavin. If he had misjudged McGavin, then there was no hope at all.

But even now, as close to death as he knew he was, he was honest enough to admit that he couldn't have told her everything. It was too complicated, his involvement too muddled with past mistakes, myriad emotions, contradictory motives. He had wanted the whole thing resolved, and then, slowly, gradually, he would have explained to her, as gently as he knew how.

But on a postcard? Or in a frantic telephone call? No, that was not his style.

Style, he thought ruefully. What the hell does style matter now? That's your problem, Cramer, always has been. It's cost you ten years of your life, and it's probably going to finish you off.

His eyes closed slowly, and eventually the shivering stopped.

4

Breaking
the Pattern

■

By Wednesday morning the rain was gone and the weatherman on the radio was promising a sunny, mild spring day for the city of Chicago. The prospect of better weather didn't help Kate Downing's disposition one bit. Impatiently, she snapped off the radio, unplugged the coffeepot, and left her cup in the sink. It pleased her to know that she was leaving the house with a dirty cup in the sink: A small act of defiance, however futile, was better than none.

She took an earlier train than the one she usually rode, but she buried her nose in a book as she always did to avoid having to watch people watching her. Ah, how vain you are, she would lecture herself, no one's looking at you; but still, she felt easier when she read.

The streets in the financial section were still practically empty and the walk to her building took less time than usual. She rode the elevator to the tenth floor and had her keys in hand as she approached the office door. She knew without touching the knob that it would be locked. Feeling somewhat like a robot, going through the motions as she had yesterday, she unlocked the door, switched on the lights, and hung her suit jacket in the corner. She crossed the room and unlocked the inner office, letting the door swing open. The room was empty. Of course; she hadn't really expected otherwise.

She had played with the notion of not even coming in today, so sure was she that Benjamin Cramer would not be there. Why should he be? Nothing had changed; his postcard had said he was staying in Wisconsin an extra week. Perfectly logical.

Only it wasn't. Something was wrong. Benjamin Cramer did not send postcards announcing an extended vacation. He did not take extended vacations. He did not address her as "Kate," just as she had never thought of calling him "Benjamin." They were Mrs. Downing and Mr. Cramer, even after all these years, and she liked it that way; it was easier. And the punctuation on that postcard, so accurate, so precise—he never bothered with details like that. It was almost as if the card had come from someone else, and yet the script was his; it was as familiar to her as her own. So where did that leave her?

I don't know, she mumbled to herself, I don't know and I'm tired of not knowing. She poured a few cups of water into the coffee maker, measured coffee into the basket, and sat at her desk, listening to the coffee perk.

The answering machine. She had forgotten the answering machine attached to the telephone. Her finger jabbed the button and she listened, but there was nothing. Of course. Why should there be? When Benjamin Cramer left the city for that cabin in the woods, his clients knew he was out of reach; it was the only way he could escape them, and they stopped calling. And he certainly hadn't called the office himself. She turned off the machine and went to pour herself a cup of coffee.

She was aware that the strain of the past two days was showing. Her shoulders, which she worked so hard at keeping straight, were slumped a little, and there were dark circles under her eyes that her makeup could not conceal. She had a headache that was resisting every known cure, and her back hurt. The knot in her stomach, tiny at first, had taken over completely, leaving no room for food, no room for the muscles to relax. The only thing it would accommodate, it seemed, was coffee, and she was drinking too much of that.

Still, as she sipped from the steaming cup, she began to feel a little better, a little more alert, at least. She had nothing to do: Her final exam was over, though it was anyone's guess if she had passed it, given her state of mind that night. There was no office work to do. So she might as well give it another try. For what seemed the hundredth time, she started at the beginning, tracing the sequence of events. Surely she had missed something. . . . Or was it, as the police had implied, a pathetic case of a sex-starved secretary trying to find a boss who was quite obviously still on vacation? Resolutely, she pushed that notion aside and thought back to March, when she had telephoned Rodney Weaver.

She could remember only two things that set that call apart from those in years past. One was that he had anticipated her request and had already checked on the cabin. She had found that amusing, but it was hardly extraordinary. Benjamin Cramer was the most predictable man she'd ever known. He had gone to the same cottage, at the same time of year, for as long as Kate had worked for him. Why shouldn't Weaver make the arrangements in advance? That was not remarkable at all, she decided. The second was even less remarkable; the rate for the cottage had gone up. The price of everything was going up.

She had mailed the check. Why to Rodney Weaver personally? Well, because she had always done it that way. She assumed he was taking an interest in an old customer; there was nothing unusual in that. Last night she had even stopped off at the library on her way home from the train station and had found a telephone directory for Eagle Hill. The address in the book for Weaver Real Estate matched the one she had written down years ago, the address to which she always sent the check, and the phone number matched the one in her book at the office.

It puzzled her that Weaver's office had no record of these transactions, but she knew that not everyone kept files as organized as her own. And, who could tell? Perhaps Rodney Weaver was not above a little slippery bookkeeping for tax purposes. There could be a hundred reasons for the absence of Benjamin Cramer's name in their files. The point was, no one in Weaver's office knew where Mr. Cramer was either.

All right, so far nothing suspicious. Now, the week before he left. Anything unusual? No, he'd been in perfect health and as efficient as ever. He seemed to be a man without moods, always even-tempered, never flustered in spite of the tension inherent in his work. He was always, Kate thought, dependably, reassuringly the same, a quality she treasured. He had spent those last few days as he always did before leaving, wrapping things up, leaving her specific instructions for anything that might arise during his absence.

And then—well, it was at this point that Kate faltered. She had

66

not received the usual postcard during the second week. But, as the police had dryly reminded her, there could be a dozen explanations for that. It might have been lost in the mail or delivered to the wrong office.

"Lady," the officer had said yesterday with ill-concealed impatience, "you got your postcard, didn't you? So what if it was late? You said yourself it's his writing. It was mailed last Friday, what more do you want?"

Kate, risking nothing because she knew he already thought her a fool or worse, had tried to argue, but how could she explain Benjamin Cramer to someone who didn't know him? How could she explain his penchant for schedules, his absolute adherence to routine, day after day, year after year? When she saw the policeman's eyebrow raised, she didn't dare produce the old postcards from her purse. She didn't have to guess what he would think of a woman who kept her employer's postcards for years on end.

Finally, in a last attempt, she asked, "All right, but look at this card that did come. It's not his style at all, the first names, the careful punctuation. And we do not have a client named J. A. McGavin. How can I cancel an appointment with someone I've never heard of? Besides, he had dozens of appointments scheduled this week. Why would he mention only one?"

The cop started shuffling papers on his metal desk, and Kate knew she was about to be dismissed.

"Ma'am, you have a postcard from a man on vacation. Maybe he had a few drinks before he wrote it, relaxed a little. What's a vacation for? And what's so mysterious—" the sarcasm in his voice as he lingered over that word was almost more than Kate could stand— "about a man you've known for ten years calling you by your first name? He tells you he's staying another week, so let him fish in peace." The officer stood up and Kate had no choice but to follow suit; he glanced over her shoulder toward the exit.

"As for the nonexistent client, I suggest you check your files again. If Cramer's as organized as you say he is, that name is in there somewhere. Now, if he doesn't show up by next Monday, and you don't hear from him, why, you just come right back here and then we'll see if we have a missing person."

Kate was furious, more at herself than at that empty-headed excuse for an officer of the law. Out of habit, she mumbled a "Thank you" as she left, but her fists were curled with suppressed anger at the way she had been treated.

No, she corrected herself as she strode down the sidewalk, at the way you allowed yourself to be treated. He looked at your legs before he looked at your face and you should have known right then that he wouldn't be any help. You should have asked to see his superior, or a detective. You should have been more forceful. You should have *made* him understand who Benjamin Cramer is. He's not just anybody, he's an important man in this city, even your business professors at school know that. You should have—

"Oh! Excuse me!" Kate walked right into someone, a man in a dark pin-striped suit, but she hardly gave him a glance. She'd just had an idea. The typing pool! Why hadn't she checked there before?

"Janice," she said, rushing into the office down the hall from her own, "I want you to check your records very thoroughly and see if the name J. A. McGavin is in there anywhere. M-c-capital G-a-v-i-n. Please, right now. It's important."

Janice stared at her from behind her electric typewriter. Kate knew she looked a mess—hair windblown, cheeks flushed—and she sensed the careful image she had maintained so determinedly had been blown away with this one lapse. She kept an easy distance with the secretaries. It was her job to supervise the work they did for Benjamin Cramer, and she tried to be pleasant, to compliment them occasionally, but she was not their friend.

Janice stared another moment, then jumped up to go to the files. She searched through drawer after drawer, until it became apparent to Kate that she was stalling.

"Not there?"

Janice turned around and looked at Kate. "No, Mrs. Downing, I'm sorry. I double-checked every possibility I could think of. No J. A. McGavin. I'm really sorry. If you want to look for yourself—"

"No, of course not." Kate's voice was returning to normal, soft and a little less demanding. "You know those files better than I do." She turned to leave.

"Mrs. Downing, excuse me, but is there anything I can do?"

Surprised, Kate said, "Do? No, thank you, Janice, I was just hoping . . ." Her voice trailed off, and she opened the door abruptly and left the office.

She hadn't even noticed that four typewriters had stopped their clicking the moment she'd entered, and that the other three typists had joined Janice in staring open-mouthed at the new Mrs. Downing. Their typewriters were still silent, though the typists were not, when the door opened again and there was Kate.

"I was just thinking . . . Did anyone stop in here this morning? Or yesterday? Anyone looking for Mr. Cramer?"

The typists looked at one another, saying, "No, I didn't see anyone, did you?" and "No, but I went across the hall to Mr. Bishoff's office, remember? Did anybody—" and "No, I'm sure, I was here all day, ate lunch at my desk—" until finally Kate interrupted.

"Oh, well, I just thought that while I was out, someone might have . . . Thank you." And she wandered out again, as quietly as she had come.

"McGavin," Kate mumbled to herself, heading back to her own office. "J. A. McGavin. . . ."

That had been yesterday. Now it was Wednesday, no McGavin had appeared, no new postcards, no telephone messages. She pulled out the postcard from her purse and was staring at the familiar handwriting when the outer door swung open. She lifted her eyes expectantly, but it was Ernie, the mailman.

"'Morning, Mrs. Downing. Boss back yet?"

"No," she answered, "he's still on vacation . . . I guess."

"Sure not like him, is it?" Ernie said, making conversation as he sorted through a handful of letters.

"It certainly isn't," Kate said promptly. At least she wasn't the only one who thought it odd. "It's not like him at all, and to tell you the truth, I'm a little worried about him."

"Hmm?" Ernie looked up. "Why's that?" He handed her several envelopes.

"Well, you know how he is. He loves his routine and—"

"*His* routine?" Ernie chuckled. "When it comes to routine, Mrs. D., you're the champ. Look at yourself now, lost without him."

He missed the frown that appeared on Kate's face.

"Now, listen, I wouldn't worry about him. He works hard and he deserves as much time as he wants away from all of this, eh? Why don't you just relax and enjoy it, nice and peaceful in here for a change," and he was backing out the door, still sorting the letters in his hands.

Kate detected a patronizing note in his voice and found it remarkably akin to the policeman's. She squeezed the mail in her fingers.

"Yes," she said coldly to the closing door, "that's a brilliant idea."

Great. First the police, now the mailman. Maybe she really was worrying about nothing.

And what did he mean by saying she was "lost without him?" That was a ridiculous notion. Benjamin Cramer was her boss, nothing more. Of course she admired him, and of course she had time on her hands when he was away.

He was part of her life, certainly. But there were other concerns, other people. Her classes had taken a great deal of her time, counting the studying she did. And there was Sonia, another widow. Kate had met her in a night class and then they'd had another class together. Sonia was a part-time student, too, working during the day and going to school at night. Occasionally they met after work for dinner, and once in a while they went to a concert together. But Sonia lived on the south side, a good distance from Kate, and she had two children, so they were far from constant companions.

But Kate had pleasant neighbors, especially Jeff and Karen Martin, who had bought Ted and Jane's house. They always included her in their backyard barbecues and their annual Christmas party. And Marie Donahue, who worked in Kate's building. They sometimes went shopping together on their lunch hours.

Kate's mental list came to an abrupt halt. That was it. She was not good at making friends. She wasn't glib or witty; she had no children to talk about. And she dreaded, always, the point where life stories, however brief, were exchanged. She would not discuss her past with anyone. That was one reason she was so comfortable with Mr. Cramer. And, oh, all right, maybe a little, just a tiny bit uncomfortable without him around. But not lost. Definitely not lost.

She flipped through the mail rapidly, realizing she was looking for another postcard. There was none, and, feeling a bit sheepish, she started over. There were two envelopes with letterheads she didn't recognize, and she opened them first. But they were only introductory letters from new clients, both routine. The rest was junk mail: a plea from a charity organization—Mr. Cramer was on all their lists, so she supposed he was a regular contributor—an invitation to attend the grand opening of a new office building, and a once-in-a-lifetime chance to buy health insurance. The name she was looking

70

for was not on any of them. She put them aside and picked up the postcard again.

By now, she knew the words by heart, but she read them again, examining every word, as if by sheer concentration she could extract some special meaning.

Dear Kate,

I've decided to stay an extra week. The weather is bad, but the fishing is fine. Please reschedule appointment with J. A. McGavin for Tuesday, 30 May.

As ever,
Benjamin Cramer

"'Dear Kate,'" she mumbled to herself. She got up and poured another cup of coffee. "Preposterous."

"'The weather is bad, but the fishing is fine.'" Bad weather . . . hmmm. Well, why not? Once before, with far less reason than she had now, she had checked his weather report. She looked up the number for the National Weather Service.

"Hello? I need some information, please. Can you tell me what the weather was in north-central Wisconsin last week? In the Eagle Hill area. Yes, I'll wait. Thank you."

She sipped her coffee and stared at the postcard.

"Yes? Oh . . . no rain? None at all. . . . And the temp— oh, that's normal for this time of year? Oh. A little above normal. You're sure . . .? Yes, yes, of course. Thank you."

She replaced the receiver slowly, biting on her lower lip. Perfect weather. So why would he write just the opposite? Unless it was a clue. Unless he was trying to tell her something. . . . Unless he was in trouble.

It was the first time she had admitted that possibility to herself. Oh, she'd gone through the motions with the police, but she hadn't believed, not really, that anything bad had happened to him. It was just odd, that's all, this break in routine. . . . But now, well, now she was beginning to think there might be more to it than that. And this matter of J. A. McGavin; that was a complete puzzle.

She put down her coffee cup, closed her eyes, and tried to picture him. McGavin . . . J. A. McGavin. It was no use. She was sure she'd never met him. Him . . . well, it didn't have to be a man, did it? They had a few women clients, not as many as men, certainly, but there were some. Why couldn't it be a woman?

She opened her eyes. It was not a woman. She knew all their clients, and she took a particular interest in the women. Some were widows with inherited money, but there were a few OMOs among them. On-My-Owns, she called them, and she respected them very much because they were making it on their own, just as she was trying to do. It was a funny thing, but every one of those women, in her limited dealings with them, treated her as if she truly were an administrative assistant and not a flunky secretary who did nothing but answer the phone and make the coffee. As a matter of fact, Mr. Cramer made the coffee when he was here, so there.

Well, this wasn't getting her anywhere. McGavin, McGavin. She stared at the postcard again, and she knew what she was going to do. It seemed fruitless—she had already done it yesterday—but she was going to go through her own files again. She had no other leads, this was the only thing she had to go on, and there was nothing else to do anyway. First, she rechecked the appointment book, going all the way through the week this time. Maybe McGavin was coming in another day. But no, she would have written it in herself, and she knew she hadn't. There was a block of empty time on Friday afternoon, but it was a holiday weekend. Mr. Cramer had told her not to schedule anything that afternoon; she'd assumed he wanted to be free to leave the office early if his work load allowed. In any case, the name was not in the appointment book. So back she went to her filing cabinets.

By one-thirty—it never occurred to her to stop for lunch—Kate had reached the last drawer and the last pile of folders. They were ancient history, a yellowing assortment of Benjamin Cramer's first accounts, and the folders were slim. He had been an unknown then, new in the business, and he had taken almost anything that came his way. Mostly they were one-shot assignments—check this stock company, determine the availability of office space in that building—nothing assignments that had, nevertheless, been carried out with painstaking attention to detail. On these cases, slowly but deftly, Cramer had built his empire, as Kate thought of it, and as she read through them a vague feeling of wistfulness came over her. She found herself, foolishly, wishing that she had been with him in those early, tentative days, sharing his struggles and triumphs. Instead, she'd been dodging Mr. Ingram down on Delaney Street, biding her time until Jim would get home from Vietnam.

The last case in the drawer was one of the first she had typed, and she remembered as though it were yesterday how frightened she had been, of both Cramer's imposing demeanor and her own shaky confidence. She had spent hours typing this account, proofreading it half a dozen times for errors, and had been rewarded only with a grunt.

Kate sighed and closed the folder. Nowhere, in any of these hundreds of case files, did the name McGavin appear. There was nothing even close, except a Gavin Harris, a client who'd died years before. She'd examined that folder extra carefully, but it had been a routine transaction. Harris had come to Cramer on the recommendation of his attorney, who happened to be Milton Rissman, Cramer's own attorney. He didn't hold much with outsiders, he announced, and high-falutin titles such as "financial consultant" gave him the willies. But, he admitted, hunching over his cane, he was getting on in years, and he had some peculiar relatives who never would learn to handle money as he had. Seeing as there was no one else to leave it to, he wanted to make it easy for them, but they weren't to squander away his entire fortune before they left his funeral. Did Cramer have any ideas about that?

Cramer did, good ones. Both he and Kate liked the old man and worked especially hard to devise a plan to suit him. Kate researched his holdings herself and reported her findings to Cramer who, as usual, seemed to already know everything she had learned, and then Cramer drew up his recommendations for Harris. Within a matter of weeks the changes had been made; shortly after that Harris had died; Mr. Cramer had told her to put his file in the inactive drawer, and the account was closed.

Still, Kate fingered the postcard, willing it to say Gavin, not McGavin. Even if the man were dead, it would be some kind of clue. But no. That part of the card was perfectly clear; it said "J. A. McGavin." Apparently, Mr. Cramer had scheduled an appointment with him himself, for sometime this week—but so far he had not appeared.

Kate pushed the file drawer closed with a slam. She was totally frustrated, and rather than sit still and go slowly berserk, she picked

73

up that day's mail and went into Cramer's office to leave it on his desk. The stack was growing. He'd be swamped when he came back. She gazed at his desk a moment, then shook her head and leaned against the window to look out at the sunshine pouring down into La Salle Street. It looked so orderly from up here, the traffic moving in precise patterns. It did not scare her at all, and yet she could remember vividly the first time she had seen that street.

It had been hot and muggy that day, and she'd worn an ugly beige dress, the best she had then. Jane's scarf had been the only touch of confidence. She had been afraid of everything then.

Sometimes I think I still am, she mused, her forehead pressed against the glass. Sometimes it seems I'm still waiting for Jim to come back and take care of everything. He was so good at taking care of things.

Even in Vietnam, she knew from his letters, although he was only an enlisted man who had to follow orders from practically everyone; still, he had found his own ways of doing things. He and that friend he had made over there, the one from the small town. They had invented ingenious ways of coping with the insanities of requisitions and red tape. Jim and his best friend, John, yes, that was his name. John something, he used a middle name, too—

Kate froze at the window. Slowly, her eyes widened.

"John!" She said it out loud. "His name was John, oh, it flowed, that name, John Andrew, no, that's wrong, John Arnold? No, no, it was smooth, John *Anthony* McGavin! J. A. McGavin!"

She nearly shouted it in her shock.

How could she have forgotten? With a memory like hers, the worst problem was trying not to remember so much. She knew the weather was hot the day she met Benjamin Cramer, and what she had worn. She could describe, right down to his freckled hands, an old man named Gavin Harris, who had come into the office exactly twice. So why had it taken her three days to link up the client of Cramer's postcard with a friend of her late husband's?

I know why, she thought, it's because there's no link, no connection between Jim and his friend John and Mr. Cramer. They never met, Jim and Mr. Cramer, and John McGavin isn't a client. The postcard implies he's a client, but he isn't, I'm sure of it. Why didn't I remember this sooner?

Oh, it didn't make any sense at all. Her husband's best friend?

Impossible! But it had to be . . . J. A. McGavin, the same name. How did Benjamin T. Cramer, Chicago financier, know John Anthony McGavin, Jim's war buddy from ten years ago? And why put his name on a postcard, indicating he was a client, and instruct her to reschedule an appointment she'd never scheduled in the first place? It was crazy, she knew that, and yet she couldn't stop herself. She knew what she had to do now. Finally, after days of inaction, there was something she could do.

She raced back out to the outer office and, in a rare lapse, she said, "Damn my own efficiency," but she couldn't help it: she took time to turn on the telephone answering machine, unplug the coffee maker, turn out all the lights, and lock both offices before she raced down the hall. But she left her half-filled coffee cup on her desk.

She reached the typing pool office and stuck her head inside the doorway. "I'll be at home if anyone needs me," she shouted to the first face that looked up, and then she flew back down the hall to the elevator and jabbed at the button as if constant punching would make the elevator arrive sooner.

After what Kate thought was an interminable wait, the elevator arrived and she pushed the LOBBY button. This was not a peak hour, early in the afternoon, and she silently urged the machine to hurry. Please, everyone, wait until I'm off this thing before you need it. But it stopped three times to admit passengers on the way down, and Kate was at the screaming point as the doors slid open at the lobby.

"Excuse me, please, excuse me," and she was running across the polished tile, past the same green padded bench on which she had cowered that first day, past elegant men and smartly dressed women, but now she was one of them, and the only reason she gave them any thought at all was that they were obstacles in her way. Then she was out in the sunshine and she realized she had left her jacket up in the office. Well, no matter, she had another—several, in fact—at home. Many things had changed since that first day ten years ago. Still, she slowed down a little, breathing hard. She was out of shape. Three mornings this week she'd been in her car and half way to the train station before remembering her resolve to walk. Well, she would, she would start tomorrow, but now she wished she could move faster. By the time she reached the station she was perspiring.

Then—agony! she thought, I can't stand this!—she had to wait nearly thirty minutes for a train. She felt as if she'd been sitting all day, and even though her legs were tired, she kept moving, pacing the floor, for once not giving a moment's thought to who might be watching her or what they might think. The name, John Anthony McGavin, consumed her brain, and she was furious with herself for not having recognized it right away, the moment she read the post-card. All this time wasted!

At last the gate opened and she boarded the train. It was nearly empty, and she took a seat near the door. She opened her purse to make certain the postcard was there. Yes, she'd snatched it from her desk on her way out of the office. It seemed very important that she not lose that card. It was as if it were her only, her last link with Cramer. It, and the name he had provided on it, were all she had to go on.

She didn't know why, but Mr. Cramer wanted her to contact McGavin. She thought she knew how to find him. Oh, it's crazy, she told herself again, this whole thing is simply beyond reason. But if Mr. Cramer wanted her to find somebody named McGavin, then she would try.

Benjamin Cramer was, she might as well admit it, more than her boss. He was a kind man, a superlative businessman, her mentor, and he had, however unintentionally, rescued her from an abyss of self-pity after Jim's death. He had, even if without knowing it, pointed the way for her, showing her strengths she hadn't known she'd possessed, intelligence she'd buried in Mr. Ingram's suffocating little office.

She owed him for all that. She would find J. A. McGavin, no matter how crazy it sounded.

She nodded to herself—she was still a nodder—and slipped the card back into her purse.

5

The Letters

•
———

Kate Downing had a fine appreciation for the permanence of the written word. She was entranced by the notion that an idea, once declared on paper, became an irrevocable and accurate reflection of a single moment in time. Whether wise or foolish, a single written sentence was more valuable to her than any conversation.

For that reason, she did not do much writing herself. She had a reluctance to commit herself on paper to an emotion that could change before the ink was dry. She had made an exception when Jim had been away and had written to him almost daily, but she had not enjoyed it. Now she limited herself primarily to breezy notes on Christmas cards, and she sent few of those.

She took a secret delight that other people were not so careful. She was a voracious reader of novels and autobiographies; but she especially loved reading letters. It was unlikely that she had ever thrown away a letter addressed to her.

This was how she came to have an entire closet shelf stacked to the ceiling with neatly tied bundles of letters. She didn't often disturb their precarious arrangement, and occasionally she mocked herself for keeping them at all, but she could never quite bring herself to discard them. They were there, like old friends, comforting whenever she thought of them, a bulky measurement of the space she had filled in other people's lives.

There were letters from her mother, written to a homesick Kate away at camp for the first time, then to a wide-eyed Kate traveling out West with her Aunt Sarah, then to a quietly excited Kate in her freshman year at college. There were a few very precious letters from her father. Apparently, he had shared her caution when it came to sealing thoughts in writing, and he had written to his daughter only when his wife was unable to. There were letters from distant relatives, most now dead or lost in the gulf created by her father's death. There were letters from childhood friends, from Ted and Jane in New York, from her friend, Sonia, and her children on their vacations up in Maine. And there were, in two carefully ribboned packets, the letters from her husband.

Kate stood on a chair to reach them and pulled them off the top of one stack. She wrinkled her nose at the poof of dust that escaped with them, then climbed down and went in search of a cloth to wipe them off. She carried the letters gingerly, as if they would break should she drop them. She often felt that they were all she had left of her husband. There was no grave to visit, since he had been lost at sea, and he had never liked to pose for pictures, so she had only a few wedding photographs.

Even her memories, once so clear, had dimmed in recent years. Once she had thought she would never forget his deep, serious voice or the scratch of his whiskers in the mornings, or the guarded ways he found to pay her compliments. But now, as she brushed at the stack of envelopes with a cloth, she was alarmed that the handwriting looked unfamiliar to her. It was only for a moment, and then she knew it was his angular scrawl, the crosses on the *t*s hard and straight, and she felt a rush of relief. Of course she remembered his handwriting! It was only that it had been so long since she had seen it.

Now that she had found some action to take, however fruitless it might prove, her appetite had returned, so she stopped to make a tuna-salad sandwich and pour a glass of tea. Then she moved everything into the living room and, with her shoes kicked off and her feet tucked under her on the couch, she untied the faded blue ribbon on the first set of letters and looked at the one on top.

It had a Denver postmark, dated October 1965. It was four months after her father's death. She removed the single sheet of paper, bit into her sandwich, and began reading.

78

Dear Kate,

Have to make this short, I've got a meeting in a few minutes. It was good to talk to you the other night, but a few more phone calls like that and we'll be eating bread and water, so maybe we should stick to letters for a while.

I can't remember, have you ever been in Denver? You'd hate it, horrible smog, but the mountains are beautiful and they say you don't have to go up very far before the air clears. Doubt I'll have time for that. Don't worry, everything's fine, just feeling the pressure, I guess. I'm a little out of my element with these high-class businessmen. Should be home Friday or Saturday.

Love,
Jim

Kate stared at the letter and wondered at the marvels of time. Had all his letters been like this, so impersonal, so cool? Surely not. She certainly didn't remember thinking so when she received them. They were wonderful then, cozy lifelines between herself and her beloved husband, and she had treasured every one of them.

She picked up the next letter, postmarked San Francisco, mailed two months after the first. It was written on Holiday Inn stationery in the same careless scrawl.

Dear Kate,

Greetings from the Golden Gate. Now that I'm here I wonder if you were right. Maybe you should've come with me. You'd like the restaurants and shops. But you'd be on your own, so maybe not much fun after all.

Have met and talked the ears off of two junior execs, finally convinced them their company can't live without The Product, but it took me a week to do it. Now they've agreed to pass the idea along, but who knows how long that'll take. I'll be home in a week, with or without the contract.

Love,
Jim

Kate swallowed hard. A lump of her sandwich was caught in her throat and she had to wash it down with gulps of tea. Her appetite was gone, as quickly as it had come, and she looked away from the letters for a moment. San Francisco, she thought, smoothing back a loose strand of hair. I remember that trip. I wanted to go, I even pleaded with him, and I was sure we could afford it, just that once.

But Jim had hardly considered it, just said no, it wasn't practical this time, and she had dropped the subject. He had been strong, so sure of himself. That phrase from the first letter, about being out-classed, was a joke; he had never felt intimidated by anyone, she was sure. It was true, they hadn't had much money, but she had inherited some stock from her Aunt Sarah and they had sold it to make the down payment on the house. Then she had worked hard to make it a pleasant place, and he had lucked into a selling job. It was a new invention, some sort of duplicating machine that did twenty-nine other things at once, and Jim had believed in it. Of course, he'd had to travel; he was on the road much of the time, but once it caught on—and he'd been confident that it would—then he would be home more often.

But it had not worked out that way. None of their plans had ever worked out. Jim had come home one night and calmly announced that he had paid a call on a recruiter that day. He was enlisting in the Marine Corps. Kate had been stunned, hardly able to compre-hend what was happening.

"Why?" she kept asking, "why are you doing this?"

"Because I'm tired of banging my head against a brick wall with this duplicator thing. I'm not getting anywhere with it. Xerox and IBM have the field covered and they beat our price every time. Once I'm in the Marines, we'll have a steady income."

"But Jim, you know where they'll send you!" Kate was sobbing, clinging to him in desperation. "Men are dying over there, and for what? Darling, if you're worried about money, I'll go to work, or we can sell the house—"

"No!" Jim pulled away from her. "I won't have you working, and this house is the only decent thing in our lives. We aren't going to dump it and move back to some crummy apartment. Look, I've signed the papers. It's settled. It's the best thing for us, trust me."

Kate continued to resist, but it was an unfamiliar role for her and she was not skilled at it. He swept away every objection with simple logic. By the time he left, they were hardly speaking to each other. But he had written and she had bombarded him with long, affectionate responses, and gradually, it had seemed to her, some of the old warmth had filtered back into their relationship.

She turned now to those letters, and read through the ones Jim had sent from his various training camps in California. It was a painful exercise, and she felt a growing bewilderment. Had she really once thought these letters were warm and romantic? Had she seen something in them, twelve years ago, that she was missing now? He was more wary of emotions in writing than she had ever been. She couldn't recall when she had last read through these letters, but she had a terrifying idea that she was, at last, seeing them clearly for the first time.

In every one the tone was detached and aloof; they could have been written to anyone, a distant cousin or a casual acquaintance, for all the ardor they radiated. They were simply brief progress reports of his boot-camp training, with occasional boasts of his high marks on the rifle range. She had been very proud of him. But not once was there any mention of his loneliness or his desire to be with her. A masochistic streak drove her to search for any hint of intimacy, any tenderness. There were none. He signed the letters "Love, Jim" with a depressing automatism.

She began to read more rapidly and soon reached the last letter in the stack. It was dated December 10, 1966, and it was identical in tone to all the others. But it contained the news of his impending transfer to a place whose very name Kate had come to hate.

The word is we're shipping out next week for Nam, but no orders yet. I'll call before we leave. They've got me in disbursing, so I'll probably spend the whole tour in some office and never even fire my rifle. A few of us hope we get orders for the same unit, we plan to drink our way through the war. (Just kidding.) Merry Christmas from sunny California.

Love,
Jim

Kate shook her head in amazement and abandoned any attempt to finish her sandwich. He had called, as promised, the night before

81

he left the country. It was the last time she had ever spoken to him and now, after so many years, she could not remember what they had found to say.

The letter fell into her lap; she cradled her face in her hands and felt her eyes burning. Oh, she should never have saved these letters. They were a trap, she knew that, didn't she? Written words could lie, they could deceive you into false comforts, and then you could read them again and see right through them. And what good were they, if they caused such pain?

I can't do it, she whispered to herself. The next ones are worse; they don't get any better. They're all I have left of him, and they're destroying my memories. I can't, I won't read them, I won't do this to myself.

Abruptly, she stood up and went to the stairs, climbed them briskly, and undressed in the bedroom. Leaving her clothes in a heap on the floor, she went down the hall to the shower and let the water beat down on her skin and run through her hair. She washed away the soot of the city, the perspiration from her race for the train, the dirty shame she felt remembering the passionate letters she had sent to Jim. Maybe he had been smarter than she and destroyed her letters. She should have burned his long ago, before their solace became a mockery.

The disillusionment was still with her, but at least she felt cleaner when she stepped out of the shower and rubbed a thick, fresh-smelling towel over her skin. She wrapped another towel around her head.

She was muttering to herself as she went downstairs. Forget about the way things were, or the way you thought they were. That was a lifetime ago, when you were young and dreamed foolish dreams. Don't let it get in your way now. It's over and you can't do anything about it.

You need to find the name. That's all you're looking for, she told herself fiercely. She flopped back onto the couch and untied the second bundle of letters. She opened the one on the top of the stack and focused a businesslike attention on it. When she saw there was no reference to McGavin, she dropped it and grabbed the next. She scanned them rapidly, not bothering to replace them in their envelopes, and soon she had a jumbled pile of papers on the floor. She was beginning to think she'd been mistaken when, suddenly, there it was. Jim had been in Vietnam for eight months, assigned to what he described as a "soft job" in a disbursing office in Da Nang. He had become, in his own words, a "wheeler-dealer," trading whatever he could find for other supplies he needed. "Trying to order anything through channels takes months," he had written, "even a desk for the office, so we bend the rules a little. Yesterday we met an Air Force sergeant and traded a case of bourbon for two mattresses. Now McGavin and I are the envy of the Corps, the only men in our shack with something besides a sagging cot to sleep on."

Kate lifted the paper to catch the light from the picture window behind her and studied it closely. Yes! It said "McGavin." She was right. It was the same name!

The next letter said nothing, no names, no mention of McGavin. She tossed it on the floor and snatched up the next one. Yes, here it was. There was no mistake. His full name was John Anthony McGavin. J. A. McGavin.

This guy is weird, but I like him. John Anthony McGavin, that's his name, and proud of it. Strictly small-town, a real yokel if I ever saw one, but he comes on with that country-boy approach and before you know it the colonel is kissing his ass.

Kate winced at the expression, but she was fascinated anyway. She put that letter aside and reached eagerly for the next, but it contained nothing, nor did the next several. One of them seemed to have gotten wet; the ink was blurred. When she read it, she knew why. She had cried enough tears over this letter to wash away all the ink. It was the letter telling her that he had decided to extend his tour in Vietnam for another six months. She threw it to the floor as if she had been burned and hastily read the next. Still nothing. Now she was racing through them, wanting only to be done. She had neared the end of the stack when her patience was rewarded. In a letter dated March 5, 1968, there was a full paragraph about McGavin.

The mail McGavin gets from home is unbelievable. I'm getting to know the town as well as he does. Everybody in

83

Derrington thinks their John Anthony is fighting the war by himself. He says people in Wisconsin are like that, and I tell him I heard about a demonstration in Madison, and he says that's not Wisconsin, so how do you argue with a guy like that? He gets fan mail by the bucket, from his parents, his girl, even some old codger named Manchester who runs the town hotel. They send him food all the time. Most of it we trade off for stuff we need. I didn't know towns like that were for real. I'm still not sure.

Wisconsin? McGavin was from Wisconsin? But that's where Mr. Cramer was! If this McGavin were in Wisconsin, why hadn't Mr. Cramer just called him himself to cancel their appointment? Why send her a postcard instructing her to do it when she didn't even know the man?

Kate forced her attention back to the letter, reading it again to be sure she hadn't missed anything. She didn't agree with Jim's skepticism about small towns. She had grown up in one and had loved it, then left it reluctantly to attend college. She had planned to return, but . . . No, not now, she had to get through these letters, there was no time for more useless grieving over a past she couldn't change.

She put the letter aside, along with the others that mentioned McGavin. There were only six letters left, and she read them rapidly. The fifth made a passing reference. "John and I are getting short and making a nice profit selling off our treasures. He's as anxious to get out of this place as I am."

The last letter held no mention of McGavin, but Kate lingered over it a moment anyway. If she had any sense at all, this was the last time she would ever read the letters. His last note to her was as devoid of emotion as all the others, and it was remarkable only for what it didn't say. There was no talk of expectancy, no mention of what his hopes and plans were for when he got home, not even a casual "looking forward to seeing you." It was as if this letter, too, had been written by rote and sent only to placate her demand that he write to her as often as possible.

She let it slip from her hand and, thrusting aside a rising urge to cry or scream or both, she read through the four McGavin letters again, searching for any bit of information she might have missed.

The only fact to go on, she decided, was Derrington. That was the name of McGavin's hometown—or it had been, ten years ago. Could he possibly still live there? It was a long shot, but the only one she had.

She went to the bookshelves next to the fireplace, pulled out the atlas, and sat on the floor. She turned to the index and scanned the *D*s. Denver, DeQueen, Derby, Dermott, Derry, Derry, no wait, she had passed it, Derravaragh Lake, Derrington. It was there, and there was just one Derrington: C4, page 124. She flipped back to the beginning of the book, found the page, ran her fingers across and down and saw it, in tiny print; if she hadn't been looking for it, she would have missed it completely: Derrington. In Wisconsin.

Kate, wide-eyed, thought, this cannot be a coincidence, it just can't be. She stared at the map and read the names of nearby towns and lakes. One inch northeast of Derrington, maybe less, in a slightly darker print, she saw it, and she knew it was no coincidence. Derrington was twenty miles from Eagle Hill.

Rodney Weaver, Kate thought. And suddenly she felt a chill and she put down the book and crossed her arms, hugging them to her body. She was frightened; she was getting in over her head. She didn't understand what was going on, but her instincts told her to go back to the police and show them the postcard again, and Jim's letters. How could Benjamin Cramer be connected to her husband's best friend?

Then she pictured the policeman she'd spoken to before and she knew she couldn't do it. He hadn't believed her then and she could well imagine his reaction to her hauling out four aging letters from her dead husband and her request that he read them. Kate shook her head and closed the atlas. She slid it back into its place on the shelf, gathered up the four letters, and went to the telephone to call the information operator.

"I have two listings for that party."

"Two?" Kate repeated blankly.

"Yes, ma'am, there's a John A. McGavin, Wahomet County Sheriff's Department, and also a residential number."

County sheriff? Was John McGavin a policeman? Elated, Kate said quickly, "Give them to me, both, please," and she grabbed a pencil. Then, before she could lose her nerve, she made the call.

"Sheriff's Office, Kalowski. May I help you?" It was a rapid-fire voice, bored and automatic, and it sounded very far away.

"Yes, may I speak with John McGavin, please?" Kate felt her knees shaking, and she sank onto a kitchen chair, her hand squeezing the phone tightly.

"Sheriff McGavin's gone for the day." Kate glanced at the clock on the stove and realized with a start that it was nearly seven o'clock. "Can I help you?"

"Uh, no, thank you, I need to—um, I'll call back, thank you." Kate stood up and pressed the button down on the phone, then replaced the receiver.

Sheriff McGavin, the man had said. Not only was he still in Derrington, he was the county sheriff! She was in luck!

She looked at the note pad, with John McGavin's home telephone number scribbled on it, and hesitated. Then the moment was gone and with it her courage. How could she call this stranger on the phone and even begin to explain? She couldn't. Well, what then?

The answer was perfectly obvious. It had been in her mind from the moment she'd located Derrington on the atlas map. She gazed out of the front window at her car in the driveway and shook her head. She was too tired to drive. With a sigh—some part of her had guessed it would come to this—she opened the phone book, found the number, and called the bus depot.

6

Derrington

■

The town of Derrington, Wisconsin, was asleep when the bus slowed down for the turnoff from the interstate, chugged up the hill, rounded the tree-lined curve, and entered the main street. It turned the corner and pulled to a grinding smoky stop in front of the bus station.

Most of the residents of Derrington, even those with their windows open to the mild air of a late spring night, did not so much as turn over in their sleep. This bus, with its cockeyed schedules, had been rocketing in and out of town for years. The noises it made were as much a part of the night sounds as the crickets' chorus. Occasionally a local businessman or a county official, returning from a trip to Chicago or Milwaukee, would step down from the bus, briefcase in hand, mumbling to himself that, by God, one of these days Derrington would have an airport, see how the bus company liked that. Sometimes a sleepy passenger would hand the driver a ticket, give him a suitcase or two to throw into the luggage bin, and board the bus for a visit to a relative up in Duluth.

Once, practically the whole town had turned out at the preposterous hour of one thirty-eight in the morning to cheer as John Anthony McGavin, twenty-three and still alive to shout about it after a year in Vietnam, jumped from the bus into his mother's waiting arms. The protests on the campus at Madison were a long way from Derrington.

In the young and dark hours of this May morning, there was no war and no returning hero, thus no welcome for the single passenger alighting from the bus. Kate Downing expected none. She had never been anywhere near this town and no one here knew her. The driver, overweight and sweating, hauled two suitcases from the baggage compartment and dumped them onto the sidewalk.

"Do you happen to know where the hotel is?"

He gestured vaguely down Second Avenue and said, "The Farman, only place in town you can walk to, but it's decent enough. Turn right at the corner."

She thanked him and he tipped his hat impersonally before he climbed back into the bus and drove away. Kate turned toward the depot, a small brick building with plate-glass windows on either side of the open doorway. She stepped inside and found no one sitting on the rows of plastic chairs. The narrow space between the ticket counter and the back wall was empty, the room silent except for a faint buzz from the overhead lights. She gave the room a thoughtful glance, feeling the same tug of recognition she had sensed on the bus, peering out of the window as they drove into town.

She dragged the heavier of the two suitcases inside the door and left it there. It was too cumbersome to haul across the room and hoist into a locker. Besides, in a town like this, she knew already, the night attendant probably had gone around the corner to grab a cup of coffee, and he'd be back in a moment to keep an eye on things.

She had brought far too much with her, having lived near the city too long. Jeans, she thought now, a pair of jeans and a few clean shirts were all she needed in this town, even if she stayed for a week, and she intended to stay as long as necessary. Then, with her purse in one hand and the small suitcase in the other, she left the bus station and walked down Second Avenue toward the main street. She moved slowly, almost as if she was out for a leisurely stroll before turning in for the night. In a manner she had not expected but that somehow seemed perfectly logical, she felt as if she were coming home.

Her gaze lingered over the summer dresses in the display window of the Bell-Lynn Shop. She stopped to peer in the dimly lit window of the Book Nook and saw the best-sellers and gardening guides. When she reached the corner she just stood for a moment and breathed deeply of the night air, already rid of its brush with the bus fumes. She felt her cramped muscles relaxing.

Spotting the hotel, she crossed Palmer Highway, the main street, looking both ways—not for traffic, for there was none, but because she had never seen this street before. And yet—it wasn't her imagination; the street was familiar. Now she was glad that this was the way she was seeing this town for the first time. She had it all to herself. Unlike her suburb, one in a crowd of suburban spokes stretching out from the hub of Chicago, Derrington stood by itself, out in the country, vulnerable perhaps, but cockily independent. She was accustomed to the frantic bustle of the city and now she took an immense pleasure in Palmer Highway's three or four stoplights, all blinking yellow for the nonexistent traffic. A few moths, getting a jump on summer, circled in the glare of the streetlights.

It was a feeling she hadn't experienced in years, this sense of owning a street, not having to share it with another soul. Once, when she was ten and her mother was away, she had gone to the bank with her father, late at night, for some papers he needed. They had walked holding hands, and from the time they left home until they returned, they had not seen another person. They had owned the streets that night, she and her father, and it occurred to her now that since then she had lost something important. Some secret dream had slipped away, and she hadn't even realized it had happened until tonight.

Suddenly the small suitcase felt heavy, pulling on her arm, and she abruptly straightened her shoulders, strode down the block, and entered the double doors of the Farman Hotel. The flaps of the green awning over the entrance rippled in the night breeze.

She gave the lobby the same attention she'd paid to the depot and found herself approving of the worn maroon carpet, the old, dark furniture polished to a glossy sheen, the glass chandeliers hanging motionless from the high ceiling. The walls were lined with framed black-and-white photographs, marking the growth of Derrington from a railroad milk stop to the celebration of its centennial several years ago.

In the city, Kate thought, this hotel would look seedy. Here it had character, it was comfortable, and it suited her growing impressions of the town.

She crossed the empty room to the counter and tapped the bell.

89

After a minute the door behind the counter opened and a white-haired man hurried out.

Instantly, Kate remembered the words in Jim's letter: there was a man who ran the hotel in his friend McGavin's hometown, an "old codger." His name had slipped her mind, but now she had to wonder: Could this possibly be the same hotel, the same "old codger," still here ten years later? The man's face was a road map of wrinkles, with strong smile lines around his mouth balanced by deep creases above his nose. He was frowning slightly, and his eyes looked a bit fuzzy—had she awakened him?

"Good evening, ma'am," he said, and one hand came up to smooth back his thinning hair. "Or, rather, good morning." He smiled in a friendly way. "Do you have a reservation?"

Kate was thrown off balance for a moment. It had never occurred to her. If the hotel was full, where could she go?

"No," she said calmly. "I'd like a single."

He was staring intently at her, and there was a moment's pause.

"I beg your pardon. Do you have a room?" She spoke politely, with the barest trace of impatience.

"Yes, ma'am, we certainly do, with a view of the main street from the second floor, will that do? Quite large, very clean. Here you are, if you would sign the slip, please?"

He placed the paper on the counter and she wrote swiftly, noticing that he was almost hanging over her to see what she wrote. She began to be amused by his interest. When she glanced up at him, he drew back immediately.

"Nice weather we're having, eh?" he said.

"Yes, a little warm for this time of year," she murmured. She remembered that from her call to the weather service.

"Mmm, right you are, it's a little warm. Will you be staying long?"

Kate couldn't help it. She had to smile at the obvious curiosity that had escaped with his question.

"I'm not certain. Does it make a difference?"

The man cleared his throat, a little embarrassed, it seemed to Kate, and his tone became impersonal. "Not at all, but I notice you have only one bag. . . ."

"Oh, I've left another at the bus station. I wonder if you could send someone for it?" It was not really a question, but it wasn't quite a demand, either.

"Of course, right away. The room is payable in advance, please." She removed a slim wallet from her purse and paid him in cash. "Room two-o-nine, top of the stairs and to your left." He pointed. "Welcome to the Farman, ma'am. Have a pleasant stay with us."

Kate could see he was bursting with questions and doing an admirable job of restraining himself. She smiled again, thanked him, and turned away. There was something about him she liked: his open, friendly manner was a world away from Chicago's La Salle Street, and it confirmed her initial reaction to the town. But it was not in her nature to make small talk with strangers, so she picked up the overnight bag and headed for the stairs.

The moment Kate had disappeared from the landing on the wide staircase, the old man snatched the registration slip from the counter and examined it closely. He was staring at it when the deputy came up to the desk.

"'Evening, Mr. Manchester."

"Pete! What're you doing here this time of night? Nothing wrong, I hope?"

"No, sir, nothing like that." The sheriff's deputy removed his hat. "Just drove by the bus station and didn't see Doverman in there, so I stopped to check. There's a suitcase in there, right in the open, nobody around. Guess Doverman's gone home for the night, but—"

"Yes, his daughter, little Ellie," Manchester replied quickly. "Heard she was sick. Henry said the flu, so he probably went to spell his wife a while—"

"Yes, sir, he may have, but the suitcase—thought you might know something about it. Anybody check in tonight?"

"Very astute, Pete." Manchester nodded approvingly. "Good thing you came in or I might've forgot that bag. Belongs to our newest guest." He peered again at the registration slip in his hand. "An odd one, she is, coming here at this hour, all by herself. Looked all right, nice blue suit, good posture, no jewelry, though. Not a word of explanation, either. Didn't say how long she'd be here, though why she'd be here, all alone and a stranger and all,

91

instead of out on one of the lakes, I don't know, although she could be in sales, except that I didn't see—"

"Mr. Manchester," Pete managed to say, "the suitcase? Did she want it tonight?" He softened the remark with a grin.

"Oh, yeah, the bag," Manchester laughed self-consciously. "She says 'send someone for it'—huh!" He shuffled around the counter in his bedroom slippers and moved toward the double doors. "I guess' I'll send someone for it—me! No help this time of night."

"Be glad to give you a hand, sir. Nothing much happening tonight." Pete held the door open and together they crossed the street and retrieved the bag. Pete carried it back to the hotel, listening all the way to the speculations of Clark Manchester, a leading citizen of the town. If they still had town criers, Pete thought to himself, amused, Clark Manchester would win the job hands down in Derrington.

"You know, Pete, I'm getting up there; I admit it. These old flat feet of mine kept me out of the army, and they move slower than ever these days. But, by golly, the old gray matter is still pretty sharp, yessiree." He tapped his head. "I've been standing behind that counter forty-two years now, watching people come and go, sizing 'em up, looking 'em in the eye, and five minutes is all I usually need. Why, once, this shifty character checks in, looking over his shoulder, nervous as all get out, and I had a hunch. I called Harry—that was back when Harry Ragsdale was running your department—and Harry came right over, did a little checking, and sure enough, we had a bank robber, right in the Farman Hotel! Ha! Another time, I was shaking my head to Margaret about the man in room two-twelve when we heard a car backfire. Thought it was out in the alley. Next morning, poor Elsie Schaumberg—she was cleaning rooms for me back then—poor Elsie found the man dead on his bed, gun on the floor. Shot himself, right there in room two-twelve."

Manchester paused to shake his head, and Pete said, "So what do you think? This one a bank robber?"

Manchester clamped his lips together.

"Humph. That's what gets me. There's something, Pete, in the eyes. She's not a crook, no, but there's something not quite right there."

They reached the hotel and Pete deposited the suitcase at the foot of the stairs in the lobby. "Can you manage from here, sir?"

"Sure thing, Pete, and I thank you kindly. Wahomet County's lucky to have a fine young man like you wearing the badge of the law. I swear, between you and John Anthony and those other fine fellows, Will Kalowski excepted—" he smiled to show he was joking; he and Will were old friends—"well, I guess we're well protected from—"

Pete didn't wait to hear what evils Derrington needed protection from. Unlike his boss, John McGavin, he hadn't yet learned to fully appreciate Clark Manchester. He was a young deputy, earnest but inexperienced, so he backed away toward the doors, smiling.

"Thank you, sir, glad to help. Excuse me now, sir, still on duty, you know."

"Yes, sure, well, good night then, Pete." Clark Manchester was a little offended at the brush-off, but only for a moment. As he picked up the suitcase, his mind jumped back to the woman in 209. Her manner reminded him a little bit of Margaret, his late wife. Yes, that was it, when she'd first come to town to run the library. She'd been in her thirties then, too, and a stranger, by herself, but she'd brooked no nonsense from anyone either. She'd had the darnedest way of being firm without ever raising her voice.

He smiled to himself, lugging the suitcase up the long flight of stairs, remembering how everyone in town had been convinced that the new librarian, a haughty, self-contained woman, was doomed to spinsterhood, and not without good cause. But Clark had seen in her a quiet woman with qualities that would not compete with his own. She was dignified, which he was not; he loved her for her quiet grace and she loved him for his laughter. Their marriage had lasted thirty years, until she died, and in all that time, she had run the library and he the hotel. Between the two of them there had been very few secrets in Derrington that they had not known.

Some people, he knew, had never understood the bond that had sealed that marriage. Clark, after all, had been born and reared in Derrington, while Margaret had just shown up one day out of nowhere. Some people had never looked beyond her stern exterior to the kindness—

The door to 209 opened in response to his knock, and the woman, still in her traveling suit but barefoot now, seemed surprised.

"I'm terribly sorry. I didn't realize you'd be the one to carry this up. That was thoughtless of me." She went to her purse, dug out a few dollars, and returned to the door to press them into his hand. "Please. Let me ease my conscience. I appreciate your trouble." And with a quiet "Good night," she closed the door gently in his face.

Clark Manchester stood there, recovering. He'd managed a quick look inside the room. She had opened the window and placed her shoes neatly together at the foot of the bed. Next to them was the overnight case, still unopened.

All that was secondary, though, because in that split-second frown, Clark had recognized it, that haunting look in her eyes, so similar to the one Margaret had worn when he'd first met her. Yes, he was sure now. It was a wariness, a certain caution against giving too much of herself. Clark Manchester knew, because he had learned it from his wife, that it was an expression born of experience, unpleasant, unhappy experience.

Margaret had come to Derrington from a village near the Canadian border in Minnesota, and it was no wonder people had considered her haughty. Her defenses were high. It was only years after their marriage that she had confessed to Clark that she had fled her hometown in dishonor and disgrace because she had borne a child out of wedlock and given it up for adoption. Clark had offered only reassurances of his love and had not probed for details; he could well imagine the circumstances and had, in fact, witnessed similar cases right there in Derrington.

It crossed his mind now that Katherine Downing could have gone through a similar trauma. It was possible—but unlikely, in this day and age, when young people seemed to have such different attitudes. A hundred other things could have planted that disappointment in her eyes. Whatever it was she had weathered it, but it had marked her face.

Clark closed the door to his own living quarters behind the lobby desk and settled into his armchair. He picked up the book he was reading, an old favorite he had read perhaps five times already. He often wished he'd written it himself, for it told of two young boys in the summer of 1928, living in a small town in Illinois.

"I'll be darned!" said Douglas. "I never thought of that. That's brilliant! Old people never *were* children!"

"And it's kind of sad," said Tom, sitting still. "There's nothing we can do to help them."

The smile on Clark Manchester's face was a rueful one.

"'Never were children,' huh . . . Ah, you're wrong there, boys. I wonder what sort of childhood Katherine Downing had. . . . Did it happen to her then, or was it later, when all those childhood dreams didn't come true?

"Ah, maybe you're wrong on both counts, boys. Could be there's a way I can help. Never can tell . . ."

Immediately he thought of Aggie Patterson. She might have some ideas. And he could trust her intuitions. She wouldn't hesitate one second to tell him to mind his own business if she thought he was interfering.

He leaned back in his chair and laughed to himself. That Aggie Patterson had always had a mind of her own. She was his best friend, now that Margaret was gone; he'd known her for years and years. She and Earl Robbins, the principal at the high school where Aggie had taught, had spent countless evenings in this very room, with Margaret and himself, arguing into the night about Hemingway's heroes, Shakespeare's sonnets, and Darwin's theories. Those were rich times, Clark thought, rubbing his eyes. He had missed the benefits of a college education and was hungry for knowledge from the books he'd never had time to read, from people whose experience stretched beyond the limits of Derrington.

He had been the instigator of those gatherings, but Aggie had been the spark, with her sharp tongue and good teacher's ability to cut through the malarkey and seize upon the heart of the matter. For a moment he was tempted to call her and tell her about his new guest, but then he rejected the notion. Lord, it was half past two. Sensible people—and Aggie Patterson was nothing if not sensible— sensible folks were in bed asleep, had been for hours.

He folded his hands on his chest and closed his eyes. A minute later he was snoring gently in his easy chair, the book open in his lap.

. . .

95

Deputy Pete Iverson, back in his squad car, settled in for several more hours of patrol duty. His radio monitored the state police network, and, in a mental trick that most policemen perfect, half his attention listened for items that might pertain to his jurisdiction. The other half was free to focus on whatever he wished, and right now he wished to think about the Farman Hotel's latest arrival. He and Clark Manchester had one thing in common: They both dealt in speculation, though Pete was able to justify his own as an official duty. It was part of his job to notice unusual things, out-of-the-ordinary occurrences.

These days, he thought, driving west out of town, no one with a shred of common sense arrived in a strange town in the middle of the night and left a fully packed suitcase sitting out in an open bus station. Not unless, that is, she wasn't a stranger at all, but somehow knew that in Derrington, Wisconsin, population 7540, it probably was safe to do that. How did she know?

He assumed Clark Manchester wouldn't mind that he'd caught a glimpse of the registration slip. Pete could have asked her name, but he liked to keep his speculations to himself. Her name was Katherine Downing, and she'd given an address from some place in Illinois that Pete had never heard of.

In her room at the Farman Hotel, the subject of all this speculation was feeling an odd exhilaration. She was not the least bit sleepy, so she shook out her clothes, hastily crammed into her suitcase several hours earlier, and hung them in the closet. She put a few things in one of the drawers of the bureau and emptied the contents of the overnight bag. She was making the room her own, at least for one night.

She was determined not to fall into the old trap of introspection, not tonight. She was not going to second-guess the decisions she had made since the moment she had stood in Mr. Cramer's office and remembered the name McGavin. She would not question how she had been able to come up to this town in the middle of the night, calmly check into a hotel as if she did it all the time, and actually enjoy the experience.

This feeling, this alien sense of beginning an adventure, was like a bold stroke of bright paint, splashing across the stagnant dailiness of her life, blotting out self-doubts and petty concerns. Tonight she faced herself in the mirror and smiled at her own audacity, just for the sheer pleasure of it.

96

7

Out of Place

■

Kate awoke Thursday morning feeling more rested than she had in days. It was a pleasant sensation to wake up naturally, with no alarm clock shrieking the hour. She lay in bed, sheet and blankets drawn up to her chin, and gazed around the room, which bore no resemblance at all to the ones in sterile motel chains. No slick chrome here, no dreary uniformity. It looked like a guest room in somebody's house.

Even in the dim light she could see the worn spot in the rose-patterned carpet in front of the dresser. The furniture was dark and old, smooth and polished but mismatched. There was a rocking chair in the corner. A rocking chair in a hotel room! It had an Early-American look to it; the dresser and the headboard were more along the lines of French Provincial. The wallpaper, fresh and bright, had red roses on a green-and-white trellis background, and a light breeze was stirring the heavy, white-fringed curtains at the double window.

I like this room, Kate decided, and in the next moment she knew why. It, too, seemed familiar. The house in Elwood where she had grown up had been old and comfortable, too, on a quiet street, shaded by oaks and willows, with a screened porch sweeping across the front. The high-ceilinged rooms had been filled with odd pieces of furniture her mother had loved. The furnishings in Kate's bedroom had probably not been suitable for a child. They were dark and massive. But Kate's mother had loved them, so Kate had loved them, too. They were solid, like her parents, and just as sturdy.

Kate snuggled deeper into the bed, not quite ready to get up yet, and she tried to visualize her mother's face. It was only when Kate was twelve or thirteen that she'd realized her mother and father were different from her friends' parents. They were much older, her father already gray-haired and slightly bent from his years of responsibility, her mother comfortably plump in dresses that were too long.

Kate had adored them anyway. How could she have felt otherwise? She was their only child, a late and much-longed-for addition to their lonely life, and they bathed her in love, in doting attention, in pride at her every minute accomplishment. She had not wanted for anything, a fact attested to by overflowing toy chests, bulging closets, and a menagerie of pets inside the house and out. Her parents were rich by small-town standards. Her father, as bank president, was a respected leader in the community; her mother, with her easy manner and lack of pretension, was a popular hostess and charity volunteer. But they had lived simply, if comfortably, desiring to be a part of the community, rather than stand above it.

Kate sighed with pleasure, remembering the warmth of that family circle, and by now, after years of practice, she hardly felt the stab of pain as she recalled their deaths. It had been almost as if they had planned it, their timing as loving and considerate as all their actions toward her had been. Once she was out of their care, safely entrusted to Jim, her new husband, they had gone quickly, first her mother, with a stroke; and then, only a few months later, her father had died in his sleep, probably of a heart attack, the doctor had said. Kate did not need to know the cause, only that they had not suffered, and that one had not had to endure life too long without the other.

The real pain had come after their deaths, and Kate did not wish to dwell on that. She threw back the covers and rose swiftly, slipped out of her nightgown, and turned on the shower. Still, as she adjusted the temperature and cupped her hands under the spray, she couldn't quite shake the remembrance of shame and embarrassment when the bank examiners had released their findings. Her father, pillar of the community and family man par excellence, had not been a good banker. He had granted loans to friends that were never fully repaid, and he had made wild, speculative investments. Toward the end he had tried to juggle the books and, after the bank audit, Sam Adams, his treasurer and accomplice, was tried and sent to prison. Kate, a rich heiress one day and a penniless outcast the next, had leaned on Jim for support, grateful at last that she no longer lived in that small town and so did not have to face those people, those friends who had trusted her father and loved her mother. The house and most of its lovely contents had been sold at auction to pay off some of the debts, and after that Kate had left Elwood and never returned.

There had been one man whose debt Kate could not allow to stand. Hiram Wilcox had been her father's closest friend, loyal and forgiving even after the bank scandal was splashed across the front page of the *Elwood Gazette*. He alone had dared to defend her father, both privately and publicly. He wrote letters to the editor. He made a quiet but impassioned speech to the Chamber of Commerce, of which he was president that year. He did all he could to salvage her father's reputation by reminding anyone who would listen of the banker's contributions to Elwood. Wilcox's efforts had been lost in a tide of bitterness, and his only reward was ostracism from the very people he sought to convince. Even Kate was awed by his generosity. He himself had lost thousands of dollars, most of his life's savings, in one of her father's disastrous speculations.

So Kate had sent him the check, the entire amount of Jim's insurance payment from the government. It was not as much as he had lost, but it was all she could do. In the return mail had come one of the kindest letters she had ever received, sympathizing with her over her husband's death. He had even urged her to return home, where she belonged. It was a letter she never answered. Elwood was not her home any longer. It was outside the scope of her imagination that anyone in her circumstances, the daughter of a posthumously convicted embezzler, could actually return to the scene of that crime and face its victims. She could not do it. Elwood, along with the death of her husband, the death of her parents, and all her foolish youthful dreams, was pushed to the farthest corner of her consciousness, and she tried to forget them all.

She stepped out of the shower to wrap an old, thick towel around herself. When she glanced at her watch on the dresser, she was surprised to see that it was after nine-thirty. She dressed hurriedly, suddenly anxious to get out of this room. She wondered if the Farman Hotel served breakfast. Yes, she thought she'd seen a restaurant sign downstairs last night, and what she needed was coffee. Strong, hot coffee to fortify her for her meeting with John Anthony McGavin.

The Evergreen Room in the Farman Hotel was a Cinderella restaurant. In the evening, with the heavy, green-velvet draperies drawn across the windows and the tables graced by linen cloths and napkins, it could pass for a fine supper club. Soft music and candlelight provided a soothing background for quiet conversation.

Then, at midnight, before the help went home, the candles were extinguished and removed, the white tablecloths were whisked away, and paper place mats took their place. Now, at ten in the morning, the Evergreen Room was a rural town's coffee shop, the favorite gathering place for businesspeople on their coffee breaks and several elderly men who rented permanent rooms on the third floor of the hotel. It was brightly lit and noisy with the clatter of dishes and energetic conversation.

Kate sat alone at a small table, feeling distinctly uncomfortable. Dining out alone was one of the many fears she had been forced to conquer; she avoided it whenever possible. In the city, she restricted herself to a few places where she went often for lunch. Soon, of course, the waitresses knew her, and then she did not feel so alone. And she always took along something to read so she would not have to stare into space.

But this time she had left in such a hurry that she hadn't even thought of packing a book. She'd entered the Evergreen Room alone and unarmed, and had stepped into a circle where everyone, except her, seemed to know everyone else. The waitresses greeted all the customers by name, the customers called out to one another, and Kate sat to one side, certain that everyone was noticing her and wondering who she was.

It wasn't long before she decided that even this coffee, better than her own, was not worth the discomfort of drinking it alone. She was gathering her purse and sweater and picking up the check when a man appeared at her table.

"'Morning, ma'am. Something wrong with the coffee?"

Kate looked up into the friendly, crinkled face of Clark Manchester.

"Good morning. No, the coffee's fine, but I—well, I seem to have overslept. I, um, have some business to take care of."

"Well, far be it from me to keep you from your business." He nodded, hands in his pockets. "But I'm about ready for a cup of coffee myself, and I'd be pleased to have your company." His voice was polite, perfectly correct, and the invitation was tentative. Kate scanned his face and caught a glimmer of concern. Last night, before falling into that deep sleep, she had read Jim's letters again, the four she had brought with her that contained references to McGavin. Now she was not sure at all that she trusted this McGavin, sheriff or not. Perhaps this nice old man could help her feel her way.

"How nice of you." Kate gestured to the chair across the table and hid her amusement at the speed with which he sat down.

"As a matter of fact, I'd enjoy another cup of coffee. It's delicious."

Manchester grinned, pleased with the compliment.

"Martha Lindstrom makes it," he said proudly, and waved at the waitress passing their table. "Coffee, please, Nan."

He looked back at Kate. "Martha's been in the kitchen here for— oh, I'd guess twenty years now. Asked her once to tell me her secret. Said she'd tell me when she was good and ready. That was nineteen years ago, and I haven't found out yet."

Kate smiled, thinking, twenty years! Could this be the same man, the one Jim had mentioned in his letter?

"Well, if you ever find out her secret," Kate said, "pass it along to me, will you?" The waitress named Nan, spry step and sparkling eyes belying gray hair and careworn face, poured their coffee and said to Manchester, "Thirty cents, boss."

"Put it on my bill," he retorted, and she laughed as she went on to the next table.

So! He *was* the owner! But she asked anyway.

"Are you the owner of this hotel?"

"Yes, ma'am, I'm proud to say I am. Clark Manchester." He held out his hand and Kate shook it.

"I'm Kate Downing."

"Miss Downing, it's a pleasure to make your acquaintance. Welcome to Derrington."

"Thank you." She sipped her coffee. "Actually, it's Mrs. I'm a widow. I suppose it should be Ms., but I can't quite get used to that."

"Neither can I," Manchester agreed. "Now, I'm not one to quibble with the growth of the language, you understand. I'm all for keeping up with the times. But what in blue bells is wrong with Miss and Mrs.? So you're a widow," he continued, not missing a beat. "Now, that's something else we have in common. I'm a widower. Lost my wife twelve years ago, and I miss her to this day."

"So do I. Miss my husband, I mean." Kate wanted to change the subject and she said quickly, without really thinking, "Have you lived here all your life?"

"All seventy-two years of it," he replied. "Went to school here, held more jobs than I can remember, and wandered into the Farman one day, looking for inside work. The winters are hard up here. Zachary Farman gave me a break, taught me the business, and left this hotel to me when he died. Been here ever since. Not the same without Margaret, but I manage."

Kate looked away, feeling the anguish behind his casual tone. She sipped her coffee.

"Ah, enough of this self-pity, eh, Mrs. Downing?" He smiled cheerfully—bravely, Kate thought—and that touched her. Then he said, "You have a beautiful day for your business." He gestured toward the east windows, where the sun was pouring in.

"Yes, I do." Kate nodded and took the opening. "Mr. Manchester, I wonder . . ."

"Yes?" The expectancy in his voice amused her, just as it had the night before. All right, maybe he was an old busybody, but he could still help her.

"Perhaps you might be able to tell me something."

"Certainly," came the quick reply.

"I—I have to see the sheriff. I think his name is McGavin?" Kate's voice was low; she supposed this little item would be all over town in five minutes, but at least she wanted to be able to leave the coffee shop before everyone in it knew why she was there.

Manchester leaned forward to catch her words. He nodded. "Yes, ma'am, that's his name."

To Kate's surprise, he waited. No comments, no questions. So she would have to work for it.

"Could you tell me . . . Well, what sort of man is he?"

Manchester eyed her carefully. "Pardon my asking, but are you in trouble with the law?"

"Oh, no." Kate shook her head vigorously and frowned. "No, it's nothing like that. Really, it isn't." She noted the lingering doubt on his face and said firmly, "I am not in trouble. But—well, I have a friend—I mean, an acquaintance—oh, that does sound fishy, doesn't it." She smiled nervously again, and this time he smiled. "But it's the truth. I have an acquaintance and—well, I'm afraid he may be in trouble and I was hoping Sheriff McGavin could help me—or help my friend, that is. Oh, dear. I'm not saying what I mean at all."

"Mrs. Downing," Manchester said quietly, but his tone had an uncompromising edge to it, "I'll tell you this. If you—or your friend, all right, your friend—if either of you is in any trouble, you couldn't go to a finer man than John Anthony McGavin. I've known him all his life. Know his family, too, fine people. Matter of fact, you just met his mama."

He grinned at Kate's bewilderment.

"Nan, over there," and he nodded at the gray-haired waitress. "Nancy McGavin, a positive gem of a woman." He nodded with conviction.

Kate followed his gaze to the waitress, then looked back at him. She swallowed. She had to be sure.

"Excuse me, Mr. Manchester, but I have to ask this. It's very important. Is John McGavin an honest man?"

If Manchester was offended by her question, he managed to hide it.

"As the day is long, pardon the cliché. He used to work for me, too, here in the hotel, when he was a youngster. He was my right-hand man two, no, three summers. That's when we do our real business, tourists flocking in; they'll begin coming next week. Now, John Anthony, he just jumped right in and did it all, carrying bags, running errands, even helped with the books that last summer, and not one complaint, either from him or about him. Tell the truth, I had some hopes he might stay with me, maybe even take over the place someday, but then that dang fool war started up, and he went, and by the time he got home, he'd sort of lost interest, I guess, and

103

old Harry Ragsdale, he was Wahomet County sheriff back then, well, he knew a good man when he saw one, always did, and he stole that boy right out from under me."

Manchester chuckled, remembering, and Kate, breathless even if he wasn't, managed to smile. She was feeling less like a stranger in this town every minute. She was tempted to spill it all out, to try the story on Clark Manchester to see if it made any sense, before she went to McGavin. But then he stopped smiling and his voice became stern again.

"Ma'am, you ever been in Derrington before?"

Kate shook her head, bewildered.

"Well, now you go out that door, that's Palmer Highway, you turn right, go down to the first street, that's Second Avenue, you cross it and go to the next street, that's Third Avenue, you turn right, and there, on your right, is the Wahomet County Courthouse, and the sheriff's office is right inside the door. I imagine John Anthony's at that big desk of his right now."

He looked at her and seemed to expect some kind of an answer, so Kate smiled.

"Yes, ma'am, you go see John Anthony. Now, excuse me," he got up from the table, "but I have a hotel to run." Kate thought she caught the trace of a wink before he turned and walked back toward the kitchen.

Well! she thought. I believe I have just been put in my place. Here I am wondering if I can trust him, and it seems he's wondering the same thing about me. At least I know one thing. He thinks the sun rises and sets in John Anthony McGavin, and he knows the man a lot better than I do.

Well, then, what are you waiting for? she asked herself, then answered, I'm waiting because I'm afraid of what I might find out.

Oh, did you abandon that office and come all the way up here to be stared at in a hotel coffee shop?

That did it. She slid out of the chair, grabbed her purse and her sweater, and paid the check. Then, sure that every eye in the place was boring into her back, she went out to the street.

As she walked down Palmer Highway, she noticed that Derrington in the morning sun did not have quite the same charm it had exuded the night before. The daylight brought out the flaws, the shabbiness of some of the buildings, and she saw now the cheap tourist shops that dotted the main street. She still liked it, though. It was what it was, a small town in rural Wisconsin, making its living as it could, and not pretending to be anything else.

She rounded the corner on Third Avenue and, sooner than she wished, saw the courthouse on her right. It was a new building, a two-story red brick, and a beige-colored squad car was parked in front. Kate paused a moment, then grasped her purse tighter against her body and entered the lobby. The glass door on the right was labeled WAHOMET COUNTY SHERIFF'S OFFICE.

Kate took another deep breath, pushed open the door, and went in to meet John Anthony McGavin.

8

The Sheriff of Wahomet County

■

A long counter stretched across the entire front room of the office. Kate saw immediately that only two people were present: a middle-aged woman stood at the counter, filling out a form of some sort, and seated behind the counter, in a starched blue uniform with a shiny badge, was surely the oldest representative of the law Kate had ever seen.

He has to be sixty, at least, she thought. Surely this can't be the same John Anthony McGavin?

At once, she knew she had made a terrible mistake. This man was too old, much too old. He was the sheriff and probably he had a son—and yet, Clark Manchester had said—

"'Morning, ma'am. Help you?"

"Uh, well, um, I've come to see Sheriff McGavin. Are you—"

"His deputy, ma'am." The old man was frowning fiercely, his white bushy eyebrows a single straight line over his eyes. Kate released a silent sigh of relief.

"I see," she managed to say. "Is Sheriff McGavin in? I don't have an appointment, but—"

"One moment, ma'am, I'll see. Your name, please?"

"Oh, he doesn't know me. Uh, Mr. Manchester, down at the hotel, suggested I see the sheriff. . . ."

Kate's voice was trailing off, but it didn't matter. The mere mention of Clark Manchester was as good as waving a magic wand, apparently. The deputy was already on the phone. Kate noticed that the woman at the counter had stopped filling out the form and was watching Kate and the deputy with unabashed interest.

"Sheriff, got a lady here who wants to see you," the deputy said into the phone. "Says Clark Manchester sent her."

"Oh, he didn't exactly send me—"

"Right, John." The deputy hung up and pointed down the length of the counter. "Gate's right down there, ma'am, just go through it, through that door back there, down the hall, first door on your left."

He waited, pointing, and when Kate didn't move, he repeated, "Through that gate, straight back to the door—"

"Yes, thank you," Kate said quickly, and nearly ran to the gate.

First door on the left, Kate muttered to herself, and there was his nameplate on the door: SHERIFF JOHN ANTHONY MCGAVIN.

She knocked, a voice called out, "Come in," and she opened the door slowly.

The man behind the big oak desk glanced up briefly and waved vaguely toward a chair. "Have a seat, please, I'll be right with you." He was wearing a blue uniform shirt with sharp creases down the sleeves.

"Thank you," Kate said, closing the door. She perched on the edge of a hard wooden chair.

Now, her misgivings multiplied, she studied the man she had come to see.

The problem was that she had formed a double set of expectations without bothering to reconcile one with the other. She had dim memories of the county sheriff in Elwood, a potbellied man in his fifties who went through life in slow motion as he strolled into the bank, spoke in an interminable drawl, and tipped his hat to all the ladies. The only time he broke the pattern was when he was behind the wheel of his car, and then he drove like a maniac, using the siren and flashing lights to go home from work every evening.

On the other hand, the Wahomet, Wisconsin, county sheriff was, she was almost certain, a contemporary of her husband's and, from the description in his letters, Kate had expected a tall, swaggering man who exuded an oily charm as he politicked his way through the demands of an elected post.

Sheriff John Anthony McGavin was neither of these monsters, at least in appearance. Kate guessed, even as he remained seated behind his desk, that he was of only medium height, far shorter than Jim. He had a compact build and an unlined face. He was, she surmised, close to her own age, thirty-three, but he looked younger. His thick, neatly trimmed brown hair showed no strands of gray and his eyes, she noted as he slid some papers aside and looked up at her, held a childlike anticipation that she instinctively mistrusted. What did he have to be so happy about?

"Sorry," he said, smiling easily at her, "this paperwork never lets go. Seems the world'll come to a dead halt if I don't get this report filed today. We have a representative at the legislature down in Madison who—well, he's my problem, isn't he. What can I do for you? Are you a friend of Clark Manchester's?"

"No, I'm only a guest at his hotel."

Kate was surprised to find herself smiling back at him, but she hadn't forgotten the capsule description Jim had provided: This man was a manipulator who could charm anyone he pleased, including colonels. I believe he could, Kate thought, and in spite of Clark Manchester's assurances, she kept her guard up.

"I need your help," Kate began. "I'm looking for someone, my employer, actually. . . ." The face opposite her remained friendly and open, encouraging her confidence. Yet she hesitated.

"So," he prompted, "your employer." She nodded. "He's here in Derrington?"

"I don't know exactly. He was here, or near here, and when he didn't come back, I—well, I came here to find him. Can you help me?"

"Let's see what we have here. How long has he been missing?"

"He was supposed to be in the office Monday morning."

McGavin rubbed his chin, and Kate, sensing his objections, rushed on. "I went to the police in Chicago and they laughed at me, but they don't know him. He was on his vacation, and he didn't come back when he said he would. He's a very organized person, and he likes to keep to a schedule, and I'm afraid something has happened to him." She heard her voice rising in pitch and she stopped abruptly, fighting for control.

McGavin leaned back in his chair, giving her space, and his voice was calm, pleasant.

"You're from Chicago?"

Kate nodded. She could see he was giving her time to collect herself, and she appreciated it.

"And your employer was here on his vacation. . . ."

"I'm sure of that," she said, back on firmer ground. "I made his reservations myself. He was gone three weeks, as usual, and then—" Kate fumbled in her purse for the postcard, now bent and frayed at the edges—"and he sent me this." She leaned forward and handed him the card.

The sheriff took the card and examined both sides of it. He looked up at her, puzzled. "My name is on this card. . . ."

Kate was watching him closely, steeling herself for another rejection, and she didn't miss a nuance of the change that washed over him. The easygoing complacency vanished, his shoulders stiffened, and he looked at her with a new, closer scrutiny. He cleared his throat.

"Excuse me, ma'am, what did you say your name was?" He looked at the card again.

Kate looked at him unblinkingly, watching his face.

"I didn't. My name is Kate Downing. I believe, Sheriff, that you knew my husband, Jim Downing."

McGavin's jaw dropped and his hand fell from his chin.

"You—you're Jim Downing's wife?"

The stress was on the last word and Kate nodded, suddenly eager because she was certain now that she had found her husband's friend. He had said her husband's name. And if that was so, he must also be the J. A. McGavin of Cramer's postcard.

"You did know my husband?"

The sheriff was staring at her, dumbfounded.

"Yes," he answered slowly, "and if I may—excuse me, but when were you married? Do you mind telling me?"

"Of course not," Kate said. "We were married in June of 1965, right after our freshman year in college."

McGavin put his face in his hands. "I see." His voice was so low she could hardly hear him. "And may I ask where—" his voice caught and he cleared his throat again—"Where is your husband now?"

"He's dead, Sheriff McGavin. He died in a plane crash on his way home from Vietnam."

"Dear God." His eyes were hidden behind his hands.

"I'm sorry. I—I just assumed you knew. It was stupid of me."
Kate could see the shock she had caused. She was silent for a moment, then said cautiously, "Sheriff McGavin, I know you were good friends. Jim wrote to me about you. But—but it happened a long time ago. . . ." Kate's voice petered out. She didn't know what to say; she hadn't come prepared for this kind of reaction.

"I'm sorry." His voice was muffled behind his hands. "I didn't know. I am truly sorry."

"Thank you." What an absurd thing to say, Kate scolded herself. He's sorry about Jim, his friend. What are you thanking him for? She went on, trying to help him, "I have to tell you, I don't understand why Mr. Cramer would write your name on the postcard. You're not a client of ours, are you? Is there some other connection?"

McGavin took his hands away from his face. "No, not a client. . . . Cramer? Cramer . . ." he said again, looking down at the postcard. "Benjamin Cramer."

"Yes, my employer. You do know him?"

"No, I—um, that is, I've never met him. But . . ." His voice trailed off again, and Kate waited. Now he was looking at her as if she were an apparition, or—or something ugly, Kate thought. The look on his face is horror, she realized, and she shrank further back into the big wooden chair, pressing her handbag against her stomach.

"Excuse me a moment," McGavin said abruptly. He shot to his feet, brushed past her, and bolted for the door.

He made it down the hallway and into the men's room just in time. The waves of nausea kept coming, and he prayed no one would walk in on him and find him like this. Finally it passed, and he sank onto the cool tile of the floor and leaned against the metal partition.

Dear God, he whispered, what have I done? What have I done?

When he felt the waves subsiding, he got slowly to his feet, knees trembling, and walked unsteadily to the sink. He bent over and rinsed out his mouth, washed his face and hands with soap, then reached for a paper towel from the dispenser on the wall.

He could picture her, down the hall, perched in that chair like an injured bird, vulnerable and totally unsuspecting. But she had come up here, tracked him down with nothing more than his name on a postcard to go on, and he knew she wouldn't leave. She was still

110

there, waiting for him to come back and explain everything to her, as if he ever could.

She has a right to know!

That phrase was rocking through his brain, daring him to contradict it, and he knew he couldn't. He also knew that he was the only one who could tell her. Oh, he hated what he was about to do to her. Was there any way to make it easier? To maybe—postpone it? Just a little while, to give him time to think of what he would say.

He bent over the sink again, splashing more water over his face, dried off, and went back to his office. He still felt wobbly, but he knew that would take a long time to pass.

Kate looked up as he walked past her to his desk. His face was white. The happy anticipation was gone from his eyes and he did not look like a child anymore.

"Have a mint, Mrs. Downing?"

He had already grabbed a handful for himself and he extended the glass bowl to her.

Kate began to sense another brush-off, and she straightened in her chair.

"No, thank you. What I do want is for you to tell me if that postcard means anything to you."

"It does, in a way," he said slowly, sinking into his cushioned chair. "That is, as I said, I've never met Benjamin Cramer, but . . . I do know of him."

McGavin was speaking very slowly. Kate was tired of his doubletalk, but when she opened her mouth to object, he surprised her by asking suddenly, "Does the name Rodney Weaver mean anything to you?"

Her eyes widened at this unexpected question.

"Yes, yes," she said quickly, "he's the real estate agent in Eagle Hill who rents the cabin to Mr. Cramer."

"Okay, fill me in. Tell me exactly what happened. You said you made the reservations?"

"Yes, I always do. Mr. Cramer comes up here every year. I called Rodney Weaver in March to reserve the cabin. It's on a lake somewhere, I think. Mr. Cramer talks about the fishing—I mean, he mentions it on his postcards. He, um, he sends a card every year, to

111

the office. Until this year; this year he was gone three weeks, as usual, but he didn't send a card—until this one came on Monday."

"And this card says he's decided to stay longer."

"I don't care what the card says." Now Kate felt she really was at the end of the line. He had given her a straw to grasp by tossing out Rodney Weaver's name, so he obviously knew something. But he seemed to be playing with her, stalling, maybe. For some reason, she represented a problem to him and he didn't want to deal with it.

But if she failed here, then there was nowhere else to go. She had to get through to him. She wasn't going to allow him to politely usher her out of his office until she had some answers.

"Now that card," she said firmly, almost belligerently, "doesn't say what it seems to say. You probably have to know Mr. Cramer to understand this, but try, anyway, will you?"

Kate was lecturing him as if he were a not very bright child. "Mr. Cramer runs on a very careful schedule. He hates to waste time, and he never makes last-minute changes in his plans. I've known him ten years and he's never behaved like this before. He had a week crammed with important appointments, and those appointments mean money. He would never extend a fishing vacation and risk losing those clients! It's just absurd to even think of it.

"In the second place, there's no way you could know this, but believe me, this card is not his style at all. He wrote it, that's his handwriting, but it's not his style. Mr. Cramer is a very formal person, maybe you'd think he's a little old-fashioned, but he has a proper way of doing things and he always calls me 'Mrs. Downing,' he always has. He never uses my first name.

"Okay, third, the weather. I checked, and the weather here has been beautiful, not 'lousy.'

"And fourth, and this is where you come in, Sheriff McGavin, he tells me to reschedule his appointment with you. Well, of course I couldn't do that, because there was no appointment with you, was there?

"Therefore, I have to come to one of two conclusions. One, he wrote that card under someone else's direction, which I doubt because Mr. Cramer is a take-charge person. Or, two, he had to stay up here for some reason, but it's not the fishing, and he needs my help and yours, too, so he gave me your name.

"Not that I understand any of this, but that is a logical conclusion, don't you think? So are you going to help me or not?"

McGavin had been listening to her intently, she was sure, but she could tell nothing from his expression. She didn't know what to think of this man. In the space of a few minutes he had gone from being mildly pleasant to rushing out of the room in apparent panic to listening with a stone face. Of course, she herself had begun calmly enough, too, and she'd ended up delivering what amounted to a closing argument to the judge.

She had done her best. Now it was his move. She waited, meeting his gaze whenever he looked at her. The silence between them stretched into a minute, two, three. He seemed to be grappling with a decision, and Kate was afraid that if she spoke, said anything at all, it would tip the scales against her. Benjamin Cramer had been right about one thing: This was a woman who knew when to keep silent.

When McGavin spoke, it wasn't exactly what she'd hoped for, but it wasn't a dismissal, either.

He said, "Have you spoken with Rodney Weaver?"

"He's on vacation." Kate paused; he seemed to expect more, so she added, "I called his office Monday morning, before the postcard came. They said he couldn't be reached. And there was something very odd. . . ."

"Yes?"

Kate couldn't tell if he was interested or merely playing for time, but she answered, "No one in that real estate office had ever heard of Benjamin Cramer. I have been calling up there every year, talking to Mr. Weaver, making the reservation, and sending them a check. But they had no records of any of that."

McGavin, who had been chewing mints at a furious pace, cupped his hands under his chin and leaned his elbows on the desk. He studied her for a long moment.

Then, abruptly, he stood up and grabbed his hat from the coatrack in the corner.

"If Weaver's on vacation, then I may know where to find him. Would you care to come along?"

Kate was already out of her chair. She snatched up the postcard from his desk and hurried through the door he held open for her.

"So," she said, trying to sound as if she'd expected this very reaction all along, "you don't think I'm imagining that something is wrong?"

"I don't know what to think." He led the way to the reception room at the front of the building, and paused only for a moment to speak to the white-haired deputy manning the front desk. "If you need me, Will, you can reach me on the radio."

"Yessir, Sheriff," Will replied, and if Kate had bothered to look, she would have noticed the curiosity on his face.

But she was being escorted through the central hallway, outside, across the sidewalk, and into the squad car.

It occurred to her, as he closed her door and went around to the driver's side, that she was getting into a car with a perfect stranger, a man she'd never met before, and that quite possibly it was a foolish, even a dangerous thing to do.

"Oh, stop it," she admonished herself. "The man is a sheriff, you nitwit. 'As honest as the day is long,' remember?" She slipped out of her sweater and clutched it in her lap along with her purse.

The sheriff got in and started the engine. He made a U-turn and drove out of the business district, heading out to the interstate.

Kate, ever the efficient secretary, asked, "What about your report? For the representative?"

"It can wait," McGavin said shortly, and Kate didn't know whether to be glad that someone was finally listening to her or frightened for the same reason.

She decided to take the plunge once more.

"Sheriff McGavin."

"Yes?"

"I'd like some answers, please. I don't understand any of this, and I think you do. Can you explain?"

The sheriff glanced over at her briefly, then looked ahead again. Kate could see him swallowing, and there were beads of perspiration on his forehead.

"Mrs. Downing," he said finally, "you deserve answers to all your questions." Kate shivered at the gentleness in his voice. Was it that bad? Were the answers so hard? "But first," he said, "let's find your boss and get some answers from him. The only way I know to do that is to find out where he's staying, and for that we need Rodney Weaver."

Kate thought he said the name with something close to a sneer.

114

"Weaver's got a fancy house out on Pine Lake," McGavin continued. "If his office told you he's on vacation, that's a likely place to find him. It's several miles from here, so why don't you enjoy the scenery on the way. We have about a forty-minute drive."

He's not patronizing me, Kate thought. He's being kind to me. So why am I so afraid?

She bit her lip and looked away from him, but the beauty of pine forests and brilliant sunshine was lost on her. She had the desperate feeling that some cornerstone of her life, something so basic she had always taken it for granted, was being blown away by a picture postcard. That pretty little life she had made for herself on Rolfe Road and La Salle Street seemed too far away to ever go back to.

The sheriff was talking quietly, giving her a running commentary on everything they drove past. There was an old railway car sitting on an abandoned track, and he was telling her how the milk trains used to make their daily runs through the dairy farms.

"Now, there," he said, pointing to their right, "is one of my favorite places. Been in the Boardman family for as long as anybody around here can remember." He indicated an immense brick mansion, poised a good distance from the road, with a narrow, tree-lined lane leading up to it. "In its day, that was the finest place for miles around. A working farm, too, used to be, but now the heirs have lost interest. They rent it out to tenants who don't know much about farming. That acreage could support half the people in Derrington, if it was farmed right."

Kate looked, out of courtesy more than interest. She didn't know much about farming, but she agreed that it must have once been a magnificent place.

"Why doesn't someone buy it?" she asked.

"Ah, they want a fortune for it. Not many people around with that much money these days. I'd like to buy it myself, just to keep it from going to pot, but of course I can't. Neither can anybody else, I guess."

Kate didn't reply, and he drove silently for a while. She soon forgot the Boardman place, but she could not lose her awareness of the man driving this car, and the fact that she had willingly come with him.

Until now, although she hadn't accomplished much, she at least had been in control. She had chosen to call the hospitals, to go to the police in Chicago, to get on a bus in the middle of the night and come up here.

But now . . . suddenly, this stranger next to her, a friend of her husband's, was driving off into the country and she was only along for the ride. Clearly, he was in charge now.

What if she asked him to turn back?

"I've changed my mind," she could say. "Take me back to the hotel." She suspected he would be only too glad to acquiesce. She could get on the next bus and go back to Chicago, back to the office on La Salle Street where she belonged. What was she doing up here, anyway?

But she didn't say a word. She stared unseeing out the window and fingered the postcard in her lap. That postcard was assuming an almost mystical power. Every time she touched it she could hear Benjamin Cramer. "Reschedule appointment with J. A. McGavin." It was a muted plea, but she knew Benjamin Cramer, and now that she had found J. A. McGavin, she knew her instincts were right. Benjamin Cramer *was* asking for her help. After all he had done for her, there was no way in the world she could turn her back on him now.

9

The Weasel

■

The part of Wisconsin through which Kate Downing and John Anthony McGavin were driving was just far enough north to claim to be part of the famed "North Woods" of the state. Dairy farms and timbered acres gave it a peaceful atmosphere. The winters here were harsh, but the summer days were mild, the nights refreshingly cool. The biggest lure to city-weary travelers was the water. There were countless lakes, most of them clear and unpolluted; some of them had been seized by entrepreneurs and developed into resorts.

Pine Lake was one such property. In a span of ten or twelve years, it had grown from a nearly forgotten, somewhat swampy body of water into a multimillion-dollar recreation center. Three hotels hugged its shores. Interspersed among them were thirty or forty expensive private homes. Pine Lake would have none of the rustic cabins such as those crumbling in the woods around Baker's Lake. Here the homes were advertisements, signs of achievement and prosperity. Their proud owners, determined to keep out any more greedy developers—after all, three hotels were quite enough—had banded together to form an association. For many, this was only a summer home, or merely a weekend escape, but they were diligent about protecting their property.

The members of Pine Lake Homeowners Association elected officers and served on committees. Blueprints for new homes were examined by the building committee. Prospective owners endured rigorous, though reasonably discreet, background inquiries by the membership committee. In the summer, when the greatest number of homeowners were in residence, the entertainment committee arranged waterfront parties, cocktail hours, and formal dinner-dances. There was even talk of purchasing a lot and building a clubhouse.

The driving force behind the association, the man who had first seen the need for such a mutually beneficial arrangement and who had modestly agreed to serve as its first president, was Rodney Weaver. He had purchased a double lot and taken well over a year to build his home on it. Even now, more than six years after its completion, it remained the showplace of all the private homes on Pine Lake. He had used limestone to form the exterior walls. The house was many-sided, constructed around the trees to preserve the natural beauty of the site, and it boasted dozens of windows to accommodate the magnificent views. There were three decks as well as a screened-in porch, a regulation-size tennis court to one side, and a heated three-car garage. Inside, the house was multileveled, almost every room set off from the adjoining ones by at least a few steps. But the central staircase was open, there were railings or counters or low bookshelves in place of many walls, and the effect was one of sweeping expanses of light and air and space.

Kate was impressed, even before she saw the house. They had turned off the interstate and were following a smooth blacktop road around the lake. Through the trees, sometimes through openings in stone fences, she could catch a glimpse of one imposing residence after another.

"Is Rodney Weaver rich?" she asked, finally breaking the silence.

"I imagine so," McGavin replied. "Tell me, Mrs. Downing, how well do you know him?"

"Hardly at all. He's a telephone acquaintance. I call him every year to make Mr. Cramer's reservations and we have a pleasant conversation. I've never met him."

"Then I'd like to make a suggestion, please. When we get there, let me do the talking."

Kate looked at him quizzically, but he was following the bend in the road, not looking at her.

"All right, Mr. McGavin. You know more about this than I do, it seems." She waited for an answer, but there was none. Kate sighed and eased her grip on the postcard, still in her hand.

■   ■   ■

118

Rodney Weaver, clad in tennis shoes and a pair of plaid shorts, was sunning himself on the warmest day yet of a cool Wisconsin spring. Stretched out on a cushioned redwood lounge on the top deck, he was sipping his first Bloody Mary of the day and ignoring the aimless chatter of his wife, Louisa, as she repotted some plants into their outdoor containers. She was preparing for another summer season at the lake, watching the time closely so she wouldn't forget to drive into town to pick up the children at school. Wouldn't it be nice, she was saying, when school was out and the children could be here with her all day? Weaver didn't hear her; he was remembering last Sunday, the night he had murdered Benjamin Cramer. He shivered involuntarily.

"Chilly, dear?" his wife said, glancing up from her work, and then, "Well, I'll be. . . . That looks like a police car, doesn't it?" He was out of his chair in an instant, leaning over the railing.

"Yes, a police car," Louisa said. "I'll go down and see what they want." She pulled off her garden gloves and stepped into the house.

Weaver sank down on the end of his lounge chair and took a swallow of his drink, draining the glass. Good Lord, the police! Had they found the body so quickly? And why had they come to him? They had no proof, absolutely none, but still . . . He needed an alibi. Where had he been Sunday night? Here, of course, with his wife and children—no, wait, that wouldn't do; he'd had to make up a story to tell Louisa to explain his all-night absence. He'd told her he'd gone into town, to the office, some work he had to do, vacation or no vacation, and he'd finished late, he'd been exhausted, so he'd spent the night in town, at home. Yes, he'd have to tell the police the same thing—

"Right this way, Sheriff, he's out here. Rod, you remember Sheriff McGavin, from Derrington, don't you? I believe we met at your Fourth of July celebration one year, didn't we, Sheriff?" His wife, ever the brainless but charming hostess, was smiling brilliantly as she led the policeman out onto the deck. Her high-pitched voice was grating to her husband's ears.

"Sure, of course, hello there, Sheriff! Good to see you again—"

"And this is Mrs. Downer, Rodney," Louisa said.

"Downing," McGavin said clearly, "Kate Downing."

• • •

119

Kate stepped out into the sunshine and saw Rodney Weaver's smile slip from his face. She glanced uncertainly at the sheriff and he, too, was watching Weaver. It was only for a moment; she might have been mistaken, because Weaver was smiling broadly now and talking in a loud voice.

"Well, Sheriff, what are you doing way out here? What can we do for you?"

McGavin turned to Weaver's wife and said politely, "Pardon me, Mrs. Weaver; I'd like a word with your husband. Would you mind . . . ?"

Louisa Weaver, a tall bony woman with carefully arranged blond hair, allowed herself to look properly offended for a moment, then said, "Of course, Sheriff. Mrs. Downing?" She gestured toward the door leading into the house.

"Mrs. Downing will stay here," McGavin said firmly.

"As you wish." All the cordiality was gone and she lifted her nose as she crossed the deck. "If you need me, Rodney, I'll be in the kitchen."

"Yes, dear, that's fine." Weaver's voice sounded too loud, Kate thought, falsely hearty. "Sit down, Sheriff, Mrs.—uh, Downing, is that the name? Please, have a chair."

Kate took the chair he offered and realized it was a distinct pleasure to be letting someone else handle things. She felt intimidated by the whole situation, the house, Mrs. Weaver, and even Rodney Weaver. After all their friendly telephone conversations, why was he pretending not to know her? She supposed it was childish, but she felt a little cheated. She had thought they were telephone friends.

And, oh, he was a disappointment to look at. She had built a false image there, too, from his outgoing banter over the phone. He was in his mid-forties and very thin. There wasn't a trace of middle-age paunch; he had knobby elbows and knees. That wasn't so bad, but his hair, straight and yellow, was combed straight back from his face and wet with oil. His teeth were narrow and pointed, too small for his face. Whenever he smiled, which was constantly, it seemed, his face took on a hollow look.

She looked at McGavin again, seeking reassurance, and she could tell that he, too, was measuring Weaver and not liking what he saw.

"Drink, Sheriff? No, I see you're on duty, but maybe the

120

lady . . .?" Kate shook her head. "Well, you don't mind if I do?" He picked up his glass and walked over to the cart near the door.

"Mr. Weaver, I believe you're acquainted with Mrs. Downing, here," McGavin began, and Weaver turned his head toward them, looking puzzled.

"Mrs. Downing is Benjamin Cramer's secretary." McGavin spoke slowly, watching Weaver closely, and Weaver turned back to the cart, making his drink. Stalling? Kate wondered. Was he not even going to admit that he knew her?

"Cramer," Weaver said thoughtfully, carrying his drink back to the lounge chair. "Benjamin Cramer, you say? No, can't say the name rings a bell."

Kate sat up, indignant, but McGavin silenced her with a wave of his hand. How dare he! Kate thought. How dare he pretend he doesn't know Mr. Cramer. She sent McGavin a pleading look. She had promised to stay quiet and she would, but he mustn't let Weaver get away with these lies. She could see McGavin swallow, taking a big breath, and when he spoke the words were pained, but loud enough for her to hear.

"Mr. Weaver, ten years ago next month, I called you at your office in Eagle Hill and inquired about some lakeside properties. I didn't identify myself, but I told you I had an acquaintance who was looking for a place to spend a few weeks every year, and it had to be in a remote location with no other cabins, no people nearby. I asked if you knew of such a place, and you said you did."

Kate, seated behind McGavin, who had turned to face Weaver, was squinting into the sun. She thought the sheriff looked for all the world like a blue stone statue. His feet were planted firmly on the wooden planks of the deck, his thumbs were hitched into the belt of his uniform so that his arms formed a triangle of light on either side of his wiry frame, and he was absolutely still. His words were as cold and emotionless as his stance. Ten years ago, she thought; that was when Jim died. The connection registered, but only momentarily; she was looking past McGavin to Weaver, and she watched the innocent, hollow smile collapse into a gape of incredulity.

"You?" Weaver whispered, staring up at McGavin. "You made that call?"

McGavin nodded almost imperceptibly. Kate wished she could see McGavin's face, but he kept his gaze riveted on Weaver.

121

"If you recall our conversation," he said, "then you'll remember that I gave you Benjamin Cramer's name and the phone number of his office in Chicago, and I asked you to call him and discuss the matter with him. Now, we both know that you made that call, and that since then, you have spoken to Mrs. Downing here several times about the rental of a cabin. We are looking for Mr. Cramer, and we would like you to tell us where he is."

Why, Kate wondered, did Weaver suddenly look relieved? Again, it was only a momentary slip, but this time McGavin must have seen it, too.

"Mr. Weaver," he said, and now there was an edge of impatience in his tone, "where is Benjamin Cramer?"

Kate was astonished when Weaver finally sputtered, "Why—why, how should I know?" He was acting indignant! How could he possibly be insulted? She leaned forward again and heard McGavin, his voice still quiet but heavy with authority.

"Mr. Weaver, this is a police matter. We can handle it here, or in my office in Derrington, whichever you prefer." He waited a moment, then said, "Fine. The squad car's down—"

"Oh, all right, no need to . . ." Weaver's voice trailed off. "You know how these big-city businessmen are, Sheriff, they like their privacy. I'm sure you see that in your work all the time, and I try to— yes, yes, I'm getting to it. I did rent Cramer a cottage a few times. But he's gone. Left last Sunday when his three weeks were up."

"How do you know he left?"

"Huh?"

"Did you see him go?"

"Well, no, I mean, yes, as a matter—"

"Where's the cottage?"

"Well, it isn't much, not one of our better properties, and since he's gone—"

"Where is it?" McGavin clenched his fists and Kate could see that he was fighting the same urge she was. She wanted to take the man and shake the information out of him.

"Baker's Lake," Weaver snapped, "back in the woods off County One-twenty-three, but he's gone, I tell you—"

"Thank you, Mr. Weaver." McGavin's voice was reasonably polite again, and Kate admired his control. She was still furious. "Mrs. Downing?"

122

Kate stood up, a little dizzy from the interrogation she had just witnessed. Thank God for this man, she thought, following Mc-Gavin toward the doorway. I never could have gotten this information from Rodney Weaver, never. McGavin paused at the door.

"For the time being," he said, "I think we can keep this conversation between the three of us, don't you?" He waited for and received an assenting nod from Weaver. "And one more thing. Right now, I have no grounds to arrest you. But I'd like to request that you not leave town until this matter is cleared up. Can I have your word on that?"

Again, Weaver nodded, almost as if he were in a trance, and Kate and the sheriff left the deck.

Rodney Weaver stood in the sun and listened as they went down the stairs inside. He heard the car doors slam and the engine start. He turned and watched the squad car back out of his driveway onto the blacktop road. It was pulling out of sight as he wife reappeared at the door.

"Well?" She stood in the doorway a moment with her hands on her bony hips, looking at him expectantly. "What was that all about?" She crossed the deck to her husband. "Rodney? What did they want? And who was that woman? I've never seen her before, I'm sure; what on earth did they want with you? Rod? Rodney! Answer me!"

"Oh, shut up," Rodney Weaver said to his wife, and he walked past her into the house.

He went to their bedroom, a huge, private room on the top level, and closed the door behind him. He sat down on the king-size bed, leaning his elbows on his knees, and stared out of the windows.

Finally he picked up the telephone next to the bed and dialed the operator.

"I want to call Hong Kong, Operator." He knew it was hopeless even as he gave her the number and waited through a series of clicks. The man had said he could take care of himself, and Weaver was sure he could.

"It's too dangerous," he had said. "We can't be seen together."

The phone at the other end began ringing.

"You just stay put," he had told Weaver. "Do what you usually do, no change in routine."

"But if the police come . . . How will I find you?"

"Your party does not answer, sir." It was the long-distance operator. Weaver replaced the receiver slowly, silently, and he knew the party would never answer. Who knew where he was by now? He had left, still holding a bloody handkerchief to his right eye, and Weaver knew that the only reason the man from Hong Kong hadn't killed him was that it would arouse too much suspicion. Cramer disappearing, that was one thing; there could be a hundred reasons for that. But Weaver, too? That would be too much of a coincidence. Besides, Weaver had proved himself, hadn't he? He had taken the gun, actually aimed it at Cramer, fired, and hit him, killed him.

Still, the man had threatened him. He would know, he promised Weaver, if Weaver said or did anything to lead the authorities to him. Weaver didn't doubt him for a second.

He lifted his head and saw the evergreens outside his home and the blue sparkle of Pine Lake, and there were tears in his eyes. The man from Hong Kong was gone, leaving him with nothing, not a shred of a chance to clear himself. The telephone number in Hong Kong was all Weaver had ever had, and now there was no way to find him. He didn't even know the man's name. There was only he, Rodney Weaver, left to take the blame.

Well, what had he thought would happen? That his life would go rolling on as before? That the Downing woman, who protected her boss in her every word, would sit in Cramer's office forever, waiting for him to come back?

Weaver knew now what would happen. They would dredge the lake, find the body, and come straight back to him. Even if he told them nothing, they wouldn't let go; they'd check his business records, his bank accounts, all those unexplainable cash deposits made every year on the last day of May. They'd investigate the worth of his property, this house and the big brick house in Eagle Hill, his wife's furs and jewelry. They'd threaten him, and he knew he wasn't strong enough to withstand the assault, not alone. Look how he had crumbled just now, under a little pressure from some hick sheriff and the pleading eyes of a little snip of a secretary.

Now the tears were flooding down his face, and he was shaking. His whole body trembled and his hands were wet with icy perspiration. For the first time in nearly ten years, he was facing himself, forced to acknowledge what seemed now the inevitable result of his avarice, and all he could feel was hatred for the man he had become.

10

Abandoned Dreams

■

"Are you hungry? We could stop somewhere for lunch."

"No, I'm not hungry. Why did Rodney Weaver pretend he didn't know me?"

McGavin hesitated a moment. "Because he's in trouble, serious trouble, and he didn't want to admit anything. . . . Once you admit to one thing, it's hard to stop."

"What's he done?" Kate asked. "What kind of trouble?"

Again she had to wait. Then McGavin said, "I'm not sure what statutes he may have violated."

Kate was impatient again. What kind of answer was that? "Give me your professional opinion, then. What statutes?"

McGavin glanced over at her, then said, "I suspect he's filed incomplete tax returns, for starters. He, um, he may have harbored a fugitive, he may be guilty of aiding and abetting. Possibly—other violations."

Kate frowned. She did not understand how any of these violations were connected to Rodney Weaver, unless—

"Do you suspect him of—of having harmed Benjamin Cramer in some way?"

McGavin nodded, keeping his eyes on the road. The atmosphere in the squad car, as they sped down a county highway in a southwesterly direction, was electric, charged with Kate's plodding questions and McGavin's evasive answers. Kate sent out another spark.

"Did I understand you correctly? Did you tell him you had called him ten years ago?" Kate's posture was determinedly erect, her face a protective mask of inexpressiveness. Her hands were gripping the purse and sweater in her lap as if by sheer strength she could wring the truth out of them. Her knuckles were white.

McGavin nodded again as he braked for the turn. He drove slowly now, avoiding the potholes in the narrow road, and they entered the woods. It was darker in here, cooler, and the beads of perspiration on her forehead suddenly felt cold.

"You called him," she said, relentless, "to arrange a contact with Benjamin Cramer?"

"Yes," he said, not looking at her. He switched off the air conditioner and rolled down his window. She could smell the pines, a clean, honest scent. "I gave him Cramer's phone number—in Chicago, his office number."

Kate rolled down her window, too, suddenly needing the air. She was close to being sick all over Sheriff John Anthony McGavin's immaculate squad car. The clean air came as a reprieve. She let her stomach muscles relax. Yes, she decided, she could ask another question without getting sick.

"Why did you make that call? You told me you've never met Mr. Cramer, so—so how did you know him? And why did you want Weaver to call him?"

"This could be it," McGavin said, and he turned off the road and drove a few yards on a patch of grass and weeds. They were facing the lake, thirty or forty yards away down a rocky, tree-studded slope. Directly in front of them was a ramshackle structure, unpainted boards leaning against one another. The sloping roof had caved in on one side and the red brick chimney had crumbled away. The windows were boarded up with thin sheets of rough plywood. It looked totally deserted.

Kate was fascinated in spite of herself. Was this the place her boss had left the city for? Benjamin Cramer, tidy and fastidious, well-accustomed to cleanliness and order, had deserted the city every year to spend three weeks in this rathole? She could not believe it, and when she glanced at McGavin, she could see the doubt on his face, too.

He said, "I don't think this is it, but I'll have a look anyway." Kate opened her door and he added, "Please don't touch anything."

126

She came around the front of the car and stopped to take another look.

"No one has been here. Look, the leaves are piled up; the wind has blown them there. Nobody's been near this place for months, maybe years."

She said it half to herself, and McGavin made no reply. He walked around the shack, checking all the windows. She supposed he was looking for fingerprints in the dirty planks, garbage, anything that would indicate recent human activity. He found nothing, and when he came back to the car he said, "I'd need a search warrant to get inside. There're a few other places down the road, I think. Let's try them first. If we don't find anything, we'll go to the judge."

Kate nodded and turned away abruptly, anxious to leave this place. She had an abhorrence of rundown buildings. It was not the cabin itself that bothered her. It was the neglect it represented, the hopelessness to which its owner had consigned it. It was a perfect spot for a cabin, a wilderness refuge protected by pines and its comfortable distance from the nearest towns. But she would have preferred nothing—a bare, untouched clearing in the woods—to this stark reminder of someone's dream, begun years ago and now, for reasons unknown to her but surely not happy ones, abandoned, released from its initial promise to die a slow, unattended death. She shivered involuntarily as McGavin slammed his door and backed out onto the rutted road.

They followed the road, the car bouncing and dipping as they crawled through the woods, winding a crooked trail among the trees and shrubs. After a few minutes they came to another cabin, remarkably—sickeningly, Kate thought—similar to the first. Unpainted, barely held together, it tilted to one side at an alarming angle. On this one, even the door was boarded up, but one window, visible to them from the road, had lost its plywood shield and revealed a ragged, gaping hole in its dirt-encrusted glass.

McGavin stopped the car.

"I don't think this is it either, but I'll take a look in the window. Probably been that way for years."

Kate was so certain that Benjamin Cramer had never stayed in this horrible place that she remained in the car, watching the sheriff as he approached the window, brushed away an immense cobweb, and put his face close to the jagged opening. A moment later he returned to the car and reached under the seat for a flashlight. Kate looked at him in surprise.

"Find something?"

"No, it's too dark in there to see much."

Now Kate wanted to see for herself. She got out of the car and followed him to the window. Together, they peered inside.

The beam of the flashlight revealed a single empty room. There were piles of leaves and debris in the corner opposite the open window, and the broken remains of a sink lay on the floor in another corner. She could see the other windows, screen hanging by a wire on one, and she knew it was a one-room shack, uninhabitable in its present state. McGavin flicked off the light and walked around the hut anyway, Kate at his heels.

"There's nothing here, Mrs. Downing. You're right, nobody's been here."

Then why did you check? she wanted to scream. Why did I make myself look at this depressing place? But she knew why he was being so thorough. She had seen his concentration at his desk back in the office. She had watched him interrogate Rodney Weaver. He was a professional, good at his job. He was trained to keep his mind open to every clue, to investigate every possibility, no matter how implausible it might be. He seemed to be on her side, taking this matter seriously, and she was grateful for that, but he was so evasive at answering her questions—

"Coming?"

He was at the car, waiting for her. She gave one last glance at the abandoned hut, then hurried to join him. He started the car again and they continued down the road, following its curves and bends as it wove an uncertain path around the perimeters of Baker's Lake. Neither spoke. Kate's mind was approaching a state of numbness, partly because she was beginning to have a good idea why the sheriff was so reluctant to answer her questions and partly because she was beginning to be desperately afraid of what they were going to find.

"There."

They had reached the last stretch of road, and Kate was pointing ahead and to her left, to a clearing in the woods between them and the lake. McGavin saw it too, and even from a distance, with the view partly obscured by the trees, the difference was clear. He pulled ahead and stopped in the road and they both sat there, unable to move for a moment, seized by the realization that if Weaver had told the truth, if he had indeed rented a cottage on Baker's Lake to Cramer, then surely this was the cottage. Kate leaned to her left, straining to see past the sheriff.

Like the others, this cabin was in an advanced state of disrepair; it, too, was unpainted and sagging on one side. But in spite of the neglect, it looked livable. In fact, it looked lived-in, Kate thought. The windows were not boarded up, the glass in them was unbroken, and it revealed faded blue curtains hanging inside. She noted recent tire tracks, the chimney in good condition, the tiny front porch, sagging on one side but swept clean of forest litter and debris. Also, unlike the others, this cabin had a brightly painted LP gas tank on the far side of the porch.

Then she saw it—the key in the door—and knew that this was it. McGavin turned to Kate, grasped her arm, and said as calmly but as firmly as he could, "Wait here. Stay in the car. Do you hear me?"

Kate was staring at the cabin. McGavin got out of the car slowly. His right hand rested on his holstered revolver as he crossed the clearing and climbed the steps. He stood to one side and knocked on the door. There was no response.

"Mr. Cramer?" He shouted it and his voice lifted in the air, disturbing the perfect noisy silence of the woods and the lake. Suddenly it really was quiet: The birds stopped their chattering; the ground animals hunched their backs and raised their heads, listening, in the suspension of sound created by the shout of a human voice. Kate got out of the car and approached the door.

"Benjamin Cramer? This is John McGavin. I'm the sheriff of this county. Are you in there?"

Kate stood behind him on the porch. Now even the wind had died and the trees stood motionless, towering over the silent surface of Baker's Lake, dwarfing the cabin in the clearing. There was not a rustle in the woods, not a sound to protect or obscure, and they both heard it. A low moan rose from inside the cabin, and Kate could not tell if a man or an animal had emitted that terrible sound.

She clutched McGavin's arm, and he said to her, speaking calmly and quietly, "Go back to the car."

"No!" She whispered vehemently. "Open the door."

129

"Mrs. Downing, please, let me go in—"

"I will not stand here arguing with you. I'm going in."

He looked at her a moment, then conceded, "All right, but let me go first, and don't touch anything. Not anything, do you understand?"

"I won't, I won't, please, open the door."

He turned the key and the door swung inward, scraping gently across a wooden floor. They stepped inside and Kate drew on some special reserve of strength she hadn't known she had to make herself look.

The first thing she saw was the kitchen, a tiny area separated by a counter from the rest of the room. On the floor were three empty soup cans, a spoon, and a can opener. With McGavin stepping slowly ahead of her, she passed the counter and saw a chair overturned. At its foot was a liquor bottle, lying on its side, the neck broken off, and there was a dark stain on the floor where the liquid had run out. Then she saw a trail of dark stains, but not—oh, no, surely not blood? McGavin followed the trail across the room to a doorway and stopped, turning to her.

"Please, wait outside."

"I will not," and she peered beyond him, straight into the bathroom. It was in chaotic disarray, bloody towels on the floor, a bottle of antiseptic, empty, laying on its side underneath the sink, a filthy, bloodstained blue plaid shirt crumpled in the corner. The old footed bathtub was spattered with more blood and strewn with blood-soaked towels.

Kate swallowed the rising nausea in her throat. She wanted to turn and run, but McGavin was turning to the left, and she followed. A whimper escaped her lips.

They saw the bed, the body on top of it, but Kate could not believe it was Benjamin Cramer. The face was deathly white and unshaven, with a huge purple bruise on the nose and forehead. His lips were cracked and dry, and there was a black bandage on his left shoulder.

"Dear God," she whispered. McGavin bent over the body, blocking her view, but as he eased away the blankets she saw the wound in the leg, and she shut her eyes, leaning against the doorframe for support. She heard McGavin, his voice as calm and gentle as if he were speaking to a child.

"Mr. Cramer, it's okay. My name's McGavin, I'm a sheriff, and I'm going to call the rescue squad. I don't know how all this happened, but you're going to be okay."

Was that true? Kate didn't know how he could possibly be okay, and she thought McGavin was probably trained to speak to injured victims that way.

"He's alive. There's a pulse." He glanced up at Kate. "Open that window, please. Mrs. Downing? Can you help? Open the window; never mind about fingerprints."

She stepped inside the room and smelled it, the horrible odor of perspiration and decay, and she rushed to the window to let in fresh air. She could not get sick, not now. Benjamin Cramer needed her.

"Mr. Cramer," she heard McGavin say, "I'm going to call the rescue squad. I'll be right back." Kate glanced over her shoulder and saw him pulling the blankets back up over the legs. He left and she struggled with the lock on the window. It was rusty, as if it had been sealed shut for years. Finally it gave, she shoved the window up, and the smell of pines rushed into the room. She took a breath, testing, and felt the qualms in her stomach settle a little.

McGavin had run out of the cottage and grabbed the microphone from the dashboard in his squad car. She could hear him talking in code, using numbers instead of real words. Then she heard "rescue squad" and "critical condition" and she didn't want to hear any more.

She turned away from the window, tears streaming down her face, but for once in her life, she did not care that she was crying. She went over to the bed and knelt beside it and cradled his face in her hands and said over and over again, "I'm here. I'm here. I came, Mr. Cramer, you knew I would, I'm here. It took so long, nobody would believe me, no one would listen, I had to figure it out all on my own, but I'm here, I'm here."

She was rocking on her knees, holding his head, and the stubble of his beard was rough against her palms. She refused to think, to ponder the message he had sent or how he had known the name of her dead husband's friend, or how this unspeakable thing had happened to him or even how she had managed, against all difficulties, to find him. She would have to deal with all of that and more, and she would. But not now. In his own remote and stuffily polite way, he had been kind to her, he was a decent man, and she did not understand why he should have had to endure this suffering. Inside, her emotions roiling, she raged at the unfairness of it, and her anger blunted the thought processes that might have led to comprehension. It was enough, for now, to be here, holding him, telling him again and again, whether he could hear her or not, "I'm here, I'm here."

She stayed that way, rocking and crying and murmuring to him, while McGavin brought in another blanket from the trunk of his squad car and wrapped it gently around Cramer's body.

Cramer was unconscious again, unaware of the two people in the room. It would have given him great satisfaction to know that once again he had been right, about both his assistant and the sheriff.

After a while she heard the siren, and then the sheriff's crisp orders to the ambulance attendants to park in the road. He was back outside again, telling them not to disturb the tire tracks, yes, it's bad, two wounds, one in the shoulder, a deeper one in the leg, and Kate began talking again, to block the sound of those words.

"It's all right, they're here now, they know what to do, everything's going to be fine." Benjamin Cramer's eyes were closed, and she didn't know if he could hear her or not. Who could guess what it had cost him to cry out to them a few minutes before? She could tell he was still alive; his breathing was slow, shallow, and uneven, but he was alive.

John Anthony McGavin had to pry Kate's hands away from Cramer's face. The attendants lifted his body onto a stretcher and took him out of the room. McGavin helped her to her feet and said, "Let's get out of here," and he didn't need to say it twice. He led her back to the squad car, helped her inside, then ran around to the other side and took up the microphone. Kate heard him telling someone to send a man called Pete out to Baker's Lake.

"I know," McGavin said patiently, "he's on the late shift, but I need him now. Find him. Wake him up if you have to, Will. Tell him to bring nylon rope, lots of it, and not a word to anybody. Then call Clark Manchester and tell him I'm bringing Mrs. Downing back and she'll need someone. Maybe he can get Aggie Patterson; otherwise have him ask my mother to stay."

McGavin was speaking clearly, almost conversationally, Kate thought, and she was suddenly angry at him. How dare he be so controlled, so unfeeling? He replaced the microphone and stood leaning against the car for a moment. He was in a patch of brilliant sunshine, shielding his eyes as he gazed thoughtfully out at the dazzling lake. Then he got back into the car, saw that she was still crying, and handed her his handkerchief. She took it and rubbed it across her cheeks, not at all daintily.

"Mrs. Downing, I want you to listen to me. I have to wait here a few minutes, until another officer is here to—to keep an eye on things. But he'll be here soon, and then I'm going to take you back to the hotel. Clark Manchester is there, and there'll be someone else to stay with you, someone you can trust. No one is going to harm you. Do you understand?"

Kate nodded, immediately hating herself for doing so, and blew her nose into the sheriff's handkerchief.

"Where did they take him?"

"To Doc McCabe's clinic on Elm Street."

"A clinic?" She gave him a look as if to say, Are you out of your mind? "He should be in a hospital. Any fool could see that—"

"The clinic is closer," he answered easily, "and that clinic is equipped for just about everything. Henry McCabe's the best doctor around, and if he thinks the man needs a hospital, he'll get him there. For now, you'll just have to trust my judgment. That rescue squad got here in a third of the time it would have taken the ambulance from Eagle Hill, and the Elm Street Clinic is the closest facility. He's probably already there, and Henry's doing everything that can be done."

"Can I see him when we get back? I don't think he was conscious before, he didn't say anything. I want him to know I'm here."

"We'll see what Henry says. I have to warn you, he's fierce about the people in his care. He does what he thinks is best for them, and he doesn't much care what other folks think, even family or friends. But as soon as he thinks it's all right, then of course you can see him."

Kate had reached her limit. She was too exhausted to argue, too confused to enter into a battle of logic and wits.

"Are you feeling a little better?"

"I'm just fine," she said, annoyed. What did it matter how she felt?

"If you don't mind, there's a question or two . . ."

She shot him a withering look. "Of course, your investigation."

McGavin remained unruffled. "I just want you to think for a moment. Did you touch anything inside? I mean, besides the window?"

"I didn't contaminate your precious crime scene." Kate herself was shocked at her rudeness, but she couldn't help it. Why hadn't she gone back in the ambulance with Mr. Cramer? He needed her, she wanted to be with him. She did not want to answer any stupid questions.

"And you said Mr. Cramer didn't say anything while you were alone with him? He didn't—"

"He's dying!" Kate burst out, finally saying it. "Couldn't you see that? He's dying, and you're sitting here worrying about your idiotic report! No, he didn't say anything!"

"You don't know that," McGavin said quietly, but then he had the sense to be silent.

A few minutes later they heard another siren, which stopped abruptly as the vehicle entered the woods. A second Wahomet County Sheriff's Office squad car came roaring down the road, and Pete Iverson was still rubbing the sleep out of his eyes as he got out to greet the waiting sheriff. McGavin had left Kate in the car.

"Sheriff, what the hell . . ."

"You bring the rope?" McGavin was brisk.

"Yeah, but—"

"Pete, go into your FBI act and secure the crime scene. I want this clearing completely roped off, all the way down to the lake. A man was injured here, three, four days ago, I'd guess. We need measurements, photos, prints, the works. Pay attention to these tire tracks—looks to me like two different vehicles. Look for spent shells—he's hurt real bad, and my guess is it's gunshot. There should be at least two shells, maybe more. . . ." McGavin paused, suddenly remembering something he hadn't even realized had registered at the time. "Check the kitchen, the cupboard over the sink. I think there's a hole in it. And you'll have to look outside too, the ground, the trees. . . ."

Pete Iverson was staring at his boss in disbelief. "John, what happened here? This is Baker's Lake, not downtown Milwaukee—"

"I told you," McGavin said brusquely, keeping his voice low, "a man's been hurt. I saw enough wounds in Vietnam to recognize a gunshot injury, and that's my guess here. Pete, don't tense up on

134

me now. You're the best I've got. And one more thing: Don't let Logan come anywhere near this place." Logan was the newest patrolman on the Derrington city police force. "If he's been within ten feet of his radio for the past thirty minutes, my bet is he'll show up here, offering to lend a hand. Be firm; tell him he's out of his jurisdiction and get him out of here. I don't want him or anything else lousing up this crime scene. Understood?"

"I can handle Logan," Pete said, "but if you'd just tell me—"

"It's a crime scene, Pete." McGavin tried to be patient. "Maybe a murder scene." He glanced over his shoulder at Kate, still in his squad car. "Now, I've got to get her back to town. There's no time to explain any more. Pete, I'm counting on you."

"Well, you know you can do that."

"Good. Now pull off to the right so I can get out of here. I'll be back as soon as I can."

McGavin was relieved to see Pete finally jump into action, backing his squad car off to the right.

Kate was waiting in his car, staring off into space, numb with tension and exhaustion. She had heard only snatches of their conversation, and none of it made any sense. Somebody named Logan, what did he have to do with any of this? And a kitchen cupboard. Ridiculous. They stood there and gossiped while Mr. Cramer—

"Here we go," McGavin said, and he jumped into the car and started the engine. They roared past the deputy and down the road, past the two miserable huts, bouncing over the ruts and potholes, but Kate was barely aware of any of it.

What in God's name was happening? Why was she hundreds of miles from home, out in the woods with a Wisconsin county sheriff? Who was he, anyway, telling her what to do, asking dumb questions, treating her like a child? She was a mature woman, used to being on her own, living her structured life with quiet independence. She should be home, or at least in the office on La Salle Street, working with Mr. Cramer—Mr. Cramer. Oh, how could this have happened to him? He would never permit anyone . . . And yet he had sent her the postcard, he had given her a lead to find him, as if he had known he would need her help. And the lead was this man's name, J. A. McGavin.

She looked over at him now and was seized with an unreasoning anger. Somehow, he was the cause of all this; he understood all of it

135

and he was purposely not telling her anything. She despised him and his cool, professional detachment.

When they pulled up in front of the Farman Hotel, Clark Manchester was outside, waiting for them. His stance was casual, hands jammed into his pants pockets, and he looked for all the world as if he'd just wandered outside for a minute to check the weather. Aggie Patterson, Clark's oldest friend, was there too, her curly white hair pressed down under a red kerchief. She was still in her gardening clothes, blue jeans and an old plaid cotton shirt, but she, too, appeared calm. She helped Kate from the squad car and her tiny, pointed features were a mask of impersonal sympathy with no hint of curiosity.

Manchester introduced them. "Aggie, this is Katherine Downing, one of our guests. Mrs. Downing, this is Agatha Patterson, a friend of mine. You go ahead with her and don't worry about a thing."

"I'd like to see Mr. Cramer. If you could tell me how to find the clinic—"

"Not yet, I'm afraid." Aggie Patterson took Kate's elbow and steered her through the double doors into the hotel.

Clark Manchester didn't know much about what was going on, but he could see there was trouble. He leaned into the open window of the squad car.

"She need a sedative, John Anthony?" He thought Kate Downing had aged ten years since she'd left his coffee shop that morning.

McGavin nodded. "Don't bother Henry; he and Mary have their hands full over there. Call the drug store and ask Bert Vogen to bend the rules and send over a mild sedative. Tell him I'll get Henry to write a prescription for it later."

Manchester nodded and straightened up. "Done. Anything else?"

"No—but thanks, Clark. I appreciate your help."

"I hope you'd never expect less of me." Manchester slapped the roof of the car. "On your way, John Anthony."

McGavin sped out of town, anxious to rejoin Pete. Not that Pete couldn't manage. Besides Will Kalowski, who was too old to do anything except run the desk—and he did that better than any man McGavin had ever met—besides Will, Pete Iverson was his most trusted deputy. He was no grandstander; he would do his job quietly and professionally, and he would not be calling the

Derrington Chronicle this afternoon to give them all the details. But he was eager to see what they would come up with out at that cabin. Every crime scene had clues to yield, if only you knew enough to find them.

He tried to remember what he'd touched, if he'd disturbed anything that they might use as evidence. He'd turned the key in the lock, so that was out. He'd grasped the doorknob. He should have used his handkerchief, but he'd been arguing with the woman, trying to convince her to stay in the car, and he'd forgotten. Then, in spite of his resolve, he thought of Kate Downing, and unconsciously he shook his head.

It had been a long time since he'd underestimated anyone as much as he had her. She had come into his office as timid as a bird, clutching that postcard as if her life depended on it, and then she had dug in her heels. She had kept asking questions, kept pushing him for answers, until he had almost blurted it out, right in the car. He might have, if they hadn't found the cabin. Even then she had kept her composure better than he'd ever expected her to. It was not easy to open a door and walk through it the way they had. Even he, with all his years of experience at grisly highway accidents, and worse sights before that in Vietnam, even with the shock of finding his own father dead in his bed at home one morning, still, he had had to steel himself when he opened that door and stepped inside. And Kate Downing had been right behind him. That had taken courage he'd never guessed she possessed.

He didn't know what the sight of Cramer had done to her. Some people never recovered from a hideous sight like that. He had to hope that she would be all right.

She was in the best of care with Aggie and Clark. If anyone could help her recover, it would be Aggie Patterson.

For the hundredth time, McGavin felt a surge of pride in his town and the people who lived in it. It was true that they were gossips, stingy with their money when it came to paying their public servants, and many of them had more than enough quirks and eccentricities. But give them an emergency and they rose to it every time, with clear heads and compassion and generosity.

McGavin was well aware, as he slowed for the turn off the county highway, that he was probably going to lose it all: his job, their friendship, the respect they paid to him and his department. He was not a man given to tears, so his eyes were dry and clear, but inside he felt hollow, burned out. There was a limit, after all, to their code of acceptance. He had pushed that limit ten years ago and lived on the edge ever since. This morning, when he'd agreed to help Kate Downing, he had stepped off the edge.

Ahead, he could see Pete waving at him excitedly, and he lifted his chin a little. He was still the sheriff, at least for a little while longer.

11

The Relic

∎

When Kate woke up she was in her room at the Farman Hotel, but it took several moments for her to realize that. She was groggy, and it was an effort for her to open her eyes. The pill, that was it. The woman had insisted she take a pill and lie down. But there was something else—Mr. Cramer.

She opened her eyes and struggled to sit up. The woman was still there, in the rocking chair, and she leaned forward.

"Remember me? Aggie Patterson. I'm Mr. Manchester's friend, remember? He introduced us downstairs, in front of the hotel."

"Yes, I remember," Kate said slowly. She was having a difficult time waking up. "What time is it?"

The woman glanced at her watch. "Just after eight o'clock. Hungry?"

Kate looked out of the window, alarmed to see it so dark outside. She had slept for hours!

"No, I'd like to see Mr. Cramer. Has there been any word—?"

"He's holding his own, but he's still unconscious. There's nothing you can do for him right now, except take care of yourself. Why don't you try to go back to sleep? I'll wake you if—"

"No." Kate shook her head, resenting this interfering woman. "I really have to see him. I have to ask him—"

"Mrs. Downing, he can't answer your questions or anyone else's yet. Dr. McCabe is with him, and he says absolutely no visitors. You'll have to wait."

Kate looked at Agatha Patterson; she was a tiny woman, with white, frizzy curls, dressed in baggy blue jeans and red tennis shoes. Why, she wondered, am I letting this peculiar woman boss me around? She met the woman's uncompromising gaze and gave up, too tired to argue.

"But, if you're rested up," Aggie said smoothly, "how about dinner?"

"I don't think so." Kate was ravenous. She could not remember the last time she had eaten. But she pictured the coffee shop downstairs, lined with curious eyes and wagging tongues. She couldn't endure that, not tonight. But a shower, she needed a shower—

"Well, suit yourself," Aggie said lightly, "but I have a friend in the kitchen, Freddy Albers. There's no room service here, but I think I might convince him to bring something up. I'm famished, myself." She had picked up the telephone and was dialing.

"Hello, Freddy. Miss Patterson here. Yes, I'm in the hotel, and I'd like some dinner. What's the special tonight? Seafood platter . . . sounds good. Salad, rolls, a little white wine." She held up two fingers in Kate's direction, questioning, and Kate nodded, resigned. If she could eat in the room, that would be better.

"Make that two orders, Freddy. Bring it to room two-o-nine. Thank you." She hung up and grinned conspiratorially at Kate. "Poor boy, I helped him get that job and now he thinks he's in my debt."

Kate smiled in spite of herself. "And you've never bothered to set him straight?"

"One of the privileges of old age. He was in my class, five, no, six years ago. Fancies himself a chef now. We'll see."

"You're a teacher?" Kate asked, making polite conversation and wishing she could just leave this room and the woman and be by herself for a while.

"Latin, in the early days. When that went out of style, I turned to mathematics. They're quite similar, you know: lots of rules and sensible limits. I'm retired now." She stopped abruptly, looking closely at Kate. Then she said energetically, "Mrs. Downing, would you like to freshen up? Freddy was a slow student; that dinner will take him a while. Go on, step in the shower, change clothes if you wish.

140

You've had a long day, and you'll feel better." She smiled brightly, but Kate sensed she was daring Kate to disagree with her. Well, it was what Kate wanted anyway, so she would do it.

She collected some clean clothes and stepped into the bathroom.

The moment the door closed behind her, Aggie was on the phone again, whispering hoarsely to Clark down at the front desk.

"She's awake, Clark, seems to be all right. I'm having Freddy bring up some dinner. Any word from the clinic?" A frown creased her forehead, and she said, "Doesn't sound good, does it? Well, she's fighting to see him, and I've stalled her for a while, but sooner or later—yes, well, I'll do what I can. Keep me posted. . . . Oh, bosh. I'm glad I could help out. I owe you, after that wonderful dinner out at the Norwood last week." Aggie was smiling as she hung up the phone.

She turned on another lamp, straightened the bed, and cleared a space on a small table. Then she sat back in the rocker and planned her strategy. This young woman needed their help, that was evident. She had come up here alone, searching for her boss, and boy, had she found him. Clark had spoken to Mary McCabe, Henry's wife, over at the clinic. The man they had brought in this afternoon was near death, and apparently the young woman had seen him. She had been in shock when she got out of John Anthony's car, Aggie was sure of that. Such goings on, right here in Derrington! And Aggie was right in the middle of it, just where she liked to be.

The problem was, how to help? The young woman was reluctant to confide in her, she could see that. So, the indirect approach. A hot meal, a little wine, a bit of subterfuge . . . all for her own good, of course. She couldn't carry this burden alone, and she didn't have to. Aggie Patterson was there to help.

When Kate stepped into the room she could see the old woman's face had softened. She did not look so bossy. Well, Kate thought, there was no need for her to; she had gotten her way. They were having dinner.

"Feeling better?"

"Yes," Kate admitted. She perched on the edge of the bed.

"Excuse me, Mrs. Downing. I'm not trying to pry, but is there someone I can call for you? A relative or—"

"No. Thank you, there's—there's no one to call." Kate stood up, restless. "I'm really all right. I appreciate all you've done, but it's not necessary for you to stay."

"What, and miss that seafood platter? Please, don't boot me out of here now." She smiled sweetly, and Kate, astonished, found herself feeling guilty. She really hadn't meant to be rude, but— "Tell me, Mrs. Downing, do you have a garden?" Aggie leaned back in her chair, and Kate tried to hide her surprise at the abrupt change in topics.

"A small one. More flowers than anything else." Kate began prowling the room, absentmindedly touching the objects, wondering why she liked this woman at all. She was pushy, overbearing—

". . . tomatoes," Aggie was saying. "Every year I swear I'll cut back. I live alone, always have, and I usually end up giving most of it away. But then comes a day in May, like this one . . ."

Kate was trying to figure out how to get rid of this chatterbox when there was a knock at the door, and then it was too late. A young man stood there, balancing a large tray in both hands. He was staring openly at Aggie, who had come to the door behind Kate.

"Freddy, how good of you. Put it on the table here, please." She produced a bill from the pocket of her blue jeans.

"Oh, wait, I'll pay for this." Kate looked around for her purse.

"You most certainly will not, Mrs. Downing. I've invited myself, so it's my treat. Freddy, thank you very much." She closed the door in his face and turned to Kate. "Ah, feast your eyes on this!"

Kate had to admit it looked good, and the wine was white and very cold. Once again she reluctantly submitted, and they sat down to eat. Aggie, still smiling a good deal more than was her custom, raised her glass.

"To gardens," she said, "and the pleasures they bring us."

Kate managed to smile in agreement as their glasses clinked.

"Did you see Freddy's face?" Aggie chuckled as she speared a bite of lettuce on her fork. "I have this image, you see, the staid and proper schoolteacher. Jeans don't fit the image."

Kate murmured, "Surely in this day and age . . ." She was attacking the fish. Oh, she was hungry.

"The younger teachers do as they please, within reason. As long as they don't get arrested, no one blinks an eye. But we relics—no,

142

it's true, I'm a fossil, and they think I should behave as I did forty years ago."

Kate smiled, but remembering her own childhood in Elwood, she saw the truth in her words. Small towns . . .

"But now—" Aggie shrugged— "what I do is up to me. Still, habits die hard. It's difficult to change. But I'm trying to live a little more on impulse. Finally realized I do exactly that when I'm traveling. I've had the most marvelous adventures on my trips, all because I let go a little."

Kate watched her pop a bit of bread into her mouth, and saw traces of her Aunt Sarah in this woman, an unmarried schoolteacher who was apparently satisfied with her life. She liked to travel, too, just as her Aunt Sarah had. She began to appreciate this chance for some comfortable, normal conversation. The woman had not asked a single personal question and that, perversely, made Kate wonder if she wouldn't make a good sounding board.

"You know, Mrs. Downing," and what she said made Kate wonder if she was a mind reader, "I've had a wonderful life, but if I had it to do over, I'd take more chances. I'd have risked a little more. I think—yes, I would have been braver." She nodded, as if to herself, as she placed her wineglass on the table. Then she averted her gaze and waited.

"Miss Patterson—"

"Oh, why don't we make it Aggie? Really, a lifetime of 'Miss Patterson' from nearly every soul in Derrington is quite enough."

"Yes, Aggie. My name is Kate. I—I could use . . . um . . . I wonder, if we might talk. . . ."

"Kate. A lovely name. Let me say something. I know you think you're alone up here, but that's not true. And I can almost guarantee that you won't shock me with anything you might want to tell me. I wager I've heard it, or something similar, before. Perhaps I can help."

So Kate poured it out, uncertainly at first. It had been ages since she'd confided in anyone, and the whole story was preposterous. It sounded impossible, even to herself. But Aggie was a patient listener, and when Kate's rambling discourse rolled to a halt, she leaned forward.

"Let's see what we have here," she said, as if she were bending over a student's paper. "Your husband has a friend, our county sheriff, but you've never met him and you're sure you never mentioned him to your employer, Mr. Cramer. Then Mr. Cramer sends you a postcard, mysteriously worded, but nonetheless clear enough to lead you to Sheriff McGavin. Ergo, Cramer must know McGavin also."

"Yes, but—"

"So it's certain he knows the sheriff. Now then, you go to John Anthony and—let me be sure I have this right—he mentions Rodney Weaver first? You're sure?"

Kate frowned in concentration. "I'm positive," she said. "He asked me if I'd ever heard the name."

Aggie nodded, looking oddly pained for a moment, Kate thought, but then she said, "So, the two of you went to see Mr. Weaver, and the sheriff told him he had called him years ago, to arrange a cottage rental for Mr. Cramer?"

"Yes," Kate said.

"And then Mr. Weaver told you the location of this cottage."

"It wasn't that simple, but, yes, he did tell the sheriff that the cabin was on Baker's Lake. But he insisted that Mr. Cramer had already left."

"And you found him there, where Mr. Weaver had said, and he was—ill. Seriously ill."

Kate felt the tears coming again. "I—I've never seen anything like that before. He looked—like something had attacked him. The blood, the smell—"

"Yes, you mentioned that." Aggie quickly poured more wine into Kate's glass and handed it to her.

"Kate, here's the way I see it. These three men are connected, and the only link is you—you and your husband. Don't you see? You work for Benjamin Cramer, you speak to Mr. Weaver every year, and Mr. Cramer directs you, however obliquely, to go to John Anthony."

Kate was rubbing her temples, trying to think clearly.

"I understand some of these connections, but—but why? Why did Mr. Cramer send me to the sheriff? I've never met him until today, and I'm sure I never mentioned him to Mr. Cramer, so how did he know I'd find him? It doesn't make sense."

"I'm sure that's not true, it's only that we don't see it, not all of

144

it. But I know who can help us." She paused. "John Anthony McGavin."

"Don't think I haven't tried! He won't tell me anything!" Kate nearly screamed it. She was beginning to panic again, and Agatha reached over and seized her hand.

"He will tell us." The emphasis on the last word was a life pre-server, flung when Kate needed it most. Kate took a deep breath.

"One of your students?"

Aggie grinned a little lopsidedly. "One of my best. Oh, not the brightest, no, there were others who did better in their studies. But John Anthony . . . well, he was a late-bloomer, you might say, a promise looking for a purpose, and in the years since he left my classroom, he has measured up." There was a distant look in Agatha's eyes, but Kate was too distraught to notice it. Aggie contin-ued, "If I ask him, he may tell us what we need to know."

"Can you call him?"

Aggie released her grip on Kate's hand and glanced at her watch. "It's late, almost ten o'clock. . . ."

"Please call him. If he says no, I'll have to wait. But he might say yes."

Aggie sighed and went to the telephone. She opened the cover of the directory, explaining, "I'm not in the habit of calling the police!" She dialed the number. "Ray! Yes, Miss Patterson here. No, no, I'm fine. Is John Anthony in, please?"

There followed a protracted silence, during which Aggie's face, pink from a day in the sun and two glasses of wine, turned white. She sank slowly onto the bed, and Kate rose from her chair.

"Yes, I see. No, don't bother to leave a message, don't bother him. This can wait. Yes, tomorrow . . . Thank you." She hung up slowly and Kate saw that Aggie was having trouble meeting her gaze.

"What is it?" Kate held her breath, staring at Aggie. "Aggie— Miss Patterson . . . Please, what is it?"

Aggie was staring toward the window. She cleared her throat. "There's been an emergency. John Anthony's gone up to help."

"Gone where?"

"Pine Lake." She closed her eyes a moment, as if gathering her strength, then looked directly at Kate. "They found Rodney Weaver tonight. . . . In his bedroom. He—he hung himself from a rafter."

145

Kate's hand flew to her mouth to stifle a gasp.

"No," she said, almost wailing, "no, dear God, no." She sank down on the bed beside Aggie.

Aggie was beginning to recover. She straightened her back to its normal ramrod posture and said slowly, "It's rather timely, eh?"

"What?"

"Perhaps an unfortunate choice of words . . . But surely it's not coincidence. . . . This morning you and our sheriff pay a call on realtor Weaver. First he pretends he's never heard of you or your employer, Benjamin Cramer. It is only when John Anthony applies some pressure that the man admits that, yes, indeed, he has rented a summer cottage to Mr. Cramer. You find Mr. Cramer in that very cottage, from all appearances fighting for his life. And the next we hear of Mr. Weaver is that he has taken his own life. Do you doubt the connection?"

Aggie's calm, quiet recital of facts, in a tone suggesting only an idiot would not agree, had mesmerized Kate. Part of her was repulsed by the cold-blooded practicality of the woman, but for the most part she was experiencing an enormous sense of relief. For the first time in days, in fact since this whole miserable journey had begun, she had met someone who seemed to be totally on her side. Not once had she raised an eyebrow or in any way indicated that she doubted Kate's sanity or the truth of her wild intuitions.

"All right," Kate said, rubbing her face, "so there is a connection. But—but—hanging himself: Aggie, it's too horrible to comprehend. If I thought I had caused that—"

"Oh, bosh," Aggie said, rising from the bed. "I can tell you're a courageous young woman, and not without a healthy intelligence. But, frankly, you do show a tendency to blame yourself for events over which you have no control. You must stop carrying the weight of the world. Haven't you learned yet that we all lead double lives?"

This remark lost Kate completely. "What on earth are you talking about?"

"Double lives, Kate. Secret lives. All of us, even you. We have a public person and a private one, and the ability with which we balance the two is a measure of our stability. Now, take Mr. Weaver. Publicly, from what you've told me, he had everything. Elegant home, beautiful wife, apparently prosperous business. Privately? Well, obviously the man's soul was not in tune with all this grandeur. The thing that drives a man to suicide, Kate, is hopelessness, an unshakable conclusion that his life is unbearable and that there is nothing, absolutely nothing, that can make it bearable again. If, indeed, it was your visit that pushed him over the edge, then you must see that he was on the edge to begin with. You had no way of knowing that. For heaven's sake, child, you'd never even met the man! Give him your pity, if you wish, but you needn't sacrifice your own integrity in the process."

Agatha, schoolteacher extraordinaire, stopped to take a breath, then grinned a bit sheepishly. "And that concludes our lecture for today. Class dismissed." She went to the table and took a sip of her wine. "Ugh. Warm. How about a walk before you turn in? Derrington is a pleasant place in the evening."

"I know." Kate was feeling an absurd urge to cross the room and hug this wise and generous woman, but she resisted it. "I came in on the bus last night and felt as if I were coming home." They left the room and went downstairs.

"Home? Are you a Wisconsin girl?" The lobby, dimly lit by the glass chandeliers, was empty, and they went through the double doors out into the cool air of the night.

"No, born and raised in Illinois. I live near Chicago now, but I've never liked it very much. I need space around me, open fields, woods, uncrowded places. Like Derrington. It reminds me of El-wood, in southern Illinois, where I grew up."

Aggie nodded. "The phenomenon of a small town is one to which I've given some thought," she said easily, strolling along with her hands thrust in the pockets of her jeans. "I chose this town, Kate, as an escape at first, but it became my home, and now I couldn't think of leaving it."

"An escape?" Kate regretted the question immediately. That was none of her business, but Aggie only nodded.

"Yes. You may doubt the truth of this, but I was once a young woman! There was a man, chosen by my father as the perfect husband, but I had other ideas. He would have cramped my style, as they say nowadays. Married ladies did not work in those days, not unless they had to, and this young man would certainly never have permitted it. For that matter, what school board would have hired me? But I had visions, Kate, dreams if you will. More than anything else in the world, I wanted to teach. So I left it all—my infuriated

147

father, my sobbing mother, and that poor, uncomprehending suitor, and came to Derrington. I've never regretted it."

"Did they forgive you?"

"Oh, eventually they seemed reconciled to it. He married someone else soon enough."

"My husband was a little like that. I mean, after we were married, he didn't want me to work."

"Ah, and did you want to?"

"Oh, yes," Kate said with a vehemence that surprised even herself. "Yes, I wanted to very much. We needed the money. Even if we hadn't—" and again Kate was surprised at the admission—"I still would have enjoyed having a job. I worked in my father's bank during the summers, before I started college. I loved it. And my job with Mr. Cramer—well, it's a blessing. But Jim would never have permitted it."

"Your voice sounds a bit rusty when you mention your husband. How long did you say . . .?"

"Ten years."

"Still grieving?" Aggie kept her tone as impersonal as the question allowed. They had reached the city park and they stopped to sit on a bench facing the bandstand.

"Aggie, the strangest thing has happened." Kate spoke slowly, looking at her hands in her lap. "All these years the memory of my husband has been such a comfort to me. But when I read his letters the other day . . ."

"A new perspective?" Aggie prompted.

"A scary one. The man who wrote those letters sounded a lot different than the man I thought I married. . . . I really loved him. We met when we were freshmen at Northwestern. He seemed so strong to me. He hadn't had an easy life. His father was unemployed a lot of the time, and he lived in foster homes sometimes. His only brother was killed in a motorcycle accident. But Jim didn't seem bitter—he was quiet, and proud, and determined to make something of his life. He came to Northwestern on a basketball scholarship. I went to some of the freshman games with my roommate because her boyfriend was on the team, and that's how I met Jim. Oh, he was handsome, and a loner, not flashy at all, and that appealed to me. And then he met my parents and I could see that he longed to be part of a real family.

148

"Everything seemed perfect. We got married in Elwood, and at first we lived in a tiny apartment near the campus, but then my aunt died and left me a little money, so we bought a house, and everything was wonderful.

"And then—then, everything just collapsed. Jim lost his scholarship, and my parents died, and the money ran out. We couldn't afford for both of us to stay in school. Jim didn't want me supporting him while he went to school—he was too proud for that—and as for me . . . hmmm. To tell you the truth, I think he didn't like the idea of me getting an education if he couldn't."

Kate stopped abruptly and shook her head. "Oh, dear, what made me say that?"

"Probably it's the truth," Aggie said quietly.

"Anyway—" Kate rushed on, anxious to finish—"he enlisted and he went to California and then to Vietnam. He—he was practically on his way home when he died—not in battle, I don't think he had much to do with that part of the war. He died in a plane crash."

"Yes, ten years ago," Aggie said. "This month? Yes, that's when John Anthony came home, too."

"They were friends, Aggie. I know that from Jim's letters. He said Sheriff McGavin—of course, he wasn't sheriff then—had charm. They had a lot of adventures together. Jim said they were always short of things they needed, and they set up some sort of barter system, trading things."

"John Anthony wrote similar things to Nancy, his mother," Aggie said. "She used to share parts of his letters with everyone in the coffee shop, so of course I heard about them from Clark. But it was still a war. It couldn't have been easy for any of them. And, oh, how I worried about that boy when he came home. He made light enough of that terrible place, even told funny stories. But—well, he was different. He was closed off, somehow, from me, anyway. Seemed to avoid me for a long time. For a while, I chalked it up to my own ego problem. I fancied I'd been his favorite teacher, and I was hurt when he no longer came to see me. So one night in the Evergreen Room, I cornered him, asked him outright, 'What's the problem, John Anthony?'"

"What did he say?"

Aggie screwed up her face, obviously trying to recall his exact words.

149

"At first, he said there was no problem, he'd been busy. But he wouldn't look me in the eye, so I just waited. Just sat there and waited for him to level with me."

Kate could well imagine that.

"At last, he admitted it. He said, yes, it was true, and he knew he owed me an apology. And then he said, yes, I'm sure, he said, he never could lie to me, and he hoped I'd never ask him about that year in his life. I tell you, Kate, the pain in that boy's eyes . . . well, I hope I never have to see that look again on anybody's face. That boy had been in hell on earth, I'd swear to it.

"I never asked him another thing about it. But things were never the same with us after that. That easy relationship was just gone. We spoke, of course—he even stopped by to see me now and again—but the barrier was there. Still is.

"Clark said he felt the same way; the boy avoided him for weeks, and then he went to work for Harry at the sheriff's department."

"Mr. Manchester told me that," Kate said. "He said he wanted Mr. McGavin to work for him at the hotel, like he had before Vietnam."

"Oh, yes, Clark had it all mapped out. Thought he'd found the successor to the throne," Aggie said wryly. "But John Anthony just didn't read that map. He turned inside himself for a while, almost like he couldn't face some of us. He'd dated a nice girl before he left, Betsy Chaney, but even that seemed to fall apart when he came home. She went down to Milwaukee and never came back. So there John Anthony was, the whole town his friend, but somehow he didn't have any friends. Just closed himself off. I never did understand that. He had an honorable record; he'd done nothing to be ashamed of."

"Public and private, Aggie. Double lives, remember?"

Aggie glanced at Kate with appreciation. "Right you are, my dear. I'm trying to merge my own double lives a bit." She rubbed her thighs contentedly, enjoying the feel of the rough denim.

"That's what I started to tell you a moment ago," Kate said softly. "All these years, since I lost Jim, I've had this perfect public image, the grieving widow, and I looked at myself that way, too. It—well, it made things easier sometimes. But then I read his letters again and—and I felt—betrayed. All this time, I believed I had the perfect marriage, the perfect husband. . . ."

150

"One of the hardest lessons in life. Nothing is perfect."

"But how could I be so wrong? His letters—they were robot letters, no affection, no emotion. I—I loved him so much—"

"And no doubt he loved you, also."

"I—I don't know anymore. I thought he did, but—I'm starting to remember things, some things I never even noticed at the time, but now I look back and I—well, I'm ashamed, but I'm starting to doubt other things about him. He changed, and I think I know when it happened."

"When?"

"When my father died. No, it was a month later. We—we lost the bank because my father—he—"

"Another double life?"

"Exactly." Kate silently thanked her for her keen perception. It had saved her from an explanation too painful to give.

"When Jim found out there was no money—I remember this now, I'm sure of it—he started drinking, something he'd never done before. Then we had to leave school, and he took this ridiculous job. Oh, it sounded fantastic; he was getting in on the ground floor, he said, and I believed him!"

Kate's voice had risen in pitch. "I believed him, Aggie! A wild scheme, selling some wonderful copier machine, and he started traveling, taking business trips, and they got longer and longer, he was gone more and more, and all I did was sit in that house and wait for him to come home!"

"I'm sure you did what you felt was right at the time. That's all any of us can do."

"Oh, Aggie, that's not the worst of it." Kate sniffed and wiped her eyes. She was gulping air, trying to compose herself. "Today, in that cabin, when we found Mr. Cramer, I realized something else. I don't know when it happened, and I'm sure it's not reciprocal, but—somehow, I've fallen in love with him." She tried to laugh. "Isn't that absurd? I'm calling him Mr. Cramer, but I love him. At first I was afraid of him, he was so stern and he demanded so much. But he had more confidence in me than I did in myself. He was like a teacher, expecting me to do my best, and we worked well together. And then, today, when we found him, something in me just—exploded. Nothing else mattered, not how foolish I might

151

sound, or what he might think of me. . . . I just knew, when I put my hands on his face . . . I love him."

"You've never socialized with him? Never dated . . .?"

"Not once in ten years. Think of it! All that time wasted. . . ."

"You met him right after your husband died?"

"Yes. It was funny. I needed a better job and my neighbor knew Mr. Cramer was looking for a new assistant, so I went in for an interview, scared to death. He was wonderful even that first time, easy to talk to. He hired me right away, without a typing test, even, and that did wonders for—"

"No typing test?" Aggie said, puzzled.

"Aggie, he made it so easy for me. I didn't even have a résumé prepared, and he never asked for one."

"A little strange, don't you think?"

"You don't know him. He's very decisive, and he makes up his mind about people in a snap. He's good at that. I suppose he just knew . . ."

"Knew what?"

"Well, that I'd be a good secretary. Ted had recommended me to him. Why else would he have hired me?"

Aggie let that question go with a small shrug. "I don't know, maybe I've read too many mysteries. It just seems a little odd, that's all."

Kate hated to admit it, and aloud she didn't, but what the older woman said made sense. In fact, the more she thought about it, the more it puzzled her. Benjamin Cramer, who checked and double-checked his recommendations to clients, who researched every detail, had not even asked if she could type.

"I've got to see him," she said.

Agatha shook her head and stood up, stretching her arms. "Sorry, but when it comes to his clinic and everything in it, Henry McCabe's word is law. If he says 'No visitors,' you couldn't get in if you were the governor of Wisconsin." She smiled a little to soften the words. They began to walk slowly back to the hotel.

"Small towns," Agatha mused. "They're fascinating. I've never been bored here in Derrington. I've seen cruelty here, and short-sightedness, and even a spark of violence every now and then. But, all in all, I believe in this town. Most of the people here are kind. Everyone has his own domain. Henry over at the clinic, Clark at the

Farman, Bert Vogen at the drugstore, even me when I was in my classroom. Somehow, we all work together, and we make a town of which I'm proud. I'd trust Dr. McCabe with my own life. Never known a more capable medical man. Same with Clark Manchester. I'd take his business advice any day, over any so-called expert's." She blinked once or twice. "If I could do it again, I might do it differently, but one thing would be the same. Whatever I did, I'd do it in Derrington." She snapped her mouth shut, and they walked the rest of the way in silence.

At the entrance to the hotel, Aggie asked, "Would you like me to stay? I'd be happy to—"

"Oh, no. Aggie, I can't thank you enough. I don't know what I'd have done without you tonight, but I'm tired again. I'll have no trouble falling asleep."

"Tell you what. Come for breakfast tomorrow. I'll call you in the morning and give you directions to my house. Then we'll check on Mr. Cramer and track down John Anthony for some answers."

Kate was nodding, biting her lip to keep back the tears. "Aggie, I—I—"

"I know, dear." In a rare gesture, the older woman patted Kate's arm. "See you in the morning." She turned and crossed the street, shoulders back, chin in the air, and Kate no longer found her even remotely absurd.

Kate entered the lobby and climbed the stairs slowly, exhausted. The woman had called herself a relic. If that was true, Kate decided, entering her room, then she was a relic of better, saner times, when people cared and helped each other.

A relic, she thought, as she got into bed and pulled the sheet up to her chin. I hope that's what I'll be someday, a relic, and I hope I'll die in a town like Derrington.

12

Confession

•

It was Friday morning in Derrington, Wisconsin, the twenty-sixth of May, a day that began with cool breezes as the sun lifted itself over the pines. By seven o'clock, the rays touched the Elm Street Clinic, shooting through the Venetian blinds in the back room.

Mary McCabe rubbed her eyes wearily. They burned. She got up from her chair, adjusted the blinds, and left the room for a moment to wash her face and squeeze some drops into her eyes. Peering into the mirror, she shook her head at her disheveled appearance and bloodshot eyes. Her body ached and she knew why. It was that girdle, a new one not yet stretched accommodatingly to her own bulges, and she'd worn the thing all night long.

Reentering the back room, she bent over the patient again. He was quiet at last, after a night of struggle, of wild talk and tortured whispers. She went to the office and called her husband, Henry, at home. It was his turn.

At the Wahomet County Courthouse on Third Avenue, a patrol car was pulling into the narrow alleyway alongside the building. It came to a stop in the parking lot at the back and Pete Iverson emerged. He crossed the lot and entered the building through a back door.

He had pulled a double shift, and he knew the sun wouldn't keep him from sleeping this morning. He just hoped his wife could keep their three-year-old twins quiet and his boss would leave him alone

154

the rest of the day. Walking along the hall on his way to the front desk, he was surprised to see McGavin already in his office. He leaned against the doorjamb and yawned.

"'Morning, Sheriff, I think."

McGavin looked up. "Everything quiet?"

"Yep," said the deputy, yawning again. "For the moment, anyway. Guess that doesn't mean much."

"Sit down a minute. I know you're beat, so am I, but this will take just a minute. I've been reading your notes—"

"Give me a break. You'll get your official report soon enough, how the hell could I sit here at a typewriter and patrol at the same—"

"Sit down, please."

Pete Iverson had heard that tone once or twice before. He sat down.

"Your notes are fine for the time being. Very thorough. I just have a couple of questions. You found only one bullet?"

"Yeah, behind the cottage in a tree. It's in the evidence locker, along with the one Doc McCabe took out of his leg."

"Fingerprints?"

"Sent 'em out last night. I called the lab, asked them to rush it."

"Good. About this trail up the slope . . ." McGavin was studying his deputy's notes.

"It's not really a trail. You want my guess?"

"Let's hear it."

"It happened in the woods near the lake. The guy spent some time in the water. His clothes, the shirt and pants he left in the bathroom, are full of weeds and sand. I'd guess he runs into the water, then he climbs out and goes up the hill, but not right to the door. I'm sure of that, anyway. Don't ask me why, but the blood on the ground says he went from the lake to a boat. It's in the bushes behind the cottage, on the side facing the lake. Then he goes to the door and inside."

McGavin thought a moment, then said, half to himself. "Why would he go to the boat first?"

"Search me." Iverson shrugged his shoulders. "I didn't say it made sense, I'm just telling you what happened. You got a better theory?"

Tired as he was, the deputy would have willingly sat there for as

155

long as it took to have the sheriff explain this one to him. They had had one brief conversation last night, but the Pine Lake suicide had interrupted them.

"Nope," said McGavin, ignoring his deputy's sarcasm. He knew they were both tired. "If you say he went to the boat first, then that's what he did."

It worked. He could see the deputy relaxing. "Now, then, one more thing. Any sign of a vehicle? There were tire tracks in that clearing, and Mrs. Downing says she's almost positive Cramer drove up here."

"I checked the road all the way to the highway, couldn't find any tracks at all leading off into the woods. If he drove, the car is somewhere else."

"Send a Teletype message before you leave, Pete, to the state police in Illinois; see if anything's registered under his name. We gotta know what we're looking for. Then put out an APB on it."

"Right, anything else?"

McGavin rubbed his forehead. "Not for the moment, but I don't guarantee you'll get a full day off, not the way things have gone the last twenty-four hours. You did well, Pete. Thanks for your help."

Iverson realized that the sheriff was not going to say another word about the Cramer case. He stood up.

"All in good time, right, boss? Okay, I'll wait. Hey," he stopped in the doorway, "by the way, Logan pulled a beaut last night. You may get a call on it."

"Logan's the city's problem, not mine. I wouldn't have hired that jerk if he'd been the last man in Derrington. What do you mean, *I* might get a call?"

"It's the Fergusons—"

"Sam and Gertrude? They okay?"

McGavin expected the worst. Logan was a local joke, a true Keystone Cop, but mere inexperience wasn't enough to explain away some of his colossal errors, let alone excuse them. One day, McGavin was convinced, Logan was going to hurt somebody.

"The Fergusons are fine," Pete assured him. "They weren't even there when it happened."

"When what happened?" McGavin prodded. Sam and his wife, Gertrude, were an elderly couple who owned a nursery just west of

156

Derrington. McGavin had grown up with their youngest son and he was fond of them.

"Breaking and entering," Pete said. "They went to the church supper at First Lutheran last night. When they got home, about ten o'clock, the back door of the greenhouse was open, and when they called it in, I was still out at the lake, so Logan came running."

"I'll bet he did," McGavin said dryly. One quality Logan possessed in abundance was enthusiasm.

"First," Pete said, "he puts his hand right on the doorknob."

McGavin groaned. "No prints."

"Only his own. Then he trips over a hose on the floor, falls into a plant rack, and he and the plants end up sprawled all over the floor."

"No footprints."

"If there were, they got lost in the potting soil."

"What was taken?"

"Near as Gert could figure, couple of small evergreens and two twenty-pound bags of peat moss."

"Okay, keep your eyes open for a yard with new landscaping, but it's not likely anyone in Derrington would risk it. Probably they're in somebody's backyard in Eagle Hill by now. That Logan . . . I don't suppose he got hurt and will be out of service a few weeks?"

Pete laughed. "You know Logan. Indestructible."

"Well, thanks for letting me know. I'll try to give Sam a call sometime today. Now, go home and get some sleep. And thanks again."

Pete nodded, then said tentatively. "Ah, I'm not all that tired. Anything else you want me to do? I could—"

"If you don't get some shut-eye, you're going to be worthless to me and everybody else. You get some rest. I'll see you tonight."

Pete nodded silently and left the office. What the hell, if the sheriff wasn't ready to talk yet, he had his reasons.

John Anthony McGavin swiveled in his chair to face the window behind his desk. Across the parking lot, in back of the building facing Second Avenue, he could see the garbagemen, banging cans as they started their morning pickup. He heard the phone ring out at the front desk. He pictured his mother walking to the hotel in her uniform, worrying about him, probably. He'd had to cancel their dinner together last night.

157

He saw Dan Little, their youngest deputy, cross the lot and get into the squad car, starting the day shift. A typical day in Derrington, everything the same. Yet nothing was the same. He dreaded this day as he had dreaded no other. After a time, he shook his head abruptly and swung back to the desk. He dialed the clinic.

"Mary? John Anthony. How is he?"

He listened patiently to her report.

"Look, I'd like to talk to you, get down in writing exactly what he said, before you forget. Can you stay there? All right, see you in a few minutes."

He punched a button on his telephone. "Will? 'Morning. Fine, thanks. Yeah, it's been a beaut. Look, I'll fill you in later. I'm heading over to the clinic—yes, he's still alive. Call me there if anything comes up. After that, I'll be at the Farman." He left the building through the back door and drove to the clinic.

In the back rooms at the Farman Hotel, Clark Manchester was shaving in front of the bathroom mirror. His mind was elsewhere, on last night's lengthy telephone conversation with Aggie Patterson. She'd called the moment she got home, and her story had fulfilled his richest expectations. Of course he felt sympathy for Mrs. Downing, but part of him, as always, stood back a step or two, observing and learning.

This beat all, he decided, splashing water on his face. He thought he'd seen and heard it all, but this was a humdinger, yessiree. He rubbed his face dry and dressed mechanically, pondering the pieces of the puzzle.

This man Cramer, to start with. Clark wondered if he'd ever met the man. It was certainly possible. Aggie said he'd been coming up here for years, renting that cottage out at Baker's Lake. Always in May, before the tourist rush that started on Memorial Day weekend. Chances were, he'd come into Derrington on occasion, maybe even to the Evergreen Room. Of course if he was what Mrs. Downing said he was, a quiet businessman who kept to himself, then maybe no one had noticed him.

Still, there was more to him than quiet and businesslike. Right this very minute that fellow was over in Henry's clinic, pretty bad off, too.

And Katherine Downing! Clark pressed his lips together as he put

158

on his shoes. He'd been right about her, all right. What a burden she'd carried, losing her folks and then her husband like that, and now getting tossed in with this character Cramer.

The single most bewildering aspect, though, was the McGavin boy. How on God's green earth had he got caught up in all this? Aggie'd said that John Anthony had been the original contact between Cramer, down in Chicago, and that real estate man, Weaver, up in Eagle Hill. But he'd told Mrs. Downing that he'd never met Cramer himself. So—the logical conclusion was that John Anthony had acted as some sort of go-between. Somebody'd given Cramer's name to John, and John had put Cramer and Weaver in touch with each other.

And look what it got Weaver. John Anthony shows up to ask a few questions about Cramer, and Weaver goes and hangs himself. 'Course that had happened up in Eagle Hill, not here in Derrington, but it was too darned close.

And the whole thing raised more questions. Who had given the sheriff Cramer's name, and why had he wanted to make that call to Weaver? And if Cramer and the sheriff hadn't met, why had Cramer sent that postcard to Kate Downing, sending her straight to John Anthony?

The answers were there, Clark knew. But he also knew that they really weren't his problem. He had other concerns that required his attention. The meeting this morning, for one thing. It was the last planning session for the Memorial Day celebration coming up on Monday. There'd be the parade, of course, and the memorial service over at the band shell. He hoped this latest turn of events wouldn't keep John Anthony from being there. The county sheriff always had a special part in the service, right at the end, where he said a few words about pride in country. The fact that this sheriff was a veteran himself lent a special poignancy to the old words.

By golly, if Clark Manchester had his way, and he usually did, this celebration was going to be the best one yet, and John Anthony was going to be there. It was tradition.

He nodded to himself and left his apartment, waving vaguely to Barry Barris, the new desk clerk he'd hired a month ago. Now there was another problem. The kid tried hard enough, Clark admitted, but he wasn't showing much promise. Ah, for the days when John Anthony had been with him. There was a boy with promise.

The hotel owner was muttering to himself as he entered the Evergreen Room. A moment later, Kate Downing came down the stairway and left the hotel, on her way to Aggie's house.

Over on Orchard Lane, Aggie Patterson was in her kitchen, at the back of the house. She sniffed the air with satisfaction. An unbeatable combination, she decided: freshly brewed coffee, homemade rolls from her freezer now heating in the oven, and the Derrington morning breeze. If all that didn't help Kate Downing, nothing would.

The girl would be all right. She and Clark would see to that. Last night she had been tired and confused, as she had every right to be. What a mess she had made of her young life! Aggie sighed unconsciously, remembering the way she had watched Kate come to terms with past dreams and illusions. It made her wonder where she herself had found the strength, the temerity, to say no to her own parents and that predictable young man, no to the life they and everyone else expected of her.

I, too, Aggie thought now, could have led that desperate existence, waiting away the days and the years. But I came here, met new friends—

"Hello?"

It was Kate, calling from the front porch, and Aggie brushed away her pity. Strength, that's what was needed now, and she went to open the door.

"'Morning, Kate! Sleep well?"

"It's a good thing you called, or I'd still be dead to the world. What was in that pill you gave me, anyway?"

"Come on in," Aggie said. "Oh, a sedative of some sort. You look better today."

"I feel better," Kate said. It was true. Aggie's prescription of a good dinner and a leisurely walk had helped her fall asleep, and there had been no bad dreams. This morning, with clean hair still damp from the shower and clean slacks and lacy T-shirt, she felt human again. Her color was back, her mind was alert, and nothing, least of all some crotchety country doctor, was going to keep her from seeing Benjamin Cramer.

Aggie was leading the way through the living room to the kitchen, and Kate said, "What a pretty house." She liked it immediately. The rooms had a clean, well-swept look, with floors polished to a hard gleam and walls graced with a few colorful paintings. There were lots of green plants and some odd mementos, from her travels, Kate guessed. "You really do have a green thumb, don't you?"

"I wasn't born with it," Aggie said. "Coffee?"

"Please." Kate sat down at the kitchen table.

"I attacked the art with a vengeance," Aggie said. She poured two cups of coffee, then went to the stove, turning up the heat under the eggs.

"Got tired of all my plants dying with frightening regularity," Aggie said, tossing cheese into the pan. "So I went out to Sam and Gertie's nursery and yelled 'Help!' They were good teachers, I must say. When I went to Mexico last year, Gert came in every day to check on my plants. They were thriving when I came back." She piled the eggs into a bowl and brought the rolls to the table. "Eat, Kate. We need our strength today."

"Have you called the clinic?"

Aggie shook her head. "Breakfast first. I've heard nothing, so that's good news. Mary would have called if—"

"Mary?"

"McCabe, Henry's wife and prize nurse. She's a bit rough around the edges; inside, soft as a marshmallow. She's a fine nurse."

Kate was enjoying the gossip in spite of herself. How different from yesterday morning. Then she had been an outsider, an alien in this closed community, shrinking at a table in a coffee shop. This morning, here she was in someone's home, eating a home-cooked breakfast and listening to small-town gossip. She thought of the office on La Salle Street where she usually spent her mornings. She felt at home there, too, but the minute she left the building she was a stranger again, a visitor in the city. What a pitiful way to live. . . .

"Aggie, may I use your phone? After we're finished, I mean. I'd like to call my office."

"Of course. The telephone's in my study. More eggs?"

"I can't resist. Surely you don't eat like this every morning?"

"Oh, often enough to remind myself I'm worth it." The older woman smiled a little, and Kate laughed.

"Take my word for it. You're worth it."

Aggie inclined her head, and Kate realized they were both a little uneasy. The intimacy of the night before, fostered by stress and exhaustion and a good bottle of wine, was thinner in the clear light of morning. Once again they were just two women, separated by age and background, thrown together by circumstance. Kate wondered if Aggie was now regretting her impulsive kindness to a stranger.

"The study is just down that hall, on the right." Agatha pointed. "Here, take some fresh coffee with you." She refilled Kate's cup and handed it to her.

"Aggie—if—if you'd rather—well, why don't I just go back to the hotel? I could call my office from there and then go to the clinic—"

"Oh, dear, am I interfering too much? I do have a tendency—"

"No, it's not that, not at all. But—well, you hardly know me—"

"I assume you told me the truth last night. You are alone? There's no family, no one you can call?"

Kate shook her head.

"Then don't be so afraid of accepting help. If I'm in the way, tell me so. But if you think I can smooth the way a little, help you with John Anthony—"

"Yes, I do! I can't get him to tell me anything!"

"All right, then. Go make your phone call. And no more of this blubbering. When I've had enough of your company, I'll let you know."

Kate was red in the face. "Yes, ma'am." She left the kitchen and found the study. She placed her cup and saucer on the desk blotter, sat down in the leather chair, and leaned on her elbows.

What had happened to her these past years? How had she become so stubbornly independent, so doubtful of other people's good intentions? It had been a long time since she had felt intentional cruelty from anyone. No, it wasn't that, it wasn't that people were cruel. It was life that had been cruel, disappointing her when she had done nothing to deserve such treatment. It was anger.

Anger? How silly; she seldom got angry about anything.

Yes, but you feel it, she told herself, you've been angry since Jim died and left you alone.

But he couldn't help that. He didn't take his own life, he was killed in an airplane crash.

But you still feel cheated. You got a raw deal, something you didn't deserve.

162

Yes, and how did I face it? Like the groundhog. I saw my shadow, what my life was supposed to be, what it would have been if not for my father—and then if Jim hadn't died—and I couldn't stand it, so I went into a hole. Only I never came out. Everything was waiting for me. There was Benjamin Cramer, and my job, the city, my neighbors, all those people at the university—a whole world for me, and I barely touched it. Because it wasn't what I had planned.

Kate sat in front of the desk like a statue, motionless, her face stony as she came to grips with what she had done.

Slowly, carefully, she said the words to herself: You never admitted that you are worth caring about. When all the people who loved you were gone, you never learned that you still deserved to be happy.

"It's awfully quiet in there. Everything all right?" Aggie's voice floated down the hall.

Kate blinked and cleared her throat. She unclenched her fists and wiped at the tears on her cheeks.

"Yes, I'm fine. Be with you in a minute."

She picked up the receiver and dialed the long-distance operator, making the call collect.

"Kate Downing? Yes, I'll accept the charges! Mrs. Downing?"

It was Janice, from the typing pool.

"Yes, Janice. Is everything going smoothly this morning?"

"As smooth as you could expect with both you and Mr. Cramer gone." Her tone was laden with questions she didn't dare ask.

"I need the number of Mr. Cramer's health insurance policy. In the employee file, in the corner cabinet. Look it up for me, will you?"

"Yes, ma'am, right away."

She was back in a minute.

"Here it is, Mrs. Downing." She read the number. "Anything else?"

"Neither of us will be in today," Kate said. "You have a key to our office, don't you?"

"Yes, ma'am, there's one around here someplace, I think—"

"Please find it and take some of your work down there. You can use my typewriter. Mainly I want you there to answer the telephone. And I think you'd better cancel all of Mr. Cramer's appointments for the next two weeks. Don't try to reschedule them yet."

163

"Okay, I'll go down right now. But—excuse me—are you okay?"

After years of not listening, Kate heard, for the second time in less than an hour, a voice of concern—concern for *her*. How many such voices had she missed?

"Thank you, I'm fine." Kate spoke slowly, choosing her words carefully. "Mr. Cramer is—ill. He was injured in an accident, and it's going to take a while for him to—recover."

"Oh, no, gee, that's too bad. What can we do? My sister works in a doctor's office, maybe—"

"No, Janice." Kate stopped. Listen to yourself! The girl is trying to help! "Thank you very much, that's very thoughtful of you, but the accident occurred in Wisconsin, so a doctor here is treating him."

"Wisconsin! Are you in Wisconsin, Mrs. Downing?"

"Janice, please," Kate said, as kindly as she could, "please lower your voice. Yes, I'm here, and I expect I will be until Mr. Cramer is able to travel. So I'm counting on you and the others to keep things going. Can you manage?"

"Sure we can! I mean—well, it won't be the same, but you don't have to worry about us, we'll be fine."

"I know you will. And there's one more thing. You must be very careful what you say about this. You know, many of Mr. Cramer's clients are—well, they have a bit of the stuffed-shirt quality, and they aren't going to like it when you cancel their appointments. You must be very courteous, but be firm, and there's no need to gossip about this. Simply tell them that Mr. Cramer became ill on his vacation and is recuperating. And you needn't tell them that I'm with him. If anyone asks to speak to me, just tell them that I'm away from the office. If they want any more details, you're sorry, but that's all you know."

Which, in fact, was all Janice did know, Kate realized.

"Can you do that for us?"

"Yes, ma'am, I sure can. And I'll tell the other girls. And Mrs. Downing—we'll be here. If you need us for anything, just let us know."

Again there was that note of genuine caring. Kate swallowed.

"Yes, I will. Thank you."

"Mr. Cramer's going to be all right, isn't he?"

"I don't know yet. I pray that he is. I'll be in touch."

Kate hung up quickly, before her voice broke. She realized that she really was praying, for the first time in years. She was skeptical about the chances that anyone was listening, but what else could she do?

A moment later she caught herself. There was plenty she could do, and she would begin with herself.

Her gaze fell on the single wall in Aggie's study that wasn't lined with books. Sipping her coffee, she began reading the diplomas, the certificates of excellence, the honors accumulated by a woman on her own. Here was the proof, right in front of her, of what one woman could accomplish.

Ten minutes later Aggie appeared in the doorway.

"Did you finish your call?"

Kate looked up, and Aggie did not intimidate her anymore. She was a kind, elderly woman, that's all. A friend.

"Yes. I called collect. We have a typing pool—wonderful secretaries—and I gave them instructions. Canceling appointments, that sort of thing. Now then. Do you think we should call the clinic or just appear on Dr. McCabe's doorstep?"

She saw the surprise on Aggie's face and almost laughed out loud. Already she felt different, and it was making a difference with Aggie. Had she really never been so forceful before? Well, it was a tiny risk. Let's see where it led.

Wordlessly, Aggie picked up the receiver and dialed the clinic.

"Good morning, Henry. Aggie Patterson here. Where's Mary? . . . Ah, I see. Well, that's why I'm calling. I have a friend of your patient here, and she'd like to see him as soon as possible." Aggie listened.

"Well, Henry. Maybe you'd better tell her that yourself. . . . Yes, but I don't think that's going to matter to her. She just wants to see him. I'm sure she won't disturb him in any way. In fact, it could help. . . . Yes. He asked her to come up here before the accident. . . . Yes, I thought so. Very well. Be there in ten minutes."

Aggie hung up the phone with satisfaction.

"He's still unconscious. Henry is moving him up to Eagle Hill this morning, but you can see him if we hurry."

"Thank you. I'll find a way to repay you for all this, I promise." Kate was already sailing down the hallway, and Aggie was swept along with the tide.

■　　■　　■

165

The Elm Street Clinic was a yellow brick building set close to the street. Outside, it looked deceptively small. Inside, it stretched back, a long, narrow collection of rooms. It smelled of antiseptic and floor polish.

"Well, Judith, good morning. I didn't know you worked here."

"Oh, Miss Patterson!" Judith Barnes, a chubby, dark-haired woman in her early twenties, jumped up from her seat at the reception desk and smoothed her white uniform. "I don't really work here—the children keep me too busy, you know—but Mrs. McCabe was up all night and she asked me to fill in for her today. Have you heard what happened?"

"That's really none of our business, is it, Judith," Aggie said smoothly. "This is Mrs. Downing. She would like to see the patient."

"Yes, Miss Patterson." Judith was blushing and looked away. "Dr. McCabe said you—well, this way, please."

Kate turned to Aggie and mouthed, "Student?"

Aggie winked and nodded and it was all Kate could do to keep from laughing as she followed the nurse down the hall. What a bear that woman must have been in the classroom!

Judith knocked softly on the door at the end of the hall, and Kate was momentarily surprised when John Anthony McGavin opened the door.

"Sheriff McGavin?" She found herself whispering. "He hasn't—that is, he's still alive, isn't he?"

McGavin, face haggard, nodded. "Yes. Come in."

Kate turned to thank the nurse, but she was already gone, off to attend to her duties, presumably, under the watchful eye of Agatha Patterson, who had remained in the waiting room. Kate stepped past the sheriff and saw a bulky man in a white coat bending over a bed. When he straightened, she could see the equipment, the machines and tubes, and then she saw Benjamin Cramer. How pathetic he looked! Except for the terrible bruise on his nose and forehead, he was ghostly pale. His body seemed to have shriveled up, and it occupied the bed like a doll, limp and lifeless. He appeared ancient and childlike at once, and that pitiful vulnerability was what disturbed Kate the most, because it was so totally unlike

166

him. She walked over to him and touched his hand with the tips of her fingers.

"Mr. Cramer?" she whispered. "Don't worry about a thing. I've called the office and everything is fine. You're going to be fine, too. Everyone is taking good care of you. And I won't leave; I'll be here whenever you need me. You just concentrate on getting well."

She touched his hand again, willing his fingers to move, his eyes to open, any response to show that he had heard her, any sign that he knew she was there. But his fingers remained limp on the sheet, his eyes stayed closed. She turned away.

"Are you Dr. McCabe?" she asked, still whispering.

The man in the white coat, a halo of salt-and-pepper hair framing his round face, bobbed his head and gestured toward the door, and Kate followed him out. McGavin joined them in the hallway, closing the door behind them.

"Doc, this is Katherine Downing. She works with Mr. Cramer down in Chicago."

They shook hands.

"Let's go into my office," the doctor said, and led the way. "Have a chair, please." He closed the door.

"Doctor, is he going to be all right? He looks—terrible."

The doctor, seating himself behind his desk, studied the woman opposite him for a moment. He cleared his throat and glanced at McGavin, who nodded and took a chair behind Kate, near the door.

"I don't know yet," Henry McCabe said slowly. He folded his big hands on the desk. They did not look like a doctor's hands. The fingers were fat and stubby, but, Kate guessed, they were skilled, and as gentle as any patient had ever required. "He has two wounds, and he lost a great deal of blood before he got here."

Kate interrupted. Her voice was low, calm.

"What kind of wounds?" she asked.

McCabe hesitated only a moment. "He was shot. Twice." He was watching her carefully, but she didn't cringe. She was leaning forward in her chair, listening intently. "One bullet passed through his left shoulder. The damage there is—uh, severe, quite severe, but with proper therapy he could regain at least partial use of the arm." McCabe cleared his throat.

"And the other wound? You said there were two."

167

"The other bullet," Henry McCabe said, "lodged in his left leg, ten and a half inches above the kneecap. I've removed the bullet, but it did its damage. It wasn't attended to as soon as it should have been."

"Meaning?" Her tone was almost conversational, but there was a challenge behind it.

"There's no way we can be absolutely sure—until he tells us what happened. But it looks as if he received those wounds Monday. Possibly Sunday. Between that time and yesterday, when you found him, he spent too many hours outdoors, he lost too much blood, he—well, frankly, I'm surprised he's still alive."

"I'm not," Kate said quietly. "Why are you moving him?"

McCabe glanced at the sheriff again. "He—well, he's going to lose the leg, Mrs. Downing. I don't have the facilities here to do that kind of surgery and give him the intensive care he'll need. It's dangerous to move him, but more of a threat, I believe, for him to remain here, and the hospital in Eagle Hill—"

"If we had found him sooner?" Kate was trying very hard not to picture Benjamin Cramer in a wheelchair.

"That's a guessing game," McCabe said. "The point is, we—we may lose him anyway. But we certainly will if we don't amputate the leg. I'm sorry."

"No—" Kate waved away his apology. "I want you to be truthful with me. Will you do the operation? I've heard nothing but praise about you, and I'm sure Mr. Cramer—"

"No, Dr. Kulik has agreed to perform the surgery. He's a very skilled surgeon, Mrs. Downing. He had experience in Vietnam, and he's much more qualified than I am. I recommend him without any reservation. I'm a family practitioner, not a surgeon."

Kate gazed at him for a moment, weighing his words.

"All right," she agreed, as if she had any choice. Clearly the matter had already been decided, and she would have to trust his judgment. "What time will the surgery take place?"

"This morning, eleven-thirty."

"I'll be there," Kate said, more to herself than to the doctor. Then, looking at him, she asked, "Has Mr. Cramer been unconscious all this time? I mean, has he said anything . . .?"

McGavin spoke for the first time. "Only gibberish, Mrs. Downing. Nothing that has any coherence."

168

She looked at the doctor for confirmation, and he nodded.

"He's in shock, and I have him under heavy sedation. My wife is a nurse and she was with him all night. Nothing he said made any sense."

"Take a look." McGavin had half expected her skepticism, and he handed her his clipboard. There were two pages of notes attached to it. "This is what Mary McCabe told me this morning."

Kate read the notes carefully and had to concede that they were right. These were the delirious ramblings of an incoherent man. "Yes, I'll be careful. Watch out! No, sir. Call—" here there was a blank; apparently, whatever followed had been unintelligible— "tomorrow . . ." It went on, and all it revealed to Kate was the degree of pain he was suffering.

"Thank you." She gave the clipboard back to McGavin and spoke to the doctor. "Mr. Cramer has insurance. I called the office this morning and got the policy number." She opened her purse and took out her note. "Are there forms you'd like me to fill out? I have his power of attorney, if that's necessary."

The doctor nodded. "I'll have Judith prepare them for you by this afternoon. It might help if you went up to the hospital in Eagle Hill and checked him in. They're sending an ambulance down to pick him up."

"Yes, of course, I'll help in any way I can. But when I come back," and Kate rose to face McGavin, "I'd like to speak with you, Sheriff. Will you be free later this afternoon or this evening?"

"You can check with the department when you get back. If I'm not there, they can reach me. Thanks, Henry." McGavin left the office.

"Doctor, I appreciate your candor. And thank you for all you've done for Mr. Cramer." Kate shook his hand again and went to join Aggie in the waiting room.

Dr. McCabe watched her from his office door. An extraordinary woman, he decided. Remarkable composure. He wondered if she'd ever been a nurse. Probably not. She'd have made a fine nurse, but if she'd had the training, she would have heard what he was trying to tell her. That man down the hall, Cramer, was very likely going to die today. Still, Henry McCabe had seen miracles before, and he knew that when you give up believing in miracles, you might as well give up the practice of medicine. He wasn't ready to do that.

But there were to be no miracles that day, at least not for Benjamin Cramer. At twelve thirty-two, on an operating table in the Eagle Hill Public Hospital, the chief surgeon, Dr. Kulik, pronounced the patient dead. But he had talked before he died.

Later, Kate wondered what would have happened if, at the last possible moment, she had been unable to convince the ambulance attendants to allow her to ride to the hospital with Benjamin Cramer. Would McGavin have ever told her the truth? Eventually she knew the answer, but on that Friday in May she was certain only that Benjamin Cramer, knowing somehow, through the fog of pain and shock, that he was going to die, had found some hidden reserve of strength to rise to consciousness one last time and whisper a tortured confession.

The ambulance, lights flashing and siren screeching every time they neared an intersection, was racing northeast to Eagle Hill. Inside, with one attendant at the wheel, the other perched near Cramer's head, Kate knelt next to the stretcher, holding Cramer's hand and occasionally speaking to him. She didn't think he could hear her, but, if only to reassure herself that she was doing all she could, she continued to talk, calmly and soothingly. Her eyes never left his face and when his eyes fluttered and opened, she saw it before the attendant did.

"Miss Down . . ." His voice, slurred and fuzzy, came from some distant plane of consciousness. She bent over him and smiled.

"Yes, Mr. Cramer. Benjamin."

"Sorry. . . ."

"Don't be silly—"

". . . your husband."

Kate closed her mouth. Unconsciously, she tightened her grip on his hand.

"Husband . . . still . . . alive." Cramer sighed and coughed, and the attendant tried to wave Kate out of the way, but with a rudeness she would have later denied, she shot him a vicious look and leaned even closer to Cramer. She must have misunderstood. He was delirious. It couldn't be—

"Nam . . . caught me . . . Found me in . . . shcago. . . . Made me do it. . . . So sorry. . . ."

"I—I didn't hear," Kate whispered. "Who—who is alive?"

"Didn't die . . . like you thought. Stu . . . stupid edgers."

"Edgers?"

"Made me hire you . . . glad . . . love . . . love you . . ." His eyelids fluttered, and Kate feared he was slipping away.

"Mr. Cramer? Did you say . . . my husband? He's alive?"

"Watching you . . ." His words came in sighs, barely audible.

Kate's eyes were wide, and suddenly her knees grew weak and she sank back on her heels. Dear God, this was wrong, all wrong; it was impossible. Her husband was dead, the Marine Corps had told her that.

"Gun . . ." Cramer tried again, and Kate could feel hot tears spurting from her eyes. "Had . . . gun."

Gunshot wounds. The doctor had told her that. But—

"Did he do this?" Kate hardly knew what she was asking. She dared not think of the enormity of that question. If Jim was alive, then . . . No, no, he would never . . . But if he was alive . . . ?

Cramer's breathing was labored and she waited for an eternity. He wasn't going to answer, he couldn't.

Then his eyes opened. He looked at her clearly, and there was no mistaking what he said.

"He knows . . . I love you. . . . Came to cabin. . . . Weaver! Both there. . . . Gun . . . shot me. Think I'm dead." A ghost of a smile fled across his face before he started coughing again. He closed his eyes, and at last the attendant prevailed. He grasped Kate's arm and lifted her out of the way so he could attend to his patient.

Kate sank onto the floor of the ambulance, tears streaming down her cheeks, rocking herself. She crossed her arms and held onto her elbows for dear life. She had never felt more lost, more alone in the world, than at this moment.

"Jim!" She was moaning softly. "Jim, no, you're dead, all these years. . . . I've been alone, you're dead. . . . Some—somewhere in the ocean, all this time. . . . Why didn't you come back to me? I kept the house, your letters, I was there all the time, why didn't you come home?"

Finally the attendant had done what he could for Cramer. He had slipped into unconsciousness again, and the medic turned to Kate

171

and helped her up onto the metal bench on the other side of the ambulance.

"You okay, lady?" He pulled out a paper tissue from somewhere and handed it to her. He said to the driver, "Hey, Tucker, step on it, will you? The dame's falling apart; I told you we shouldn't have let her come."

He turned back to Kate as if she couldn't have heard what he'd said. "That's it, wipe your face, take a deep breath. Take another one. Look, if you wanta help your friend here, just sit nice and quiet, okay? We're almost there."

"Leave me alone." Her voice was fierce. "Just take care of Mr. Cramer. Do your job, that's all I ask. Just take care of him and leave me alone." She blew her nose into the tissue and looked at Cramer. His face had changed, she thought. He looked almost peaceful, and, for no good reason she could think of, that made her angry, too. The siren was wailing as they wheeled around a corner, and she thought her head was going to explode. What more? she thought. What more can happen to blow my world apart? Every assumption I've made for the past ten years was based on a lie, a monstrous lie! Jim is alive—oh, God, I think it's true; Mr. Cramer wouldn't lie to me now, not at a time like this. Jim is alive and Mr. Cramer knows it! He's known it all along! And the gun—those wounds, those terrible things that happened to him—was it Jim? Jim and Weaver? No, maybe Weaver, but not Jim. He was gentle with me, he made love to me, he—

"Okay, lady, we're here." The ambulance screeched to a halt under an awning, and the attendant jumped up to grab the end of the stretcher. The doors flew open; another attendent hopped up to take the other end of the stretcher, and they rushed into the hospital. Kate cowered on the metal bench a moment longer. Then she got out of the ambulance, feeling numb, and went through the double doors.

She was no help at all to the woman at the desk, with her pages of forms and endless questions. Childhood diseases? Allergies? Age? Kate wasn't even sure of that. At the moment, she couldn't have told them her own date of birth.

When Aggie Patterson, a sensible driver no matter what the circumstances, reached the hospital in her own car and at last found Kate in a waiting room on the third floor, Kate reached out for her hand. She squeezed it as if it were a lifeline—which, indeed, it was—and offered no excuse or apology. They sat together, on a couch, until Kate spoke.

"My husband is alive." Her voice was hoarse, scratchy with ten years of grief and a hundred conflicting emotions. "He's alive, Aggie. Mr. Cramer told me." Her voice rose with wonder. "Mr. Cramer said he's—watching me."

"Dear God in heaven," Aggie said, under her breath. Kate had been staring into space, almost talking to herself. Now she looked into Aggie's eyes and saw all the woman's objectivity fading away. She was no longer, Kate sensed, a teacher guiding a stumbling but promising pupil. The limits she had imposed on herself to stay strong were disappearing. Still, she tried.

"Kate, the man is in shock. Think what he's been through! People in that—that condition—their minds wander; you can't—"

"Jim is alive!" Kate gripped Aggie's hand harder. "I know it. I believe him, he told me the truth! I know it!"

"That's impossible," Aggie persisted. "He died ten years ago. The Marine Corps verified it, didn't they?"

"There was no body, I told you. His plane went down at sea. They didn't recover any bodies. So—so maybe he wasn't even on the plane, Aggie; that would explain it, he wasn't on the plane, don't you see? He's still alive. And that's not all, oh, there's something worse. He said Jim —and Weaver, Jim and Weaver—he said they—there was a gun, at the cabin. . . ."

Kate couldn't help it; she could see that cabin as if she had just stepped inside it, and the horror of it came flooding back to her. Those stains on the floor, they *had* been blood, and the bathroom, his clothes, more blood, and the smell, Mr. Cramer in that bed, sick and alone, and all because of Jim? Could he possibly have done such a thing?

Aggie wrested her hand from Kate's grip and fought the numbness in her fingers as she searched her purse for a handkerchief.

"Here, dry your face. It'll be all right. There, there," and Kate could not have anticipated the tenderness in Aggie's voice. She put an arm around Kate's shoulders and held her tight. She didn't ask any questions or offer any more objections. Kate knew that even

Aggie Patterson could not deal rationally with the impossible. But she could offer comfort, and Kate took it, sobbing in her arms.

Why? she kept thinking. Why would he do this? Why would he let me think he was dead?

The question pounded at her, and she began to feel bruised, body and soul battered by a force she had no way of controlling. It was almost as if she were in the cabin with Cramer, suffering the same violence, feeling the same excruciating pain, and she was defenseless. He could not protect her; there were no more barriers between her and the pain. The sobs racked her body, and all she could do was hide in Aggie's tiny, strong arms and wait for them to stop.

Finally, when she felt she was close to suffocating, when there was no breath left to feed the punishment, Aggie said gently, "There now, that's better. It's out now, it's gone, you're going to be all right." Kate sat up a little and saw the tears on Aggie's face. Kate sniffed, and Aggie handed her a paper tissue. For the moment, it was over.

Kate found the ladies' room and washed her face, splashing cold water into her eyes until they stopped burning a little. She barely glanced at herself in the mirror because she knew what she would see: the Kate of ten years ago, desperate and lost, unable to cope. She couldn't bear to see that face again.

She rejoined Aggie in the waiting room and they sat silently, not talking, until Dr. Kulik found them.

His abrupt announcement of Benjamin Cramer's death came as an anticlimax. Kate had guessed it, even yesterday, the moment she had seen him; Aggie had seen Henry McCabe's face when she left the clinic, so she was not surprised, either. The surgeon wanted permission to perform an autopsy. The final indignity, Kate thought, but what did it matter now? She signed the paper and assured him that she would make all the other necessary arrangements tomorrow. Then she and Aggie left the hospital slowly, in a near stupor, supporting each other.

Aggie's aging Ford had no air conditioning, so they rolled down the front windows. Clean, woodsy air swept their faces as they drove back to Derrington. Kate spoke first.

"Do you know what else he told me?"

The older woman kept her eyes glued on the curving highway. "What?"

174

"He said he loved me. . . . Imagine that. After all these years. I thought he never even noticed me." A choking sound, a weak attempt at a laugh, died in her throat. "Do you know what I think? I think Benjamin Cramer has known all this time, since the day he hired me, that Jim was alive. He said Jim made him hire me, so he has known all this time, and he never told me.

"What kind of a man could do that? Tell me, will you? How could he know my husband was alive and not tell me?"

Kate's bitterness cut into the sweet-scented air. Aggie rubbed her nose and squinted a little into the glare of the strip of pavement.

"I suppose—the worst kind of man, Kate," she said lamely, then hastened to add, "but we don't know why yet. He must have had a compelling reason. Try not to judge him yet, until—"

"Until Sheriff McGavin can explain." Kate's voice was sharp with cynicism. "Oh, you bet I'll wait. I'm going to find that sheriff of yours, and I don't care if the town is burning, he is going to find time to talk to me. Care to join me?"

This time it was not a desperate plea for help. It sounded like an invitation to attend an execution.

"If you wish."

"I wish," Kate said grimly, and then they were silent, each considering the dying words of Benjamin Cramer.

175

13

The Lawyer

▪

Milton Rissman swore softly under his breath as another car cut in front of him, narrowly missing the front fender of his own car. The traffic on the Tri-State inched its way north from Chicago, a massive exodus at the beginning of the Memorial Day weekend. Rissman tugged at his tie to loosen it and unbuttoned his shirt collar. There, that was a little better. He turned the air conditioner up and decided that yes, barring a collision, he would make it home safely, sanity relatively intact. At last he joined the line of vehicles in the exit lane for Deerfield and, the necessity of total concentration on driving somewhat reduced, he pondered the cause of his entrapment in one of the year's worst traffic jams.

He'd planned to leave his office in the city by noon, one o'clock at the latest, and be home in time to supervise the filling of his backyard swimming pool. Expansively, he'd told his secretary to take the afternoon off, an offer she'd enthusiastically accepted, but not before reminding him of his three o'clock appointment with Benjamin Cramer.

Damn, he'd forgotten that. It was just like Cramer to make a Friday afternoon appointment weeks ahead of time with no concern that it was the beginning of a holiday weekend. The man seemed oblivious to the fact that other people occasionally needed time off, even if he didn't.

Captain Cramer, Rissman called him, though only to himself.

Such was Cramer's reputation in the city that Rissman kept his joke private. He'd hardly expect anyone else to understand the respect and even the measure of affection it conveyed. Rissman had heard or read somewhere that Cramer really had been a captain once, in the Marine Corps, and the title still suited him: He ran his business like a command post, every aspect neat and orderly and carefully disciplined.

Well, Captain Cramer was wheeling and dealing again, no doubt. He hadn't specified the nature of his business; he'd only requested this appointment several weeks ago. Maybe he wanted to buy another building. Rissman had heard that the Latham Complex might be going up for sale.

Milton Rissman would have suffered the shock of his life if he'd ever learned that Benjamin Cramer had made the appointment to discuss with his lawyer certain ramifications of the statute of limitations and divorce laws in Illinois. He was spared the shock because Cramer failed to keep the appointment.

Alone in the office, Rissman was mildly annoyed when three o'clock came and went with no sign of Cramer. After all, the man was a walking stopwatch himself, and it was rather presumptuous of him to be late. By three-thirty, his annoyance now exasperation, he dialed Cramer's office.

"Mr. Cramer, please," he said shortly, skipping the usual amenities. He was quite fond of Kate Downing, even intrigued by her, but he was in no mood for idle chatter this afternoon.

"I'm sorry," an unfamiliar voice purred. "Mr. Cramer is out. May I take a message?"

"This is Milton Rissman. He had an appointment with me for three this afternoon, but he isn't here yet."

"Oh, dear! Oh, dear, I'm so sorry, Mr. Rissman!"

"Say, who is this?" Rissman demanded. "Where's Mrs. Downing?"

"Oh, she's gone too, sir. Neither one of them came in today. You see, first Mr. Cramer decided to take an extra week's vacation and Mrs. Downing canceled all his appointments—well, she didn't cancel them, not at first, just rearranged them, but I don't see your name on the appointment schedule at all, so I guess she couldn't cancel it, or, I mean, schedule it for another time, but I'm awfully sorry—"

"Are you telling me Cramer's on vacation? He's not in Chicago today?"

"Well, no, I mean, yes, he's still in Wisconsin, but—"

"Thank you." Rissman dropped the receiver and sought to bring his temper under control. He refused to think about it as he rode the elevator to the basement garage, retrieved his car, and battled his way to the Tri-State. By the time he reached the exit ramp and knew that he was only eight minutes from his home, his beautiful wife and, God willing, a swimming pool filled with water, he was calm enough to allow a margin of concern to take the edge off his anger.

Cramer certainly had his share of quirks, but flighty? Undependable? Never. And his assistant, Kate Downing, was the perfect match for him. Together they were quite a team. Rissman had once told his wife that they were a symphony of efficiency, and at least twice he had hinted to Cramer that should he ever let the woman go, he, Rissman, would hire her in a minute. Cramer had carefully ignored him both times. Apparently the Captain knew what an asset his First Mate was to the running of the ship.

Then, of course, nearly five years ago, Cramer had changed his will and Rissman understood. Or thought he did. That was another oddity. Cramer allowed him to get only so close and then—wham. Up went the storm wall. Rissman had given him every chance to confide in him, but there were never any explanations, not even a wink or a nod to confirm Rissman's suspicions. Still, it pleased him to think that two people he genuinely liked had found each other, though why Cramer didn't marry the woman was beyond Rissman's comprehension.

But now, this afternoon, that romantic symphony had sounded a distinctly sour note. That excuse for a secretary on the telephone . . . Rissman managed a little chuckle as he pulled into his driveway. Cramer didn't deserve that caliber of help and Rissman would tell him so when they did finally get together.

He resolutely put the entire matter out of his mind as he went in the side door and called to his wife. He had a three-day weekend ahead of him and, by God, he was going to enjoy it.

"Peggy? . . . Peg, you home?"

"In here, dear. Telephone for you." His dark-haired wife, slim and, at forty, still stunning, appeared in the arched doorway leading

178

to the study. She kissed him on the lips. "It's a woman, Miltie, long distance. Velly eenteresteeng." She was laughing up at him as she took his briefcase.

"You know perfectly well you'll get a full report." He pulled her back to him for another kiss. "Kids home?"

"In the pool, of course! I'll fix you a drink out there, so make it short."

"Two minutes."

She went down the hall and Rissman crossed the room to the desk and picked up the receiver.

"Hello."

"Mr. Rissman?"

"Yes."

"This is Kate Downing calling. I'm sorry to bother you at home, but this is rather urgent."

He hardly recognized her voice, and a frown creased his forehead. The usual throaty quality he found so pleasant was completely gone, and in its place was a clipped, almost harsh abruptness. What in the world . . .?

"Mr. Rissman?"

"Yes, I'm here. I had an appointment with your boss this afternoon, but he didn't show up."

"Mr. Cramer is dead, Mr. Rissman."

The flat, emotionless finality of that statement, without benefit of preamble, jolted him upright in his chair. He gripped the phone tightly. There was a moment of silence as he groped for something sensible to say, but she saved him the effort.

"He died late this morning, in Wisconsin. I'm up here now and I'll take care of things here, but I'll need your help when I come back. You are still Mr. Cramer's attorney, aren't you?"

"Yes," he managed, thinking furiously, "yes, certainly I am. But—how? I mean, how did he—he seemed in perfect health—"

"Yes, he was. It was—he had an accident, and he was out in the woods. He couldn't get help in time. Mr. Rissman, I need to know if—did Mr. Cramer have a family? I don't know whom to notify."

Still that crisp, level tone, so distant that it begged him not to ask any more questions, and Milton Rissman, knowing all he did, thought he heard grief in every perfectly controlled word. He was burning with questions, but it was clear that this wasn't the time to ask them.

"No, he didn't. No family at all. It may reassure you to know that he left a very specific will. He has kept it up to date. Thad Brewer over at First National is the executor."

"A wise choice, as usual," and Rissman at last detected the faintest shadow of the wry humor he had come to expect and enjoy in this woman. "Do you happen to know if there are burial provisions in the will?"

"I believe there are, but I'll have to check, and the will is at my office." The thought of returning to the city caused him to slump in his chair, but there was no choice. "I'll have to call you back. Give me your number—"

"Would tomorrow morning be better? The holiday traffic must be awful down there."

Rissman marveled at her ability to think of anything as mundane as traffic at such a moment.

"Yes, tomorrow would be better for me. And Mrs. Downing, may I tell you—Benjamin Cramer was just about the finest businessman I ever knew. I liked him tremendously. I—I'm very sorry."

"Thank you. I'm staying at a hotel in a town called Derrington. If I'm out when you call tomorrow, you can leave a message." She gave him the telephone number, then added, "Can you think of anything I should take care of up here?"

"Do you have a death certificate?"

"Tomorrow. After the autopsy is completed."

"Autopsy! Why—Mrs. Downing, excuse this one question, please, but exactly how did the Cap—how did he die?"

"He had an accident. It's quite complicated; I'd rather not go into the details over the phone."

Was it his imagination, or did he detect annoyance in her reply? Oh, slow down, he told himself, the woman's under a terrific strain.

"All right, but please be certain the certificate is legible, and signed by a medical doctor. Now then, have you considered the funeral arrangements?"

"No. . . . If he didn't specify anything in the will, I'd rather— could we just bury him?"

That took Rissman completely by surprise. "Just bury" Benjamin Cramer? Without a service? Preposterous. Perhaps she'd change

180

her thinking if she knew the provisions of his will. Well, they could settle all this tomorrow.

"I suggest we work this out tomorrow. I'll get back to you as soon as I can."

"Thank you, Mr. Rissman. Until tomorrow."

He heard her hang up at the other end and, slowly, he replaced the receiver and sat staring at the telephone. He knew that instrument could play tricks, and although he spent half his time using it, he had an instinctive distrust of it. He liked to look people in the face during a conversation, to be sure he was getting his point across. Thus, it was hardly fair to make a judgment based on a telephone conversation; but Kate Downing had certainly sounded odd. Grief, yes, and an understandable amount of reluctance to discuss details. But that abruptness, when she'd always been polite above all else; well, that was damn peculiar.

Rissman leaned back in his swivel chair and rubbed his forehead.

"Ben Cramer is dead." He said it to himself over and over. He guessed that he and Cramer were about the same age, and it shook his complacent acceptance of his own rich, full life. Cramer dead!

Well, he had certainly left his estate in good order. True to form. Rissman couldn't recall all the particulars, but he had been impressed with Cramer's finesse and attention to detail when the will was drawn up. Most men, if they bothered to make a will at all, left everything, the whole ball of wax, to their wives or "to be evenly divided" among their heirs. Evenly divided! Hah! Rissman shook his head as he rose from his chair and went to the bedroom to don his swimsuit. He had seen perfectly lovely people become snarling tigers as they fought to "evenly divide" the possessions of the deceased.

Cramer had certainly taken precautions against that fiasco. True, he had no family, but he had bequeathed donations to several persons and charities, and it was all spelled out in excruciating, under any other circumstances amusing, detail.

Rissman felt a twinge of alarm as he struggled into his swim trunks. Had they shrunk since last summer? Or had he really gained several pounds over the winter? He would have to start watching his diet, he told himself as he went out to the pool. Had Cramer gained weight? No, no, it was an accident, she'd said, but still, it wouldn't hurt to shed ten or fifteen pounds.

He stretched out in a deck chair and sipped on his drink. But the commotion of children in the pool, the alluring scent of his wife nearby, even the prospect of a long weekend—nothing could distract his thoughts from the image of Katherine Downing. He was picturing her, not at her desk, not ushering him into Cramer's office, not even alone at some hotel up in Wisconsin. No, he was anticipating the look that would spread across her face when she heard him read Benjamin Cramer's will. That moment alone, he decided, would make his trip back into the city tomorrow worthwhile.

He was imagining, first, her incredulity, and then her pleasure when she learned that Benjamin Cramer had left the bulk of his estate, well over two million dollars, to his able administrative assistant, Katherine Downing.

14

The Nightmare's Echo

·

Kate hung up the telephone in her room at the Farman and lay back on the bed. Milton Rissman was going to be a problem, she could tell already, but there wasn't much she could do about that now. She reached back and loosened the knot of hair, letting it fall away from her face as she rested her head on the pillow. There, that was better.

Her eyes still burned, and she closed them, not with any hope of sleeping, but because it suddenly required too much effort to try to keep them open. Her energy was depleted, spent in the turmoil of emotions she had never felt before, intensified beyond any previous experience.

Was it only this morning that she had stood in Aggie's study, filled with determination to control her own life? It had actually seemed possible then. She was going to talk to Mr. Cramer, get all the answers from him. Well, he had given her answers, hadn't he? He had given her the truth, ten years late, but the truth, nonetheless.

Deep inside her, at the very center of her being, in the place she had thought was dead at last, Kate felt a tiny stirring. Ten years late . . .

Aggie's words from the night before came back to her. "No typing test?" she had asked. And Kate remembered that brief interview, and how surprised she was when he offered her the job. She re-

183

membered the efficient woman who had shown her into Mr. Cramer's office, and the organized files she had left behind for Kate.

So he knew then, Kate thought, and the stirring sensation began to grow. He said it himself, in the ambulance this morning: He had to hire me. Because Jim made him? Yes, because Jim made him do it. I don't know why yet, but it makes sense.

He treated me decently, she told herself. More than fairly. She had trusted him, grown to depend on his approval, his guidance. . . . For ten years she had admired his integrity. She felt her heart begin to pound, coming back to life again.

And to think I was ashamed, she thought, to tell him about my father! My own father, who lived a good and honest life until he tried too hard to help his friends and ended up in disgrace.

It wasn't the money, she insisted. She had lived without it and she didn't need it. But her father's duplicity, whatever his motives, felt like a slap in her face, even after all this time had passed. If he had come to her and told her everything, she would still have loved him, stood by him and supported him in any way she could have. She still loved him. Nothing could cancel that. But she was still angry with him, too.

The sensation was spreading now. She felt her limbs coming back to life, surging with a tingling sensation.

Her thoughts came to Jim, at last, and now she felt ready to deal with them. There were questions she couldn't answer, but she suddenly knew what she felt, what this odd sensation was all about. It was anger, a rising tide of healthy, lifesaving anger, and the greater portion of it was directed at the man she had married. He had stripped her, she thought. She had given him love and passion and trust, the three most intimate things one human being could impart to another. She had held nothing back. If he had died, it would still have been a violation, but a crime of nature, not of human blame. But he was alive! She had given him her grief! For ten long, empty years she had looked over her shoulder, seeing him still there, and lived in a manner that she hoped would please him.

How ironic, she thought. I wouldn't let you die, Jim, and all that time you were still living! Isn't that a joke?

A tiny sob escaped her lips. She felt her fingers curling inward, making tight fists. How dare you! she raged against him silently. How dare you! She sucked in her breath, feeling the tears about to

184

start again, when there was a quiet knock at the door. She sat up, startled.

"Who is it?"

"Freddy Albers, ma'am. From the kitchen?"

The young man from last night. Kate swept her hair away from her face and got up.

"Yes?" He was standing there with a cloth-covered tray.

"I'm sorry to disturb you. Mr. Manchester thought you might like some supper. He said nothing heavy, so I brought you some soup—it's fresh vegetable tonight, real good, I made it myself—and a sandwich, ham on whole wheat. Does that sound good?"

Kate had to smile at him, he was so earnest. "What a nice thing for you to do. Here, put it on the table while I find my purse."

"Oh, no, ma'am, Mr. Manchester was real clear about that. This is on the house." He put the tray down and darted for the door.

"Thank you," Kate said lamely as the door closed.

She lifted the cloth, and there was also ice water, a soda of some sort, cookies, and a pot of coffee. She smiled at the coffee. Clark Manchester had not forgotten her.

Should she eat? Somehow it seemed sacrilegious, she thought, the way eating after funerals had always seemed wrong. At Jim's parents' house, after his memorial service, she had felt that way. But when she looked at her watch and saw that it was after six, she was suddenly hungry. She was alone; there was no one to watch or judge. And Clark Manchester had thought of her, sent this food to her. She sat down and began eating with gusto.

Jim's parents, she thought suddenly. Did they know? Had they been in on this charade, too? No, she didn't think so. Their grief had been as real, as bewildered as her own. She had lost touch with them over the past few years. She would have to find them, tell them. But tell them what? How could she explain that their son was alive? They would want to know the same thing she did: Why had he done it?

Was it me? she wondered. Did he not want to come back to me? And she thought of the mistakes she had made, the safe route of submission she had chosen at every turn. He might have wanted more from her, more spirit, more excitement. But she had given him what she was, a child of her parents and her upbringing and the times. What else could she have done?

Had she made similar mistakes with her father? She had readily accepted his perfect image and never hinted to him that her adoration depended not on his bank or his money, but on his character. And with Benjamin Cramer; had she been at fault there, too? She had maintained that stiff, wounded-widow image with him. She must have made it very hard for him to confide in her, to tell her anything unpleasant, let alone as shocking as the news that Jim was still alive.

And yet—she could hear Aggie's voice in her ear, cautioning her against carrying all the blame. She took a sip of Martha Lindstrom's good coffee. All right, so she had not been perfect. She should have done some things differently. She should have been stronger. Did that mean she couldn't start now? Was she going to live whatever life was left to her wallowing in remorse? If she saw her weaknesses, couldn't she change them?

Kate sat in the rocking chair, drinking her coffee, feeling its invigorating warmth. She had tonight to get through, and then the funeral, and the office to take care of. Then she would be free. And she suddenly knew exactly what she wanted to do first.

She left her room and started downstairs, eager now for her encounter with John Anthony McGavin. She knew that this newfound anger was a dangerous ally. She could not cling to it too long or it would consume her. But, for now, she was almost enjoying it. She would let it go, soon enough. She was not so stupid as to think she could use it forever.

She tapped on the door behind the counter that led to Clark Manchester's apartment. *Stupid* . . . Mr. Cramer had uttered that word this morning. Something about stupid edgers. What had he—

Manchester opened the door and ushered Kate into the room.

"Thanks for dinner," she said, and he beamed in reply. Oh, he was a gentle soul, she thought. I'd like to get to know him better.

Aggie Patterson was already there, seated on an old and comfortable couch. There were no windows in the sitting room; dim light filtered through the doorways leading to the bedroom and the bath. When Clark switched on a lamp in the corner of the room, Kate saw McGavin, dressed in slacks and a sport shirt. He looked smaller to her than ever, his tense, wiry figure perched in a low chair, leaning forward with his forearms resting on his knees. It was a defensive position, Kate thought. She sat down on the couch with Aggie, and

Clark took a chair near the door. He was there, she assumed, at the sheriff's request. McGavin had requested this meeting place, and it was fine with her. Aggie had come because Kate had invited her.

But they were bystanders, as far as Kate was concerned. This was McGavin's show. He knew things she wanted to know, and she had no intention of letting him leave this room until he had told her everything. And then she had a surprise or two for him, unless Aggie had already told him. She doubted that. Aggie had stepped back this morning, seeing Kate's newfound confidence. She would let Kate handle this in her own way.

Clark drew his chair into the circle of light and cleared his throat.

"Mrs. Downing, may I say how very sorry I am about Benjamin Cramer. I didn't even realize until a few minutes ago that I had met him and I—"

"You knew him, Clark?" Aggie said, surprised.

"I met him in the coffee shop, just a few days ago. We had a pleasant conversation about—um, about you, John Anthony, matter of fact. But I didn't know his name until I saw tonight's newspaper. His picture's on the front page. And I—I'm especially sorry that it had to happen up here. But I'd like you to know," he said to Kate, "that we'll do all we can to help. I spoke to Curt Owens this evening, at the funeral home. If you wish, he'll make arrangements for moving the—uh, for driving you and Mr. Cramer back to Chicago.

"But as far as we're concerned—" here he gestured to include Aggie—"we want you to know that you have a room in this hotel, or with Aggie, for as long as you want it. We hope you'll come back as soon as possible and stay with us awhile. You—you're going to need some friends, and I'd just like to make this as clear as I can: You have friends here."

He cleared his throat again, apparently embarrassed by his own little speech. Aggie nodded her head in agreement. John Anthony McGavin stared at the floor.

Kate hardly knew what to say. Were these people real? She was nearly a stranger to them, yet they were opening their homes and hearts to her as though they did this sort of thing every day. Who knows, she thought, perhaps they did.

When she spoke her voice was low, and she tried to keep it under control.

"Thank you, Mr. Manchester, Aggie. You've both been kinder to

187

me than I have any right to expect. But there are—details . . . things I have to attend to, at the office and—elsewhere. I'd appreciate your help in returning to Chicago tomorrow. I expect the lawyer to call me in the morning, after he's reviewed Mr. Cramer's will, and then we can—finalize those arrangements. If you'll have my bill ready—"

"There's no charge—"

"I insist." Kate's tone brooked no argument. "You are hardly responsible for any of this." Up to this point, Kate had studiously avoided including McGavin. Now she looked at him directly, her face hardening, and she gripped her hands in her lap.

"Sheriff McGavin, I'd like to tell you, without interruption, everything I know about this. Then you will fill in the gaps." He nodded, an assent she hardly required, and in a low, distinctly impersonal tone, Kate began reciting facts as if by rote, like a child reciting a memorized poem, the words of which had only the remotest connection to her own life.

"My husband and I met when we were both freshmen in college at Northwestern. We fell in love and were married that summer. It now appears that we did not wait long enough, because the man I thought I knew turned out to be someone quite different. When we were married both my parents were alive and my father was a banker—well-off, we thought—and he wanted Jim, my husband, to work for him after we finished college. I fully expected to work there, too, for a time, and then have children and grow old gracefully in a small town." A tinge of irony crept into her voice, but it was gone in the next instant.

"But soon after we were married both my parents died. We lost the bank, and suddenly we had no money and no safe, comfortable future. So we quit school. My husband went to work. I can see now that he began to change then—or perhaps he stopped pretending, I'm not sure which. Anyway, against my wishes, he enlisted in the Marine Corps. The day he left for his basic training in California was the last time I saw him."

Kate paused a moment, but when she sensed that Aggie was about to speak, she raised a hand. "Please, Aggie, I'm all right. Sheriff, I'd like to know if you met my husband in California."

Speaking for the first time, McGavin's voice was stronger than anyone in the room had expected.

"No, ma'am. We figured out later that I got there at about the time he left for Nam. We were assigned—"

"Later, please. Were you also an enlisted man?"

"Yes."

"Then perhaps you could tell me. Is it customary—or was it then—that is, did you have a chance to come home during your training, before you left for Vietnam?"

McGavin frowned, trying to remember. "I'm not sure. . . ."

"Kate, if I may?" Aggie made it a question, and Kate nodded. "That was nineteen sixty-seven, John Anthony, and you came home in March. I remember it because we had a terrible snowstorm, and the schools were closed the following Monday. You and Betsy came over and shoveled my walks."

"Right, I remember now—"

"Then, in your opinion, Sheriff, it's quite possible that my husband also had leave?"

"Well, it wouldn't have been in March—he enlisted before I did—but, yes—he should have had a week or two sometime before he shipped out."

"Thank you. He did not come back to Illinois, as far as I know. He certainly didn't come home. So I—I have to assume that he didn't wish to see me."

"Mrs. Downing, please—"

"Mr. Manchester, these things have to be said. I want to get this absolutely clear in my mind."

Aggie gave a small signal to Clark; Kate caught it and smiled. Aggie was trying to tell him to stay out of it.

"Of course, I did get letters," Kate continued. "And I believe he left California for Vietnam in November of nineteen sixty-six. It was before Christmas—at least he said—"

"That's right. He went over in November and I got there about six months later, in May."

"And you were with him the entire next year?"

"Yes."

"When was the last time you saw him?"

McGavin swallowed, and even in the dim light Kate could see beads of perspiration forming on his forehead. It was warm in the room, and stuffy, but Kate wasn't going to ask Clark Manchester to

189

do anything about it. She had no intention of making this easy for McGavin.

"Do you remember the last time you saw my husband, or don't you? It's a simple enough question."

"Yes, Mrs. Downing, I remember, but I'd like to explain—"

"I spent several hours yesterday asking you questions, Sheriff McGavin, and you declined to answer or explain anything. I think you can wait a few more minutes. When did you last see my husband?"

He sat silently for a long time, but at last he spoke, choosing his words very carefully.

"The last time I saw your husband, Mrs. Downing, was in May of sixty-eight, the day your husband left Vietnam."

The Sheriff, tight-lipped, was sweating profusely now, but Kate was relentless.

"You haven't seen him since?"

McGavin hesitated. "You want just an answer, no explanation?"

Kate nodded.

"No, I haven't seen him in ten years."

There was an odd emphasis to his words but Kate, satisfied, sat back on the sofa and returned to her recital of facts.

"That May, when Jim was due home, I was told that he had died in a plane crash. They said the plane went down at sea and it was impossible to recover the bodies, but that there was no doubt that there were no survivors. So I thought Jim was dead.

"It wasn't very long after that when a very lucky thing happened to me. I didn't realize until last night just how lucky it was." Kate glanced at Aggie. "A neighbor and friend of mine, Ted Young—by the way, does that name mean anything to you, Sheriff?"

It was a shot in the dark, and she knew it, but still . . .

McGavin shook his head. Kate paused a moment, giving him time to consider, but he said, "I never heard of the man, Mrs. Downing."

"Hmmm . . . Well, my neighbor heard about a fantastic job opening. It seemed a coincidence at the time. Benjamin Cramer needed a secretary and I desperately needed a better job, so I interviewed for it and I got it. Just like that, not even a typing test. I worked my head off and I kept that job for nearly ten years. In all that time Benjamin Cramer never mentioned my husband. He never indicated in any way that he knew Jim or had the slightest interest in him. I never thought this was odd. Mr. Cramer is—Mr. Cramer was a businessman, I was his assistant, and we seldom discussed anything other than business.

"There was one exception. Rodney Weaver. As far as I knew, Mr. Cramer's only dealings with Weaver were to rent a cottage from him every year, always for the first three weeks in May, and Mr. Cramer always had me make the reservation and send the check in advance. So I did that again, this past March.

"Now, Sheriff McGavin, I believe you know everything that has happened since then, except that Mr. Cramer spoke to me this morning, in the ambulance."

The look on McGavin's face showed that this was indeed a surprise to him. Kate, glancing at Clark, guessed correctly that Aggie had filled him in, but apparently neither of them had had an opportunity to tell McGavin.

"He spoke to you?" McGavin was clearly astonished. "He came to? What did he say?"

Kate had to wonder if his sudden eagerness came from his professional interest or an absurd hope of being absolved by her. She took a breath.

"First, I think you should know that the ambulance attendant also heard Mr. Cramer. I don't know his name, but I believe Dr. McCabe knows him. At any rate, he should be able to substantiate this." She was daring him to doubt what she was about to tell him.

McGavin nodded impatiently. "Please, what did he say?"

"He told me my husband is still alive, Sheriff McGavin."

She was watching him intently, and his reaction didn't surprise her at all. He looked relieved. That's right, she thought bitterly, you do know, don't you, but now you've been spared the ordeal of telling me yourself.

Aloud, she said, "You're not surprised, are you?"

McGavin admitted it. "I told you that the last time I *saw* your husband was the day he left Vietnam. That's true. But I knew he wasn't on the plane that crashed because I've *spoken* to him since then. He—he called me on the phone, right after I came home from Vietnam."

"Where was he?" Kate asked quickly. "Why did he—"

"He didn't say, and I didn't ask."

So I was right! Kate thought. He wasn't on that plane! It's not just

Mr. Cramer's wild ranting, it's true. Jim didn't die. She tried to pay attention to what McGavin was saying.

". . . haven't seen him, or even heard of him since then—until you came into my office yesterday morning.

"You have no idea where he might be?"

"I don't even know for sure if he's still alive. I suspect he is, but I can't prove it."

"Oh, he's alive, Sheriff." Kate's voice was bitter. "He's not only alive, he's been at Baker's Lake."

"What?" McGavin sat up again. Oh, he'd make a lousy poker player, Kate thought. His face was as easy to read as a child's. He hid nothing, and this time she could see that he was genuinely surprised.

"He was there, with our friend Rodney Weaver." She paused, trying to form the next words, and he helped her.

"Did Cramer say they shot him?" he asked quietly.

Kate nodded, pressing her lips together, fighting for self-control. "He—he tried to tell me everything, but he couldn't breathe very well and he was coughing. He was very weak. The stupid attendant kept trying to push me out of the way, but I was close to him, I practically had my ear over his mouth, and I heard what he said. He said the word *gun* very clearly, he may have said it twice. He said they were both there, Weaver and—and Jim. He said they thought he was dead, that they had killed him."

Kate was about to lose her grip on herself when she saw McGavin making a move to rise, and her anger came pouring back, rescuing her.

"Don't you dare leave this room!" She nearly shouted it, and he froze. "Your idiotic reports, or whatever you have to do, can wait! They can wait a few more precious minutes, damn you! You knew my husband was alive! You knew from the time I met you yesterday, and you didn't tell me! You've run out of time, Sheriff. I'll call the state police if I have to, or whoever exercises any authority over you, to keep you in this room. My—my husband killed Benjamin Cramer, and I want to know why! Not ten minutes from now, not tomorrow, not some convenient time for you. Now!"

Aggie sat forward and made a placating gesture toward Kate, but this time it was McGavin who stepped in.

"She's right, Miss Patterson. I do have reports to file, an APB to

192

get out, but they can wait. He's long gone by now; another hour or two won't make much difference." He was speaking quietly, in a reasonable tone, and Kate resented his composure when she was losing hers. But it had the desired effect: Aggie sat back, Clark stayed silent, and Kate began to catch her breath. "Is it all right," he asked Kate, "if I start way back at the beginning? I'm not stalling, I promise you, I just want to tell it in sequence. Can I do it that way?"

Oh, he's clever, Kate thought, substituting procedure for substance. But I'll get it out of him, the truth, if it takes all night.

She nodded, and he looked directly into her eyes. As far as Kate was concerned, they were still the only two people in the room, though she knew he was very much aware of Clark and Aggie. Their being there made it harder for him, but he plunged in anyway.

"I'd never been further from Derrington than Chicago, and there only once, on my senior-class trip. Then I flew out to San Diego for my boot camp, and six months later they sent me to Vietnam. I was scared, but I was excited, too. I was in great physical shape and the Marines had taught me how to survive. I was determined to come back alive. I wanted to finish college and come back here to the Farman, to work for Clark Manchester."

He glanced briefly at the hotel owner, but Kate's gaze never left McGavin's face.

"I thought I was prepared for that place. And physically, I was— except for the heat. When we landed in Da Nang, that heat was like a blowtorch. I can remember stepping off the plane and that torch blasted me in the face. I'd never felt anything like it before— haven't since.

"The next thing I noticed was the smell. I had a girl friend then— her name was Betsy—and she said she could still smell it on me when I came home and got off the bus. I—well, I won't describe it, I'm not sure I could, but that's what I remember about that first day, the heat and the smell.

"And one other thing—that night, my first night in Vietnam, I met your husband.

"They gave me a cot in a tent—this was still during the big buildup, and they were bringing in hundreds of Marines every day and putting up tents, huts, anything they could, as fast as they could. Everything about Da Nang looked temporary, then. They could put up a tin warehouse in less than a week.

"First thing I had to do was report to the office where I'd been assigned. It was a personnel office, and my job was to fill out leave papers and passes. It was boring, but it beat the hell out of carrying an M-16 into the bush.

"Well, I made up my mind, that very first day, that I was going to stay busy, I wasn't going to give myself one extra minute to sit around and think about all the things that could happen to me. We weren't in combat, you know, like you see in the movies. But we got mortar and rocket attacks almost every night. The Vietcong would send those things in from just outside the camp perimeter. You could hear a swishing sound first—it's hard to explain, it doesn't sound like anything else—but I learned fast. I had to. I heard that noise no matter how much other racket there was, and when I heard it I flew into the nearest bunker."

McGavin's eyes had left Kate's face and were staring behind her, into the wall, into the past, obviously remembering things he thought he had managed to forget. But her eyes were burning into him; her whole being was focused on his words.

"The only reason I mention all this is because that's how I met your husband. In the bunker, that very first night.

"It was late and real quiet. I was on my cot, not asleep, just trying to figure out how I was going to stand that heat and the smell for thirteen months.

"Suddenly the guy next to me jumps out of a dead sleep—I mean, that guy was snoring one second and the next he was three feet in the air and then I heard it, too. It was that swishing noise, and I followed him out of the flap of the tent and threw myself into the nearest bunker. I landed right on top of the first guy and he started yelling at me, and then a third guy landed on top of both of us. The third guy was Jaycee. . . ."

McGavin's voice faded into silence. Finally Kate said, "J.C.?" and McGavin jerked his attention to her.

"Jaycee Downing. Your husband."

"But my husband's name was Jim. Maybe—well, you must be thinking of the wrong man. . . ."

McGavin shook his head.

"I know his name was Jim. James Crawford Downing—"

194

"Yes, Crawford was his mother's maiden name, but—"

"Initials J.C. But he spelled it J-a-y-c-e-e. Nickname he used in boot camp. Also, I think he said his brother used to call him that."

"I never heard that nickname."

Was it someone else? For a moment hope rose in her heart.

"Mrs. Downing, do you happen to have a picture of your husband?"

"No, he didn't—wait a minute, I do. A wedding picture, in my billfold—wait, let me find it—here. It's not very good, it's so old—"

She held out her open billfold and McGavin came over and held it under the lamp. She read his face and felt the knot in her stomach tighten.

"That's him," he said. He looked at Kate. "I'm sorry, it's him. I'm sure of it."

Kate closed her billfold and put it back in her purse without speaking.

"Do you—do you want me to go on? We could do this later—"

"What happened in the bunker, Mr. McGavin?" Kate's voice was low, resigned. She had asked for this, hadn't she?

"Well—he was cool as you please," McGavin said, returning to his chair. "Here we were getting the daylights pounded out of us, and this other guy was yelling at me to get off his arm and I was just clamping my teeth together to keep 'em from chattering. And Jaycee—he pulls out a bottle of Chivas Regal Scotch and offers me a drink. I'd had one bottle of warm Tiger beer that night, and here he is with a whole bottle of the finest Scotch on earth.

"And he says—I can remember this like it was yesterday—he said, 'Have a drink?' like we were in somebody's living room for cocktails."

McGavin's voice, and the hint of awe that produced a twitch of a smile, told Kate he still admired that kind of courage.

"So you had a drink?" she asked impatiently. She was morbidly fascinated in spite of herself. Everything he was telling her had occurred after she had last seen her husband. She found herself hungry for every minute detail of his life after that.

"You bet I had a drink," McGavin said, grim once again, "more than one. And of course," he added, his voice disgusted, "I had to ask him where he got it. I was just making conversation. I mean, here was this guy, absolutely cool in the middle of a mortar attack, and in between blasts he's offering me a drink. He had this—well, a demeanor about him that demanded I act the same way.

"The other guy was hunkering in the bottom of the bunker, still swearing at me 'cause I'd jumped on his arm. He was scared out of his mind. So was I, but there was no sense in arguing with him, so I asked Jaycee, 'Where'd you get this?' He said he bought it with a stack of lumber."

"Lumber?" Kate echoed.

"That's just what *I* said." For a moment Kate resented the implied suggestion that she and McGavin had reacted identically, but he was continuing, "See, a new shipment of lumber had just come in. That stuff was like gold then, they'd been waiting for that shipment for months. Somehow—well, I know how, now, but anyway he—your husband—excuse me, Mrs. Downing, but you said you want to know everything—he swiped a pile of those boards and he sold it to another unit. They wanted it to build something, and they'd put in an order months before, but no lumber arrived. So, when they got an offer they took it, and they paid him with a case of Scotch. One of the men in their unit was a bartender at the officers' club. That's how they got the Scotch.

"And that's how Jaycee came to have a bottle of it in his hand when the first mortar came in. He'd been drinking with a buddy in a tent near mine, and he didn't stop to put it down, he just started running, and when he landed in the bunker, there was that Chivas Regal, still in his hand. I don't think he spilled a drop. That's called guts, Mrs. Downing. Keeping your cool under pressure." Again the admiring note had crept into his voice and Kate felt an odd, detached sort of pride in her husband. She brushed it aside, loathing her momentary lapse.

"Excuse my stupidity, but I'd like to be sure. That was illegal, wasn't it? That is, he stole the lumber to get the Scotch, which was also stolen?"

McGavin nodded. "Yes, ma'am, it was illegal. But—now please, I'm not excusing anything I did"—here he glanced quickly at Clark and Aggie—"there's no excusing any of it. But I want you to understand how it was over there.

"You think you're prepared, but there's just no way I know of you can really prepare a man for war. You teach him how to shoot a gun and how to follow orders and how to dive into a bunker. But how do

196

you teach him not to think about death? You know that every night you're going to be pounded with mortar and rockets, and along about five in the afternoon you see the sun getting lower and lower. And you just wish you could stop it, keep it from going down, because when it's gone it gets dark, and then the rockets come." He was talking faster now, and Kate could hear the panic he had felt, watching the sunset, unable to stop it.

"You could be doing everything right, just the way you were trained, not taking any chances at all. And then one night you just might not hear that swish soon enough. You might just be in the wrong place. It's all luck.

"And even though you know it's dangerous to think like that, you get scared.

"Well, it took exactly fifteen minutes in that bunker for me to make up my mind. I was going to come out of there alive no matter what.

"When you make a decision like that, the line between right and wrong gets hazy, in a hurry."

McGavin's voice had sunk lower and lower. Kate strained forward to hear.

"It sounds pathetic now, I know. . . . But I guess I sold out for a bottle of Scotch. No," he corrected himself, for now he was almost speaking to himself, as if he'd forgotten the others, "no, it was what that Scotch represented, it was the way Jaycee had found to live in that hell."

And as McGavin stared into space, picturing his old friend and the bottle of liquor, the others shared his nightmare vision, seeing things a decade ago as if they were right now in front of their faces.

Kate, especially, could picture her husband. His cool, vague letters had never described the searing heat, the stink and the sweat and the sinking sun, the rows of tin warehouses and canvas tents. He'd never mentioned the second sense of hearing that listened, even in sleep, for a swishing warning. Never before had she shivered at the terror of diving into a hole and huddling there while the ground shook and pieces of shrapnel flew in the air and a cracking explosion announced the destruction of a nearby warehouse.

At last, after all these years of thinking she'd understood, she was in the bunker with a brave and cocky Marine, awestruck at the

197

bottle of Scotch in his hand. Her whisper, a tremulous thread of compassion, reached across the room to John Anthony McGavin.

"I see."

It was all she could say. She and Clark and Aggie were like stone statues. They were immobilized by the memory of a night eleven years before, reincarnated for them at their own insistence.

When Aggie broke the silence, her voice sounded normal, but Kate saw her touching her eyes with a white, old-fashioned handkerchief.

"Clark, if we might have some iced tea?"

It took him a moment to answer.

"Hmmm? Tea?" He scratched his ear. "Hmmm, yes, certainly." He got up slowly, feeling every one of his seventy-two years in his leg muscles. He crossed the room to the door and opened it, spoke quietly to the desk clerk, and stood there waiting, his back turned to the others. Aggie reached up and turned on another lamp and the first thing she saw were the tears spilling down Kate's cheek. She reached across the sofa and patted her arm.

"I never knew, either, Kate," and Kate nodded and sniffed as she reached into her purse for a tissue. Neither of them dared look at McGavin, but his face would have told them nothing. Kate sensed, though, that the worst was still to come. That blank expression, she thought, was his shield against feeling too much.

Clark took a tray from Barry, closed the door, and distributed the glasses. McGavin drained his glass almost immediately and plunged ahead.

"That's how it started. Just a bottle of Scotch. After a while the rockets stopped and we climbed out of the bunker, but before I went back to my tent I'd agreed to look up your husband the next day. He worked out near the airfield, at a disbursing office. I'd had to stop in there earlier, right after I got off the plane, so I knew where it was.

"That bottle just may've kept me alive. Here I was all set to spend thirteen months chained to a desk, filling out forms till I either went blind or nuts. Then I meet your husband, Jaycee, and he'd found a better way to live. So I went to see him the next day and he said there was a new shipment in, some tools, hammers and saws, that kind of stuff, and he says he's got a buyer. I said, what do we get in return? and in two words, that line was gone. In two words, there

198

was no right or wrong. I said, 'Jaycee, what do we get for these tools?' He said, 'Fresh eggs.'

"Fresh eggs," he repeated, sensing Kate's skepticism. "They served up warm Kool-Aid and powdered eggs every morning, and here's a guy telling me if I swipe a few tools I can eat fresh eggs. So I got the tools, and that night we ate real eggs. Don't ask me where he got them, they were rarer than Scotch or lumber, but he got them, off and on, the rest of the time we were there.

"After that night it got to be a game. I know how that sounds now, here in this nice, comfortable room, with clean glasses and sugar and fresh lemon in our tea. But over there—well, it was a way to survive. If we could get eggs and liquor, then maybe we could get clean blankets, and when we got those everybody else in our unit wanted them, so we went into business. There were four of us at first, me and Jaycee and two other guys, but one of them volunteered to ride shotgun on a truck to Dong Ha and he got wasted so then there were just the three of us, Jaycee and me and another guy named Deck. He was from Philadelphia. But Jaycee was the brains of the operation. I'm not *blaming* him, you understand, or trying to make my part in it seem less than it was. But Jaycee was the thinker, the dreamer, I guess you could say, and he had big dreams."

McGavin stopped abruptly, and Kate thought he was finished, that he'd told her all he meant to tell. Then she saw him working his lips, biting them, and she knew he was only searching for a way to go on. Her voice was as gentle as she could make it.

"Please, whatever it is, I want to know. All of it."

He searched her face. "All right. Now, I don't expect you to believe this, Mrs. Downing, but it's the truth. I swear to God, it's the truth. Until you walked into the office yesterday, I never knew Jaycee was married."

His expectation had been correct. Kate stared at him in total disbelief.

"Mrs. Downing, it wasn't just me. I don't think anyone else knew he was married, either. He—he never talked about himself or his past, his family—once he told me he had a brother who had died, but that was all. I—well, I just thought he was single. So did everybody else."

Kate found her voice at last, and she flung away his assertion with her questions. "But you were friends, weren't you? You said you were together the whole time, a year! Why wouldn't he tell you? Besides, I wrote him almost every day, surely you saw the letters—"

"Sure I did. I razzed him about those letters all the time. He'd never show them to anyone, not even me. He said . . ." McGavin looked away; Kate had to pull it out of him.

"He said what?"

"Well—I—well, he told us those letters were—from a cousin, a cousin of his in Illinois, some kid who—well, he said she thought she was doing her bit for the war by writing to him every day. To tell you the truth, some of us thought she was a weirdo, but we never said that to Jaycee. He wasn't a man you wanted to argue with. Oh—I didn't mean that—"

"Of course you did," Kate said, disgusted. "That's a fair description of him. But I don't understand—why wouldn't he want anyone to know he was married?"

McGavin was ready with his answer. He straightened up in his chair. "At the time, I wasn't suspicious. I mean, he had this weird cousin, or we thought so, anyway, but it never occurred to me that he was married. Now, when I look back on it, I can see what he was thinking, or I can guess.

"I said Jaycee was a dreamer, and in some ways, I was, too. We'd talk about after Nam, what we wanted to do. Mostly I talked about Derrington, and Mr. Manchester here, the hotel and everything. But sometimes we'd dream up crazy plans, about how easy it'd be to just fade into the tangle of paperwork and red tape over there, and go into business together in some exotic place, like Hong Kong or Bangkok or Singapore. For me it was a joke, something to talk about besides the monsoons or the VC—you know, we'd have a few drinks and start weaving those crazy dreams, but I never took them seriously. But Jaycee—"

"Jim didn't want to come back." It was a flat statement, drilling into him with precision and persistence.

"Well, he had these plans, you see?" Kate thought McGavin was softening the truth as much as he could. "He—well, he got caught up in those games and the dreams and he started to think that they were real, that life was one adventure after another, that the whole world was ripe for the picking. There he was, outwitting the whole military system, bending their rules to suit himself, challenging the

200

odds. . . . It was a heady experience to pull the stunts we did and get away with them. I tell you—well, I was just a runner, I never had the brains to work out that system in the first place or to keep it going, but Jaycee was smart, he was thinking all the time, figuring the odds, always looking for bigger deals. That was his life. I don't think he could have come back and gone to an office every day. Not after the way he lived over there."

Kate nodded in acknowledgment of that line of reasoning. To her own surprise, it actually made sense. Was she going mad?

She looked at Aggie. Did this make sense to her, too?

"It sounds like psychosis," Aggie said quietly. "When the real world isn't enough, replace it with a fantasy. Finally the fantasy becomes the only reality."

"But—this fantasy—do you think he intended—from the beginning—"

"I don't know when he decided not to come back—but I'd guess he was thinking about it, at least, when he first got there. Then—well, there's one more part, Mrs. Downing. At the end, he didn't feel he had a choice."

"Why not?" Kate lifted her chin, readying herself for another blow.

"Like I said before, I think he was playing with the notion of just fading away. When his tour was up, he was going to stay in Southeast Asia. There were a lot of—opportunities for a guy like Jaycee."

"None of them legal, I suppose?"

McGavin ignored her comment.

"Then a terrible thing happened. It was only a week or two before he was supposed to leave. He—well, he was arrested for selling grass. After everything else we'd done, it was ironic that he'd get caught for that. In a way it was nothing, compared to some of the other deals."

McGavin paused a moment and looked at Aggie.

"Miss Patterson, I know it doesn't make a whit of difference, but I didn't have any part of that drug deal. In fact," and he looked back at Kate, sparing Aggie the necessity of a response, "I didn't even know Jaycee was into that kind of thing. We drank a lot, but we never smoked grass or used any other drug.

"Well, anyway, he got caught. He went to the brig. And his lawyer was talking about a five-year prison sentence."

"Five years!" Kate was astounded. "Why, that's ridiculous! For one marijuana sale?"

"Mrs. Downing, this is nineteen seventy-eight. That was nineteen sixty-eight. Ten years ago. There were two drugs coming into Da Nang then, grass and heroin, and in the eyes of the Marine Corps there wasn't much difference. They just didn't tolerate it, not any of it, and they meant to punish anybody they caught with it, especially the sellers."

"All right, all right, I believe you," Kate said, impatient again. "He was in the—brig? Then what happened?"

"Well, a few days after he was arrested, one of the brig guards going off duty came by my tent and told me Jaycee wanted to see me. So I went over there before I went to work. Deck was leaving as I went in, and he was laughing. I didn't see anything funny about Jaycee being arrested, but Deck said something like, 'Just wait and see what Jaycee's cooked up this time!' So I figured he'd found a way to beat the rap.

"Well, he had, but he needed my help. He said he wanted a simple favor and would I help him out?

"Now, here's a guy who's kept me going through twelve of the worst months of my life. I'm gonna turn him down? No way.

"He wanted two things. One of them I understood right away. He wanted me to get some leave papers for him from the personnel office where I worked, for an R and R in Bangkok. He wanted them dated that day. He asked would I type out a set of orders, get the right signatures okaying them, and give them to Deck? And I—well, I did it.

"The other thing he wanted I never did understand. In the disbursing office there were two logbooks he wanted. They were old pay records nobody cared about anymore, but he wanted them. So I went over there at lunchtime and hid in the head—excuse me, in the men's room—until all the clerks left on their lunch hour, and then I found the logbooks. I hid in the men's room again until the place filled up after lunch and they were real busy. Then I just put those stupid ledgers inside my uniform shirt and walked—"

"Wait a minute," Kate interrupted. "What did you call them? What were they?"

"They were pay records," McGavin repeated. "You know, accounting ledgers they—"

"Ledgers!" Kate exclaimed. "Not edgers, ledgers! Mr. Cramer said something about stupid edgers, and it didn't make any sense. He meant ledgers! He knew about those books!"

McGavin looked puzzled. "Maybe so," he said slowly, "but I don't see how they could have had anything to do with Benjamin Cramer, or even Jaycee, for that matter. They were just old records, accounts that were closed out before Jaycee even got there. But—but what matters here is, they were the property of the Marine Corps and I—I stole them."

Kate had been struck with a glimmer of understanding at the mention of the ledgers. They were the connection, she sensed, the link she had been looking for that would explain some of the mystery. But at the sound of McGavin's voice, she glanced at Clark and Aggie and saw that one mystery, at least, was solved. They had not known until now about this incident, and the look on McGavin's face, his utter misery, explained why he had withdrawn from them so many years ago. Aggie had thought he'd done nothing to be ashamed of, but he had, and it had nothing to do with the heat of battle. It was not so easily dismissed from his conscience.

McGavin looked down at the floor. "So . . . That afternoon I went over to the airfield and found Deck. I gave him the R and R papers and the ledgers. I didn't stick around to ask him any questions. I didn't want to know what Jaycee was going to do, but of course I guessed part of it.

"Late that afternoon, they were sending Jaycee to Okinawa. There was a brig there, where he'd wait for his court-martial. And his—his plane took off, the one he was supposed to be on.

"But the next day we heard that it had crashed at sea and everybody on it had been killed. So everybody thought Jaycee was dead. . . . Everyone but Deck and me. I avoided Deck from then on. I didn't want anything to do with him. . . . I almost made it, too," he said wistfully, "until my last night there." His voice became hard again, and Kate could hear his self-hatred in every word.

"We were having a party. A lot of guys in my unit were going home the next day, and we were celebrating. Deck showed up. I tried to ignore him, but he was drunk and loud and he kept saying he had to talk to me, and some of the other guys started looking at me suspiciously. Here Deck and I had been good friends, and now I wouldn't have anything to do with him. So, to get him out of there, I went outside with him.

"He said he had a message for me. I said I didn't want any messages. He said, oh, it was a short one: Jaycee sends his regards.

"I said something brilliant, like 'Bully for him,' and turned around to go back into the tent, and Deck said, he was whining, that he deserved some of the credit, too, it wasn't fair for me to think I'd done it on my own.

"Credit! God, how warped can you get? I turned around and just stared at him, and he said something like, 'I'm the one who fixed the plane, you know, you couldn't have done that, you're not smart enough.'

"And I said, 'No, I'm not very smart,' and I started to turn away again, but I wasn't fast enough. I heard what he said then, and I've wished to God ever since that I'd never left that tent with him. He said his timing had been perfect, he'd adjusted the fuel gauges just right and put just enough fuel in that plane to get it out over open sea. He was laughing, and I just kept walking away from him, but I still heard what he said, and I can still hear him laughing."

For the first time, Clark spoke up. "John Anthony, you mean that boy purposely sabotaged that airplane?"

McGavin winced. "That's exactly what I mean. Deck was an airplane mechanic. He knew how to do it. He set the gauges to read full, and then he put in a quarter of the fuel, or however much he figured would get it off the ground and out in the middle of the South China Sea. No place to make an emergency landing, nothing out there but water, and with the fuel gauges still reading three-quarters full, the pilot wouldn't even know what the problem was.

"Not counting Jaycee, because of course he wasn't even on the plane, there were sixteen men, and every one of them died." McGavin was still talking to the floor. He rubbed his eyes, and Kate began to wish she hadn't wolfed down that big ham sandwich. Her stomach was churning.

"John Anthony, what about the guards?" Clark asked quietly. "Surely they didn't just open his cell and tell him to get himself over to the airfield and catch a flight to Okinawa? He was a prisoner. Wouldn't they have escorted him, made sure he got on the right plane?"

"I thought about that a lot," McGavin answered, not looking up, "and I think I know what he did. Half the Marines in Da Nang owed Jaycee a favor. He had a talent for making people feel that way, even when he got the best end of the deal, which he always did."

That was true, Kate realized, surprised. She remembered how she had tried to keep him from enlisting, and how she had somehow ended up feeling guilty about it. She had spent the next two years atoning for that guilt in her letters to him.

"And believe me," McGavin was saying with conviction, "if he'd been selling drugs for a year and a half, he had the money to pay for those favors. He probably even concocted a story for those guards to tell the authorities. He couldn't tell them the plane was going to crash, that they'd be dead in a few hours and never have to explain anything. So he probably said they could tell everyone he'd bailed out of the plane before anybody could stop him, and short of jumping out after him, there was nothing they could do. Perfect alibi for them, and perfect for him, too. It'd look like he committed suicide rather than go to prison.

"And don't think for a minute that the MPs were above a bribe. They were kids, like we were, and it was a war. Everybody I know sold out over there, one time or another.

"So the MPs got on the plane without him. There were sixteen of them, mostly boys, really—there probably wasn't a guy over twenty-five—they all got on the plane. But not Jaycee. He caught another flight—no problem, I had written his R and R orders myself—" Kate heard his voice catch on a sobbing gasp before he went on. "Jaycee just flew to Bangkok and disappeared."

McGavin had his head in his hands, and his sobs were silent ones now, but Kate could see his shoulders shaking. In that moment she felt her hatred for him slipping away. She shed it like a useless layer of skin; she not only didn't need it anymore, it was an encumbrance. She supposed she should have been more outraged than ever, but she was learning, quickly, how to direct her anger.

"You didn't know," she said, hoping desperately that she was right, "when you gave him those R and R papers that anyone was going to die because of them."

She waited a long time for his answer, and she knew it was because he was searching his memory, his soul, for the truth. "I knew," he said finally, "that I was helping a prisoner escape. I knew he had kept me from losing my mind, maybe even my life, in that place, and that I owed him for that. I didn't let myself think any further than that. I got him the papers, and I knew he would use them to go to Bangkok instead of the brig in Okinawa."

"But who fixed the plane?" It was Clark now, his tone reasonable.

"Deck."

"His own idea, do you think?" Kate's anger was beginning to show.

"Jaycee's," McGavin said quietly. "I'm sure of that. Deck and I did what we were told. Jaycee was the one with the ideas."

"Who bribed the guards?" Aggie chimed in.

"We did it!" McGavin said loudly, finally looking up to face them. "The three of us, we killed those men!"

"My husband did it," Kate said, because she knew neither Clark nor Aggie could say it. "He was responsible." She felt cold inside, her senses feeding on the anger. "He killed sixteen people," she said, astonished, "and he got away with it."

"There was nothing Jaycee couldn't get away with," McGavin said sadly. "He'd had two years of practice over there—"

"And many more before that," Kate said shortly.

"Do you want to hear the rest of it?" McGavin looked at Kate, and now she almost wished she could stop this thing, because she could see what the telling of it was costing him, but she had to know all of it. She felt so foolish, so naive, for having been so gullible. She had believed the Marine Corps, never questioned their information. She had accepted Benjamin Cramer and his job offer at face value. For ten years she had been a puppet, dancing aimlessly at the flick of someone else's fingers, and now she was on the verge of cutting those strings. She had to go on.

"Just tell it," she said to McGavin. "If you can."

He searched her face for a moment, glanced at Aggie and Clark, then swallowed hard.

"All right. I—I came home. I actually lived through that hell and came home alive. I went to spend some time with my mother while I tried to decide what to do. And one night I got a phone call. It was two, three o'clock in the morning, and guess who it was. My old friend, Jaycee. He wanted one last favor. I said no. He said it wasn't illegal, he just wanted me to help a friend of his. The friend's name was Benjamin Cramer."

Kate's eyes widened in astonishment. "Benjamin Cramer was a friend of Jim's?"

"Mrs. Downing, I have no idea. All I know is that Jaycee said he was a friend. They could've been bosom buddies or never met each other. All I know is what Jaycee told me. He said Cramer needed a place in the woods, a cabin he could rent for a few weeks every year, and did I know of such a place?

"Well, I didn't, and I told him so, but—he kept pushing. He reminded me of all the times in Nam—see, I owed him, like everybody else did. I still said no.

"Finally he gave up on that approach. He told me there were ways of anonymously informing the military authorities about all those deals we'd pulled. Of course that would incriminate him, too, but he was officially dead. I was a sitting duck. If I didn't want to answer for all the charges that would be brought against me, I'd just have to help him this one last time.

"So—I agreed. He gave me Cramer's telephone number in Chicago, and said I should call Cramer when I had something lined up."

Without looking up, McGavin added, "That was the last time, Mrs. Downing, that I ever spoke to or heard from your husband." He paused a moment, then cleared his throat.

"I made a few telephone calls the next day—nobody in Derrington, everybody knew me here, but I talked to a few real estate agents up in Eagle Hill. When I called Rodney Weaver he said he had just the place. I gave him Cramer's number, but I never told him who I was.

"I don't have any idea how Cramer figured out the connection. I never even met him. But—but somehow, he must have known about me and he put my name on that postcard he sent to you. And God knows why, but he must have trusted me enough to believe I'd help you."

Clark coughed and squirmed in his chair. "John Anthony, I believe I can explain that—or part of it, anyway. When Mr. Cramer came into the Evergreen Room last week, we talked about you. He was very complimentary about our town, how clean it was, how well-run it seemed to be, low crime rate, all that sort of thing. And I naturally said the last part, the crime rate, was due to you, and he asked about you, very politely, and you know me, John Anthony, I'm so darned proud of you and too fond of the sound of my own voice, and—well, I s'pose I told him everything he wanted to know about you. . . . I can't bear to think I'm responsible—"

"You're not!" Aggie and McGavin spoke together.

"Mr. Manchester, please, don't make this harder for me." The sheriff sounded almost desperate. "Nothing was decided by your conversation with him last week. He's had ten years to find out about me, and I'm sure his decision to trust me wasn't based only on a few words from you. Now, please—let me finish this."

Now McGavin's voice was so low that the others leaned closer to catch his words.

"The only person I ever talked to about any of this was Harry Ragsdale. He was still the county sheriff back then, and he was an old friend of my dad's. You remember, Clark, he was a vet, saw a lot of action in the Pacific. He picked up on me right away, saw something was wrong, and he wormed it out of me.

"And he—well, he didn't seem to think it was all so bad; he found a million excuses for what I did. And he came up with an idea. He said if I really wanted to make up for it, I could do it by coming to work for him. He said he'd teach me everything he knew and I could work the other side, enforcing the law. So that's what I've been trying to do, but—but nothing can erase what I did. I—I've cheated every person in this town, and—and just as soon as I wrap up this investigation, I'm going to resign.

"This afternoon I called the Naval Investigative Service down at Great Lakes. I have an appointment next Tuesday, and I'm going to tell them everything. I guess the statute of limitations applies here and they aren't going to lock me up for swiping some old pay records and not reporting that I knew Jaycee didn't die in that plane crash. But I mean to set the record straight, anyway."

He stopped and, in the silence, Kate glanced over at Clark and Aggie and knew that they, too, felt it, this bond of sorrow. They had heard the nightmare's echo and, like the dreamer who wakes but still remembers, they knew that sleep would not come easily that night.

Kate could not take her eyes from the bent head and slumped figure of McGavin, crouched in shadow in a corner of the room. She had studied him closely yesterday, and listened to him tonight, hearing things he'd been too decent to say as well as the words he'd spoken aloud. She had seen him try to maintain his objectivity as an officer of the law. He had kept his professional poise while she had fallen apart. He had tried to spare her the pain of what he knew, and when he could no longer do that, he had somehow managed the trick of softening the facts without distorting them. He was an extraordinary man, and it occurred to her to wonder how in the world he and Jim had ever been friends. They were as different as any two people she had ever known. John Anthony McGavin was far from perfect, but Kate was beginning to understand the wisdom of Aggie's words. "Nothing is perfect," she had said last night, and Kate could see now that it was dangerous to believe otherwise. She had let herself be consumed by that falsehood, demanding perfection from her father, her husband, her boss, and, worst, herself.

She felt an overwhelming sadness settle on her. It didn't crush her—nothing, she swore, would ever crush her again—but, looking at McGavin, she wanted to tell him how she felt, to make things better for him. And she would, but not tonight. Here in this room with her new and, oddly enough, she felt, her most loyal friends, she sat in silent rapport. She was still hearing the nightmare's echo, and its reverberations filled her with resolve. She was not defeated, not yet. There were actions she could take now that she knew the truth, and as soon as Benjamin Cramer was buried, she would begin.

15

The Will of Benjamin Cramer

■

When Milton Rissman telephoned Kate on Saturday morning, she had already been up for hours. Dressed, with suitcases packed, she was sitting on the edge of the bed in her room at the Farman, staring vacantly out of the window. In the street below, there was a minor traffic jam as the tourists poured into town. Some of the local residents had compounded the problem by stringing a huge, colorful banner from one side of the street to the other. WELCOME TO DERRINGTON DAYS, it proclaimed, and below that, HAPPY MEMORIAL DAY.

Aggie, the night before, had announced that she was accompanying Kate to Chicago.

"Do you think I'm going to let you go through all that alone?"

"I've done it before, Aggie." Kate paused on the landing on the way up to her room.

"I don't care." Aggie smiled sweetly. "Call me after you've heard from the lawyer. Good night." And she was gone before Kate could offer any further objections.

As it turned out, Kate would not have been alone. Milton Rissman had matters well in hand. By the time he called Kate he had contacted a mortuary, located a cemetery where Benjamin Cramer owned a burial plot, and scheduled a service for two-thirty Sunday afternoon.

"A service? Is that really necessary?"

"Yes, it is." He had made up his mind about this. "It is necessary."

Kate only wanted to be done with it, all of it. How could Mr. Cramer have lied to her? she kept asking herself. How could he have pretended, all those years, that he did not know her husband still lived? And how could she appear at his funeral, feeling the way she did?

And yet—Rissman was right. Benjamin Cramer had been an important businessman in Chicago. There had to be a funeral, and it would cause even more questions if she did not attend it.

"Very well," she said, reluctantly. "Meet us at the mortuary, then—"

"Us?"

"I'm bringing a friend."

"Good. Very good. How soon can you get here?"

"No, I meant tomorrow, for the—"

"Nonsense. How long does the drive down here take?"

Kate knew it was useless to argue. She told him when they would be there, then called Aggie, and soon they were on the road, riding in the front of the hearse with Curt Owens. Kate thought it was the longest trip of her life.

When they reached Chicago and found the mortuary, Rissman was there, and he and Aggie were suddenly co-captains of the team, making suggestions that Kate dazedly approved.

Rissman dropped them off at the office on La Salle Street at five o'clock. The financial district was virtually deserted, but Aggie was fascinated anyway. In her many visits to Chicago, this was a section she had never explored, and she was brimming with questions.

"Some other time, Aggie, do you mind?" Kate asked as kindly as she could.

"Right. Let's tend to business," Aggie replied with a salute. She was trying to lighten the mood, but Kate remained unreachable.

They spent only a few minutes in the office, just long enough for Kate to leave written instructions for Janice. On their way out, Kate grabbed the suit jacket she had left behind on Wednesday, and it jarred her to remember that it had been only three days ago. Then they were on the train, and then in a taxi for the short ride to Kate's house.

Kate led the way in the front door, and felt a sudden, totally

211

unanticipated wave of revulsion, for her house and much that was in it. Aggie took over in the kitchen and managed to produce a decent meal that neither of them ate.

Kate grew increasingly irritable, but it wasn't until the next morning that she admitted, out loud and to herself, that she she didn't want to live in the house any longer.

"Kate, you've done wonderful things—the drapes, the wallpaper. How long have you lived here?"

Kate looked up from her coffee; and the words that came out of her mouth surprised her.

"I hate this house," she said slowly.

"Oh, come now, it's perfectly—"

"Awful," Kate interrupted. "Do you know what, Aggie? Everything about this house is a joke. It was supposed to be very special. We made the down payment with three thousand dollars my Aunt Sarah left me when she died. It was every penny we had, but it was the least foolish of all the crazy ideas Jim had for spending that money. I thought we should use it for school, but Jim wanted to invest it in some preposterous land scheme down in Florida or take a trip around the world. The house was a compromise. . . . At least it turned out to be a fair investment."

"I should think so," Aggie said, wondering where all this was leading.

"Less than a year after we bought it, Jim left for boot camp. He never came back. But the place is full of him." Kate rose and moved restlessly about the kitchen. "We planted that maple tree," she said, gesturing vaguely out of the front window, "and he built these shelves. He pounded nails in the walls to hang the pictures and—"

"Well, of course he did." Aggie kept her tone very calm.

"I hate it. Everywhere I look, he's here, even after all these years."

"Kate, come home with me tonight."

"Oh, I can't—"

"Why not? I'm dreading that bus ride, and you haven't a thing to hold you here. You said your exams are over?"

"Yes, but the office—"

"Why do you think I asked Mr. Rissman to drop us off down there? You've taken care of everything. The typists can hold down the fort for a few more days."

212

"Yes, but our clients will be calling—"

"With all sorts of nosy questions. The typists only know he had an accident. It will be easier for them to handle those calls. Come home with me."

Kate had stopped roaming and was leaning wearily against the refrigerator. "You're a bossy woman."

"Yes, I am."

"You don't take no for an answer."

"Not very often."

They were both beginning to smile.

"All right, boss, on one condition. I'll drive. We can go in my car. I don't like the bus any more than you do."

"Agreed." Aggie cleared the coffee cups off the table. "Now, then, Mr. Rissman will be here soon. Let's get dressed."

There were 214 people at the funeral. Kate was astonished. How had they found out so soon?

"I called the newspapers," Rissman told her later, and she was furious at his audacity.

She knew many of them. They were clients, and as a distraction from the hideous farce of some minister (also Rissman's doing) spouting praise for a man he'd never met, she spent the time trying to assess the total of stocks and properties owned by the gathered mourners. Her feelings about Cramer were in turmoil, and it pleased her to put her brain to more efficient use. She would have time to mourn him, if it ever came to that.

When the service was over, Rissman drove them back to Kate's house.

"You've been very kind," Aggie said as he opened the car door for her. "Won't you come in for coffee?"

"Thank you, Miss Patterson, I will," he said, to Kate's annoyance. He brought his briefcase in with him and he and Kate sat in silence as Aggie prepared the coffee. He made several attempts at conversation, but found it impossible to carry on a monologue.

"Here we are." Aggie came in with a tray. "Cream and sugar?"

Kate shook her head and watched silently as Rissman made a small production of spooning sugar into his cup and stirring it. He sipped it, nodded appreciatively in Aggie's direction, then said tentatively, "Miss Patterson, I wonder if I might have a few minutes alone with Mrs. Downing?"

"Certainly." Aggie rose from her chair.

"Why?" Kate asked abruptly. She knew she was behaving worse than a child would, all this frowning and pouting. She was being downright rude, and it was so unlike her. Yet she couldn't help herself.

He made his tone as reasonable as possible. "Mr. Cramer left a will, as I told you. . . ."

"Surely that can wait?"

"I'd rather not. When do you plan to return to Chicago?"

"I don't know," Kate answered honestly.

"Yes, well, the terms of the will directly concern you."

"Is that so. . . ." Kate said slowly.

"I'm going out to take a look at your garden." Aggie started to leave the room.

"No, Aggie, please. I want you to stay. Mr. Rissman, I have nothing to keep from Miss Patterson. So if you don't object?"

"Of course not," he said easily. He put his coffee cup on a table and, opening his briefcase, drew out a sheaf of papers as Aggie returned to her chair. He put on his wire-rimmed glasses, thumbed through the papers, and cleared his throat. He looked up at Kate, who was silently screaming at him to stop the ceremony and say his piece.

"Benjamin Cramer has modified his will several times, but the last time was only two or three months ago. As far as I know, and as indicated by the will, he had no living relatives."

Rissman paused, evidently awaiting a confirmation, but Kate said nothing.

"Of course," Rissman continued, "long-lost relatives have a way of coming out of the woodwork for estates like this one, but Mr. Cramer didn't leave them many loopholes to crawl through." He permitted himself a small smile, but Kate's unchanging expression erased it.

"As I said, he recently updated the will. He wanted to include a complete list of all his property and holdings. He did this on a regular basis. I won't read the entire list to you right now—unless you want me to? It's quite lengthy—no, all right, then. Now, according to his own and, I suspect, highly accurate estimation, Mr. Cramer's estate is worth approximately two million seven hundred thousand dollars."

214

Kate's eyes widened in astonishment. I had no idea! she thought.

"This figure, I might add, is what he estimated the heirs would receive. It is an after-taxes figure."

Kate's eyes grew wider still. Rissman permitted himself a tiny smile.

"He has bequeathed," he continued, obviously enjoying himself, "somewhere in the neighborhood of six hundred thousand dollars to various charities, universities, et cetera, et cetera, and I must say some of them show a very wide range of interests on his part—and a bit of eccentricity, if you'll pardon me for saying so. I wonder, Mrs. Downing, do you happen to know where Mr. Cramer was from? I don't believe he was a local—"

"I have no idea," Kate said flatly.

"Hmmm, well, among his donations is a sizable one to the University of Minnesota, another to Northwestern, and a third—"

"Excuse me. You said Northwestern?"

"Um, let's see, yes, that's right. It's a scholarship endowment to the business department."

"I see." Kate kept her voice noncommittal, but she couldn't help being curious. That was her school, the one she'd had to drop out of when her father died, and the one she had returned to after so many years. Was it possible there was a connection?

". . . University, as well. There is also a sizable bequest to one Penelope Withers, last-known address, Bensenville, Minnesota. Ever hear of her?"

Kate shook her head.

"Yes, well, the remaining sum includes his condominium near Lake Michigan, his furniture, books, rugs, automobile, stocks and bonds, cash and savings accounts, some vineyard acreage in New York State, and part ownership in his office building on La Salle Street. Their total value comes to just over two million dollars. . . . Not bad for a man who never saw his fortieth birthday."

Rissman looked up from his papers, removed his glasses, and smiled at Benjamin Cramer's secretary.

"This sum, Mrs. Downing, Benjamin Cramer has bequeathed to you. Along with some very sound advice on how to pay the taxes."

Kate gasped out loud. She saw Rissman grinning like the Cheshire cat, and she hated herself for reacting in precisely the way he had obviously expected her to. Benjamin Cramer had said he loved her, but it had never once occurred to her that he would do any-thing like this. She covered her mouth with her hand, suddenly feeling desperate, trapped.

"I don't want it," she cried, "not a single penny!"

She squirmed around on the sofa and looked out the window into her backyard, fist pressed against her lips, but she was not seeing the yard at all. Her vision was crowded with the faces of the three men she had loved: her father, her husband, and her boss. In a puzzling but somehow logical way, she could not seem to separate those three faces, from one another or from the money they had worshiped. She wanted none of that. Even more, she refused to allow Benjamin Cramer to control her life from his grave as easily as he had controlled it from his desk at the office.

In a moment of yearning so intense that she almost winced, Kate would have given anything for her mother to be here, still alive, to help her through this time.

"Mr. Rissman, excuse me." It was Aggie, far abler than Kate's mother ever would have been, if Kate had only known, to take charge at such a moment.

"I know this matter is none of my affair. But Mrs. Downing, as I'm sure you can understand, is under a great strain. It was she who found Mr. Cramer in his cabin, and since then she has literally had not a moment's peace. I intend to see that she gets nothing except that, when she comes home with me."

Aggie paused briefly, but when he didn't take the hint, she said, "I'll give you my address and telephone number. If something par-ticularly urgent comes up, you may call."

Aggie stood up and gestured the bewildered Rissman toward the front door.

"Are you aware of anything in Mr. Cramer's estate that requires her immediate attention?"

Rissman, trying to stuff his papers back into his briefcase, shook his head. "No, there's nothing at the moment, but Mr. Cramer did leave something else—"

He found it at last as they reached the front door. It was a long white business envelope, and he handed it reluctantly to Aggie. "He brought this envelope to my office one day five years ago. It was inside another envelope, and the instructions were that I should keep it in a safe place and only open it in the event of his death. I

216

did, and, as you can see, it's for Mrs. Downing. I really should give it directly to her—"

Aggie took the envelope. "I'll see that she gets it."

She found a pad and pencil and wrote down her address and phone number. She handed it to him and opened the door. Rissman glanced over his shoulder toward the living room.

"Miss Patterson, I am sorry if I chose the wrong time, but really, an estate of this size . . . If you, or Mrs. Downing, had told me more details of Mr. Cramer's death, perhaps I—"

"The details are quite simple. Mr. Cramer had an accident, he needed medical attention, and he was unable to get it."

"Yes, I understand that much, but why—"

"Mr. Rissman. What did you think of Benjamin Cramer?"

"What?"

"Did you like the man?"

"Why, yes, of course I did. I was quite fond—"

"Then I beg you," Aggie said, her voice more commanding than pleading, "to let this matter go. The man is dead and there is nothing we can do to change that, is there?"

"Well, but Mrs. Downing—she seems so—I thought she'd be so pleased—"

"I can assure you that Mrs. Downing will be quite all right. She is a very strong person, and Derrington, Wisconsin, is the best medicine I know of for a grieving heart."

Rissman nodded dubiously and pushed open the screen door.

"Mr. Rissman?"

Rissman turned. "Yes, Miss Patterson?"

"While she's away, I'm sure she wants you to carry on as her attorney. Keep a sharp eye on that banker Mr. Cramer named as the executor of his will. If you see him doing anything that could be remotely construed as against Mrs. Downing's best interests, you must call her immediately. Will you do that?"

It was hardly a request, but he answered anyway.

"Certainly."

Little more than an hour later, at around six o'clock, Kate and Aggie came out of the house. They put their suitcases in the car and Aggie waited while Kate went next door to the Martins' house. She made the conversation as brief as possible. Her boss had died, she told Karen, and she was going up to Wisconsin, she wasn't sure for

217

how long. She gave her Aggie's address, asked her to bring in the mail, and silently thanked her for not asking too many questions.

Then they were on the road, with Kate behind the wheel, driving north on the Tri-State. They stopped for gas, then hamburgers at a McDonald's. Aggie never broached the subject of the will; Kate never gave her a chance. She kept up a stream of chatter and led the conversation in a new direction whenever it wandered too close to the topic she wished to avoid. It was as if Milton Rissman had never come into her home and delivered such an astonishing announcement. She spoke, instead, of the funeral service, giving Aggie capsule descriptions of many of the people there.

"There was one man I was really surprised to see. Harvey Schmidt, that little bald man in the brown-check jacket. Did you happen to notice him?"

"The one who looked like a mad scientist? Tie askew, rumpled hair, vacant look in the eye?"

Kate smiled. "That's Dr. Schmidt. A dear man. He's not a scientist; he's my favorite professor at Northwestern."

"Well, I was close. All teachers are a little mad."

"He's brilliant, a born teacher, and rather famous in academic circles. I was very lucky to study with him. I took every course with him that I could, and last fall I had an independent study with him. I got to know him pretty well. I suppose that's why he came to Mr. Cramer's funeral. It's funny, though; I don't recall ever telling him where I worked. I wonder how he knew? . . ."

Kate stepped on the brake suddenly, swerving to avoid a car cutting in too close in front of her, and was silent for a moment.

Aggie eased her grip on the armrest and chuckled. "All good teachers have a secret weapon. It's to know more about our students than they know about us."

Kate smiled again. "I suppose you're right. He certainly knew my capabilities better than I did when he encouraged me to write that paper for independent study. It was an unusual topic for an undergrad, you know. I knew about real estate and a little about stocks and bonds, and I'd taken a few courses on straight business finance, but Dr. Schmidt said I needed to widen my horizons, not limit myself yet, and besides, I knew it was a special interest of his, so—"

"Excuse me, what was?"

"Finance in higher education. It's a huge problem these days, and it's going to get worse. It costs a fortune to keep a college or university going, even with state and federal funding. Dr. Schmidt gave me a whole semester of independent study to research and write the paper, and I spent a lot of weekends visiting colleges in the midwest to talk to people."

"Sounds like a dissertation."

"It nearly was; I got carried away. It was so different from everything else I'd done. And Dr. Schmidt was right, of course. A college is a business, you know, and by the time I finished that paper, I knew enough to set up my own business."

"And Professor Schmidt gave you an A," Aggie smiled.

"I earned it. I only wish—"

"What?"

"Oh, it was foolish. . . ."

"You wish what?"

"It's stupid, especially now, after everything that's happened, but I sort of wish Mr. Cramer had known."

"About the paper?"

"Yes, and all the other papers and tests and courses. I don't know why I kept it all from him."

Aggie was amazed. "You mean you never told him? About going to school, working toward your degree?"

Kate shook her head and pushed a stray lock of hair away from her face.

"Why on earth not?"

"I have this stubborn streak. I wanted to do it all on my own, without any help from anyone, especially Mr. Cramer. He could have opened doors, put in a word for me here and there. He often spoke at the university, he knew some of the people in the business department. Hmm, I guess he knew Harvey Schmidt, too. But I didn't want any special favors. And then, when I learned I really could do it by myself, that I was smart enough—"

"Of course you were!"

"—and could swing the tuition, it got to be a challenge. I wanted to just walk into his office one day and show him my diploma! I thought he'd be so proud of me. . . . And all that time, from the very beginning, he—"

"He was giving you work, meaningful work. He was paying you an honest salary. He was giving you new purpose."

219

Kate was silent for several minutes. They were still on the interstate, a few miles south of Derrington, when she realized she was reaching a decision. She tested it out loud.

"Have you ever been to Bangkok?"

Aggie looked at her in concern. She did not like this idea.

"No," she said carefully.

"How'd you like to come with me? Benjamin Cramer paid me well. I'm going to sell my house. We can go without touching that inheritance. How about it?"

She said it as if she were going to the supermarket. Aggie said firmly, "There's no need to rush off to Bangkok. John Anthony said he might be there, but it was ten years ago—you don't know if he's still there—"

"I have to start somewhere." Kate slowed for the exit from the interstate.

"And what if, against all odds, you find him? What good—"

"I want a divorce, Aggie. But first I want to look him in the face and ask why. I don't want him back—whatever love there was is gone—but I have to know why he let me think he was dead all these years.

"And there's something else. He had something on Benjamin Cramer. I don't know what it was, but he had enough leverage to make Mr. Cramer hire me. If Jim could do that, then he could keep an eye on me, through Mr. Cramer. Mr. Cramer said it himself, in the ambulance. He said, 'Watching you,' but I didn't know if he meant himself or Jim. Well, it was one and the same.

"I have to know if there's an explanation for that cruelty. I have to know—why."

"Those are big questions," Aggie said. She opened her purse to check on the envelope Rissman had given her. "Can you live with the answers?"

They were driving up the hill now, around the curve, and into the downtown streets of Derrington. The streets were quiet, as they always were late at night.

"I'm not sure I can live without the answers," Kate said finally. She drove the few blocks to Aggie's house on Orchard Lane, and parked at the curb, behind Aggie's Ford.

"Well, then, this may help." Aggie took the long white envelope from her purse and handed it to Kate.

"Mr. Rissman left this for you. He said he got it from Benjamin Cramer five years ago. He was to give it to you when Mr. Cramer died."

Kate peered at the envelope in the darkness. She opened the car door, the inside light came on, and she could read, in Benjamin Cramer's familiar, careless scrawl, the words on the envelope. "Katherine Downing. Personal."

"Aggie? What's this all about?"

"Search me," Aggie said. "Give me the keys to the trunk; I'll get the bags."

"No, wait, I'll do it, but—do you think . . . I mean, he tried to tell me everything he could, in the ambulance, but what if . . . ? Five years, Mr. Rissman said?" They retrieved the bags and Kate followed Aggie inside. "What if he knew, Aggie, even then, that something might happen. What if he wanted to tell me, but he couldn't, so he wrote this . . ."

"Don't get your hopes up," Aggie said briskly. She snapped on a lamp in the guest room across the hall from her study. "It's not much," she said, gesturing around the small room, "but it's yours, for as long as you want it."

"It's fine; it's exactly what I need right now. If you can bear with me a little longer—"

"Nonsense. We're both used to living alone, so we both know how to stay out of each other's hair. Now then, you can sleep in tomorrow if you wish, but I'm getting up to see the parade. Want to join me?"

"Parade?"

"It's Memorial Day. Listen, we may be country bumpkins up here, but we like our parades. Starts at ten o'clock. Then there's the picnic in the park, by the band shell."

"Oh, I'm not sure . . ." Kate said doubtfully.

"Don't worry about it! If you're sleeping in, I won't wake you. If you're up and want to come, fine; otherwise, you can stay here, or go wherever you like. Sleep well."

Aggie closed the door and paused a moment in the hall, considering. She stepped into the study, closed the door quietly, and went to the telephone.

"Clark? Still awake?" She kept her voice barely above a whisper.

"Well, you'd better sit down for this one. First, please promise me again . . . I know, but it's different this time, it's really a private matter. . . . No, not even John Anthony, this has nothing to do with him, at least not yet. . . . Good. Oh, Clark, you won't believe this, but I heard it with my own ears. . . ."

She didn't think Kate would really mind. After all, she had no one else. If she and Clark didn't look after the girl, who would? Milton Rissman seemed a decent enough man, but he was a big-city lawyer with lots of other concerns. And the world was full of scoundrels, Lord knew, opportunists who would do anything to get their hands on two million dollars. Now, more than ever, Kate needed help. And Providence—what else could it be? Aggie asked herself—had once again placed her right in the middle of things. Oh, life was rich.

But she couldn't do it alone. Of all the people she knew, Clark Manchester was the one she trusted most. Earl Robbins, the high school principal, had been a dear friend and companion, but he was gone now. She was still angry that he had died long before she wished him to, and she still missed him. But Margaret was gone now, too, and Aggie and Clark made quite a team, she thought. So it was with the barest twinge of guilt that she related every detail of her trip with Kate. She left out nothing, not even Kate's chatter on the way home that night.

When she was finished, she was not the least surprised to hear Clark say, "Schmidt? I've heard of him. Management seminar I went to, years ago, down in Evanston. . . . Hmmm, I have a wild idea! It would be a monumental project, but . . ."

Aggie decided it was a good thing she was speaking to Clark over the telephone. Had they been face to face, she wasn't at all certain she could have resisted the urge to reach up and hug him. She was tired of her old image, the stern and bossy teacher role she had played for so long. Tonight she would have let down her guard, had he been here with her. She sighed.

"Thank you, Clark. I'll see you in the morning."

"Aggie, you were right to call me. Good night."

Was she imagining it, or did his voice sound—tender? Gentler than usual?

Oh, bosh, she scolded herself, hanging up the phone. You're a foolish old woman and you're up past your bedtime.

Still, a tiny, youthful smile escaped from her lips as she went down the hall to her bedroom.

Kate settled into bed, the pillow propped up behind her. In spite of the drive, she felt wide awake, and the envelope from Benjamin Cramer was on the nightstand beside her. In the lamplight, she could see that it had yellowed a bit. She picked it up and examined the back of it. Still sealed.

And then she couldn't resist it another minute. She despised her own eagerness. She shouldn't want any more to do with this man, but she tore open the envelope and drew out several pages of heavy bond paper. All of them were filled with Cramer's familiar scrawl. She smoothed the fold creases in the papers and began to read.

June 1, 1973

My dearest Kate,

I hope you shall never have to read this, but if you do, I beg your forgiveness and understanding. I have perpetuated a monstrous hoax, and that I continue in the name of love, rather than the fear with which I began, can hardly excuse my actions.

I have just returned from the cabin at Baker's Lake. It is one of the most perfect spots on earth and I hope someday you may enjoy it with me. It is spoiled by only one thing, my annual "conference" with a man I believe to be your husband. He wears a disguise, but I am sure he is James Downing. The reasons that prevent me from disclosing this fact to you this very day are so complicated that they may defy my powers of explanation, but I shall make an attempt anyway. You may naturally think this explanation entirely self-serving, but I shall make it as honest as I can.

You may or may not know that I was raised an orphan. I have no idea who my parents were. My earliest memories are of an extraordinary woman, Miss Penelope Withers, who ran the Bensenville Children's Home in Bensenville, Minnesota. She taught me basic arithmetic when I was four years old and continued to take an avid interest in my education. When I was in my last year at the local high school, she approached one of a number of well-to-do persons in the area and secured for me a privately funded scholarship that supplemented a loan I took out to defray some of my expenses at the University of Minnesota in St. Paul. I later learned that she made similar arrangements for many others in her charge. Upon graduation, she urged me to attend the Wharton School of Finance and Commerce at the University of Pennsylvania for my master's degree, and she helped me secure a sizable loan to do so. She then suggested military service as a vital step in my education. She was quite sincerely patriotic, and although I frankly loathed the prospect, I could hardly ignore her counsel when I owed all that I had achieved to her.

It was thus that I found myself the captain in charge of a Marine Corps disbursing office near Da Nang in 1965 and '66. My debts were considerable; my pay did not begin to cover them, and I resorted to some elementary juggling of pay records to increase my income. I have compiled an account of these ill-gotten monies and will attach it to this letter. If, at the time of my death, there are sufficient funds to meet this expense, I ask you to repay this amount, plus the current rate of interest, to the United States Marine Corps Finance Center in Kansas City, Missouri.

When I returned to civilian life in the fall of 1966, I was nearly free of debt and resolved to establish an unimpeachable reputation in the field of finance. The fact that my earlier nefarious activity would prevent me from ever feeling that I deserved such a reputation has only gradually been made painfully apparent to me. I opened my office in Chicago, worked as diligently as I knew how, and was, I blindly believed, at the beginning of a brilliant career.

It was then that I first was contacted by your husband, though I had no idea at the time who he was. He had recently left Da Nang and he had somehow not only discovered my illegal bookwork in Vietnam, but also obtained those very books and tracked me down.

He was very clever. He sent one incriminating page from the ledger. It arrived in the mail with no explanation whatsoever, only the illegal entry circled in red ink, and he let me stew about it for a week. There was a Bangkok postmark on the envelope, but no return address. Then, one night at my apartment, I received an overseas telephone call. In the briefest of terms, without identifying himself, he told me he had thirteen months' worth of phony pay records. This covered my entire tour of duty in Vietnam. He was prepared, he said, to send them immediately to the proper authorities with a complete explanation of how I had bilked the U.S. government. If I wanted to obtain the ledgers, however, he was willing to help me do so.

It was very simple. I was to contact a certain man in my office building, arrange some pretext for a meeting, and during the course of that meeting I was to drop the fact that I needed a new secretary. In due time, a woman would apply for the position. I was to hire her immediately. She would be, he assured me, an excellent secretary, and she was to know absolutely nothing of this arrangement.

Thereafter I was to meet with him once a year. He would give me pages from the ledgers in exchange for my reports on the secretary's activities. At the end of five years I would have all the pages from the ledgers, and I would never see or hear from him again.

Of course you know that the businessman I contacted was Ted Young. A few days later, just as promised, a capable woman applied for the job: you, looking scared out of your wits.

I have to tell you, I wondered, at first, if you might be in on the scheme. So I watched you very closely, and I met with Ted again. He disclosed to me his and his wife's genuine concern for your health and well-being; and I began to notice your eyes, and then I knew that you were an innocent party to this evil scheme.

After that, even before I knew my blackmailer's identity, I did what little I could to protect you from him. I tried to help you equip yourself to deal with the world on your own. I held back some things I knew about you, the men in the building you occasionally dated, personal things he had no right to know.

But now the situation has become more serious. Three weeks ago, at our annual meeting at Baker's Lake, he reneged on his promise. He has extended the terms of our agreement for five more years. I still have only half the ledgers.

And now I am convinced of his motives. If, indeed, he is your husband, he has been keeping his eye on you through me, monitoring your activities. He is obsessed with your personal life, with the remotest hint of a new romance. It is clear, though not understandable, that he does not wish you to know he is alive, but he does not wish you to remarry. I think if you were to consider that, he would find a way to stop it.

And so I stand in the middle, trapped by him and trying to protect you. I fear that if I withdraw from the picture, he would only find some other means to control you. This in no way excuses my own guilt, but until I can find the means of conquering him, I will protect you from him, for he is far and away the most dangerous man I have ever encountered.

If, after my death, you wish to locate him, I urge you to do so with great caution. I have traced him as far as Hong Kong, but he travels under several assumed names and I do not know if that is his final destination. Rodney Weaver has, all this time, acted as intermediary. I don't think he knows much, but he may be able to help you, and that is why I've established the annual contact between you and him.

There are two other persons who may be able to assist you. One is Randy Daniels, a private investigator in Chicago who has been in my employ for the past several years. It is his diligence that has provided me with such information as I have, and he will provide whatever help he can. He is a man of scrupulous discretion and you can trust him.

The other possible source of help is the sheriff of Wahomet County, Wisconsin, John Anthony McGavin. Daniels has ascertained that McGavin was stationed in Da Nang at the same time as your husband was and that they knew each other. It may be coincidence that the site of my annual meeting with your husband is only a few miles from McGavin's hometown, but I doubt it. We have made several inquiries, as discretely as possible, and McGavin seems to be an honest man, well respected and liked locally. I suspect that his involvement, if indeed any exists, has been under duress, but I continue to seek confirmation of this. Approach him warily if at all.

I have two final requests, which of course you are under no obligation whatsoever to honor:

First, I hope that you will continue with your studies at the university and obtain your degree. (Yes, I know, and have known since the day you enrolled. Harvey Schmidt is an old friend.) Penelope Withers taught me the value of formal education, and although I have not lived up to her expectations of me, I have never doubted her wisdom. You will need that degree and you will never be sorry you got it.

The second request involves the matter of my will. You will know, by the time you read this, that you are my chief beneficiary, and, by now, you will have rejected, I am sure, all thoughts of accepting whatever wealth I may have accumulated. I beg you to reconsider. My estate, with the exception of the amount I have asked you to remit to the Marine Corps, was honestly obtained. In every business transaction I have conducted I have been, without exception, as fair and as aboveboard with all concerned as was humanly possible. This estate is not tainted. It is yours, free and clear, to use in whatever good and honorable ways you see fit. You may trust Milton Rissman, and Thaddeus Brewer at the bank; they are men

227

I am sure of, and you may rely on their judgment. But don't rely on them entirely. Your own judgment is as reliable as theirs. Trust your own good instincts.

It is my most fervent wish that this letter never reach you. I am even now searching for a way out of this impossible, depraved situation. But if I should fail, it is with whatever shreds of integrity I have left that I tell you I love you,

Benjamin Cramer

The sixth and final page of the letter contained a precise accounting of the stolen Marine Corps funds. By the time she reached it, Kate was reading through a blur of tears. She was crying for lost chances, for roads not taken, for secrets untold. The letter was self-serving, that was true, but it was painfully honest, as well.

She was haunted by the image of that cabin at Baker's Lake, such an unlikely place for the terrible events it had served. Benjamin Cramer, alone up there, struggling to protect his business, his reputation, even her, from a man who was supposed to be dead.

A "dangerous man," he had called him, and he didn't know the half of it.

She buried her head in the pillow to stifle her sobs. "Jim, Jim," she whispered, "what happened to you? Were you ever the man I thought you were? I opened my life to you, I pulled you to me, I gave you my heart and body and soul! I want them back! Do you hear me, wherever you are? I want them back, and I'm going to get them!" She pounded the pillow with her fist. "I'll find you, Jim Downing, if it's the last thing I do in this life, I swear I'll find you. The strings are cut, do you hear me? I'll find you!"

Gradually her sobs subsided and then she could hear the night bus, several blocks away, plowing its way into the sleeping streets of Derrington.

16

The Man from Hong Kong

▪

"Don't forget to take those pills, sir, three times a day, until they're all gone. You don't want that infection coming back."

"Right. Thanks a lot." Jaycee left the hospital and found his rented car in the parking lot. The glasses were gone, broken beyond repair and thrown away, but his black mustache and wig were firmly in place. He started the car, rolled down the window, and found his way back to the interstate.

Good-bye, Madison, he said to himself as he left the city limits. Good-bye, Wisconsin. Good-bye, USA. He was on his way to get her now, and nothing would stop him this time. The flight to Zurich, with two first-class reservations in one of his false names, didn't leave until Tuesday morning, but he couldn't wait any longer. He'd canceled the first reservation, thanks to Cramer and the damned fishhook, but now he was on his way again, the blood poisoning under control, the antibiotics on the seat beside him to keep it that way.

He'd had nearly a week to get over his anger at Cramer. Who would have thought the sap would have tried to pull a stunt like that one? Never a peep out of him, all these years, and suddenly he's threatening to move in on her. He'd had it so easy, too. All he had to do was leave things the way they were. She wasn't going anywhere; Jaycee didn't need him keeping tabs on her any longer.

But the fishhook, that still rankled him. The rod had been one thing, a wild swing to knock his aim off. But the hook, a double one with triple prongs, had flown loose from the eye on the reel and sailed right into his eyelid. God, the blood! It had blinded him, thrown him into a panic, and that worthless Weaver had let Cramer escape out the window.

That's what had caused all the trouble. If he'd been able to get to a doctor right away, not in Derrington, but somewhere else nearby, there would have been no infection, no time for the blood poisoning to set in. He would have had nice, neat stitches instead of this gaping scar. He still couldn't fully open his eye. He'd got there too late for stitches. "Can't do it," the doctor had explained, "it'll seal in the infection and it'll never heal. Why'd you wait so long to come in, anyway?"

Jaycee had been forced to think of an excuse, some line about how it hadn't seemed that serious until he began to feel sick. He *had* been sick, hardly able to drive away from the cabin and down to Madison, and it was Weaver's fault. Those hours in the boat! Jaycee cursed under his breath, then told himself, oh, let it go, Cramer's dead, that's all that matters. Weaver's scared out of his mind; he's not going to squeal. Everything was wrapped up nice and neatly, the way he liked it.

They'd kept him in the hospital six days, and all that time he had thought about her, imagining her reaction when she saw him. The more he had been away, the more he realized how much he wanted her. He felt an old, familiar longing, and he pressed down on the accelerator. He would have to explain, very carefully, why she couldn't call anyone. What reason could he give her? She had to leave the house with him, go to a motel near the airport, and stay put until Tuesday morning.

You should wait, he told himself. Wait until Monday night; don't give her a chance to question it.

Even as he thought it, the resolve slipped away. He couldn't wait! He was so close now. Cramer had forced him to act; it was Cramer's fault that the time had to be now.

Jaycee pounded the steering wheel with his fist. Cramer! He had ruined everything! Jaycee hadn't wanted to risk another trip back to the States. Once, he was sure, he'd been followed all the way back to Hong Kong. After that, he'd been extra cautious, but, still,

Cramer was getting nervous. Jaycee had felt it, with that sixth sense that had kept him alive and out of prison all these years, and he had learned to listen to those warnings. Who knew what kind of trap he might set at that cabin?

So Jaycee had decided not to give him a chance. He had amassed a pretty good sum, and all of it was safe in Swiss accounts. Within a few months, he could wrap up all his deals in Hong Kong, relocate to Switzerland, and send for her.

But Cramer hadn't even given him a few months. "The chicken is flying the coop." Oh, he was cute. Real clever. He knew how to get Jaycee to that cabin. But he wasn't as clever as Jaycee. True, he'd made some money in Vietnam, but nothing compared to what Jaycee had made.

Ha! Jaycee liked the irony of it. There was an officer, a college-educated whiz kid, juggling pay records, and getting away with it, but then he leaves the books behind. Stupid! Along comes Jaycee, cheated out of an education by a banker's untimely death, and he perfects the system and expands it beyond even Cramer's imagination.

Short-sighted. That's what Cramer had been, Jaycee decided, short-sighted and stupid. He'd left the ledgers right there in the disbursing office, where any guy with a little ambition could pick up his method.

Well, Jaycee was not stupid. And he looked to the future, protecting his investments. A clerk in that office had become suspicious, and Jaycee hadn't waited around to see where those suspicions might lead. A warehouse had gone up in flames one night——obvious sabotage by the enemy—but nobody could figure out why that kid had been in there. Too bad.

Jaycee felt no remorse at all for that kid. But sometimes he missed Deck Bannister. He was the only one Jaycee had stayed in touch with after his escape from Vietnam. Deck had also found that part of the world to his liking, and had settled in Okinawa after his tour in Nam. There was a ready market there for guns and drugs, and Jaycee had supplied them. They had made a lot of money together. But when Deck had gotten greedy, Jaycee had been forced to act. He didn't share his profits fifty-fifty with anyone! Another fire, this time in Deck's apartment building, and Jaycee was safe.

But Cramer, Jaycee thought, Cramer made him maddest of all. How dare he imply that Kate would leave? Jaycee knew her better than anyone. He was the man she loved, the man she had married. He was the only man she'd ever wanted, couldn't Cramer have seen that? She belonged to Jaycee, no one else, and he had protected her all these years. He wouldn't share her, not one percent of her, with anyone!

He'd had to leave her; he would make her understand that. The idiotic job, the crummy house—it was a dead-end life. He'd had to leave to find something better, something where he could breathe again, and time had shown he'd been right. He'd found something better than she'd ever dreamed of: excitement, adventure, wealth. He had taken a thousand risks, met every challenge, become rich.

He'd wanted a few more months, but Cramer, greedy to the end, had denied him that. Well, no matter. He had what he wanted. After ten years of living like scum, first in Bangkok and then in Hong Kong, he had built his fortune, stashing it all away, planning for this day when he would see her again. When she heard what he had done, when she realized all the sacrifices he'd made, she'd fly into his arms, and they'd go off to Switzerland, to his money. There'd be no more sharing of anything with anybody. She would truly be his again.

His mind was made up. He had decided in the hospital, and he wasn't going to wait any longer. She was his wife, and the waiting was over. He would reclaim his prize possession, and she would adore him for what he had achieved!

A few more hours, he cautioned himself. You can't go in there in broad daylight, even in the disguise. The neighbors, he remembered, emptied out of their houses on Sunday afternoons, cutting grass, washing cars; it was a regular circus, and a stranger on the street would be the star attraction.

But Chicago was a dangerous place for him. So he pulled off the highway into one of the suburbs, parked behind a tavern, and went in where the lights were low and the patrons were cheering the hopeless Cubs on television. When the game was over he moved on, finding another dark place to eat dinner, and then he sat in his car and counted the minutes.

At nine-thirty, when he couldn't hold back any longer, he started the engine and drove slowly to the suburb, feeling his way by memory and instinct. In all his trips back to the States, he had never once allowed himself to come this close to her, but he found the neighborhood and turned onto Rolfe Road. He was surprised at how small and shabby the houses looked. Somehow, when they'd first moved in, it had seemed a decent enough place to live, especially to her. Now it was strictly lower middle class, the houses like blocks, nearly identical, and he felt his confidence soaring. When she heard where they were going, the kind of life they were going to lead, she wouldn't even stop to pack a bag. He was her ticket out of this dump.

He braked to a stop down the street from his house. No car in the driveway. Where in hell was she? It was Sunday night; she never went anywhere on Sunday. Maybe the car was in the repair shop. Yeah, that must be it. He inched the car a little closer. In the dark he could see that there were no lights on, inside or out. Finally he parked and walked slowly across the street and up the short walk to the cement doorstep.

He knocked and waited. Maybe she was already asleep. He tried again. The clang of the brass knocker rang out in the quiet evening air.

"Yoo-hoo! She's not home!"

Jaycee spun around and saw the shadowy figure of a woman coming across the lawn. He squinted in the darkness, trying to make out her face. The neighbors! Jesus, of all times. If Jane what's-her-name saw him, he was cooked. He began silently cursing his own stupidity. Why hadn't he just gone around back and looked in the shed for the extra key? She probably hadn't changed the hiding place.

"Are you looking for Kate Downing?"

"Yes," he said shortly.

"Well, she's gone. Left a few hours ago. Can I help you?"

Finally she was at the front step and Jaycee found himself in the awkward position of trying to get a good look at her face without allowing her to see his.

"Yeah," he improvised, "I'm an old friend of hers, in town for a couple o' days, and I thought I'd drop by. Name's Jordan Willis."

"I'm Karen Martin." Immediately, Jaycee silently let out his breath in relief. He didn't know her. "I'm afraid you won't be able to see her this time, Mr. Willis. She's up in Wisconsin for several days."

"Wisconsin?" Jaycee echoed dumbly.

"Yes, a place called Derrington. She's had a real shock, you know—oh, you wouldn't know, would you? Her boss, the man she's worked for for ten years, well, he died. She told me, and I'd read it in the papers. Poor thing, here she is, left with no job. But anyhow, they left this evening and she didn't say when she'd be back, and you know, for the life of me, I cannot understand why she'd want to go back up to that town. Why, I'd—"

"They?" Jaycee cut in.

"Hmmm?"

"You said 'they.' 'They left.' Who was with her?"

"Why, I don't know, some elderly lady. She came down with Kate yesterday, then they had the funeral this afternoon, and then they left and drove back up there tonight."

"Um, yes, I see. Thank you." Jaycee was backing away from the woman, edging toward the street.

"I'll tell her you came by, Mr. Willis. Jordan, is it?"

"Right, thanks again."

Jaycee got back in his car, seething, and drove away.

Back out on the interstate, a highway he was rapidly learning to loathe, he tried to tell himself it was just as well. It'd be easier this way. Away from her home and the nosy neighbors, there'd be no need for explanations. She could just get in the car and leave with him.

But Derrington! Of all places! He'd have to be careful. If they knew Cramer was dead, then they'd found the body, somehow. That worried him. Did dead bodies really float? He'd always heard that, but he didn't know. If the body had floated to the surface, somebody—but there was never anybody out at that lake. Weaver had promised him that, over and over. So who had found the body? And could they tell he'd been shot? Sure they could; even if he drowned, there'd still be the bullet.

So. The cops would be all over the place, and he would have to be more careful than he'd been in years. Well, he could do it. He'd been in worse scrapes than this one, far worse, and he'd always come out clean. He could do it again, no problem.

He rolled down the window and turned on the radio. It was a long drive to that hick town, but once he found her, everything would be all right again.

234

17

Memorial Day

▪

It was 1:38 in the morning of Memorial Day. The bus from Chicago, Milwaukee, Fond du Lac, and a dozen other smaller towns, the bus that Kate heard from her room in Aggie's house on Orchard Lane, left the interstate, climbed the hill, and rounded the curve into downtown Derrington. Right behind it, in his rented blue Mustang, with the windows rolled up to keep out the bus fumes, came Jaycee. He followed the bus as it turned off onto a side street and rolled to a stop in front of the tiny depot. No one got off or on, and a few minutes later the bus chugged away from the curb.

Jaycee cut the lights and the engine and rolled down his window, tossing his cigarette away. He listened for night sounds. It was still, the air heavy and warm. He could hear the bus, half a mile away, as it accelerated down the hill, heading back to the interstate. Otherwise, the night was absolutely silent, and it made him uneasy. He was accustomed to Asian city nights, filled with the noises of street markets and motorcycles, fist fights and screaming domestic quarrels.

And then he began to relax. He'd been away so long he'd lost his perspective. This town wasn't going to be swarming with cops; they probably had one or two on the night shift. Nobody was looking for him, and even if they were, he had his disguise; they wouldn't recognize him if they tripped over him. This was going to be easy.

Okay, first he needed a place to stay. He couldn't sit here in his car all night. Well, McGavin had talked about a hotel; it shouldn't be hard to find. He started the car and headed back toward the main street.

Clark Manchester was roused from a light sleep a few minutes later by an insistent tapping of the bell out at the front desk. Pulling a robe over his striped pajamas, he shuffled out to the desk and pushed a registration card across the counter.

"You're in luck," he yawned. "One room left. How many nights?"

"Just one," the dark-haired man replied. He didn't look up as he quickly filled in the blanks on the card. "How much?"

He paid in cash, took the key, and waved his thanks as he walked to the stairway. Clark stuffed the card in a box without even glancing at it, locked the money in the cash drawer, and went back to bed. He was too tired for guessing games tonight.

When he rose at five, there was no time to ponder the latest guest to check into his hotel. He was everywhere at once, enjoying the rush of activity, solving the dozens of minor problems that arose. Then, as the diners began streaming out of the Evergreen Room, he joined Aggie outside and settled down to watch the parade. Within minutes the Evergreen Room was nearly deserted.

At a round table in the corner, one last family with several small children struggled to finish their meal without breaking any more dishes or spilling another glass of milk. And at the counter was a single customer, a tall, black-haired man with a thick mustache. He had strolled in a few minutes earlier and ordered breakfast. When the remaining waitress refilled his coffee cup and joined the cook at the windows behind him, he had, in the mirror along the wall behind the counter, an unobstructed view of the door.

The women at the front window were chatting about some activity out on the main street. Apparently, there was a parade of some sort. Yes, he heard drums, and now the marching music, and the women provided a running commentary of the procession.

He picked up a newspaper someone had left on the next stool. The *Derrington Weekly Chronicle* was a slim publication, filled with local merchants' ads and chatty reports on the garden club, city-council meetings, and high-school sports. The front page headline read, MEMORIAL DAY PLANS FINALIZED.

Memorial Day? The parade. Of course. And there had been some sort of banner out in the street last night. No wonder there were so

236

many people in this hick hotel. It had nothing to do with a dead body being found. It was a holiday.

Jaycee scanned the front page, wondering how he was going to find her. She could be outside right now, watching the parade, but he didn't want it to be that way. It should be private—

He jolted upright on his stool and squinted at the front page. What was this . . .? A small article, near the bottom of the page: CHICAGO MAN FOUND INJURED HERE. There was a photograph of Benjamin Cramer. Injured? Impossible. Weaver had said he got him, he was sure of it. But . . . The article said he was being transferred to the county hospital in Eagle Hill. Still alive! No, no, wait, the neighbor down on Rolfe Road—she had told him the boss had died. That had to be Cramer. So what . . .? There had to be an explanation.

He reread the article, and when he reached the last sentence he got another shock. "According to Wahomet County Sheriff John Anthony McGavin, the matter is under investigation."

McGavin? A county sheriff?

Jaycee nearly laughed out loud. McGavin, his partner and buddy in stealing the Marine Corps Supply Depot blind, had crossed the tracks. Now he was a cop on the take; he could probably lead Jaycee right to her, with the right persuasion. . . .

"More coffee, sir?"

"Yeah, sure." He ground out his cigarette in an ashtray and studied the waitress a moment.

"Too bad about this guy," he said, tapping the newspaper.

"Who's that?"

"This, uh, Cramer," Jaycee said, pointing to the picture.

"It certainly is." She shook her head. "They say he never had a chance."

"Well, if he's in the hospital . . ."

"Oh, my, he died. He was out there for days before anyone found him. The newspaper," she said, for he was looking puzzled, "it's a weekly, and that's three days old. Friday edition. He died, Friday, I guess it was, yes, Friday afternoon. They've already buried him."

Jaycee's breath came short with relief. "His family . . .?"

"No, as I understand it, he didn't have anyone. Poor soul. No, his secretary took care of the funeral. 'Course, we helped all we could."

237

The pride of the small town, lending aid in time of crisis, was evident in her voice.

"I'm sure you did. Terrible responsibility. She must have been pretty upset."

"The poor child . . . She found him, you know, she and John. . . . He was afraid to leave her by herself for a minute; she took it real hard."

Jaycee didn't need to ask who John was, and he marveled at the amount of information she gave him so readily. But then, she was not the sort he usually dealt with. She obviously had nothing to hide, nothing to gain, and nothing to trade.

"Nan, come look! There's Buddy Fitzgerald in that funny getup again!"

"Coming, Martha." The waitress named Nan smiled at Jaycee. "Can I get you anything else?"

Jaycee took out his billfold. "The secretary," he said casually, "do you happen—"

There was a crash, and Jaycee spun around.

"Billy Taylor, that is absolutely the last straw!" A child began to wail, and his older sister screamed, "It wasn't his fault, Mommy, Joey did it—"

"Excuse me." The waitress smiled apologetically. "That's the third glass. Have a pleasant day." She hurried over to the corner table.

Jaycee cursed under his breath and strode out into the lobby. She was here in this town, he could feel it; she was here, waiting for him. . . . He spotted the kid who'd been behind the counter earlier. Now he, too, was watching the parade, from the windows at the front of the lobby. Jaycee approached him.

"Hey, kid."

The young man, his face eager to please, said, "Yes, sir?"

"I'm looking for a woman named Downing, the secretary of that man they found—Cramer, the one who just died."

The kid's face turned doubtful, and Jaycee thought fast.

"Sorry, should have introduced myself." He stuck out his hand. "Dave Streeter, *Chicago Tribune.*"

"*Tribune?* Wow, glad to meet you! I'm Barry Barris. Wow, the *Trib?*"

"Right, we're doing a story on Cramer, and we'd like to get the secretary's angle. Understand she came up here last night. Do you know where I can find her?"

238

"Gosh, I'm not sure. I haven't seen her this morning. I don't think she's staying here—hey, I got an idea. Why don't you talk to Miss Patterson?"

"Who's she?"

"She's my teacher, I mean she was, she retired—"

"What's she got to do with—"

"Oh, she's been taking care of Mrs. Downing. Hey, I bet that's where she is. She is probably staying with Miss Patterson. You could ask her, she's right outside, for the parade—"

"Yeah, I'll do that. Thanks, kid."

Jaycee slipped out the door and scanned the crowd on the sidewalk. He didn't see her, and he was glad. He wanted her alone, all to himself. He had to find out where this dame Patterson lived. Maybe Kate was still there, and he could go inside, find her, take her in his arms. . . .

Suddenly his mouth was dry, and he moved as quickly as he could through the crowd. He was in a hurry now, he was so close.

A block and a half away he found Vogen's Pharmacy and he saw what he wanted through the front window: a pay telephone. He went in and nearly tore apart the slim local directory looking for *Patterson*. There it was, only one, Agatha B., and he was sweating now; he could almost see her, almost hear her voice, smell her clean hair, feel her skin, her breasts against his chest—

He dropped a dime in the slot and dialed the number. It rang once, twice, forever; damn, she wasn't there—

"Hello?"

It was her voice. He had never forgotten the husky tone of that voice, and he guessed he had awakened her; that was the way she sounded early in the morning, when they were still in bed. Sometimes—

"Hello?"

Christ, how had he stayed away so long? He'd had to do it—there'd been no other way—but there wasn't another woman in the world like her. None of them, before or since, had given themselves so completely to him, aroused him the way—

"Who's there?"

And suddenly, if there'd been any doubts, they were gone. He was right to have come back; it was past time, but he was ready now, oh, he was ready for her—

There was a click. She had hung up, and it came like a slap in his face. He flipped to the front of the phone book and tore out the page with the city map on it. Then he nearly ran back to the hotel, taking a back street to avoid the congested sidewalks. He went in the back entrance and took the steps two at a time. In his room, he threw the few items he had unpacked back into his suitcase. He ripped off the wig and the moustache and tossed them in on top. He might need them tomorrow at O'Hare, though how in hell he'd explain that to her—well, he'd think of something.

He went to the Mustang, parked in the lot behind the hotel, and studied the map. Orchard Lane, the phone book had said, and there it was, just a few blocks away, a snap. But he had to circle the parade route; he got fouled up on a one-way street and he rounded the corner to Orchard Lane just as John Anthony McGavin approached him from the opposite direction.

It had to be him! He was wearing a blue uniform and, even with his cap on, shading his face, Jaycee recognized his old friend. He stopped the car down a few houses and across the street and saw McGavin turn up the walk to the Patterson house. He knocked, and eventually someone inside opened the door. He couldn't see, but it had to be her, he'd just heard her voice, and then McGavin stepped inside. The screened door swung closed.

Jaycee hesitated. He could still go in, confront them both, and take her away. McGavin was a cop now, he could even help them, but what if . . .? He was in uniform, he had a gun, and Jaycee wished to hell he hadn't already disposed of his own weapon. He'd bought the magnum in a gun shop down in Milwaukee, on his way to meet Cramer for the last time. Of course, he'd used a false ID, but when he'd had to go to the hospital he couldn't take it in with him, and he didn't want to leave it in the rental car. What if they towed it away, looked inside? So he'd thrown it into a river on the way to Madison, out in the country where nobody could ever find it.

What if McGavin had a sudden attack of conscience? He'd had them all the time in Nam; what if he decided to draw the line?

Jaycee rubbed his forehead. McGavin had been the last real friend he'd ever had. He could kill McGavin, he knew that, but he didn't want to. And it would add to the risk of getting out of the country. It wasn't that he feared risks; he'd taken plenty of them in the past twelve years; they'd become a normal part of his life. But he hadn't made a fortune and stayed alive by taking unnecessary ones.

Besides, this wasn't the way he had planned it. She had to be alone. It had to be just the two of them, because the minute he saw her he wouldn't be able to hold back, there'd be no reason to. He wanted her alone.

Jaycee turned off the ignition, lit a cigarette, and stared through the hazy sunshine at the house across the street. He would get to her, one way or another.

Twenty minutes earlier, Kate had been awakened from a restless sleep. There had been a pounding in her head, like the beat of drums, ta-dum, ta-dum, ta-dum-ta-dum-ta-dum, and then she had seen the men. There were hundreds, thousands. The column stretched on forever, and they were marching right past her house in Elwood. She and her mother were waving gaily at the men in uniform—soldiers, sailors, marines—and some of them would call out admiringly, "Look at that woman's dress!" and Kate felt so proud of her mother in her dress that was too long. Some of the men were carrying flags, but some of them were waving dollar bills instead, fistfuls of bills. And then she saw her father, marching proudly with the rest of the men, and he had more dollars than anyone.

"Daddy!" she called. "Daddy, give some to Jim! He's right behind you!" And sure enough, there was Jim, tall and oh, so handsome in his uniform, but he had no flag and no money, only a gun, and it was ten feet long and he carried it like a fishing pole, slung over his shoulder. The end of it, the barrel, bobbed up and down in the air, and the men in line behind him had to keep ducking as they tried to stay in step.

"Oh, Mother, there's Mr. Cramer!" He was behind Jim, trying to dodge that long gun, but he couldn't seem to avoid it. Every time he raised his head, bam!—the end of the gun would bob down and thunk him on the head.

"Oh, that's not fair!" Kate cried. "Mother, make him stop!"

But when she turned, her mother was weeping into a white, lacy handkerchief, and the bank examiner was leering above her. "Fair!" he was shouting. "I'll show you what's fair! Take 'er away, men!" And the moving men, huge and sweating, picked up her mother and carried her off down the street, behind the column of marching men.

"Mother, come back! Please, come back!" Kate was crying, standing at the front gate, but no one could hear her because now the band was playing, the drums were louder than ever, and she was the only one left behind. Everyone else in Elwood had followed the marching men off to war.

At the very end of the line, wearing his blue uniform, was Sheriff John Anthony McGavin, and she cried out to him, "Sheriff McGavin! I want answers now! You're not one of them, you don't belong with them, tell me the truth!" But he was calling cadence into his radio microphone, "Hup, two, three, four, hup, two, three, four," and he couldn't hear her. No one could hear her.

Then the telephone in the house was ringing and she thought, I've got to answer it, there's no one else to answer it, and then she realized the telephone really was ringing. She sat up slowly, and gradually the room came into focus, the present came flooding back, and she remembered where she was. She clambered out of bed and made her way across the hall to Aggie's study.

"Hello?" She was still half asleep and her face was streaked with tears. She stood barefooted, in a short cotton nightgown, trying to clear the cobwebs away from inside her head. In the distance, she could hear a band, and she remembered then that there was a parade this morning because it was Memorial Day.

"Hello?" she said again, but there was no answer. "Who's there?" She heard only silence and she replaced the phone and rubbed her eyes. She went to splash some water on her face and brush her teeth, then wandered down the hall toward the kitchen. There was a note on the table, next to a clean cup and saucer.

> Gone to parade. Coffee ready. Come to the picnic!
> Aggie.

Kate poured a cup of coffee and sat at the table, gazing out of the window into Aggie's tidy backyard. Two cardinals, one fiery red, the other a dull orange-pink, were perched on a bird feeder. Kate watched as the male poked his beak into the tray, came up with a seed, and presented it to his mate. She took it in her beak and cracked it open.

That's one lucky lady cardinal, Kate thought briefly, and then, abruptly, she reminded herself. "That's the last thing you need, Kate Downing. You are making it on your own just fine, and there's no reason you won't continue to. You are an OMO. On my own, and don't forget it."

Determined to really believe that, she examined her future as if it were one of the financial portfolios she had prepared so objectively for Benjamin Cramer. On the plus side, there were certainly no financial worries. His letter had dented her resolve to reject the inheritance. She needed more time before she decided, although she was still inclined to refuse it. Even without it, she could go on living as she had for several months. Or she could sell the house, empty her savings account, and take off for Hong Kong—not Bangkok; she would start in Hong Kong—and look for Jim until the money ran out or she found him. She could even take Aggie with her, and then scramble for a job when she got back. She had her degree, or would have it in a few days. With that, and the contacts she had made working for Benjamin Cramer, she felt confident about finding a good job with a decent salary.

Why, then, when she had all these pluses going for her, did she feel miserable about the future? It depressed her to imagine herself trudging back to La Salle Street day after day, or anywhere else in that city, for that matter. She had never truly enjoyed it; she'd enjoyed only her work with Benjamin Cramer, and that was finished now.

Well, it didn't have to be Chicago. What if she went somewhere else . . . out west, maybe? Or south? What if she found a fantastic job, a new apartment? What if she really tried to go out and meet people, to make new friends?

"Baloney."

She said it out loud and rose to pour herself another cup of coffee. She looked around Aggie's tiny kitchen, neat and immaculate, and thought of the living room with its beautiful Mexican rug on the wall, and the wall in the study lined with diplomas and autographed photos of some of her students who had achieved varying degrees of fame and accomplishment. And she thought of Aggie, full of purpose and energy and—alone. Alone in this house, all these years, because she had made a very hard choice, right at the beginning.

She didn't know where the idea came from, or when it started.

243

Perhaps it had been born that first night, when she had climbed off the bus and had the streets of Derrington to herself. It had been simmering beneath her consciousness ever since, and now it seemed obvious. Not necessarily logical, but it made perfect sense to her.

She wanted to live in a place like Derrington.

No; she refined the notion. Not a place *like* Derrington. She wanted to live *in* Derrington.

Why move and start over in a new town where she knew no one? She would be looking for people like the ones she had met here, people who still cared about fresh air and quiet nights, people who chose to lead productive lives outside the frantic pace of the cities, people who made time for each other. Look at Aggie. She was hardly alone—she was surrounded, in fact, by friends and acquaintances, people who liked and respected her. Of course, she had been here a long time. It would take time, Kate knew, to build those relationships, but suddenly she wanted to do it. She was sick of her cloistered existence. For the first time, she felt hemmed in by the walls she herself had built. They had been founded on fear and shame, and she no longer felt afraid or ashamed.

Kate shook her head unconsciously, wondering at the person she had let herself become. She had been disgusted with herself, with her father's crime, and with not preventing her husband from going to a war that had taken his life. Well, she was no longer ashamed of crimes she hadn't committed, and her husband had not died in the war. She remembered the demons she had fought those two years before his death; all this time she thought she had conquered them, but she had been wrong. They had been winning after all. But not any longer.

She had already begun, she realized, to tear down the walls, to slay the demons, one by one. She had left her safe nest in the suburbs and come up here to find Benjamin Cramer. She had let herself open up to Aggie and ask for her help. She had listened to John Anthony McGavin in Clark Manchester's apartment three nights ago and had allowed herself to reach out to him in understanding. It had been years since she had let that happen with anyone.

Kate was remembering that moment, visualizing his face, when there was a knock at the front door.

"Mrs. Downing?" His voice drifted through an open window.

"Yes, I'll be right there," she called, and she rushed down the hall to the guest room and rooted through her suitcase for her robe. The light cotton duster she pulled out of the bag was a mass of wrinkles. Well, she had to put it on, she had nothing else, and she ran a comb through her tangled hair before she dashed down the hall and through the living room. She unlocked the front door and opened it.

"Oh, you caught me—um—"

John Anthony McGavin was staring at her, his mouth slightly open, and she could feel her face flush.

"I could come back later," he said, but he didn't sound as if he wanted to.

"No, it's okay, come in." She opened the screen for him and he stepped inside. "Would you like, uh, coffee? Or is it lunchtime?"

"Almost, but coffee's fine. Did I wake you up?"

"Oh, no," Kate said, awkwardly touching her hair. She brushed it back from her shoulder. "I've been up," she said, leading the way to the kitchen, "sitting here, enjoying the birds in the backyard. And Aggie's good coffee."

She opened a cupboard door, looking for the cups, and he said, "You missed the parade." He sounded tentative and she glanced at him. He was leaning against the doorframe, as if he was ready to leave the moment she asked him to.

"Is it over?" Kate realized she could no longer hear the drums and the music. "Now, where does Aggie keep—oh, here they are." She produced a cup and saucer for him and poured the coffee, refilling her own cup. "Cream? Sugar?"

"Black," he said, and he sat down across the table from her. "Yes, it's over."

Kate said nothing and nodded. She sipped her coffee.

"I'm glad you're back." In the sudden silence, his voice came out unnaturally loud.

"So am I," Kate said. "My house, um, my house didn't—it was nice of Aggie to invite me." She was looking past him, at the green in Aggie's backyard, at the starched white curtains at the window, at anything but him. She wished she was dressed, not in this thin robe and nightgown, her hair loose instead of neatly knotted at the back. It had been years since she had sat in a kitchen like this, with a man she liked. . . .

"I've been worried about you," he said finally. Again his voice was tentative, almost asking her permission to speak at all.

"You have?"

He nodded, looking at her face. "The things that happened to you . . . They shouldn't happen to anyone, but especially not—not you." He paused a moment, as if considering whether or not to continue. "I've seen it before, in my work. People in the wrong place . . . You deserve better."

"Oh, I believe people usually get what they deserve, Sheriff McGavin." She wrapped her fingers around her coffee cup and studied the kitchen sink.

"John. Please call me John."

"But you're in uniform," she said, as if that carried its own set of rules.

"This morning I was working. Now I'm not. I—I should have changed before I came over here. I'm sorry."

"This isn't an official call?"

He shook his head. "I didn't intend it to be."

"What, then?" The words were out before Kate could stop them. "Paying your respects?"

"In a way," he said, unrattled. "I'm very sorry, sorrier than I can tell you—"

"I don't want or need your pity." Her voice was soft, barely above a whisper. Please, don't pity me, she thought.

"I wanted to say that I'm sorry we met the way we did. I wish the circumstances had been different."

"But they weren't." She was studying the refrigerator, aware of its quiet humming. Oh, if things had been different . . .

"No, and there's nothing I can do to change that, but . . ."

"What?" Her voice was low, and now she was staring at the saucer in front of her, fingering its delicately scalloped edge.

"Please don't go to Bangkok."

"What?" Kate raised her head in surprise and finally looked at him.

"Simple deduction. You think Jaycee—I mean, Jim—you think he's in Bangkok, and you are not the sort of woman to let loose ends dangle. You want to find him, don't you?"

Her eyes dropped, but her voice was firmer. "I'm going to start in Hong Kong. Mr. Cramer traced him that far."

"Do you still love him?"

"That's none of your business." She stood up abruptly and took her cup to the sink. No! she wanted to scream, I hate him! But she kept her face averted so he couldn't see her anguish.

"Yes, it is," he said quietly.

She was facing the sink, her back to him, and she heard him get up from the table. When he spoke, his voice was in her ear.

"Please turn around and look at me."

Kate was trembling. She was surprised to find her eyes suddenly full of tears. A gentle voice, intimate almost, after so long . . .

"You pity me," she whispered.

"The morning you came into my office and told me who you were, I pitied you. Not anymore. I ache for you, I'm angry for you, and I have no right at all to expect you to feel anything but contempt for me, but—will you turn around?"

His voice sounded almost helpless, as if he hadn't expected to be saying these things, but there they were anyway.

"I don't want anyone to take care of me." Her voice was still a whisper. "I can take care of myself." I can, she repeated silently, I can.

"I know that, I've seen it. I don't want to protect you. I want to be with you."

Kate could almost feel his breath on her shoulder. Her stomach was touching the edge of the sink in front of her, and the tears were sliding down her nose. She wondered why she didn't feel trapped, caught here in the kitchen with him. She remembered the first time she had seen him, behind his desk in his office, and how innocent his eyes had looked at first. She had spent the next two days watching that look disappear as they searched for Benjamin Cramer, found him, then watched him die. She had seen the terror in his eyes as he relived Vietnam, and she had tried to reach out to him then, to let him know she understood, as well as anyone could who hadn't been there. It was the most natural thing in the world, she thought, that he should come to her now. In a way, she had invited him.

"Mrs. Downing?" he said softly, and she could hear it in his voice, the anger and the admiration and, most especially, she could hear tenderness, a gentleness so great that, at last, after what seemed a lifetime of holding back, of waiting, of hiding behind walls, she had

247

to gather every bit of courage she possessed. She took a deep breath.

"Why don't you call me Kate?" she said, and when she turned around his arms wrapped around her, not trapping her, but welcoming her, and then they kissed hello. She felt her fear melting away, another wall crumbling, another demon disappearing for good.

"John, there's so much I want to tell you—"

"Kate, I want to talk to you about—"

They spoke at the same time and they laughed and then they just clung to one another without saying anything for a long time.

Kate was feeling a jumble of emotions, but to feel anything at all was such a new experience for her that she hardly cared if she didn't understand them. She didn't know how she felt about John Anthony McGavin, except that she trusted him and she liked him and the sensation of being in his arms was something she needed very much right now. He was a good and decent man, she was as sure of that as she was of her own name.

For once, she told herself, I don't need to calculate, to think of plus or minus, to protect myself no matter what the cost. He's not perfect, and I wouldn't want him if he were. He's a smart and good and gentle man, the finest I've met in a long time, maybe ever. And he's here! In my arms! Here, in this sunny kitchen, the most wholesome, nonthreatening place imaginable. My room is just down the hall. . . .

She began to feel an odd sensation, and when she realized what it was, she began to smile.

"What? . . ." He drew back to see her face.

"No," she said, almost to herself, "not yet. . . ." Not, she told herself, while Jim is still alive, not until I get that finished. But soon . . .

He was looking at her oddly, trying to read her mood.

"Isn't there a picnic today?" Kate said quickly. She stayed in his arms, smiling up at him.

"Every year," he answered easily, going along with her. "We could—no, wait, I have a better idea. Let's have our own picnic."

"I have one question," Kate said. She was suddenly so happy she wanted to laugh again. "Are you a rich man?"

"I'm an unemployed pauper, or I will be as soon as I resign. Are you a rich woman?"

"No," she said. It was the first and last lie she ever told him. "I don't have a job, either."

"I knew there was something I liked about you."

Outside, in his rented car, unnoticed by a resort town overflowing with early summer vacationers, Jaycee smoked his cigarettes, stared at the little white house on Orchard Lane, and waited.

It was past noon when Aggie Patterson decided she couldn't stand it any longer. She rose from the lawn chair Clark Manchester had thoughtfully brought along for her, and gazed around the park.

"Clark, where's the nearest phone?"

"Gettin' antsy, aren't you?" He remained seated, grinning up at her.

"So what if I am? It won't hurt to call, just to be certain she's all right."

"John Anthony's there. She's fine."

"Well, what if he left? I'm going to find a telephone and—"

"Woman, you always were a stubborn so-and-so." Clark glanced at his watch and stood up. "Time for a shift change in the Evergreen. I'd best make sure they all show up. C'mon, you can call from the hotel."

They left the park together, Clark assuring everyone they passed that no, they weren't leaving for good, they'd be back in a few minutes.

"I wish she'd come here with us," Aggie said, frowning. "She needs people, needs to laugh a little and enjoy herself."

"Who says she can't do that with John Anthony?"

"Hmmm? Well, of course, but—John Anthony? He's hardly the best of company himself these days, or haven't you noticed?"

"I noticed," Clark said shortly. "I noticed everything."

"Well, then, you know that—" Aggie stopped short and looked up at him. "What's that supposed to mean? 'Everything'?"

Clark smiled benignly down at her. "I do believe," he said, "that nature is taking its course. Finally."

"Oh, speak English, Clark. None of that homespun philosophizing with me."

"Add it up for yourself," he drawled, walking along beside her, hand on her elbow. "The minute that parade was over, there's John Anthony, finding us in that crowd, looking for Mrs. Downing. The minute you tell him where she is, he's off to see her."

"And why not? He has reports to write; no doubt he has papers for her to sign."

"Hmmm, maybe."

"You think it's more than that?" She was beginning to smile.

"I do."

"And I say, nonsense. They're both miserable—"

"Loves company, Aggie. Misery loves company. Weren't you watching them the other night in my apartment?"

"I saw everything. She threw enough daggers at him—"

"I mean later, woman. At the end. The way she looked at him. He noticed, I'm sure of that."

They went in through the double doors of the hotel lobby and Aggie was about to offer another protest when Barry rushed up to them.

"Mr. Manchester! Miss Patterson!"

"Barry," Clark acknowledged calmly. "Everything under control?"

"Yes, sir, quiet as a church. And guess—"

"I'll be back in a minute, Barry. Have to check on the shift change."

"And I need to make a telephone call. May I?" Aggie was already at the counter, lifting the telephone.

"Yes, ma'am, of course, but—"

Aggie held up her index finger.

"John Anthony? You're still there, good. How's Kate?" She listened a moment. "Glad to hear it. Say, the picnic's in full swing. Bring her over and we'll—oh? Hmmm . . . But—I see. . . . Well, certainly, but Clark has had a marvelous idea, he needs to speak with her—then—well, yes, John Anthony. If that's what you and Kate have decided. Yes. All right, then—no, I won't. Good-bye."

Aggie had a dazed expression on her face as she hung up.

"Humph!" she said, to no one in particular, but Barry said, "Anything wrong?"

"What? Oh, Barry. No, everything's fine. . . . I think. Oh, how would I know?"

"Yes, ma'am." Barry backed away. He had seen that look before on his math teacher's face. Nearly all her students had, and what it said was, don't cross me. Barry had no intention of crossing her, but he had news, and it was nearly killing him not to be able to tell her.

"Well, Barry." Aggie crossed her arms and leaned against the counter. She seemed to be recovering from whatever had upset her. "Are you enjoying your new job?"

"Um, yes, ma'am. It's real exciting. Gives me a chance to be right in the middle of everything, you know?"

"Yes, I suppose it does," Aggie mused. At the moment she had the distinct feeling of being on the fringe.

"'Course, you'd know more about that than I would." Barry smiled.

"Whatever do you mean?"

"Well, gosh, Miss Patterson, it's not every day you get interviewed by a big Chicago newspaper, is it?"

"Barry, what on earth are you talking about?"

"The *Tribune,* of course! The reporter!"

"What reporter?" She sounded exasperated. "Make some sense, boy."

"Mr. Streeter, ma'am. From the *Chicago Tribune.* He was looking for Mrs. Downing, so I sent him out to see you. Didn't he find you?"

"No. Suppose he wants an inside sob story." Aggie wrinkled her nose in disgust. "Humph. It's a good thing he didn't find me, for I'd have given him a piece of my mind. The idea!"

"But the *Tribune*—"

"—is just a newspaper, Barry. Big city, yes, but apparently—oh, Clark, there you are. Listen, I have to talk to you. I just spoke to John Anthony, and it's the strangest thing. You know, I believe he very nearly put me in my place? Now, I don't want to say he was disrespectful. I don't expect John Anthony could ever be that, but . . ."

Clark was grinning over his shoulder as he led Aggie across the lobby and out the door.

"I'll be at the park, Barry, if you need me!" He was laughing as the door closed behind them.

"Yes, sir," Barry mumbled to an empty room.

Well, so much for his big announcement. Jeepers, a reporter from the *Chicago Tribune* comes all the way up to Derrington for a story, and she acts like the guy committed some kind of crime! He was lucky he hadn't found her, the mood she was in. Mr. Streeter seemed like a nice guy, and she would have torn him up and tossed him away like she was disposing of a bad test paper from a student. Whoo-ee.

Barry shook his head and returned to his post behind the counter.

Kate Downing and John Anthony McGavin left the house together. They turned out of Aggie's front walk and came straight in Jaycee's direction.

Jaycee had only a second or two to be sure it was Kate before he ducked. Yes, damn it, it was Kate! She looked exactly as she had the last time he had seen her, thin and graceful, hair full and hanging to her shoulders—she hadn't changed a bit in all these years.

He stayed low, bent across the front seat, and through the open car windows, he could hear the murmur of their voices as they passed down the other side of the street. When the voices faded he raised his head and saw them rounding the corner. He started the car, turned around in the nearest driveway, and drove to the corner. There they were, still walking, and they were holding hands. Jaycee cursed as he lit a cigarette. He turned the corner slowly, staying a block behind them. They crossed the street, not even looking his way, still walking away from the business district, and he edged to the corner and looked to his right. He could see them entering a house down the block.

What were they up to? Was McGavin making a move on her? Well, not for long. Jaycee took furious puffs on his cigarette. There was nothing he could do except wait.

Inside the house on Calvert Street, McGavin was supervising the preparation of a picnic supper. He came up from the basement with a cooler and emptied some ice into it.

"What'd you find? Anything interesting?"

"Your mother must have the best-stocked refrigerator in the state

252

of Wisconsin," Kate said, laughing. "You name it, she's got it—ham, cheese, lettuce, tomato, some kind of salad in here—"

"Well, throw it all in, and there should be some beer in there—"

"Here it is." Kate pulled out a six-pack and put it in the cooler. "Bread?"

"Homemade," McGavin answered, and he handed her an unsliced loaf wrapped in a plastic bag. "Let's see, napkins, knife for the bread, forks for the salad, hand me the mustard, aha! Cake!"

"Hey, wait a minute, surely your mother had plans for all this food? We can't just leave her with an empty refrigerator."

"This is standard operating procedure for her, Kate, she—"

"John? Is that you?"

"Ah, the cook returns! In the kitchen, Mom!"

Nan McGavin, still in her waitress's uniform, appeared at the kitchen door.

Kate, suddenly feeling awkward, closed the refrigerator door and looked at McGavin.

"Mom, I have a very special lady I'd like you to meet. Kate Downing. Kate, this is my mother, world's finest cook."

"Kate, I'm so glad to meet you." Mrs. McGavin's voice was warm. "I've seen you at the hotel. I—I'm very sorry about your employer."

"Thank you." Kate hugged her elbows and smiled nervously. "I'm afraid you caught us raiding your refrigerator."

"Oh, going to the picnic?"

McGavin spoke. "Uh, no, Mom, we thought we'd take a drive and, uh . . ."

"Then you'd better get going, the day's half over! And what about your speech?"

McGavin spoke casually. "I asked Mr. Manchester to fill in for me this year." He ignored his mother's frown and said, "But what about your plans? We don't want to leave you stranded—"

"You're not," his mother said easily. "I'm meeting Gertie and Sam at the park, but I did promise to bring that cake with me. Oh, not to worry, son," Mrs. McGavin said. "Here, I'll just wrap some up for you. Now, what else do you need?"

"A change of clothes," McGavin said. "Back in a minute." He left the kitchen through the back door and climbed an outside staircase to his apartment above the garage.

"Well, Kate." Nan McGavin was slicing the cake. "I'm glad you

253

and John are getting away for the afternoon. He hasn't had a day off in ages. Takes his job much too seriously!" She smiled as she wrapped the cake and placed it in the cooler. "Somewhere along the line, he got the idea that he's indispensable around that sheriff's department—"

"But he's so good at his job." Kate felt almost defensive.

"He certainly is. Best sheriff we've ever had. That's not just a mother's pride speaking; everybody thinks so."

Kate wondered how much John's mother knew, and as if by telepathy, her question was answered.

"You and John seem to be on good terms," Mrs. McGavin said. She was smiling.

"Yes. We are."

"That's good." She nodded, and went to the sink to wash the knife. "Are you going to be here long—in Derrington, I mean?"

"A few days, at least. I'm not sure yet—"

"The place grows on you, I'm warning you!" Nan dried the knife and placed it in the cooler. She snapped down the top and locked the handles. "Stick around awhile," she said. Then she turned around and faced Kate.

"Tell me, am I the only one who thinks a single year in a boy's youth should not haunt him the rest of his life? There isn't a person in this town who hasn't benefited from his efforts to wash away his guilt. And I never even knew it until three days ago."

"You mean you don't want him to leave his position at the sheriff's department?"

"Not in disgrace. If there's something else he wants, something better, a greater challenge, then I'm all for it. Can you talk to him?"

"Ready, Kate?" McGavin came in the back door, wearing jeans and a cotton shirt.

Instantly his mother was smiling again.

"All right, scoot, you two." She made a show of shooing them out of the house. "Have a good time!"

18

Old Debts

•

"Tell me more about the Boardman place."

Kate was leaning forward to gaze through the windshield of McGavin's car as they drove north out of Derrington. The hazy sunshine of the morning was clouding a bit, but it was still a warm day, and they had the windows open to the clean breeze. Kate's hair, free of its customary restraint, blew away from her face, and she was enjoying the unfamiliar feeling. She felt wonderful, almost euphoric, setting off on a holiday picnic. There was not a thing she could do about her travel plans until tomorrow, and today she felt like a child with a day off from school.

McGavin glanced at her face and caught her mood.

"The Boardman place," he said, in the tone of a tour-bus director, "is one of the landmarks of Derrington, Wisconsin, ladies and gentlemen. The main house, constructed in the late nineteenth century of natural red brick, has twenty-seven rooms. The property, which includes numerous small outbuildings, is composed of four acres of landscaped lawns and gardens and some six hundred acres of some of the finest farm and dairy land in the state. The house, although far from architecturally perfect, has a charm of its own, as each wing has a story of its own. Take the kitchen, for example—"

"Forget the kitchen," Kate interrupted, laughing. "Where did the Boardmans get their money?"

"Lumber, my dear lady, log after log of it. And when the country

255

stopped building during the depression they turned to anything they could get—building roads, washing floors—they did whatever they had to do to hang onto their land, because they knew it was the only thing they had of lasting value. They kept it, somehow, and then the last one—Rupert—he nearly—"

"Oh, who cares about Rupert?" Kate sensed a swing in his mood and tried to steer him away. "I'm thinking about supper, especially since I never ate breakfast. Do you think I'm crazy, wanting to go back to Baker's Lake?"

"Yes." McGavin smiled at her tactics, but he was serious.

"Please don't tell me you're superstitious. It's a beautiful place, quiet, and we can sit down by the lake and watch the sun set and eat ourselves into oblivion. Not a bad way to spend a holiday, is it?"

"No . . ." McGavin was slowing for the turn off the county highway. "But after what happened up here, I'd think—"

"Mr. Cramer left a letter for me," Kate said abruptly. "His lawyer gave it to Aggie, yesterday, after the funeral. I read it last night. It explains a lot of things."

McGavin's eyebrows were raised in surprise. "When did he write it?"

"Five years ago, right after he'd seen my husband."

"What?" McGavin jerked his eyes away from the rutted road to look at her, and the car bounced over a pothole.

"John, they came here every year. They met in Rodney Weaver's cabin, and they talked about me. Remember the ledgers?" He nodded grimly. "Mr. Cramer had been in Vietnam, sometime before Jim got there. He juggled those pay records, and when Jim went to work in the same office, he found out about it. So he tracked down Mr. Cramer, and there he was, a perfect pigeon, and he made him hire me. Every year up here, Mr. Cramer would—would report to him on me, and get some of the pages from the ledgers."

"You mean Jaycee came back, every year?"

"Cozy little arrangement, wasn't it?" Kate could not keep the bitterness out of her voice.

"But think of the risk," McGavin said. "He could have been recognized—"

"Mr. Cramer said he wore a disguise. He hired a private detective to find out who was blackmailing him. In fact, I'm going to call him. He could help me—"

256

"Those guys bounce around a lot, Kate. He may not even be in Chicago anymore. Or he may be out of town."

"Mr. Cramer said he might be able to help me find Jim."

The car came to a bumpy stop in the clearing and McGavin turned off the ignition. Except for the fluorescent strips of plastic rope that Pete Iverson had strung up to cordon off the area, the place looked exactly as it had the first time Kate had seen it. The woods were deep and green with early summer foliage. The cabin, leaning a little to one side, still managed to look habitable, cared for. The blue water of Baker's Lake sparkled at the foot of the slope beyond the cabin. It was as serene a setting as one could ask for.

She turned to McGavin. "He—he loved this place, in spite of everything. He said he hoped I'd see it some day. I brought his letter with me and—I know this sounds crazy, but I'd like to read it in his place, and try for once and all time to understand him and what he did. Then I can put him away, like a bad piece of clothing that doesn't fit anymore, and be done with him. Can you understand that?"

"Be done with him. . . . I vote for that." He gave in, and they got out of the car. "The cabin—we went through it, pretty much took everything, but still—"

"Oh, I don't want to go in." She shuddered. "I'm trying to block it out, just forget it. You know what I'd like?" She smiled and touched his arm. "I'd like to go down to the lake and sit in that hazy sunshine and listen to Benjamin Cramer one more time." Her voice quavered, and she put her fingers on his lips. "Please? I'm fine. I just need a little time, do you mind? I'm grateful to you for bringing me here."

He studied her a moment, then said, "Okay. Go ahead. I'm going to take down these plastic strips, but I'll be right here—"

"I know." She turned away and walked past the cabin, hardly giving it a glance. She smelled the pines, taking a deep breath, and already she could feel the peace of this setting sweeping through her. It's as pretty as a postcard, she thought. He gave me those, every year, and now she knew that he had done it on purpose, set up another routine too obvious for her to miss, all a hedge against the time when he might need her help. She hadn't understood soon enough, but she could give him this afternoon, read his letter in his place, try to replace anger and hurt with understanding and forgiveness. Then she would truly be free of him. Her debt would be paid.

She settled on the dock, crossing her legs, and took the letter out of her purse.

McGavin, standing in the shade of the pines and birches surrounding the cabin, watched her move down the slope, light and sure and graceful on her feet, and settle on the wooden pier at the edge of the lake. He knew her mood had darkened; she looked as though she was preparing herself for an ordeal. She took out an envelope from her purse, and he prayed Benjamin Cramer would give her the answers she needed to hear, so that she could bury him for good and get on with her life.

He leaned against his car, looking at the cabin, and shook his head. Cramer and Jaycee, meeting up here every year, right under his nose! What had gone wrong this year? Why had Cramer been killed? Had he refused to cooperate any longer? Hadn't he known how ruthless Jaycee was? He was lucky to have survived at all, even a few days. There had been a battle in that cabin. He'd been right about the cupboard door; the hole in it matched another at the back, on the outside wall; the bullet had gone right through it and was out there on that slope somewhere. There was a hole in the ceiling, too, from another wild shot. He wondered what kind of gun Jaycee had used. Lab reports were slow because of the weekend and the holiday, but they had the bullet from Cramer's leg; that would help. But where was his car? And where was Jaycee? Back in Southeast Asia, where he'd always wanted to be? What would he do, now that Cramer wasn't there to keep tabs on Kate?

McGavin felt his own mood darkening. He was responsible for all of it. Without the ledgers—

"Wahomet-One, Wahomet."

He heard the squawk from the police radio installed in his car. Now what? It must be important or Will wouldn't bother him, not after all the time he'd put in during the past few days. He reached in the open window and grabbed the mike.

"Wahomet-One. Go ahead."

"We found the car, Sheriff." It was Will Kalowski, the bushy-browed desk deputy who had been on duty the day Kate had first

258

gone to see McGavin. "Plates are gone, but make and model match the info we got from the Illinois boys. We're pretty sure it's his."

"Cramer's? They found it?" He was excited; this could be a real lead.

"Wipasaukee River, Sheriff, four miles south of town. Two kids fishing spotted it, only the antenna sticking up out of the water. Wrecker's on the way, but everybody's tied up with an accident out on twenty-three, and I figured you'd want to know."

"Who sent for the wrecker?"

"Logan."

McGavin moaned to himself. Derrington's youngest city cop, so green behind the ears he hadn't even learned to call signals yet. Everything he touched or even approached turned into mass confusion. Look what he'd done at the nursery. . . .

"I'm on my way, Will. Get Logan on the radio. Tell him to do nothing until I get there. Nothing. Got that?"

"Ten-four, Sheriff." Will's voice sounded like that of an ogre. If that didn't keep Logan at bay, nothing would.

McGavin replaced the mike and went down the slope to the lake. "Kate?"

She jerked her head around.

"Sorry, I didn't mean to startle you."

"He's got me mesmerized," she said ruefully, waving a sheaf of papers, the letter from Cramer.

"Kate, they found Cramer's car." He watched her eyes widen in surprise.

"Where?"

"In a river, south of town."

"Are you sure it's his?"

"They think so. It's evidence. I have to go down there. C'mon, I'll drive you back to Aggie's, or we can find her at the park."

"No, I'll stay here. Just leave the food." She grinned.

"I'm not going to leave you here. I could be gone for hours."

"How long does it take to pull a car out of a river? Go ahead, I'll be here when you get back."

"It could be dark by then, probably will be. Come on, let's go." He bent to help her up.

She shrugged him off. "I can take care of myself. I like it out

259

here. I like the quiet. I'm perfectly safe. It's been ages since I just sat out in the middle of nowhere and watched the sun set. We city folk don't get a chance to do this very often." She was smiling up at him. "I need this time and I'm going to be selfish and enjoy it. And when you come back I have some very interesting things to tell you about Chicago's leading businessman. I may even ask for a little advice."

"You can tell me on the way."

She shook her head. "No, it'll keep. Besides, it's a long, sad story. The man rambles on forever. A guilty conscience will make one do that. Now go on, just leave me something to nibble on, and I promise I'll save some cake for you."

She dismissed him with another smile and bent over the letter again.

He remained a moment, staring down at her, but she did not look up again, and finally he turned and trudged back up the slope. She was right, he told himself, she was perfectly safe here. Weaver was dead and her husband was in Bangkok or Hong Kong or some other far corner of the world.

He pulled the picnic cooler out from the backseat, placed it beneath a tree, and climbed into his car.

You should make her come with you, he told himself as he started the engine.

I can't protect her from a danger that doesn't exist, he argued.

He debated it all the way to the highway. It was wrong to leave her alone, something told him that, but what choice did he have? Logan would mess things up, McGavin knew he would, unless he got there in time to supervise things himself. But Jaycee could be anywhere. . . . No, not Jaycee. He was too smart to hang around and watch the results of his murder act. He was long gone, back in his old haunts, making his drug deals while he figured out a new angle for keeping an eye on Kate.

His mind made up, McGavin felt the wheels hit the pavement of the highway and he pressed the accelerator to the floor.

Perfect! This was just perfect!

Jaycee was jubilant as he turned into the woods. Familiar territory! He'd hardly been able to believe his luck when he'd seen them turn down this road. He'd gone ahead half a mile, turned around, and sat for a few minutes, planning his strategy. McGavin, he'd decided, was expendable, a risk worth taking. He'd been in civilian clothes when they left the house on Calvert Street. He'd left his gun behind, and Jaycee was confident he could handle him. But then, just as he'd been about to drive back, here had come McGavin's car, and Jaycee was close enough to see he was alone. He'd left her there! Jaycee knew that road. There was only one place it led, one place she could be. At last she was alone.

The puzzle was coming clear. He didn't have all of the pieces yet, but he had enough to make a few guesses. Cramer hadn't died here. Somehow he had survived, and they'd found him out here. They'd taken him to some clinic in Derrington and then they'd moved him to a hospital up in Eagle Hill. He had died there, the waitress at the hotel had said that.

And now his loyal secretary was here, his devoted employee, and she wanted to see the place where they'd found him, where he'd spent his vacation every year. So McGavin had accommodated, driven her out and dumped her here, then went about his business.

No doubt he'd be back, but not soon enough.

No matter what McGavin might have told her—and if he was smart, he'd have kept his mouth shut—still, no matter, when she saw her husband Jim, alive and in the flesh, the last ten years would just dissolve, and he'd take her to Switzerland and then they'd really start living. Oh, yes, she'd see what living could be when you had plenty of money. He'd taken care of her all these years, even if she didn't know it, and he would do even better now. He'd buy her whatever she wanted, they could travel, they would mix in the best circles. She would have furs and jewels, and she'd be so grateful to him that he would forgive her for her father dying the way he had. He would write it off; he could afford to now. He could afford just about anything he wanted, for a while, at least. And when what he had ran out, he would have thought of something, a good plan.

He left the Mustang a few hundred yards away from the cabin and began to walk the rest of the way. It still amazed him that Cramer had actually seemed to enjoy this run-down place. He hadn't been required to stay three weeks. Jaycee needed only one night of his time, but Cramer had spent three weeks here every year, fishing, puttering, doing God knew what,

It hadn't mattered to Jaycee, just as long as Cramer was here the

261

night Jaycee wanted him. Originally Jaycee hadn't wanted to risk staying in Chicago a minute more than was absolutely necessary. He knew too many people there who might recognize a man who was supposed to be dead. Flying in and out of O'Hare was a huge risk in itself, and he had pressed Cramer to come to Southeast Asia instead, or at least move the meeting site to California or Mexico.

But Cramer, even backed into a corner as he was, had drawn the line. Jaycee gave him grudging admiration for that. Cramer had first insisted on Chicago and they'd finally compromised on this place. Well, it had worked out, Jaycee reflected; it had worked out better than he had hoped.

He stopped behind a tree and studied the cabin in the clearing. The door had a piece of paper tacked to it, probably a police order to keep out. McGavin's fluorescent strips were still stretched between the tree trunks. Where was she? He moved past the clearing, looked down the slope, and saw her, sitting on the pier in the sun, her back to him. They were alone—there wasn't another person within miles of this place—and suddenly he knew he couldn't wait another second. He thrust his hands in his pants pockets to keep his excitement from showing, and went down the slope to get his wife.

Kate was holding the last page of Benjamin Cramer's letter in her hand, but she was staring out across the lake, squinting a little in the glare of its reflection, trying to comprehend the mind and motives of the man she had once respected.

"Kate."

She had not heard him coming down the slope, hadn't even heard his car. Was John back already? When she swung her head to look up at him, there were tears in her eyes and the glare from the lake and the hazy sunshine blurred her vision. But it wasn't John. He was taller, blond—

"Jim!" She gasped it and he bent down and took her shoulders, pulling her up to him. He was smiling.

"No!" She twisted away from him, and one of the pages of Cramer's letter slid off the pier and floated onto the water. She clutched the last page in her hand, and her fingers formed a fist as she swung at him. Jim! It was impossible, he wouldn't come back here—

262

"Kate, easy, hold it, now." His fingers closed around her wrist. "What kind of reception is this?"

"You," she gasped. "Let me go. How dare you come back here!" Her instincts told her to run and she tried to break away from him, but his grip was strong. "What are you doing here, you—"

"I came back for you." He sounded as if it were perfectly logical. "C'mere, Kate, it's all right—"

"Take your hands off me!" She was panting, struggling to get away from him. "I mean it, Jim, let go of me. You have no right—"

"I have every right in the world. You're my wife." His voice was sharper now, harder, and his fingers squeezed tighter.

"You bastard, you filthy—"

"All right, that's enough." He shouted it and jerked her arm, turning toward the cabin. His foot pushed another page of Cramer's letter into the water lapping the shore.

"Let me go!" she screamed. "No! No-o-oo!" He was dragging her up the slope toward the cabin, and she fought him, the page from Cramer's letter crumpled in her fist.

"He's gone; he can't hear you. We're alone, just the way I planned it, and you're going to listen to me."

"He's coming back," she panted, still trying to twist away from him. "He'll be back any minute, and if you're still here—"

"Then he'll be sorry he came back. He'll be sorry he ever met you." His voice was that of a stranger. He didn't sound anything like the man she had fallen in love with and married, a basketball player from Seattle who had charmed her and her parents, the first man she had ever—the only—

"No!" She cried out again and dug her elbow into his stomach. "Let me go, you have no right, how dare you—"

"Shut up." He took both her shoulders and shook her. "Kate! Look at me! Listen! I came back here for you and I'm not going without you. Now, let me explain—"

"Explain?" She spit it out, furious. "You can explain leaving me, and the men on the plane and Benjamin Cramer? And Weaver? You can explain murder? Do you think I'm a fool? Do you think—"

"Will you shut up?" He snarled it, losing patience, and dragged her up the steps to the cabin.

"We can't go in there—" Kate began, but when the knob

wouldn't turn, Jaycee kicked the door violently and it swung open. He jerked her arm, pulling her inside, and the last page of Benjamin Cramer's letter flew from her hand and dropped to the ground next to the porch.

McGavin and Iverson had been in to gather evidence. The cans were gone from the kitchen floor; the glass from the broken bottle had been picked up. As Jaycee pulled her across the room and all but threw her into a chair, Kate caught a glimpse of the bathroom. They had taken his clothes, too, the bloody towels, and the first-aid kit. It was almost as if nothing unpleasant or evil had ever happened here. But Kate was shivering as the horror of that day came back to her. To be left in this cabin, alone and dying in pain. . . . A shaft of weak afternoon sunshine came through the door, and she could see the bloodstains on the hardwood floor. She looked at Jim, towering over her, and her terror began to grow.

She had meant to find him, but not here, oh God, not here, and not by herself. She would have the police with her, or maybe that investigator, Randall, Daniel, whatever his name was; at least Aggie would be with her, someone, but not like this. Dear God, not like this. She shrank back in the chair, trying to calm herself, trying to keep her head clear, but inside she was screaming, "John! John, please come back, come back, hurry!"

"Now you're going to listen to me." Jim had his feet planted on the floor, standing over her. The blue curtains were all drawn closed and in the dim light she could hardly see his face, but his voice, hard and confident, struck her like a blow. She was trapped. "I can explain everything, and you're going to listen. You owe me that."

Kate couldn't help it. In spite of her fear, she snapped, "Owe you! I owe you nothing, except what you're going to get. Justice—"

"Stop it!" He yelled, "Stop it, just *shut up!*" He leaned down toward her and she could see his face, contorted with anger. He had an ugly scab on his right eyelid, and she could smell him, tobacco and sweat, and she clamped her lips together.

"That's better," and she hated the smugness in his tone, but then he straightened up and she found she could breathe again.

He lit a cigarette and his words came out in a stream of smoke.

"I meant to come back," he said, "sooner, and I would have, but not to that dump on Rolfe Road, not to selling door-to-door crap.

264

We needed money, Kate, to travel and live the way we should. I mean a mansion, with servants, and furs and diamonds. That's the way you should live, and I needed money for that, and I saw a way to get it—"

Stall him, Kate thought. Try to reason with him, stay calm, and John will come back.

"I never asked you for those things," she ventured. "I never wanted them! I just wanted you—" and her stomach twisted with revulsion. It sickened her that she had wanted this man so much.

"But *I* did! Damn you. *I* wanted them! And with the bank, we would have had them—"

"Is that why—" His language scared her—he had never sworn at her before—but she had to ask, she wanted to hear him say it. It was the first block, the foundation, in the wall of hate she was building against him. "My father's bank, is that why you married me?"

"No! It was you, and the bank, hell, all right, that too, but it was you, Kate; you looked so innocent, but in bed—"

"Stop it!" She couldn't bear to hear him say it. She loathed herself; the passion she had felt for him sickened her now, because it had been born of her innocence and based on a lie. "It was the bank," she cried, "and when we lost it—"

"Then I found another way." He sounded very satisfied with himself. "I heard there was a fortune to be made in Vietnam, just so long as I stayed out of the infantry and didn't let them teach me how to fly. And it was true! I thought I could make enough in a year, but, shit, it was so easy I decided six more months, and then they fouled me up. I couldn't come back to you, so I went to Bangkok and—"

"Aren't you forgetting something?" she said bitterly.

"Kate, I couldn't come back just then—"

"The arrest." She spat it out, hating him. "The court-martial. The plane, oh, tell me about that, Jim, sixteen men, boys, on that plane—explain that away, will you? Sixteen men!"

"I never touched that plane—"

"No, you didn't have to, you found someone who could do it better than you, and sixteen people died!"

"How the hell did you know about that?" He sounded as if he was ready to deny it.

"Your old friend," she said angrily, "John Anthony McGavin."

"I might have known," he muttered. "What other lies did he tell you?"

"He told me everything," Kate said triumphantly. "And I believe him, every word." Suddenly she was tired of this, tired of his attempt to explain the unexplainable, tired of his self-serving lies. He sounded calmer now; maybe he would listen to her.

But before she could speak, he said, "None of it matters now, Kate, don't you see that? It's over, all the waiting is over. I have tickets, first class, to Zurich. We leave tomorrow—"

Kate lost it. All her control, her struggle to contain her loathing, exploded at this final proof of his arrogance.

"Mr. Cramer!" she cried out. "What about Benjamin Cramer? You killed him, you shot him right here in this cabin, you murdered him!" She made a move to rise from the chair and he pushed her roughly back down.

"He double-crossed me, Kate!" His voice was low, menacing, and she cringed at the sound of it, at the suffocating feeling that pressed in on her as he bent over her chair. His face was only a few inches from hers, and she could see the fury in his eyes. "We had a deal—"

"It was blackmail," she whimpered, and now the tears were coming. "He was a decent man who made a mistake, and you blackmailed him."

"Damn right I did." His voice was strong with conviction. "I needed somebody to keep an eye on you until I could get back, and he was perfect. When I found those ledgers and figured out what he'd done—man, he had a real system—"

"And you perfected it," Kate guessed. She could see the truth register in his eyes, but he rushed on.

"—and there was his picture in *Time* magazine; he'd won an award. He was out of the service by then, right in Chicago—"

"Right where I was." Kate was crying hard now; she could hardly breathe. She remembered that award; the secretary before her had clipped the article, and he had a plaque on his office wall, Young Businessman of the Year, from the Chicago Business Alliance. He'd won it a month before she went to work for him.

"It was perfect, can't you see that?" He stepped back and lit another cigarette. "I had something he wanted. All he had to do was hire you and make sure—"

"Make sure I didn't find somebody else?" Her voice came back,

266

strong with outrage. "Make sure I didn't start over and make a new life, a better one, without you?"

"I was coming back," he insisted, "can't you get that through your head? All he had to do was make sure you were all right, but no, he had to mess everything up."

"What did he do?" Kate sat forward, her voice intense. "Did he finally call it quits? Did he finally hate himself so much that he decided anything was better than—"

"It doesn't matter anymore!" he roared, stamping out his cigarette on the floor. "We have to think about *us* now!"

"*Us!*" Kate sputtered. She tried to swallow the sour taste in her mouth. She felt sick, dirty, just being near him. "There *is* no us, don't you see that? You killed it, Jim, a long time ago; you kill everything you touch! Do you think I want anything to do with you? You killed the men on that plane, you killed Benjamin Cramer, and I'm supposed to welcome you back and go off to Europe with you? Are you insane? Do you really think I could do that? There isn't a woman alive who could do that! Do you know what?" Kate's anger pushed her up from her chair, knees trembling, and she stood with fists clenched, her face contorted with wrath. "I wish you were dead. God help me, I've never in my life wished that for another living soul, but I swear I wish you were dead. You are dead to me, can't you see that?"

He took her shoulders again and held her there. "Listen to me, Kate. I did this for you. Do you think I've been living it up all this time? Do you know what it's been like? I lived in the sewers, ratholes that would turn your stomach, and I did it for us! I saved every dollar I could, and now we've got it made! There's nothing for you here; you're out of a job, and people are going to ask questions. How the hell are you going to support yourself? I got you that job in the first place, don't forget that, and it's not going to be easy now, but you come with me and—"

His voice dwindled off as he saw the look spreading across her face.

"I'm beginning to understand," she said, amazed. "It's preposterous, but you think I'm the same person you left, don't you? You remember that Kate, crying and sniffling at your feet, killing herself to please you. I couldn't decide what to wear without asking you first. And you liked it, oh, it was just what you wanted. Well, let me tell you something." Kate straightened her shoulders and he dropped his hands.

"I've changed," she said steadily. "It took me a long time, but I grew up, because I had to and because Benjamin Cramer demanded it and because you weren't there to prevent it. You got me that job, thanks to Ted—oh, yes, I know about that, too." She acknowledged his surprise. "You must have felt so clever when you found out Benjamin Cramer had an office in Ted's building. All you had to do was arrange for them to meet. Poor Ted; you used him, like you use everyone, and he never even knew it.

"You got me that job, but you're forgetting one thing. I'm the one who kept it, and the hammer you held over Mr. Cramer's head had nothing to do with that. He could have shuffled me off to some corner and paid me to stare at the wall, but he didn't. He made me an executive secretary, and then his assistant, and I earned those titles and every cent he paid me, and I did that without any help from you."

Her voice was rising to a fever pitch. For days now, since the time she had dusted off his letters and begun to doubt him, her anger had grown from a tiny seed of mistrust to a revulsion for all that he stood for, all he had done. Ten years of misplaced grief, her shock and disillusionment, her utter loathing of him, rushed out of her like a flood tide. There was no way she could stop it. She felt it consuming her, and releasing it now was no longer a choice. He had set it in motion, fueled it with his every action, compounded it with arrogance beyond the scope of her comprehension. She saw him actually begin to back away from her and, feeling almost triumphant, she fired her last volley, the killing blow. She wanted to hurt him now, and she knew this would do it. What mattered most to him, what had always mattered most, was money, and wasn't it ironic that she could use it against him now. She took a breath and tried to steady her voice.

"I don't need your help, not now and not ever. I can support myself, Jim, oh, yes, I could, but do you know what? I don't have to! Do you know what you did when you killed Mr. Cramer? Oh, you'll love this, Jim, it's perfect. You set me free! I don't need you; I don't need anyone. He left me his money, all two million dollars of it, and it's mine! It's all mine!" She was laughing and crying now, hysterical, and she missed the look that passed over his face.

"What did you say?" The tone of his voice stopped her cold. She wiped her eyes with the back of her hand and felt her heart stop. His eyes, oh, there was more than fury in them now. It was a look she'd seen before, not in his eyes, but—dear God, that was the look of a fanatic, a maniac, a person whose obsession has erased his touch with reality. He's crazy, she thought, he is really crazy.

And suddenly she knew she had gone too far. She tried to speak, to think of some way to undo the damage, take back the words, but it was too late; she had made a terrible mistake. Nausea rose in her throat. Her arms came in close in a self-protective motion and she took a faltering step back, away from him.

"That double-crossing maggot left *you* two million dollars? *You?*"

"Keep away from me, Jim," she whispered, "just keep away from me. . . . It doesn't matter anyway," she said, louder, "I won't take his money. Not his, or yours, or anyone's; it doesn't matter, Jim." She was pleading now, horrified by the crazy glint in his eyes, and she took another step backward, toward the fireplace and the low row of bookshelves beside it. She glanced toward the bathroom, remembering the horror of that day when she had found Mr. Cramer here, and a scream began to rise from her throat.

"Jim, it's time to go now. John's coming back any minute." Oh, where was he? What was taking him so long? She could see the open doorway beyond Jim; it was nearly dark outside now, he should be back—where *was* he? "He's coming back, you have to leave now, it's better that way, just go, please, just go away."

She hated the way she sounded, terrified out of her mind, but that was exactly the way she felt. The look on his face, watching her, frightened her out of her wits. He was calculating, finding the best angle, the way he always did, and she knew what he was thinking. She would never go with him, he knew that now; they would never share the inheritance. But if she were dead—could he claim it? No, he was supposed to be dead himself, he couldn't—

He would find a way, Kate knew. Hadn't he found a way, all these years, to get exactly what he wanted? He had lied and stolen and murdered. It was just like Aggie had said, when John had been trying to explain to them what happened to Jim in Vietnam. He had closed out the real world and created a fantasy, where he was powerful and got whatever he wanted. He would find a way, she knew, to claim Benjamin Cramer's money, with or without her. He was

269

already rich, he had told her that, but with him it was never enough. Eighteen months in Vietnam had not been enough. Dear God, ten years since then had not been enough; the only reason he had come back now, he had admitted, was that Mr. Cramer had refused to cooperate with him any longer. There was no one left to blackmail, no one to keep her from marrying someone else. So he had come back, she realized, with enough in his Swiss account to get by on for a while, but it would never stop, she knew; his insatiable greed fed on itself.

She took another step back and felt the stone wall of the chimney behind her.

"No, Jim, please, it won't work, it'll never work, you can't—"

"It's the only way." He was coming toward her slowly, and he sounded almost resigned. "Everybody tries to cheat me, do you know that? You're not the first. My old man was a welfare bum who couldn't even buy me a pair of shoes. My brother taught me to play basketball and fooled me into thinking I could do something with it, and then he goes and gets killed on his damn motorcycle. Then your old man promised me his bank, and it turns out he's already picked it clean. Cramer— well, never mind him. But I'm through with it. No more cheating. If I can't have you—"

Kate sucked in her breath. He didn't need to finish the sentence; she knew what he was thinking. If he couldn't have her, then no one could.

Her eyes, wide with terror, pleaded with him to stop, to try to think clearly, but there was no reaching him. He had been out of reach for a long time.

The only thing to do now was scream, scream as loud as she could and pray someone heard her. But there was no one; that was why she had wanted to come here, to be alone, and now he was raising his hands and she gasped.

He was going to kill her. And there was no way on earth she could stop him.

19

A Matter
of Timing

∎

The three-day weekend was drawing to a close and traffic was
heavy, even on the county highways that McGavin was traveling.
He did have a portable red light on the floor of the car, but he was
reluctant to tear through the countryside with lights flashing. He
was scrupulous about using it only in genuine police emergencies,
and the discovery of Cramer's car in the mud of the Wipasaukee
River was hardly an emergency. Of course, Logan had the capacity
to make it one, but even he would have a hard time making it a life-
threatening situation.

So, anxious as he was to get there and then back to Kate,
McGavin followed the flow of cars. He skirted Derrington and
drove south on County 18, following its course as it ran parallel to
the river. He wondered if this was the same route Weaver had
taken—or had it been Jaycee?—as he drove Cramer's car from
Baker's Lake and looked for an out-of-the-way place to abandon it.

Even before he reached the spot, McGavin knew he'd found the
right location. Several cars had pulled to a stop on the road shoulders and a crowd of onlookers had gathered, their interest drawn by
the flashing red lights of a Derrington City Police car and a huge
yellow crane parked on the bank of the river. Wrecker, Will had
told him, but Logan had found a crane!

"Logan!" McGavin was yelling even as he jumped from his car
and pushed his way through the crowd. Now he was positive he had

271

done the right thing in leaving Kate to come down here. Logan was the only law-enforcement official on the scene and he had conveniently ignored the order to wait for the sheriff's arrival. The salvage equipment operators were already hooking up the chains.

"Logan!" the sheriff thundered, "I told you to wait!" As he reached the banks of the river, two divers emerged from the water.

"Aw, Sheriff, no harm done. See? You're right on time!"

Logan's hat was pushed back on his head and he grinned delightedly.

"Okay, boys!" he yelled, waving to the equipment operators, "bring 'er up!"

"Logan," McGavin said between clenched teeth, "damn you, shut up!"

"But, Sheriff—"

"I said shut up!" McGavin kept his voice low but there was no mistaking the intensity. He was livid and, though he was the smaller of the two men, it was Logan who began to back away.

"Just stay out of this. You are out of your jurisdiction! Do you understand that?" McGavin waited until he got a reluctant nod from the young policeman, then turned to face the suddenly silent crowd. Like moths to a flame, they were invariably and disgustingly drawn to any sign of tragedy. Flashing red lights were a beacon, bringing out a morbid curiosity in otherwise sane people.

As McGavin surveyed the crowd, his demeanor underwent a transformation. Still in command, he put aside his frustration with Logan, and the expression on his face became calm and impersonal. His voice, loud enough to carry to the road, where more people were arriving, was pleasant but authoritative.

"All right, folks, move back, please. This is no emergency, nobody's hurt, just a vehicle we have to get out of the river. But it's a tricky operation and we need room. That's it, keep moving, somebody get those kids back, thank you, sir, that's it," and although they groaned with disappointment, they obeyed.

"Now, I want you to listen to me," McGavin yelled, still facing the crowd. "This is very important. When that car comes up, we're going to hook it to the tow truck here and haul it away. I don't want anybody touching the car, do you hear me? It is evidence in a criminal investigation. If one of you, just one, touches that car, you will be subject to arrest for interfering with an official investigation. So just stay back and let us do our work."

He turned to the salvage operators and spoke quietly with them for a few minutes. Then he walked to the edge of the river and conferred with the divers, nodding once or twice. At last he gave the signal to the machine operator, who started the engine. It roared into life, and the driver threw the gear shift into reverse. Slowly, the machine edged away from the river. The crowd watched as the chains grew taut. When the chains began to squeak under the strain, all heads turned to the river.

"There it is!" someone in front shouted, and a cheer rose as a luxury-model black sedan emerged from the muddy depths of the Wipasaukee River.

McGavin turned to Logan. He kept his voice low.

"If anybody from that crowd so much as looks like they're going to touch that car, I will hold you personally responsible. Do you read me?"

"Right, Sheriff." The patrolman was subdued, but only for a moment. "Okay, folks, stand back," he yelled to the crowd.

McGavin supervised the rest of the operation, and when the black sedan was hooked to the tow truck he left Logan in charge of dispersing the crowd. Then he got into his own car and led the way back to Derrington.

They locked the sedan in the county garage, where a team of Wisconsin state crime lab technicians would pore over it in the next few days. The possibility that any fingerprints remained was almost nil. Several days in the river would have taken care of that. But he hoped the car might yield some other sort of clue.

McGavin drove past the city park on his way out of town. It was packed with people and several of them, grouped around the picnic tables nearest the street, called out and waved to him. He returned their greetings but didn't stop. He had his own picnic waiting for him, out at Baker's Lake, and a beautiful woman besides.

It was dark by now, and he hoped Kate wasn't too uneasy. If she hadn't already eaten, maybe they would take the cooler down to the lake and sit on the pier, where they could catch the pine-scented breeze. They would talk about everything and nothing, about Cramer, if she wished, and he would tell her what he had thought of her that first day when she had hesitantly entered his life, so prim, so meek.

Ha! That was a good joke. He told himself that now, once and for all, he should be cured of making snap judgments. Kate was strong and independent, and he admired that tremendously. In fact, he would tell her so, as soon as he got to the cabin. If she wasn't ready to hear it, that was too bad. For ten years he had been treading water, waiting either to sink or for the water level to drop. Now, he wasn't exactly sure which had happened, but he was going to swim with the current. Kate Downing was the best thing that had happened to him in a long time, and he wasn't about to lose her.

20

The Fire

■

―――――

At the moment when Cramer's black sedan emerged from the river, Jaycee made his move. His hands gripped Kate's head like a vise and banged it back against the stone chimney.

Kate opened her mouth, but no sound came out. Her knees collapsed and she sank to the floor in a crumpled heap. She lay there, barely conscious, defenseless against the next blow.

The gun, she thought. He had shot Mr. Cramer and now he was going to shoot her. She should run, get up and run away from him, at least make an attempt. But she felt smothered; her body was dead weight. She could hardly breathe. She couldn't open her eyelids, let alone stand up.

She heard a sound—the click of the gun? Did it have a safety catch? Was he pulling it back, pressing his finger on the trigger? She tried to open her mouth, make her tongue work, say something to stop him. But nothing would work; her strength was gone. In the darkness of the cabin, behind the swirling blackness in her head, there was a lifting of the veil, the barest lessening of the dark, but she couldn't open her eyes.

His footsteps moved around her, past her. They crossed the wooden planks of the cabin floor and stopped. Was he leaving?

Clank!

No! He was still here!

The noise, harsh and grating, sent waves of pain through her head, but it brought her back from the edge of unconsciousness. Her eyes fluttered open. Outside it was totally dark now, but there was a dim, flickering light inside the cabin. In the shadows, Kate saw her husband leaning over the stove near the door.

Phooo! Phooo!

She heard it distinctly, once, twice.

Then he straightened up, his back to her, and clank! His hands shoved the top of the stove back into place.

He turned around to look at her and she wondered if he could see her eyes, wide open with terror, staring at him. Did he think she was already dead? She held her breath, her arms and legs at odd angles on the floor, waiting for him to come back and check, to finish the job.

Then he spun on his heel and adjusted the knobs on the stove before he went out the door, pulling it closed behind him. She could hear him on the steps of the porch, and then he was gone. Her eyes closed in relief and she let out her breath in a long sigh. He thought he had killed her. He was gone.

Her head felt as if it were spinning and her fingers grasped at the floor. The whole cabin seemed to be spinning, around and around, and there was a terrible pounding in her head—oh, no, his footsteps? Was he coming back? Was that what she heard?

She forced her eyes open again. She was afraid to look, but it was worse not knowing, worse imagining. . . . The room slowly stopped spinning. The pounding, she slowly realized, was only in her own ears, and it was caused by the waves of pain in her head.

The door was still closed. She was alone. But there was still that dim, flickering light. The space in her line of vision was empty. She struggled to lift her head and turn it.

Then she saw it. It was a candle, a fat, white candle, the kind her mother had called a storm candle. It was meant to be used in emergencies, when the power failed. It was on the low shelf next to the fireplace, at the end of a row of paperback books, and it was burning brightly.

Kate rested her head on the floor, but her eyes remained open, mesmerized by the flame of the storm candle. That clicking noise . . . it wasn't a gun; it was his cigarette lighter. But why would he light a candle?

He was gone, she was sure. The cabin was empty. But what had he done? What sounds had she heard?

He had slammed her head against the stone chimney, oh, it hurt, like nothing she'd ever felt before, and she had slumped to the floor. Then the click—he had lit the candle. Then he'd left—no, wait, something else. Some other noise, near the door. The stove?

She tore her eyes away from the candle flame and slowly moved her head. She gazed across the floor of the cabin and tried to bring the stove into focus. It was on the far wall of the cabin, near the door, and her view of it was partly obscured by the counter that jutted out into the middle of the room.

Think, she told herself. Try to remember. He had lifted the top of the stove, bent over it. He blew out the flames.

That was it! That *phoo!* That was the sound she had heard. Twice. And then he had replaced the stove top and turned on the burner jets.

Her head sank to the floor, but she was staring at the stove across the room. It was a gas stove. Yes, she remembered now. She had seen the tank outside that first day. It was painted orange and it had blue letters on it. LP gas. That sound—Jim had blown out the gas flames on the stove.

But that was dangerous. Her mother had taught her that. Be careful, she always said. Be sure the pilot lights are on before you turn the knob. Sometimes they get blown out, she would say. Like this. *Phoo!* Then we have to light them again.

Jim had blown out the pilot lights. He had lit a candle and blown out the pilots. But that was backward. . . . That was dangerous.

Kate moved her arms and raised herself up on her elbows. Her head was pounding and she felt dizzy again, but she forced herself to think.

It's going to explode.

The full realization came slowly, slipping in between the pounding beats of pain. This cabin is filling with gas, and it will rise to the ceiling and then it will come down—it's already coming down. When it reaches that candle there will be an explosion!

Slowly, she brought her knees up and raised her upper body, leaning on her palms, and lifted her head. The movement set off a new wave of pain, and she winced, but she kept her eyes open, her head raised.

Straight ahead of her, through an open doorway, was the bathroom. Around to the left was the bed where Benjamin Cramer had fought for his life.

Benjamin Cramer did not choose to die here, she thought. And neither do I.

She pushed her hair back from her face and put a hand on the couch nearby. Slowly, clenching her teeth against the waves of pain in her head, she stood up. Now she could smell the gas, and she knew the danger was real, and it gave her strength.

She turned unsteadily toward the door and took one faltering step. Holding her head between her hands, she took another step.

See? You can do it. It's easy. Just move one foot. There. Put your weight on it. Now the other foot. Slide it forward.

Faster. A little faster, there's the counter, now to the door, and she was past the stove. Her right hand left her head and reached out blindly for the doorknob, and the door swung open easily. Aha! He'd broken the lock when he'd kicked in the door; he couldn't lock her in.

Then she was on the porch, down one step, down another, on the ground, almost running now, and behind her there was an unfamiliar sound, a muffled *swoosh!* —

BOOM!

The glass in the windows shattered, and, immediately, flames rolled out of the windows and the door.

Kate stopped. She turned to look back at the cabin and saw Jim running toward her.

"No!" She shouted it, but the scream was swallowed up in the fire's roar. She swerved and plunged into the woods. Why was he still here? Why hadn't he shot her, unless . . .? Unless he didn't have a gun. . . . She ran away from the cabin, away from the man who had chosen death for her.

"No," she cried out, "you can't make that choice for me!"

Her hair was streaming out behind her, catching on branches, but she twisted free and kept running. She stumbled over tree stumps and through bushes and she tore her slacks and still she kept running because, behind her, she could hear him. Only the darkness and the density of the woods were preventing him from catching her.

He must not have a gun, she thought. He'd be shooting if he had one, surely I'd hear it? He doesn't have a gun, he had to find another way; but I'm out of there, I got out in time, and now I have a chance. That flicker of hope kept her feet moving.

Behind them, Rodney Weaver's humble little cabin was a torch in the night.

Deeper and deeper into the woods Kate fled, gasping for air, thinking only that she had to get away, until a terrible thought penetrated her panic: She was running the wrong way.

She had shot out the door of the cabin and headed straight into the woods. But the door faced east. The highway, the county road where there would be traffic, people who could help her, all that was to the west. She knew she couldn't outrun him forever. She had to get to the highway.

So she started making a wide arc, trying to move more quietly now. It was hard to do. The dry spring had left the forest floor hard, and the leaves, the pine needles, the underbrush were brittle. Every step, she thought, was an announcement, a signal he could follow, but still she tried to control her breathing, to stifle the panting breaths. She felt her way from tree to tree, moving to her right, until at last she could see the glow of the fire on her right. Then she moved straight ahead for a minute or two, so she wouldn't meet him head-on.

At last, when she knew her adrenaline was slowing and she was nearing the end of her strength, she dared to turn back and move to the west. The fire, roaring and crackling and hissing, was her guide. Its sounds and the light it emitted were her points of reference. She couldn't get lost now, no, she had to stay calm and somehow she had to reach the highway. In her mind there was no room for comprehension, no time for reasons or emotions. There was only the command of survival, ordering her to keep moving, and she obeyed.

The ache in her head was bad enough, but now she felt a cramp in her side. It cut into her more deeply with every step until finally she stopped. It wasn't a conscious decision. Her legs simply refused to move. She bent over, leaning a hip against the peeling trunk of a birch tree. She pressed her fist into her side and gasped for air, and at first the only sound she could hear was the beating of her own heart.

And then she heard the louder sound, a huge animal thrashing through the woods. Jim. She left the tree and, still holding her side, she started running again.

I can't make it, she realized. I'm not in shape; this cramp won't go away. I can't keep running much longer, but I have to get to the highway. There will be people there, if only I can keep running, just keep running, keep going.

She said the words to herself over and over, but she knew she would never make it. She couldn't stay ahead of him much longer.

Maybe John would come back in time. Oh, why had she let him leave without her? Why was she always so stubborn?

It was going to be such a lovely picnic, she thought. We were going to sit down by the water and eat Nan's homemade bread; we would cut it in thick slices, just the way my mother used to—

Bread. The cooler.

How could she have forgotten? The cooler! The blessed cooler!

She had asked him to leave it and surely he had, surely he had left her the cooler, but where? Not on the dock, no, he hadn't come back down the slope, so the cabin—no, the cabin had still been locked when Jim—so, where? Somewhere in that clearing, oh, John, please, that cooler has got to be in the clearing.

It was her last hope and she knew it.

"One more spurt," she told herself, "I can do it, I must do it, faster." She felt her legs, incredibly, responding to her brain, and she was running straight for the fire.

When she suddenly burst out of the woods into the clearing she had to shield her eyes from the glare. The heat burned in her face, but she wouldn't turn away from it. She was looking frantically for the cooler, a dark green ice chest with white handles. It had to be here, please—

Yes! She could see it across the clearing and she ran into the open, arms pumping, and collapsed on her knees in front of it.

John's cooler, packed with ham and cheese and beer and bread and cake for their very own Memorial Day picnic. There was ice in the chest, cold, soothing ice.

And the knife. She had seen Nan put it in—a long, serrated blade on a sturdy wooden handle.

She struggled to open the cooler, but the handles were linked at the top and she couldn't pull them apart. What was keeping them together? She lifted the ice chest and heaved it against the trunk of a pine tree. The handles flipped apart, the top flew off, and the cooler dropped to the ground, upright. She bent over it and a rush of cool air met her face.

The cooler was packed full and the contents were hardly disturbed. Carefully placed on top, right next to the strawberry cake, was the knife. She grasped the cold handle and pulled it out of the cooler.

When she looked up she was facing the direction from which she'd come. On her knees, with the cooler in front of her, she raised her head and saw a monster emerging from the woods.

In the glow of the flames and the billowing smoke, his face was red. He must have run through branches because his skin was bleeding. His short blond hair could hardly be seen; his head was smeared with dirt, and dry leaves and pine needles were matted in his hair. His shirt was in shreds.

Shoulders heaving, legs shaking, he was staring across the clearing at her. He looked like a callous hunter who had just shot a deer out of season. There was no shame on his face, no guilt, only crazed triumph.

Kate tightened her fingers around the knife and held it low, close to the ground, behind the cooler. Her breath came in short, panting gasps. She wanted to run. Every nerve in her body was tensed, telling her to run while she could, straight down that road and out of the woods. But if she got up, he would see the knife and then it would be useless. Her only possible hope lay in surprising him. She would wait, hold her ground and make him come to her, and when he was close, close enough to touch, then she would use the knife.

Dear God, he's my husband, she thought. I lived with his man, I slept with him, this is Jim—

He took a tentative step toward her, and in the glow of the flames she saw his face again and she knew that this grotesque and hideous monster was not the man she had married. That man was gone, lost in the tide of war, as surely dead as if he really had died in a plane

281

crash. In his place was this stranger, barely familiar, who was intent on killing her.

Jaycee took another step and Kate's hand squeezed harder around the knife handle.

What if he moves the cooler? He'll see the knife; I can't let him see it! Slowly, as slowly as she dared, she inched her hand off her thigh and onto the ground. Slowly, so slowly it seemed to take an eternity, she moved her hand, with the blade scraping across the ground, until her arm was twisted behind her. She dug her knuckles into the hard dirt and leaned a little to one side, just enough to slip the opposite leg out from beneath her body. Slowly, she raised her knee and planted her foot on the ground, then transferred her weight to that foot. Still crouched behind the cooler, looking as helpless as a sparrow beneath the huge Scotch pine, Kate was ready to spring.

Jaycee took one more step.

In a movement so sudden and swift it made her jump, he thrust out a leg and kicked the cooler aside. The contents came spilling out and lay scattered on the ground.

Please don't see the knife, she prayed silently. Don't see the knife, it's all I have. If you see it, you'll take it away from me, and I'll die in this fire. I don't want to die like this. Is this the way that Benjamin Cramer felt?

Now she thought of Cramer, and a rising wave of anger rushed through her. It seized her mind and her body and she knew, without any doubt at all, that this creature looming over her was not her husband. He was not even human. He was an animal gone mad. The anger gripped her muscles and strengthened them.

When he took the final step and bent to seize her, she was ready.

The knife, driven by a force outside her body and beyond her control, flashed in an arc from behind her, sliced through the smoke, and plunged into his stomach. She didn't feel it going deeper and deeper; she didn't feel anything except her own fingernails cutting into her palm as her fingers squeezed the knife handle.

She heard a grunt, an animal's moan—not human, surely—and then a heavy weight fell onto her, crushing her to the ground.

She could hear a gurgling sound, and something hard was digging into her stomach. She couldn't breathe. The flames were coming closer, snaking across the dry pine needles on the ground, dancing

282

in the trees over her head. Everywhere there was smoke, and a crackling noise, like the sound of an old hag laughing. It was the dry branches snapping above her.

She felt the weight on top of her sag down more heavily and that hard object punched deeper into her stomach. The knife handle. Her fingers were still closed around it; they seemed to be glued to it. She couldn't seem to move at all.

A spark of tiny flame landed next to her head, and then another. Then a third spark fell and it dropped into her hair, and she smelled it immediately. With one violent push, she shoved the weight to one side and wrenched herself free. Her fingers, still coiled, slipped away from the knife, and she rolled across the ground.

She lay there. Her mind was empty; all she could do was struggle to catch her breath. Then she felt the sparks again. They were falling faster now, and it seemed that a hundred tiny fires were circling in on her, pine needles sizzling as they burst into flame.

She curled up her knees and rolled over onto them, then used her fists to push herself upright. She turned uncertainly away from the flames, where minutes ago there had been a cabin, and once more willed her legs to move, away from the fire, away from that monstrous form on the ground.

Don't look at him, there, you're past, move, just move, the road is right over here, another step, another step, another—

"Kate!"

She spun around, and in the orange and yellow glow, framed like a silhouette, was the dark shape of a man, teetering on his feet, but upright, in a crouched stance. One hand was clutching his stomach, but the other, held out to his side and near the ground, brandished the knife.

"Kate."

She did not even recognize his voice, but the sound of it, and the image of a body risen from the dead, was enough to paralyze her. The heat was burning in her face and her brain was screaming at her to run, but her body was frozen.

She watched in a trance as Jim took a lunging step closer to her. He was doubled over even lower now, one arm bent across his stomach, but his head was raised and his eyes never blinked.

Kate willed her feet to move. Running—that was her only hope now and even then she wasn't sure she could outrun him, or even get out of the clearing. All around them, flames raged. The fire had jumped from tree to tree, bush to bush, and sparks were flying everywhere.

Run! she screamed to herself silently, and still her legs did not move.

He took another halting step closer.

Then, above the noise of the roaring fire, she heard a crack. It came from overhead and it made a thunderous noise and they both looked up. The tree nearest the cabin, a huge Scotch pine, already dying and ridden with dry, rotted branches, succumbed to the fire raging through it. A shower of flaming branches, as if felled by a lumberman's precision, came plummeting down, a streak of fire falling in the night.

It landed with a terrible crash and the silhouetted figure, still gazing up, still clutching the knife in one outstretched hand, was crushed beneath it.

Above the crash, above the roar of the flames, Kate heard one last anguished scream, but she was never sure if it had come from the man in the flames or from herself or from both of them.

McGavin almost ran her down. He had seen the orange glow in the sky from several miles away and had already radioed for the fire department and the Eagle Hill rescue squad. He made the turn off the county highway on two wheels and was roaring down the rutted lane into the woods when his headlights caught a stumbling figure in the middle of the road.

She reeled to one side, he swerved to the other, and then he was out of his car, holding her, supporting her. She was trembling and all she could say were two words.

"He's dead."

Her voice was raspy from the smoke and her face was streaked with dirt and blood. Her hair, so clean and shining only a few hours before, was a dirty, tangled mane of leaves and pine needles. She had lost one shoe and her clothes were hanging in shreds on her scratched and bleeding body.

John Anthony could only hold her and tell her, over and over, "It will be all right. It's all right now, you're safe."

It is not all right, he thought. Good God, it's a disaster; she's been attacked by someone or something, the woods are burning down around us, and somebody is dead.

Even as he held her, as he had longed to do, he wondered if anything would ever be all right again.

EPILOGUE

1985: On My Own

The bus pulled off the interstate, climbed the hill, and rounded the curve into the downtown streets of Derrington. It was eleven o'clock on a Saturday morning in May, and the bus was full. Most of the passengers got out when it pulled to a grinding halt in front of the bus station. The majority of them would board another, local bus for the short ride out to the campus.

One passenger, an eighteen-year-old girl, collected a small, worn suitcase from the pile on the sidewalk and stood apart, clutching a shoulder purse in one hand and pushing her brown hair out of her face with the other. She was supposed to meet someone, a Mrs.—

"Hello! You must be Cindy Fletcher! You look just like your picture!"

"Yes," came the girl's voice, flooded with relief, "I'm Cindy. I was afraid you—"

"Oh, I was almost late, wasn't I, but you see we have a bus, so you could have found your way to the campus, right? Just one suitcase? Smart traveler. Now, come along, the car's right over here—"

"We're not taking the bus?"

"No, even though the bus is free—though I should warn you, we may have to charge a fare by next year—but right now it's still a free service we like to offer. We don't like our students to feel isolated at the university. Our location is remote enough as it is—which you'll find has many advantages—but the town plays a big part in our operation, too, and the bus service fosters the connection. That's why I want to show you the town first. I want you to see it, get the feel of what it's like to live here, before you see the campus. Here we go."

The older woman opened the driver's door of a light blue sedan. There was a navy-blue emblem on both front doors, indicating that the car was an official vehicle of the University of Wisconsin–Derrington. Cindy Fletcher put her suitcase on the backseat and got in front with the woman who had come to meet her.

"Oh, just a minute. There's someone I want you to meet. Aggie! How are you this morning?" She got out of the car and came around to Cindy's side, near the sidewalk. Cindy didn't know if she was supposed to get out, too, or stay where she was. She compromised by rolling down her window.

"'Morning, Kate! Glad I ran into you. Big news! The loan for the addition came through. Clark says we'll start renovating in September and we'll be ready for graduation next year."

A tiny, white-haired woman with a face like a prune had hurried down the street and stood talking to Kate. She moved, Cindy thought, amazingly fast and easily for a woman her age. She had to be at least seventy, but she was wearing a very smart blue-denim jumper with a red-and-blue plaid blouse.

"Aggie, that's wonderful! We're going to need all the rooms we can get. You know, Harvey Schmidt is faculty chairman of the first commencement committee, and he's already planning an extravaganza. So they liked the architect's plans?"

"Yes, Milton Rissman came through again. That city feller he recommended turned out to be one smart cookie, I'll admit it. I guess he knows how to deal with loan officers, even ones as stingy as— say, who's your friend?" Aggie peered into the car and Cindy knew she was under inspection. She suddenly felt intimidated by this munchkin of an old woman.

"This is Cindy Fletcher, Aggie, from Mount Jeffers, Illinois. I told you about her. She accepted us sight unseen, and now she's here to look us over. Cindy, I'd like you to meet Mrs. Manchester."

"How do you do, ma'am?" Cindy Fletcher had never used that phrase in her life. She clutched her purse in her lap and tried to meet the old woman's sharp eyes.

"Cindy, it's a pleasure to meet you. Yes, I remember now, you won your school's mathematics prize this spring, didn't you? Congratulations. We're glad to have you with us.

"Stop by the Farman any time you want a decent cup of coffee. That watered-down mud they serve at the student union may keep you awake for exams, but that's the only recommendation I can give it.

"Have to run, Kate. You're coming for dinner?"

"Yes, and John, too. We'll see you, Aggie."

288

Kate started the car and pulled out of the new parking lot adjacent to the bus depot.

"Mr. and Mrs. Manchester own the Farman Hotel," she explained to Cindy, and she pointed it out as they reached the corner. "They bought that building next door and they're going to enclose the alleyway and make it into an arcade, then renovate the offices into more hotel rooms. Business is booming here, as you might guess. The first time I saw this town, it was a sleepy little village with a fair tourist trade during the summer months. When the campus opened three years ago, Derrington became an instant metropolis. The people here are very supportive of us, but they're cautious, too. We want to keep Derrington a small college town if we can. We're their life's blood now, and our enrollment's growing faster than our dormitory space, so lots of students live in town.

"There's the bank, and the post office, and that shop there, Goodman's, just opened. Nothing but jeans, every size and style you could want.

"There's Fergusons' Flower Shop, that's new, too, open about six months now. Gertie has beautiful fresh flowers there, all year 'round, and they have a large nursery on the other side of town. They have a sale on houseplants out there in September, so you can—now here's the Elm Street Clinic, hope you never need it. We don't have our own yet, but Dr. McCabe is an excellent physician and he has two other doctors in his practice now. Of course, your fees will cover most medical expenses. . . ."

Cindy Fletcher struggled to follow the rapid-fire delivery of information, swerving her head from one side to the other, following the direction of Kate's pointed finger, but what she wanted to look at was Kate herself. Her photograph in the college catalog didn't do her justice. She was a striking woman, Cindy thought, and there was no way that a camera could capture the sheer forcefulness of her demeanor, the confidence and self-assurance that accompanied every gesture.

Cindy had read all the UW–Derrington brochures, and she knew the admissions director's credentials: ten years' business experience on La Salle Street in Chicago; bachelor of arts in business from Northwestern, master's degree from the Wharton School of

289

Finance, and a Ph.D. from the University of Wisconsin–Madison in counseling.

She personified success, Cindy thought, tall and slim and beautifully dressed in a light gray suit, hair short and smooth and smartly styled, eyes alight with purpose and enthusiasm.

Cindy shrank lower in her seat and curled her fingers around the strap of her purse.

"You see how short the distance is," Kate was saying, and Cindy thought, the distance is not short at all, I'll never make it, and then she realized Kate was speaking in terms of walking distance. "The campus is close enough to walk into town when you want to. Now, here's the Boardman Building." Kate parked the car in the slot marked ADMISSIONS DIRECTOR in the row of spaces in front of the building.

"Take a moment, Cindy, and look at this building." They got out and stood in front of the car.

Cindy obediently looked, hoping she would see what the admissions director expected her to see.

"It's called the Boardman Building because a man named Jeremiah Boardman built it," Kate was saying quietly, "in 1889. He built it as a home for his family—he was a dairy farmer and a lumberman—and as the farm prospered, he kept adding on to the house. He ended up with twenty-seven rooms, plus the cellar, which is now our student union. This wing, on the far end, he built as a ballroom. Look at the lines, Cindy, at the way he forces the eye to look up, and then you notice the frieze. The man was a farmer, Cindy. . . ."

They stood in the warm May sunshine and looked at the building, and Cindy began to appreciate its massive size, the strength of its solid red bricks, the symmetry of its windows, all trimmed in fresh white paint. She felt her gaze rising, just as Kate had said, placing the building in its surroundings—huge oaks, green pines, and peeling, white-trunked birches.

"We rescued this house from the demolition team," Kate said proudly. "Isn't it magnificent? Jeremiah Boardman put his roots down here, and now we benefit from his foresight. He built this house to last beyond his own lifetime, and that's what a university is all about. It helps you find the building tools and it teaches you how to use them. You're going to be very busy here, Cindy, but when the pace gets too frantic, and it will, just take a moment to look at this building again. It'll remind you why you're here and—hello there, gentlemen! Oh-oh, you caught me in the act."

Cindy jerked her eyes away from the roof and saw two men approaching them. The taller of the two, with red hair and a smiling, freckled face, was introduced to her as Randy Daniels, the campus security director.

"And this is John McGavin, a friend of mine." Kate was positively beaming, and Cindy noticed that as he extended his right hand to her, McGavin's left arm slipped easily around Kate's shoulders. "We used to be lucky enough to have this man as our county sheriff," Kate was saying, "but the politicians in Madison stole him away from us. Now he's so tied up with the State Crime Commission, the Parole Board, and half a dozen other projects, that we make appointments with him, just like everybody else."

"But this is still home," McGavin said, and Cindy believed him. She recognized love when it was obvious.

"Ladies," McGavin went on, "we are on our way to lunch. Care to join us?"

"Decided our stomachs couldn't take one more dose of student-union food," Daniels said, "so we're going to the buffet at the Evergreen Room."

That sounded wonderful to Cindy, but Kate spoke up.

"Oh, you tempt us, but we'll resist today. We have a schedule. I want Cindy to meet Dr. Schmidt before he leaves for the day. He promised he'd wait for us. And then—"

"Okay, I know when I'm outranked!" McGavin was laughing. "Another time, Cindy?"

"Of course," she managed to mutter.

"But we're still on for dinner, right?" McGavin said, looking at Kate.

"You bet we are." Kate kissed him lightly on the cheek, and turned to enter the building.

"See you soon, Cindy." Randy Daniels flashed his open grin again and waved as they parted. Cindy waved, too, suddenly feeling not quite so far from home, and followed Kate up the wide steps to the veranda and through the double doors into the building.

Just inside the entrance, on the right-hand wall, was a plaque emblazoned with gold lettering. Ahead of her, Kate was breezing right by it, but Cindy paused to read it, and slowly, her mouth fell open in astonishment.

Kate glanced back, and a flicker of annoyance darkened the lively gray eyes.

"Come on, Cindy, that's not important."

"Dr. Downing? Is that the same—that is, is this you? It says Katherine Downing—"

"One and the same," Kate said briefly. "Now, Dr. Schmidt's office—"

"But, Dr. Downing, I thought you were the admissions director."

"I am. Please, Dr. Schmidt will be leaving soon—"

Cindy couldn't stop herself. "But it says here that you donated the land for this campus. It says you renovated this house."

"So?" Kate did not intend to sound rude, but she was clearly annoyed.

"But—but then why . . ."

"Why what?" Kate had been forced to retrace her steps so that they wouldn't be shouting to each other, and now she stood next to Cindy in the entryway.

That explained it, Cindy thought. That was why Dr. Downing was so smartly dressed, so self-assured. She was rich, filthy rich, and this branch of the university, three years old now, was her toy. When you had money, the kind of money that could bring a branch of a state university into existence, you could look and be any way you wanted.

Kate scrutinized the girl's face, and she knew she was going to have to explain. She'd had to before, but she still detested trotting out her life story for strangers to gawk at. But this girl, the daughter of a man who fished in the summer and led goose-hunting parties in the autumn and trapped in the winter, was going to get away from her unless she relinquished a piece of her privacy. Kate sighed inwardly. She might as well hear the story straight instead of through the campus gossip line. She kept it as brief as she could.

"Seven years ago I was a secretary in Chicago, Cindy, living on an adequate salary, hoping I could pass my last exam for a bachelor's degree. I owned a six-year-old car and a small two-bedroom house with a mortgage, and I had worked very hard to keep both of them.

"Then I—I inherited a large sum of money. Not from my family, from a friend. At first I didn't want it and I nearly turned it down.

292

But finally I decided I could put that money to better use than the lawyers and the executors and the vultures who come out of the woodwork whenever an estate is up for grabs. I will tell you what I did with my inheritance.

"First, I paid a debt incurred by the person who left me the money.

"Second, I convinced the University of Wisconsin Board of Regents to open a branch in Derrington. I did that by buying this property, which had fallen into disuse, and donating it to the state, with the condition that it be used only as the campus for the new branch. Clark Manchester gave me the idea, and it was as smart as any notion he ever had. The state could hardly afford to turn me down.

"Third, I continued my education, and at a very accelerated rate, because I wanted to be a part of this school and I wanted to be qualified for the position I now hold. Hiring me was not one of the stipulations of the donation. By the time I had finished my Ph.D. the papers had been signed, the land belonged to the state, and they had no compulsion to hire me. I competed for this job, and I'm very fortunate to have it. I'm single and I have to support myself.

"Fourth, with the money that was left—and there wasn't much, compared to the amount I began with, but it is sufficient—I established the scholarship fund that is going to pay for the greater part of your education here. Every last penny of my inheritance is invested, and the income goes directly to the scholarship fund. I couldn't touch that money even if I wanted to, which I don't. I live on my salary, which is, again, adequate.

"I have to admit I get an immense amount of selfish pleasure out of that scholarship fund. As admissions director, I see all the enrollment applications that come in—that's why I wanted this job—and every year I select three young women and offer them a chance they might not otherwise have. This year you are one of them."

Cindy Fletcher had had the decency to look away as Kate made what was obviously a painful explanation. What had possessed her to push Dr. Downing into such an embarrassing position? She hung her head and stared at the polished wood planks of the floor and wished she were back in Mount Jeffers, where no one took any notice of her at all.

"Do you know why I selected you?"

293

Cindy shook her head.

"Look at me, child." Kate put her finger beneath the girl's chin and raised her head. "You are a straight-A student and you want a degree in business administration. Your application said your career goal is to run a livestock-breeding farm, but you want a degree in business first. Do you know the sort of practical imagination that shows? You are exactly the kind of young woman I want to see succeed."

"But I—um, I'm not what you call a leader. I wasn't president of anything or—"

"Oh, other people take care of the leaders. I'm interested in the quiet ones, the ones in the back of the crowd, who only need a little help in clearing the path. But not just any quiet ones. Only the ones with potential."

"You think—me?"

"Certainly. Don't you?"

"Well, yes, but in Mount Jeffers, well, um—"

"Oh, I know about the Mount Jeffers of the world. They're wonderful places, and that breeding farm is going to open their eyes. Meanwhile, you have a lot of work to do. You remember, don't you, that this scholarship isn't a free ride? You're going to have to work part-time, too."

"I know, and I'm willing, but I don't think I'm qualified to do anything."

"Now that's pure nonsense. I have several ideas—the campus bookstore, surely you can learn to operate a cash register, or one of the offices here, where you can see a practical application of all the theories your professors are going to throw at you. And we have a reforestation project out at Baker's Lake; that's good outdoors work and they have a lot of fun out there. You don't have to stick with the same task all four years; we'll move you around, give you as much experience as we can, if you agree."

"Well, of course, yes, I agree."

"Good. Now, we must hurry to catch Dr. Schmidt. He's the chairman of our business department, an extraordinary man, and he'll be assigning one of the other professors to be your advisor. Then we'll have lunch, and then I'll take you to Sharon Tyler's room over at Cramer Hall; that's our new dormitory. She's a freshman this year and you'll be her guest for the rest of the weekend. . . ."

Cindy found herself trailing along after the admissions director, straightening her shoulders as she hurried to catch up.

It was late. They had the streets to themselves and they walked slowly, hand in hand, enjoying the light breeze. The conversation at dinner had been noisy and lively, as it always was at Clark and Aggie's table, so they savored now the silence of a spring night in Derrington. Kate could feel the tensions of a long, productive day slipping away.

Something about Cindy Fletcher had struck a chord, and Kate remembered the girl who had left Elwood for Northwestern, the woman who had left the house on Rolfe Road for Derrington. She sighed contentedly, feeling her muscles relax. She had tested herself in the years since then, not just professionally, but emotionally, too. She had doubted the inclinations of her own heart, and so she had waited, wanting to be sure. She had dated other men, looking for certain qualities. Some were still her friends; most were good, kind men, but they lacked, in the end, the bond she sought, the one that would complete her spirit and yet set her free.

Suddenly she laughed out loud.

"What?"

"I just realized something."

"Hmmm?"

"I'm forty years old!"

"You're right, that's hilarious."

"It is! Don't you want to know why?"

"I always like to know what makes you laugh."

"It's funny, my darling, because it's taken me all these years to tell you this. I'm ready."

"Ready?"

"To get married. John Anthony McGavin, will you marry me?"

He stopped in his tracks and looked at her. "You're asking *me?*"

"It must be my turn by now."

He began to smile. "On one condition."

"What?"

He wrapped his arms around her so she wouldn't go away. "Are you a rich woman?"

"No." She was laughing again.

"Good. I knew there was something I liked about you."